CROSSROADS

A Novel By

ROCHAN MORGAN

Q-Boro Books
WWW.QBOROBOOKS.COM

An Urban Entertainment Company

Published by Q-Boro Books
Copyright © 2006 by Rochan Morgan

ISBN 1-933967-09-9
First Printing September 2006

This is a work of fiction. It is not meant to depict, portray or represent any particular real persons. All the characters, incidents and dialogues are the products of the author's imagination and are not to be construed as real. Any references or similarities to actual events, entities, real people, living or dead, or to real locales are intended to give the novel a sense of reality. Any similarity in other names, characters, entities, places and incidents is entirely coincidental.

Cover Copyright © 2006 by Q-BORO BOOKS all rights reserved
Cover Layout & Design – Candace K. Cottrell
Editors – Melissa Forbes, Candace K. Cottrell, Tee C. Royal

Q-BORO BOOKS
Jamaica, Queens NY 11431
WWW.QBOROBOOKS.COM

CHAPTER 1

"Get your tail up, Pooney! You hear me?" Sheila's voice was a distant distraction to her older brother, who was firmly entrenched in his favorite dream. This was the one where he was the starting cornerback for his beloved Dallas Cowboys, playing against their rival, the San Francisco 49ers, in the NFC Championship Game. The one where he intercepted an errant Steve Young pass, ran the length of the football field and through the end zone, straight into the arms of his wife, Janet Jackson. The two of them shared an intimate kiss in front of the seventy thousand screaming fans.

"You better get your butt up, boy! It's already after seven, and Mama just called and said she's on her way!" Sheila's voice was not quite as distant now, and though still asleep, Pooney sensed the urgency involved.

"Mama?" This was all his brain could muster as his eyes sprang open.

"Mama said she's on her... ooh, what happened to your eye?" The purple and green bruise under her brother's left eye startled Sheila.

"Shut up, girl! Damn!" The siren-like wail Sheila produced was more than Pooney's splitting headache would allow him to endure.

Pooney rolled out of bed and onto his feet. He stood motionless while waiting for his still uncooperative eyes to focus. Standing before his sister clothed only in his boxers, Pooney unwittingly displayed the score of welts and bruises he had acquired the night before. Sheila, two years Pooney's junior, stood wide-mouthed with amazement at the sight of her brother's battered body.

"You've been fighting!" Sheila declared.

"Shut up!" Pooney was unsure whether his headache was the result of the dozens of kicks and punches that had found their target the night before, or simply a reminder of the fifth of cheap wine he drank afterward. In either case, he felt his head would explode at any moment.

"You've been drinking, too, Pooney. I can smell it," Sheila fussed. "I'm tellin' Mama."

"I'll put my foot in your ass, too," Pooney threatened before the pounding in his head forced him to sit down on the bed.

"Well, tell me what happened then." Sheila was always willing to settle for a tidbit of juicy gossip.

"Iron my clothes and I'll tell you when I get out of the shower." Pooney was instantly energized by the secret he could dangle in his sister's eager face.

"You'd better not be lying, Pooney," Sheila pleaded unnecessarily. She was totally unaware of just how badly Pooney wanted to tell his secret.

"Just iron my clothes, girl. I'll tell you when I'm finished in the bathroom." Pooney felt powerful until he once again rose to his feet and another surge of pain threatened to decapitate him.

Pooney struggled down the hallway leading to the bathroom, pleading with his rubbery legs not to give out on him. Once inside the room, the fifteen-year-old boy jumped into the ice-cold shower. The freezing water instantly raised Pooney's level of consciousness, causing the assortment of bumps and bruises to sing loudly in unison.

Pressed for time, Pooney cut his shower short. After gently towel-drying his body, he quickly brushed his teeth. Pooney was in a real hurry now. The last thing he wanted was to explain to his mother the origin of his battle scars. He reached for a fresh set of boxers, and then realized he hadn't remembered to grab a pair.

"Sheila!" Pooney yelled through the cracked bathroom door.

"What?" Sheila was at the door instantly.

"Look in my top drawer and bring me a pair of boxers."

"Don't nobody wanna be touching your nasty, stinky drawers," Sheila protested.

"Don't you want to hear what happened?" Pooney knew he had the needed leverage to manipulate Sheila to do as he desired.

"You want too much, huh!" Sheila stormed away, fussing all the way to her brother's bedroom. "I already ironed your clothes and put those bloody sheets in the washing machine."

Sheila reappeared moments later, holding Pooney's underwear between her thumb and index finger. Her head was turned in the opposite direction as if she were trying to avoid an awful smell.

"Quit trippin', girl. They clean." Pooney was slightly irritated.

"You might have them crab things again," Sheila responded.

"Give me the damn drawers!" Pooney snatched the boxers from Sheila's grasp. "I ain't got time to be trippin' with you!"

Pooney exited the bathroom wearing nothing but his boxers. The Gap jeans and FUBU sweatshirt Sheila had ironed were lying at the foot of his linen-less bed. He dressed himself quickly as his internal clock rang loudly with the news of his mother's imminent arrival. The clock on the wall read 7:35, which meant his mother's bus would be arriving in front of Tim's store in about seven minutes.

(2)

Ms. Regina Richards stepped from the city bus in front of the convenience store located directly across the street from the Back Bay apartment complex she and her two children called home. After a twelve-hour shift at the nursing home, where she worked six days a week in order to make ends meet and keep up with the ever increasing taste her children possessed for expensive clothes, the short trek home from the bus stop to her apartment door became a major ordeal.

After struggling through her front door, Regina would take a shower, don her house robe, and collapse onto the couch under the pretense of watching the Jerry Springer Show. Regina seldom made it past the first commercial break before she was sound asleep. She would usually remain there until Sheila returned home at four o'clock. After five minutes of her daughter's prodding, Regina would lie in the bed they shared until five thirty. Then she would prepare herself for work. Of course, Sheila would have all her things ready when she awakened.

Always the "little woman," Sheila had taken the responsibility for most of the household chores many years before. If not for her youngest child, Regina would have succumbed to fatigue long ago.

Regina grimaced when her thoughts turned to her son, Allen. He wasn't a bad kid, as Regina considered her son to be a very respectable young man, but she rarely got to see her eldest child. Their schedules were such that Regina would usually see Allen only on her off days. And even then that was no guarantee. Regina had promised herself a thousand times that she would take a vacation and spend some quality time with her children. However, the fact that her job did not offer paid vacation days made her dream a very improbable one. She knew that Allen, as well as Sheila, needed much more attention than she was able to give them. However, as a single mother, she was simply doing the very best she could.

(3)

Now fully dressed, Pooney grabbed the brush   from   the television set and brushed his hair vigorously. He stole an occasional glance at his little sister, who shifted impatiently every so often to be sure that her brother remained conscious of her presence.

"You gonna tell me or what?" Sheila's impatience was now out of control.

"Yeah, girl." Pooney stared at himself in the mirror, allowing his sister to squirm a little while longer.

"Well?" Sheila glared angrily at her older brother.

"I got clicked in last night,"Pooney confessed proudly.

"You what?!" Sheila couldn't believe her ears.

"I'm   Deuce-nine   now,"   Pooney   continued enthusiastically.

"Deuce-nine?" Sheila repeated.

"Yeah. Deuce-nine Crips."

"I know what Deuce-nine is, boy," Sheila snapped. "You're stupid!"

"You don't know nothin'." Pooney was indignant.

"I know you're stupid, Pooney! Those boys ain't gonna do nothing but get you in trouble." Sheila sounded more like a mother than a younger sister.

"You don't know what you're talkin' about." Pooney resumed the attack on his hair. "I don't even know why I told your dumb ass!"

"We're gonna see who's dumb when Mama finds out."

"You tell Mama what I told you and you'll be minus some teeth!"

"I ain't scared of you, Pooney," Sheila replied to her brother's threat. "Anyway, I ain't gonna have to tell her. She's going to find out on her own when you go to jail for sellin' dope or shootin' somebody."

Pooney and Sheila's argument was cut short earlier than expected by the sound of their mother's key turning the deadbolt lock on the front door.

"Shit!" Pooney grabbed his books from the top of the dresser. "Put the window down," he instructed before raising his bedroom window just high enough so that he could climb through it.

Sheila heard her mother's summons upon discovering that the chain-lock had impeded her progress.

"Here I come, Mama." Sheila closed the window and ran quickly toward the front door.

(4)

Pooney decided against riding the school bus. Although bursting at the seams with pride over being a Deuce-nine Crip, he had no desire to entertain his peers by fielding questions about his black eye. The time on his Nike watch was 7:45. The newly christened gangbanger broke into a slow jog in order to catch up to the same city bus that had just dropped his mother off at Tim's store. He needed to get to the bus by the time it reached K-mart. Pooney knew that he was just as likely to draw the attention of gawkers among the city bus crowd, but at least he wouldn't run into any of his classmates.

Still a block away from K-mart, Pooney saw the bus coming to a stop in front of the small gathering of early-morning commuters. Accelerating effortlessly, he quickly closed the small gap between himself and the #6 downtown. As he ran, the ninth grader imagined himself streaking down the sidelines of Texas Stadium. Pooney reached the bus stop just as the last two passengers boarded the now densely populated bus.

"Hold up, youngster. Where's your fare?" the burly, hairy-faced bus driver asked as Pooney attempted to walk by him.

"Oh, my bad." Pooney flipped through his wallet and produced his bus card, and with a nod from the bus driver, he was on his way.

The only available seating was on the sofa seat at the rear of the bus. After wading through the mass of arms and legs that cluttered the aisle, Pooney's heart fluttered at the sight of the three passengers who would be sharing the sofa seat with him.

"'Scuse me, playa." Pooney deepened his voice and frowned slightly as he passed by one of the three red-clad young men and settled into the corner of the sofa seat.

Pooney opened his American history textbook and pretended to read. He tried to convince himself that the fact that all three young men wore red was merely a coincidence. His next thought, a more realistic one, was that the three young men would not recognize him as a Deuce-nine Crip, since his clothing gave no hint to his gang affiliation.

Another check of his watch revealed the time to be 7:52, just thirteen minutes before the start of first period. Being about two minutes into a ten-minute bus ride, Pooney hoped that he could make it through the morning without another tardy.

"Say Blood, what time you got?" the red-clad young man closest to Pooney asked suddenly.

Pooney cringed as the word "blood" rolled off the lips of the short, light-skinned brother. As a Deuce-nine Crip, Pooney was obligated to check the young man for disrespecting him that way.

"What?" Pooney tightened his frown.

"What time you got?" Shorty was unmoved by the attempt Pooney made to look mean.

Pooney briefly considered his options. He was supposed to represent his set regardless of the circumstances. But there were three of them. And they were bigger. At least the brother hadn't used the word again, Pooney told himself as he brought his watch-bound wrist to eye-level.

"Seven forty-nine," Pooney responded simply.

"What happened to your eye, homeboy?" The inevitable question was asked by the largest of the sofa seat occupants, a tall muscular brother seated between the other two. He was wearing a size-too-small Houston Rockets tank top, making him look even bigger than he actually was. Pooney eyed the initials W.S.B. tattooed on the man's right bicep.

"I got into a fight with a white boy at school." Pooney swallowed hard before lying.

"What? You let a white boy punch you in your eye?" the third member of the group asked before all three exploded with laughter.

"The white boy stole me, man." Pooney's lie grew in extravagance. "I put them hands on him after that. I got a cold boxing game, fool."

"I see." All three young men exploded with laughter again as the practical joker seated farthest from Pooney continued his performance at Pooney's expense.

"You go to Ball High?" the light-skinned brother asked.

"Yeah." Pooney nodded.

"Shit, when I was going to Ball High we had them white boys trained."

"They sure wouldn't pull no stunt like that at Texas City High," the muscle-bound youngster added before asking, "You play ball?"

"Yeah, I play cornerback." Pooney was happy that the conversation had turned to a topic he felt more comfortable with.

"J.V.?"

"Next season I'm playing varsity," Pooney promised.

"Startin'?"

"Right now I'm penciled in as the third corner and kick returner," Pooney explained. "But I'll start. Just watch."

"What grade are you in?" The larger young man had an approving smile on his face.

"I'm a freshman," Pooney answered.

"Yeah? What's your name, young blood? I'll watch for you in the paper next season."

"Allen Richards." Pooney answered, even though he had once again been disrespected by being called blood. Only three blocks away from his destination, Pooney saw no reason to inflame the situation.

"You bang, fool?" The comedian from earlier was now totally serious.

"Why you ask me something like that?" Pooney avoided the question.

"Youngster's a ballplayer." The muscle-bound youth came to Pooney's rescue. "He ain't no damn gangbanger."

"What? You think it ain't no crabs playin' football, Chuck?"

"I don't think this fool is a banger or a ballplayer." The light-skinned brother was desperate to add something to the conversation. "He looks like a mama's boy to me."

A block away from his stop, Pooney closed his American History book and tucked it under his arm, along with the Biology book, and two spiral notebooks he held.

"This is my stop." Pooney stepped toward the middle of the aisle. He became aware for the first time that everyone in the rear section of the bus had been watching and listening intently to the scene taking place on the sofa seat.

"Take it slow, youngster." The muscle-bound youth was the only one to speak to Pooney as he walked by them.

"You too, playa." Pooney turned around and gave the ex-football player some dap.

Pooney stood next to the double doors located at the bus's midsection as the bus slowed to a stop. He waited anxiously for the doors to open, still not feeling safe in the presence of three members of the West Side Bloods.

Pooney sighed in relief as the double doors opened. After safely exiting the bus, he started his three-block journey toward Ball High's north campus. Pooney was momentarily stricken with the urge to yell something through the bus window at the rival gang members, but the sound of the 8:05 bell made his thoughts regarding the passengers of the #6 downtown instantly obsolete.

(5)

After a few minutes of listening to Pooney's intensely inspired pleas, Ms. Dawkins, Pooney's usually unrelenting American History teacher, showed some leniency. She agreed to overlook his tardiness if he stayed after class and cleaned the chalkboard. Pooney quickly accepted his punishment, realizing it was a small price to pay.

Pooney chose a seat on the front row, hoping that none of his classmates would dare question him about his eye while he sat so close to Ms. Dawkins. He was correct. Although there seemed to be an endless procession of students traveling to the pencil sharpener next to Pooney's desk, none of them spoke a word. Their smirks were enough. The fifty-five minutes Pooney used to half-heartedly work on chapter review questions seemed to drag on forever.

Once the bell finally rang, Pooney headed directly to the chalkboard in order to avoid Ricky and Fred, the two boys with whom Pooney usually walked to his second period biology class.

"You want us to wait for you, Allen?" Ricky used Pooney's given name in Ms. Dawkins's presence.

"Naw." Pooney answered without turning from the chalkboard. "I'll catch y'all later."

"You two go ahead to your second period class," Ms. Dawkins interceded. "Unless of course, you'd like to join Allen in cleaning the chalkboard."

"No, ma'am," Ricky answered as he exited the classroom.

"See ya later," Fred added.

While continuing his task of erasing the chalkboard, Pooney turned toward Ms. Dawkins just in time to see the wide grin that enveloped her face. Pooney was absolutely positive that in the eight and a half months he had been Ms. Dawkins's student, this was the first time he had ever seen anything that resembled a smile. He had always considered Ms. Dawkins to be extremely attractive, although her usually icy demeanor thwarted any potential crush before it developed. Pooney had never questioned Ms. Dawkins about her age but she couldn't be *that old* he figured, maybe twenty-eight or twenty-nine. Ms. Dawkins had a caramel-colored complexion that Pooney found irresistible. And although the loose-fitting clothing she wore never allowed Pooney to confirm his suspicions, he was sure that Ms. Dawkins had a knockout figure.

The sight of the now smiling Ms. Dawkins, with small dimples that Pooney had just now discovered in both cheeks, was enough to stop the young boy's heart. The crush was on, and there was nothing Ms. Dawkins could ever do to make him see her as the business-only educator she pretended to be.

"Allen," Ms. Dawkins beckoned. "I want to talk to you."

"Yes, ma'am." Pooney wanted nothing more.

"Is everything OK with you, Allen?" she asked after waiting for him to be seated in the chair next to her desk.

"Yeah. I'm fine." Pooney wished she would smile once more so that he could get a closer look at the dimples which had fascinated him just moments before.

"If you don't mind me asking, what happened to your eye, Allen?"

"Oh, my eye!" Pooney quickly searched his own mind for a believable story. "I got into a fight with this man around the corner from my house."

Ms. Dawkins was momentarily silent as she contemplated the story Pooney had given her.

"He was harassing my little sister," Pooney added in an attempt to add nobility to his tale. "It's no big deal, Ms. Dawkins, really."

"Your eye looks pretty bad, sweetie." Ms. Dawkins gently touched the puffiness under Pooney's left eye. "Have you put anything on it?"

"No, ma'am." Pooney tried to sound pitiful.

"Did your mother see your eye?"

"My mother works nights," Pooney answered. "I leave for school before she gets home in the morning."

"Well, I think it would be a good idea if the nurse took a look at your eye, Allen." Ms. Dawkins reached inside her desk drawer, pulled out the school nurse pad, and scribbled furiously. "In the meantime, try to stay away from that guy. He might hurt you."

"Yes, ma'am." Pooney reached for his pass to the nurse's office then stood to leave.

"And," Ms. Dawkins said as she stood up and walked over to the chalkboard, "when you come to class tomorrow, you will have completed the chapter review questions you pretended to be working on earlier."

"OK." Pooney smiled as he headed for the doorway. "Ms. Dawkins," he called before leaving.

"Yes, Allen?"

"Can I say something without you getting mad at me?"

"Of course, Allen." Ms. Dawkins gave him her full attention.

"I think you're beautiful." Pooney declared boldly.

Ms. Dawkins's face lit up immediately. She had been caught totally off-guard by the brashness of Allen Richards. The dimples Pooney longed to see were much deeper now than they had been before. The moment was a fleeting one, however, as Ms. Dawkins quickly regained her composure.

"You won't think I'm so beautiful tomorrow if you come strolling into my classroom without your completed chapter review questions." Ms. Dawkins once again attempted to be cold, although she knew both her voice and body language betrayed her. She was rather embarrassed at having been momentarily swept off her feet by a teenage boy. "I'll see you no later than eight o'clock tomorrow morning, Mr. Richards."

With no further discussion, Pooney exited Ms. Dawkins's classroom.

CHAPTER 2

Pooney strolled nonchalantly amidst the dozen or so tardy students who scurried frantically in every direction.

"Pooney," a familiar voice called from behind.

Pooney turned in time to see Antonio Anderson sifting his way through the crowd of hustling bodies. The tall and lanky Antonio, who was affectionately known as "Crooked Tony" because of the two endless rows of uneven teeth he possessed, was Pooney's closest friend. Antonio had also been responsible for introducing Pooney to the Deuce-nine Crips.

"What's up, Tony?" Pooney extended his right hand toward Tony with his thumb and index finger shaped to form the letter C, the customary handshake amongst Deuce-nine Crips.

"What's up, cuz?" Crooked Tony returned the handshake, along with one of the Crips' many appropriate verbal greetings.

"How ya feelin', Loc?" A second young man stepped from behind Crooked Tony, also offering his hand to Pooney.

The second young man was Larry. A couple of years older than Pooney and Crooked Tony, Larry was a menacing figure as he stood in the center of the hallway with his mid-sized afro, unkempt beard, and dark sunglasses. Pooney half-expected the arrival of campus security at any moment.

"What's up, Larry?" Pooney shook the hand responsible for his multicolored left eye.

"Where you headed?" Crooked Tony asked.

"Biology," Pooney answered.

"Kinda late, ain't you?" Larry asked.

"I got a pass." Pooney waved the piece of paper in the air. "And you?"

"I just came to see the broads." Larry stroked the hair under his chin. "Why don't you really get some use out of that pass and come roll with your boys?"

"I can't, man. I need to get to class. It's finals review week."

"Finals review week?" Larry laughed.

"Missing one class won't hurt you," Crooked Tony reasoned. "We'll bring you back for third period."

"C'mon, Loc," Larry picked up where Tony left off. "Moe wants to talk to you."

Moe was the undisputed shot-caller for the Deuce-nine Crips. Pooney knew that a summons from Moe was not to be ignored.

"Aw right, cuz." Pooney reluctantly agreed. "Let's go."

(2)

Galveston is a small island off the coast of southeast Texas. In addition to the numerous activities held on the beach each spring and summer, Galveston boasts of Mardi Gras festivities and the Historical District to attract tourists year round. To residents, the summer months are known mostly for the stifling heat and humidity. Mid-May on "The Island," could be more unpleasant than the dog days of summer in other parts of the country. Although just after nine a.m., the temperature inside the air condition-less Ford LTD Larry drove was unbearable.

"Damn, it's hot in here," Pooney complained to no one in particular.

"You ain't lying," Tony agreed.

"Where y'all car at?" Larry was suddenly sensitive. "We ridin', ain't we?"

"Ain't nobody tryin' to diss your ride or nothin'." Crooked Tony was always the diplomat. "Just drive a little faster or something; maybe we can catch a breeze in this muthafucka."

The three boys laughed as Larry turned on Broadway Boulevard and headed east. Larry turned left on 29th Street, and the Cedar Terrace Housing Projects, the stomping grounds of the Deuce-nine Crips, became visible. Larry pulled the LTD close to a group of young men congregating outside the convenience store on 29th and Winnie.

"Moe been around here?" Larry asked the group of young men.

"He's at the clubhouse." A tall, dark-skinned man wearing a blue Dickies work uniform approached the car. "You done stole your grandpa's car again, huh, Larry?"

"Another damn comedian." Larry shook his head.

"What's up, Crooked Tony?" The man smiled.

"What's up, Paul?"

"Who's the kid with the black eye?" Paul's eyes settled on Pooney.

"Oh, him? He got clicked in last night."

"Yeah?" Paul smiled proudly. "Did he fight back?"

"Hell yeah, he fought back," Crooked Tony answered. "My homeboy got heart."

"Congratulations," Paul said to Pooney. "What's your name, Loc?"

"Pooney."

"I want you to remember something, Pooney." Paul was totally serious now. "Deuce-nine is for life, and you always got to represent. Dig?"

"Yeah, cuz. I dig." Pooney looked just as serious.

"The clubhouse." Paul slapped the side of "The Tank" before walking away.

"Who is that?" Pooney watched as Paul resumed his position in front of the store.

"That's Paul Scott." Crooked Tony gave Pooney a quick run-down. "One of our O.G.s. Just did six years in the penitentiary."

"Let's go." Larry climbed from the car. "We can walk from here. I just need to run in the store real quick." Larry walked toward the front of the store where a small group of men stood around socializing. After exchanging hi-fives with some, and the Crip Shake with others, Larry disappeared inside the store.

"What's the clubhouse?" Alone with Tony, Pooney allowed his apprehension to surface.

"Just a house where the O.G.s chill. It's cool."

Larry returned carrying a brown paper bag. "Somethin' to quench you boys' thirst." Larry placed the bag on the ground, reached inside, and pulled out a bottle of Thunderbird wine. "You youngsters watch closely. You might learn somethin'." Larry reached in his pocket and grabbed two packages of cherry-flavored Kool-Aid. After emptying the contents of the packages into the bottle, Larry twisted the cap tightly then shook the bottle violently with both hands. Next he took three large cups of ice from the bag, removed the lids, and filled each with his lethal concoction.

"Let's walk." Larry commanded while handing each of his companions a cup.

Pooney took a sip from the cup Larry had given him. It was sweet initially, but the aftertaste almost gagged him. The second sip was a little better and caused a tingling sensation throughout his body.

As the three of them walked through the Cedar Terrace Housing Projects, Pooney's attention was drawn to the graffiti present on almost every building. The majority of it was nothing but the spray-painted street names of neighborhood gangbangers. Other entries paid homage to dead homies, while still others professed their undying loyalty to Deuce-nine. Most of the apartments in this unit were unoccupied and had been boarded up by city workers. Many units had been unboarded by neighborhood drug users.

"It's gettin' hot as hell out here." Pooney wiped his forehead with the bottom of his shirt before taking a much bigger drink from his cup. The three of them crossed 31st Street, entering the second section of the apartment units. These were mostly occupied, and Pooney's stomach growled in protest as the scent of bacon and eggs assaulted him from an open window.

"That's the clubhouse." Crooked Tony announced as they reached the corner of 33rd and Winnie. He pointed at the white, two-story, wood-frame house directly in front of them. Larry led the way as they climbed the clubhouse stairs. Once at the top, he gave the wooden door three solid knocks.

"Who is it?"

"Larry."

"C'mon."

Pooney followed closely as Larry started forward. Crooked Tony closed the door behind them. Pooney's eyes began to burn as he struggled to see through the dense fog of marijuana smoke that hovered in the clubhouse. What he was able to make of the room was unimpressive, but he was thankful that there was an air conditioner running.

"What's up, Pooney?" Moe, whom Pooney had met just once before, spoke from the couch. Just under six feet tall with a medium build and honey brown complexion, there was nothing physically imposing about Moe. However, the extremely charismatic twenty-eight-year-old was not to be taken lightly. A veteran of over a decade of street wars, Moe had proven himself to be a formidable foe, as well as a savvy leader.

"What's up, cuz?" Pooney stood straight and tall.

Moe wore a pair of white Nike shorts and a blue Dallas Cowboys jersey. Seated to his left was a pretty girl Pooney was sure he had seen around the high school. Seated in a wooden chair to Moe's right was Big Lou, Moe's first lieutenant. Even seated, the powerfully built first lieutenant was nearly six feet tall.

"Chill out, Loc. This ain't the Army," Moe quipped to the extreme amusement of the young girl beside him. "Here," Moe offered Pooney a Swisher Sweet cigar which had been emptied of the tobacco and refilled with marijuana. Pooney took the Swisher from Moe's hand, but was reluctant to put the cigar between his lips. He had never smoked marijuana before.

"What's up, Loc?" Moe frowned. "You don't wanna smoke?"

Pooney brought the cigar tentatively toward his lips, the smirk on the young girl's face providing him with the needed motivation to take a small puff.

"Hold it in, cuz," Big Lou instructed while watching Pooney's eyes water.

Not knowing what else to do, Pooney attempted to swallow the smoke, causing himself to choke. There was a thunderous collection of laughter as he struggled to catch his breath.

"Gimme that, fool." Larry snatched the cigar from Pooney's hand.

"You all right, Loc?" Moe was still laughing.

Bent at the waist, hands on knees, and unable to speak, Pooney nodded.

"I just wanted to congratulate you and welcome you to the Deuce-nine family." Moe was suddenly all business.

After taking a sip from his drink, Pooney felt a little better, but still chose to nod instead of attempting to speak.

"We ain't had no beef with nobody lately, but that can change at anytime," Moe continued. "You're a soldier now, Loc, so be ready for war at all times."

Pooney continued to sip and nod.

"Y'all be careful out there." Moe's gaze turned from Pooney to the girl seated beside him. "Catch y'all later."

Pooney followed Larry and Tony out the front door, and just like that, their visit with Moe was over.

(3)

"Baby girl was somethin' serious, wasn't she?" Crooked Tony went on about the girl they had seen in the clubhouse.

"The hell with that hood rat ho!" Larry answered.

"What was her name?" Pooney mouthed dreamily as the three of them crossed 31st Street.

"I don't know her name." Crooked Tony replied. "But I know she somethin' serious."

"Shit, y'all busters wanna see somethin' serious?" Larry asked.

"Man, you trippin'." Crooked Tony waved his hand at Larry.

"Oh, yeah?" Larry reached in his pants. "What you marks know about this?" Larry was suddenly holding a .38 caliber snub-nosed revolver in his right hand.

"Aw, shit!" Crooked Tony shook his head as if not at all surprised by Larry's actions.

"Say, Pooney." Larry called. "Do you know what I can do with this lil' joker?"

With no idea how to answer Larry's question, Pooney turned to Crooked Tony. All Tony had to offer was the infamous "Crooked Tony Shrug." Crooked Tony had a frustrating habit of hunching his shoulders and staring blankly into space whenever presented with a puzzling situation.

"Just wait until I get to use this baby on a slob." Larry pointed the gun at an imaginary target. "Slob" was a derogatory term used by Crips in reference to members of the rival Blood gangs. "Y'all don't understand what I'm saying do y'all?" The low, even tone Larry used may have seemed harmless, but the violence in his eyes was unmistakable.

"Why don't you chill out, Larry?" Crooked Tony's voice broke.

"Chill out?" Larry smiled, looking past his friends and at the porch of a vacant apartment where a wino lay in a drunken slumber.

Pooney's pulse raced rapidly as Larry, gun in hand, approached the unfortunate soul. He thought he would faint when Larry placed the barrel of the .38 to the man's forehead and cocked the hammer. Each second was an eternity as Pooney stood with his eyes closed, silently awaiting the explosion that would take the sleeping man's life. Pooney wished with all his heart that he had attended Mr. Lankford's Biology class.

"I'ma let you make it," Pooney heard Larry utter softly.

Pooney breathed an audible sigh of relief as he watched Larry uncock the hammer and return the gun to the waistband of his Enyce jeans before strolling away from the drunken man.

"Y'all some scary muthafuckas!" Larry professed as the three of them resumed their walk toward the LTD.

"What y'all wanna do?" Crooked Tony threw his now empty cup on the ground.

"Damn. I'm late for third period." Pooney's watch read 10:15.

"You might as well chill with us, Loc." Larry reached in his pocket and pulled out an assortment of coins that he proceeded to count. "Ain't no sense in wasting your buzz at school."

"I can't miss football practice." Pooney said.

"Football practice is after school." Larry answered. "That's five hours away."

"But I got Coach Roy for my fifth period health class," came Pooney's rebuttal.

"Well, hang out until fifth period," Crooked Tony suggested.

Pooney took another sip of his cup of watered-down wine. He frowned and wiped at his brow with his hand before finally answering, "OK." He took another sip. "Until fifth period."

(4)

Cheryl Dawkins was crossing the line. She had discovered that Allen Richards had not only skipped his trip to the nurse's office, but he had also failed to show up for his second and third period classes. And this after showing up to her first period class badly beaten. All logic told her to mind her business. She was just a history teacher, not a savior for wayward children. But Allen Richards was in trouble. She had seen this story played out too many times before. It was none of her business, but she had to do something. So, after ten minutes of intense deliberation, Ms. Dawkins picked up the telephone and dialed Allen's home phone number.

The phone rang ten times before Ms. Dawkins first considered hanging up.

"Hello," came a hoarse whisper after the thirteenth ring.

"Hi, this is Cheryl Dawkins. I'm Allen's American History teacher. Is his mother in?"

"This is Allen's mother." Regina Richards's mind was slowly coming into focus, though her voice did not yet reflect that fact.

"I hate to wake you, Ms. Richards." Ms. Dawkins recalled Allen explaining that his mother worked nights. "But I think there may be a problem with Allen."

"What problem?" Regina's voice was unintentionally harsh.

"Well," Ms. Dawkins was starting to regret placing the phone call already. "Allen showed up to my class this morning pretty beat up."

"Beat up?"

"Yes, Ms. Richards. Allen had a bad bruise on his left eye, and some scratches on his face and neck."

"What in the world?"

"He told me he had a fight with an adult man for harassing his sister." Ms. Dawkins felt like a police informant.

"My daughter didn't mention it to me this morning."
Regina was clearly puzzled. Sheila didn't keep things from her
mother.

"There's something else, Ms. Richards."

"Something else?"

"Allen's not at school."

"What?"

"He left his baseball cap in my class after I had written
him a pass to the nurse," Ms. Dawkins explained. "When I went
to take it to him, I found he had never been there."

"Uh huh, I see."

"He also failed to report to his next two classes," Ms.
Dawkins continued. "Ms. Richards, I only called because I am
very concerned about Allen."

"Oh, you did the right thing." Regina contemplated the
severity of Allen's first whipping in years. "Thank you very
much."

"You're welcome, Ms. Richards. And if I see him, I'll be
sure to call back."

After exchanging goodbyes with Allen's mother, Cheryl
Dawkins placed the receiver back on its hook. It was done now.
Allen would be upset with her, but it was for his own good.

(5)

"Stay in your lane, fool!" Larry grabbed the steering wheel
and pushed hard, keeping the Ford LTD from ramming into the
curb.

"I got it." Pooney was ecstatic about his first time behind
the wheel of a car.

"Straighten this thing up!" Crooked Tony yelled from the
back seat.

Larry and Crooked Tony continued yelling instructions
in Pooney's direction as The Tank barreled down Port Industrial
Boulevard. For his part, Pooney ignored the voices of his friends,

as well as the crescendo of horns which squealed in protest of his lack of driving etiquette.

"The red light, Loc!" Larry yelled after they were already in the middle of the intersection.

As the cars to his left started in motion, Pooney instinctively pressed the gas pedal to the floor and accelerated through the intersection.

"I sure hope none of them got cellular phones." Crooked Tony looked out the back window at the mass of confusion Pooney had just caused.

"Pull this muthafucka over!" Larry had had enough. "Shit, you already pulled over. Just stop!"

Pooney pressed down hard on the brakes, sending all three young men crashing forward. Another horn blared as an angered motorist veered around the LTD shouting obscenities.

Pooney, pulse racing and breath coming in spurts, smiled as he counted to himself the dozen or so blocks he had just driven.

"Get your crazy ass in the backseat!" Larry yelled while reaching to put the car in park. He then activated the hazard switch.

"What's wrong with you?" Pooney's smile got broader as he noted the fear in Larry's voice.

"Get your ass in the backseat!"

"You trippin'." Pooney opened the door slightly and another horn blared at him.

"Don't try to open the door, fool." Larry spoke in a slow measured voice as he attempted to hide his frustration. "Climb into the backseat."

The three young men played a quick game of musical chairs that placed Larry in the driver's seat, Crooked Tony in the passenger seat, and Pooney in the backseat.

"Look at all this damn wine!" Larry wiped at the dashboard with a rag. "My grandpa's gonna kill me!"

Larry slipped the car into drive and eased into traffic.

(6)

Regina poured herself a third cup of coffee and returned to her seat in front of the television. She struggled desperately to ignore the catastrophic images her mind conjured. She turned the television to the local CBS affiliate to watch *The Price Is Right.*

The conversation with Ms. Dawkins had left Regina totally bewildered. To the best of her knowledge, Allen had never done anything like this before. *To my knowledge.* The thought almost caused her to laugh aloud. Truth be told, Regina had very little knowledge regarding the comings and goings of her fifteen-year-old son. What little she did know was courtesy of Sheila, who had obviously begun to keep secrets for her older brother. They would both have some explaining to do today.

Regina placed the empty cup on the arm of the chair and headed for Allen's room in hopes of finding some clue as to her son's whereabouts.

CHAPTER 3

Sheila beamed with pride as her classmates saluted her with a standing ovation in response to her rendition of Elton John's "Candle in the Wind."

"Well done, Sheila." Mr. Comeaux, Sheila's music teacher, applauded softly as the bell rang, signifying the end of the class.

Sheila gathered her books as her classmates shuffled from the classroom.

"Sheila," Mr. Comeaux called out as he straightened the papers on his desk. "Can I speak to you for a second?"

"Yes, sir." Sheila placed her books on top of the piano she had just played while waiting for Mr. Comeaux to close the door behind the last student.

"The song you performed," Mr. Comeaux made his approach. "Elton John, right?"

"Yes, sir," Sheila answered. "It's one of my favorites."

"Who taught you to play it?" Mr. Comeaux was obviously impressed.

"I listen to it all the time." Sheila shrugged. "The lady I babysit for has a piano. I just close my eyes and play what I hear."

"You taught yourself to play that song?"

"Yeah."

"By ear?"

"I guess so."

"Sheila," Mr. Comeaux ran his hand through the handful of wavy, jet-black hair he possessed. "Do you have any idea of the very special talent you have?"

Sheila could only smile.

"Do you have any plans for the summer, Sheila?"

"No, sir."

Are you interested in the summer music school I told the class about?"

"Yes, Mr. Comeaux. I'm very interested, but I don't know if my mother can afford it." Sheila tried in vain to hide the disappointment in her voice. "I haven't asked her yet."

"Sheila," Mr. Comeaux looked toward the door as if his next statement was extremely secretive, "forget about the tuition. Do you want to go?"

"Yes, sir!"

"Good." Sheila's enthusiasm brought a smile to Mr. Comeaux's face. "Let me give you these registration papers."

Sheila grabbed her books from the top of the piano and followed Mr. Comeaux to his desk.

"Here you are." Mr. Comeaux handed Sheila the needed forms. "Just fill them out with your mother and bring them back tomorrow."

The two of them exchanged smiles before Sheila turned toward the door and walked away.

"Sheila." Mr. Comeaux called just as Sheila was exiting the room. "One more thing."

"Yes, Mr. Comeaux?"

"You have a beautiful singing voice."

"Thank you." Sheila smiled sheepishly, realizing for the first time that she had begun to sing while playing the piano for the class. "Bye!"

(2)

Larry parked in front of the slightly run-down wood frame house that stood on the corner of 38th Street and Avenue I. "Roll y'all windows up," Larry instructed as he reached under his seat and grabbed the quarter-ounce of marijuana he had gotten on credit from a friend.

Larry swallowed the contents of his cup and immediately poured himself a refill. Crooked Tony followed suit.

"Want this last bit?" Crooked Tony asked Pooney.

Pooney, still nauseous from the wine he had drunk earlier, declined Tony's offer with a shake of his head.

"Y'all let me do all the talkin'," Larry stated. "I'll get us inside."

"Yeah, like last time." Crooked Tony laughed.

"You'll be thankin' me in a minute, cuz," Larry told him.

"How you know it's some broads over here anyway?" Crooked Tony asked.

"Leticia just had a baby. She's on homebound study." Larry took another drink, causing Pooney to marvel at the amount of wine he was capable of consuming. "The other broads hang out over here when they don't wanna go to school."

"Well, let's go." Crooked Tony smiled broadly, revealing his entire collection of oddly shaped teeth.

"One more thing." Larry's voice was humorless. "Y'all know we out of bounds, so stay ready."

The three of them stepped from The Tank and made their way toward Leticia's front door. Larry gave the door a series of solid taps before pulling a blue bandanna from his pocket and tying it around his head.

"What you doing?" Crooked Tony eyed the bandanna.

"Representin'," Larry answered before launching a second assault on the door. "Leticia!"

"Who is it?" A female voice screamed from the other side of the door.

"Larry."

"What you want?"

"Open the door!"

"For what?"

"'Cause I said so!"

"Fuck you."

"Open the damn door!"

Pooney stood stiff with apprehension when he heard the lock on the door turn.

"What the hell you want?" The door cracked.

"Get yo' ass out the way!" Larry forced his way through the door despite Leticia's high-pitched protests. "Y'all c'mon," he barked to Pooney and Crooked Tony once inside the house.

"So y'all just gonna walk y'all triflin' asses in my house 'cause this asshole said so?" Leticia stared at Pooney and Tony in disgust.

Standing in the doorway with both hands on her hips, and a black scarf tied tightly about her head, Leticia looked much older than her eighteen years.

"Chill out, girl." Crooked Tony stepped around Leticia and followed Larry.

"Excuse me," Pooney mumbled after deciding that the angry-looking young woman was harmless.

Pooney slid past Leticia and followed his two friends into the house.

"Who is you, homeboy?" Pooney heard Larry ask.

"Steve," answered a voice that startled Pooney.

"What you want over here?" Larry continued his interrogation.

"You got a lot of fuckin' nerve, Larry." Leticia brushed by Pooney and entered her living room. "Comin' in here, questioning my company."

"Your company?" Something about the sound of Larry's voice gave Pooney chills.

"I came to see Deidra." Steve spoke quickly, obviously sensing the same potential in Larry's voice.

"You ain't gotta tell him nothin!" Leticia yelled. "He don't run shit over here!"

"Where you from, homeboy?" Pooney watched from the doorway as Larry approached the man.

"La Marque," the young man answered.

"Where 'bout in La Marque?"

"Lake Road."

Larry pulled his shirt up and Pooney took a step backward as the handle of the gun became visible.

"You smoke, cuz?" Pooney opened his eyes in time to see Larry drop the bag of marijuana on the table.

Although relieved that Larry had grabbed the bag of marijuana, and not the gun, Pooney knew that the potential for danger was not over. Larry had used the word cuz to check Steve. If Steve was affiliated with a blood gang then there could be big trouble.

Steve said nothing. The stoutly built, light-skinned brother eyed Larry closely, while remaining as quiet and still as a cobra in pre-strike mode.

The room was silent as all present nervously awaited Steve's response.

"Fire it up, Loc," Steve finally answered, and the storm cloud that hung over the room seemed to dissipate immediately.

"So now y'all gonna smoke weed in my house?" Leticia continued to fuss while everyone else continued to ignore her.

Pooney leaned against the doorframe, still light-headed from the morning's drinking. He allowed himself to relax as he inventoried Leticia's living room. The furniture was modest, consisting of a matching brown-vinyl couch, love seat, and chair. Larry, Steve, and a girl Pooney assumed was Deidra, sat on the couch. Crooked Tony joined two other girls on the loveseat, while Leticia still stood in the middle of the floor, holding the same pose she had struck at the front door. There was a small wooden table in front of the couch Larry used to roll the Swishers.

"Sit down, Pooney." Larry never lifted his eyes from the table.

"Yeah, make yourself at home. Everyone else is," Leticia fussed before storming off in the direction of the crying infant who could be heard from a nearby room.

Pooney walked slowly toward the unoccupied chair. "What's up?" He spoke in the girl's direction.

The girl seated next to Tony, the heavyset one with the beautiful caramel complexion just like Ms. Dawkins, whispered into the ear of the smaller, slightly darker girl seated beside her. Then the two of them erupted into that annoyingly hysterical giggle that only teenage girls seemed able to manage.

"What y'all laughing at my homeboy for?" Crooked Tony asked.

"You need to shut up, Crooked Tony." The smaller one rolled her eyes.

"Ooh, and please shut your mouth," the larger one added, and the room quickly filled with the laughter of everyone present save for Pooney and Crooked Tony.

Pooney was one of the few people who knew how badly Tony was hurt by jokes about his teeth. His anger toward the two girls rose steadily as they continued to laugh at his best friend.

"Remember him?" Leticia redirected everyone's attention as she entered the room carrying her and Larry's infant son. "That's your Daddy." She pointed at Larry.

"What you bring him in here for?" Larry looked up from his chore of rolling Swisher Sweets.

"This is his house. He can go wherever he wanna go," Leticia said. "Here! I gotta fix his bottle." Leticia dropped the baby in Larry's lap before stomping toward the kitchen.

"I'll finish rollin'." Steve slid over the album cover containing the marijuana and cigars so they were in front of him.

"Hey man, what you been doin' while Daddy was gone?" Larry made a clumsy attempt at baby talk. "See my lil' loc, Pooney?"

"How old is he?" Pooney asked.

"Two months," Larry answered. "Wanna hold him?"

"Yeah." Pooney shrugged.

Larry handed the baby to Pooney. Once the exchange was finished, Pooney gently cradled Lil' Larry in his arms, marveling at how difficult it was to keep the tot stationary.

"Use your arm to support his neck, stupid!" The little one with the smart mouth was at it again.

Pooney followed loudmouth's instructions while staring intently at the infant in his arms. What he saw in the smiling face of Larry's little boy seemed totally inconsistent with the scene in Leticia's living room. The joy the tot exhibited was clearly contagious. Pooney couldn't help but return the baby's smile. Lil' Larry's smile grew even wider, now accompanied by a shrill of excitement as Pooney tickled him gently.

"I thought you were in here playing with the baby, Larry." Leticia emerged once more. The anger she had exhibited earlier had now been replaced by disappointment.

"Y'all fire it up." Larry took the baby from Pooney and walked toward Leticia. "I'ma help Leticia put our son to sleep."

The smell of marijuana was already filling the room as Larry and his family closed the door behind them.

(3)

Sheila unwrapped her tuna fish sandwich while her mind replayed the conversation she had had with Mr. Comeaux. Because she knew her mother couldn't afford it, she had never bothered to mention to anyone how badly she wanted to attend the summer music school.

"You listening, girl?" Janeen's voice impeded Sheila's thoughts.

"Yeah, I'm listening," Sheila lied.

Janeen was Sheila's best friend and was prone to long periods of constant chatter. Sheila had long ago mastered the art of pretending to listen to her by mumbling words of acknowledgement whenever there was a pause in Janeen's conversation. She had obviously missed a pause.

The two girls never missed a lunch together. And everyday Janeen would go on and on about the same subject: boys! To Sheila's dismay, Janeen had returned from last year's summer vacation with a fully developed chest that she loved to show off in tight-fitting blouses. Of course, Janeen's attraction to boys was mutual. There was always an endless procession of boys passing their table to invite Janeen to a party, or ask for her phone number, or just watch the way she would push her chest out even farther whenever they were around. Occasionally, one of the boys would attempt to talk to Sheila, but she just wasn't interested. At least not in any of the boys who had approached her.

"Well, does he?" Janeen was exasperated.

"Does he what?"

"Does your brother have a girlfriend?"

"My brother?" Sheila laughed. "Since when are you interested in my brother?"

"Girl, we are going to be in high school next year." Janeen was quiet long enough to strike "The Pose" for two passing boys. "I need a man with a letterman's jacket."

"And my brother is as good as any, I guess." Sheila spoke with the slightest hint of attitude.

"Girl, your brother is fine." Janeen was never discouraged. "But that don't matter as long as he has a letterman's jacket."

"You're crazy, Janeen." Both girls laughed loudly.

"Look, girl." Janeen was excited to see Charlie Williams, a real favorite with the girls, headed directly toward her and Sheila's table.

Once again, Janeen crossed her legs, cupped both hands around her knees, and poked her chest out so far that Sheila was sure her friend would explode.

"Can I sit down for a second?" Charlie Williams asked after already having pulled the chair from under the table and sitting down. "Hi, Janeen."

Sheila turned green with envy at watching Charlie speak directly to Janeen's blouse.

"Sheila," Charlie turned away from Janeen, "I came to ask if you have a date to the School's Out dance."

"No." Sheila hoped she didn't look as silly as Janeen.

"Would you like to go with me?" Charlie smiled, displaying a mouthful of braces that on any other boy would have looked totally nerdy. But with Charlie Williams, even braces were cool.

"Well...uh..." Sheila hesitated before a hard thump on her shin caused her to say, "Sure."

"Good." Charlie's smile widened. "I'll have my mom pick you up next Friday at seven."

"Seven's great." Sheila barked in fear of another kick from Janeen.

"Can I have your phone number?" Charlie asked.

"My phone number?" Sheila was caught off guard.

"So I can call next Friday night for directions." Charlie talked fast.

Sheila pulled a Bic pen and a small notepad from her purse and wrote her number down quickly. "Here, Charlie." She beamed.

"Here's mine." Charlie handed Sheila a small piece of paper with his number already written on it.

"If a guy answers the phone, it's my brother," Sheila explained. "He might try to give you a hard time."

"Don't worry. I'm good with brothers." Charlie Williams ended every sentence with a smile.

Sheila and Janeen watched as Charlie returned to his friends.

"What is wrong with you, Sheila?" Janeen was upset.

"What?"

"When a boy like Charlie Williams asks you to a dance, you don't hesitate."

"Girl, let's go." Sheila laughed. "I need to get my English book."

"Yeah, I need to stop by the restroom and check my hair." Janeen's chatter began again as they headed for the door. "I don't even have a date yet, and Charlie Williams asks you. Charlie Williams, of all people. Do you know how many girls wish Charlie Williams would ask them out?"

"I know one." Sheila laughed as they exited the cafeteria.

(4)

"Hello." Regina answered the phone on the first ring.

"Ms. Richards, it's Cheryl Dawkins." Ms. Dawkins noted the anxiety in Regina Richards's voice.

"Yes, Ms. Dawkins."

"Allen has returned to school."

"Thank you, Jesus." Regina sighed heavily.

"He showed up for his fifth period health class."

"I've been worried sick, Ms. Dawkins."

"Me, too."

"Where in the world has he been?"

"I haven't talked to him," Ms. Dawkins explained. "I just walked by Mr. Roy's classroom and saw that he was there."

"Thank you so much, Ms. Dawkins." Regina managed to control her trembling left hand long enough to sip from her coffee cup.

"I'm just glad Allen's OK, Ms. Richards."

"For now. His butt is mine when he gets home." The two women shared a brief tension-relieving laugh.

"I wish I could say he didn't deserve it." Ms. Dawkins toyed with the locket dangling from her neck.

"And he's gonna get it." Both women laughed again.

"Well, Ms. Richards, I need to get back to my fifth period class before they send a search party out for me."

"OK, Ms. Dawkins. Thanks, again."

"No problem. Just leave enough hide on him for my first period class tomorrow."

"Bye.."

"Bye."

(5)

"What the hell is wrong with you, Richards?" Coach Roy's voice seemed to have the power to raise the temperature inside Pooney's helmet twenty degrees.

The latter part of Pooney's afternoon was spent battling one misery after another. After discovering that Larry had fallen asleep, Pooney walked from Leticia's house back to school, vomiting once along the way. Next, he made it to Coach Roy's class ten minutes after class had begun, which meant being subjected to Coach Roy's policy of tardy students being the teacher's aide for the day. After forty-five minutes of writing and erasing things on the chalkboard, pointing to the life-sized illustrations Coach Roy used, and running an assortment of errands, Pooney was quite relieved when the bell finally rang and he could get to the restroom to vomit once more. Then, halfway through his sixth period Algebra class, it started, a headache unlike anything Pooney had ever experienced. This was more severe than the headache that had accompanied his sixth grade bout with strep throat.

Mrs. Guidry's seventh period English class offered some relief. Pooney had at least been able to doze off for half an hour.

But now, football practice presented a misery beyond his wildest comprehension. Today, of all days, the team had been surprised with a full-speed scrimmage. So as Pooney struggled with the discomfort of being clad in full pads beneath an unrelenting Texas sun, he was clearly playing as badly as he felt.

"Why'd you turn him loose?" Coach Roy was shouting directly in Pooney's face.

"I thought I had outside help," Pooney replied.

"Outside help!" Coach Roy was enraged. "What the hell were you doing in the huddle? Cause you sure as hell weren't listening to the call!"

"Sorry, Coach." Pooney returned to the huddle.

"I know! Quit reminding me!" Coach Roy returned to the sideline.

"What's up, Allen?" Alfredo Quintana asked, clearly puzzled. Alfredo was the Tors starting middle linebacker, and the largest Mexican kid Pooney had ever laid eyes on.

"I'm all right. My bad, fellas." Pooney clapped his hands. "Let's go!"

"All right then!" Quintana spat behind him. "Twenty-seven man-cover. Twenty-seven man-cover," the middle linebacker repeated for Pooney's benefit. "Let's take it to 'em!"

The entire varsity defense clapped loudly in unison before lining up on the ball.

"I thought I had outside help," Carlton Green, the receiver Pooney was assigned to cover, mimicked as the offense lined up.

"Shut up, punk!" Pooney shot back.

"I'm taking you deep this time, Richards."

"Bring it on." Pooney backed up a couple of steps.

The ball was snapped and Green charged hard off the line of scrimmage. Instead of attempting to run by Pooney, Green ran straight at him, burying his helmet into the cornerback's chest.

Damn. Run. Pooney realized Green had bluffed him. The offense was running a sweep in Pooney's direction. Pooney worked desperately to hold his ground as Green threatened to blow him off his feet. After fighting Green off, Pooney eluded the block of the pulling guard and closed in on the ball carrier, placing himself on course for a head-on collision with a much bigger running back. After the resounding *smack* that accompanied helmet-to-helmet contact, Pooney found himself flat on his back. He somehow managed to bring the ball carrier down with him.

"Way to go, Allen!" Quintana's voice was partially obscured by the ringing in Pooney's ears.

"Good hit, Richards!" Pooney heard another vaguely familiar voice say as he was pulled to his feet.

Pooney couldn't tell if the whistle he heard was a Coach's whistle or the train that roared inside his head.

"Aw right, two laps and hit the showers!" Pooney's eyes began to focus as his teammates started running. "Richards, come here."

Pooney approached Coach Roy cautiously, not yet trusting his shaky equilibrium.

"What the hell is your problem, Richards?" Coach Roy was yelling.

"What you mean, Coach? I made the play."

"I'm not talking about the play, son. That was a helluva play you just made." Coach Roy studied Pooney's face. "I'm talking about you."

"What you mean, Coach?"

"You've been drinking, Richards."

Pooney considered lying, but the last thing he wanted was to piss off Coach Roy. Coach Roy, who had once played for the Atlanta Falcons, stood well over six feet tall, and tipped the scales at over 270 pounds. Coach Roy could also outrun most of the players on the starting varsity defense, a feat he enjoyed repeating about once every week or so. A product of the same Galveston housing projects that many of his players now called home, nothing upset Coach Roy more than squandered talent. Once, a starting varsity flanker, who just so happened to be a real speedster, tried to quit in the middle of a homecoming game. The kid had a fifteen-yard head start as he broke for the locker room. However, Coach Roy chased him down, kicked him squarely in the behind, and sent him right back in the game.

"You listening to me, Richards?" Coach Roy's voice caught the attention of a couple of Pooney's teammates as they finished their first lap.

"I'm listening, Coach."

"You've been drinking, haven't you?"

Pooney looked down at his cleats—answer enough for Coach Roy.

"So what are you trying to do?" Coach Roy was livid. "Fuck yourself up?"

Pooney looked up suddenly, taken aback by Coach Roy's language.

"That stuff is poison, son," Coach Roy continued. "What class did you cut?"

"Huh?" Pooney was dumbfounded by Coach Roy's questioning.

"You had time to get drunk! What class did you cut?"

Pooney hesitated before answering, "Second and third periods."

"Richards, normally I'd run your tongue out of your mouth, but not today." Coach Roy pulled a stick of chewing gum from his pocket, unwrapped it, shoved it in his mouth, and attacked it violently. "How much you weigh?"

"One fifty-five."

"You know, Richards, I shouldn't tell you this, but Coach Hawthorne really likes you."

"Really?" Pooney didn't even think the Tors head football coach knew he existed.

"When two-a-days start, you'll be penciled in as our top corner."

"Really?" Pooney could think of nothing else to say.

"I think you can handle the job, Richards. But it's gonna take a lot of hard work."

"I'll work hard, Coach Roy, I promise." The opportunity to play varsity football had been a dream of Pooney's since he first attended a game with his grandfather at the age of five. He promised then and there that his grandfather would one day watch him play for the beloved Tors in Public School Stadium. When his grandfather died seven years later, Pooney's desire to make varsity only grew stronger.

"Well, you can start by putting on some weight this summer. Reynolds almost killed you." Coach Roy laughed to himself while sizing Pooney up. "Ten pounds ought to do. I want to see you in the field house every day this summer."

"Yes, sir."

"Well, I guess you can start running."

"You said you wasn't going to run me."

"I'm not. You are."

"What?" Pooney was tiring of Coach Roy's riddles.

"What did you plan on telling your second and third period teachers tomorrow?"

Pooney shrugged in frustration, already knowing the coach's angle.

"For five laps, I'll take care of it." Coach Roy smiled.

"Five laps?"

"Five laps for each class. And one more thing." Coach Roy took his gum out and held it in his hand. "You pull a stunt like this again, and I'll make you regret it the rest of your life."

"Yes, sir."

"Now get going. The Astros are coming on in thirty minutes."

"One thing, Coach," Pooney started nervously. "How'd you know I was drinking?"

"You kiddin'?" Coach Roy rubbed one side of his well-groomed beard. "I smelled you as soon as you walked in my classroom this afternoon."

Pooney began his laps, wondering if there was any possible way he could finish.

(6)

Pooney stepped off the bus at the convenience store across the street from his apartment complex. He stretched wildly before reaching in his pocket and pulling out two one-dollar bills and a handful of change. As he walked toward Tim's store, so-called after its Korean owner, Pooney counted the change in his hand.

"What's up, Tim?" Pooney had always liked the Korean store owner.

"Hey, Pooney. How's it go?" Tim made his usual hilarious attempt at communicating with slang.

"Everything's all right, Tim." Pooney tried to smile. "I need some aspirin."

"Aspirin? You get punched in eye?"

"Headache. Big headache." Pooney imitated Tim's accent.

"Linebacker hit you in head?" Tim asked.

"Somethin' like that."

Pooney purchased four single Tylenols, two of which he placed in his mouth immediately, and a half-pint of orange juice which he swallowed in two gulps while standing at the store's entrance. "Later, Tim." Pooney placed the plastic carton in the trash before exiting the store.

"Later, playa," Tim called behind him.

Pooney could think about nothing but a nice, cold shower and Sheila's meatloaf as he crossed Heards Lane. Then, after completing the chapter review questions for Ms. Dawkins' history class, he would sleep until tomorrow morning. *I'll be in bed by nine,* Pooney thought while eyeing his watch.

"Honey, I'm home," Pooney joked with his sister as he walked through the front door and threw his backpack on the floor. "Where's my dinner?"

"You're gonna get your dinner all right." Pooney felt that sinking feeling in his stomach as he heard his mother's voice coming from his bedroom. "Get your butt in here!"

"What you doin' here, Mama?" Pooney was terrified.

"What in the world happened to your eye?" Regina was shocked upon seeing her son's badly discolored eye for the first time.

"I got hit at football practice."

"That's not what you told Ms. Dawkins."

"Ms. Dawkins?" Pooney felt betrayed.

"What happened to your eye?"

"I got hit at football practice." Pooney felt a combination of fear and disbelief upon noticing that his mother had his leather belt in her lap with one end rolled around her right hand. "I just told her anything because it wasn't none of her business."

"Sounds like the only practicing you been doing is lying." Regina tightened the belt around her hand. "Where were you this morning when you should have been at school?"

"I was at school, Mama."

"You'd better stop lying to me, Allen. I'm inches off your behind as it is!" Regina was irate. "Where were you?"

"I was at a girl's house." Pooney was a quick thinker.

"You mean to tell me that while I was sitting around here worried to death, you were with some pissy-tailed girl?" Regina rose to her feet and approached her son.

"Yeah, Mama." Pooney back-pedaled slowly.

"Don't make me chase you, boy!"

"But, Mama." Pooney halted. "I'm fifteen-years-old. That's too old to be catchin' whippings."

A split second later, Regina was on him like a rabid mongoose. She held him at arm's length by the back of his collar, giving herself all the room she needed to demonstrate her prowess with the belt.

"OK, Mama!" Pooney yelled as the belt started to sting the unprotected skin of his legs. How he regretted his decision to wear gym shorts home from football practice.

"OK nothing!" Regina flailed away. "I work too hard trying to keep you with the things you need to do well in school."

The lecture and whipping continued as the two of them went round and round Pooney's bedroom.

Moments later, Regina stood in Pooney's doorway, trying desperately to catch her breath, while Pooney sat on the edge of his bed, eyes watering, but refusing to cry.

"Unhook that damn telephone and put it in the living room." Regina's weapon became a clothing device again as she laid it on her son's dresser. "Get your books, do your homework, and don't even think about coming out of this room unless you are going to the bathroom! Understand?"

Pooney mumbled his acknowledgment while unhooking the telephone. He wrapped the cord around the phone and headed to the living room. Sheila was sitting on the couch. Pooney reached around her to grab his backpack. As he did, he was surprised to see her wiping tears from her eyes.

Once alone in his room, Pooney kicked his sneakers off and turned his stereo on just loud enough so his mother couldn't hear him. He reached in his backpack and grabbed the Swisher he had taken with him from Leticia's house and placed it under a section of the rug that had once served as a piggybank. He then took his American History textbook and folder from his backpack and began his homework.

(7)

Sheila knocked softly on her brother's bedroom door. "Pooney," she called softly while pushing the door open and poking her head inside.

Pooney, seated at his desk with pen in hand, was sound asleep with his face in his history book.

"Pooney." Sheila shook him gently. "Wake up."

Pooney popped up instantly in response to Sheila's touch, wiping saliva from the side of his face. "Ugh! You're nasty." Sheila turned her nose up as she pushed his book aside and placed a monstrous-sized plate, complete with meatloaf, green beans, two ears of corn, and four buttered rolls before him. She left momentarily, only to return a few seconds later with a half pitcher of Kool-Aid and a drinking glass.

"Don't make this no habit!" Sheila smarted while pouring her brother a glass of Kool-Aid.

"Where's Mama?" Pooney asked between shovelfuls of meatloaf.

"She went to bingo with Renee."

"Bingo? She didn't go to work?" Pooney poured himself a second glass of Kool-Aid.

"She said her nerves too bad to go to work." Sheila watched as Pooney devoured the plate.

"What you lookin' at me like that for?" Pooney's mouth was full of meatloaf.

"You're stupid."

"You're stupid." Pooney wasn't in the mood to hear Sheila's mouth.

"I told you those boys are gonna get you in trouble." Sheila was shaking her head. "This is only the beginning."

"That was good." Pooney scraped the last of the sauce from his plate before pouring himself a third glass of Kool-Aid. "If you wasn't so ugly, you'd make somebody a good wife."

"Forget you, punk!" Sheila grabbed the empty plate from her brother's desk. "You'd better finish your homework before Mama gets home."

"What time is it?"

"Nine thirty. She'll be here in about an hour." Sheila emptied the remainder of the Kool-Aid into her brother's glass. "Them girls been callin' here. I told them all you was sleep."

"What girls?"

"I don't know! I ain't your secretary." Sheila stood to leave. "That crooked teeth boy called, too."

"What'd you tell him?"

"I told him he already got you in enough trouble for one day."

"You what?"

"I told him you was asleep, boy. Finish with that glass. I need to roll my hair before I go to bed."

"Thank you." Pooney handed his sister the glass.

"Whatever." Sheila smacked her lips.

Pooney smiled as he watched his sister storm from his bedroom. Black women were funny that way. Loving, caring, and generous to a fault, they would, for reasons known only to themselves, prefer to project an attitude that would suggest something different. Fortunately, the only people they succeeded in fooling were themselves.

CHAPTER 4

Regina peered out the passenger side window of Renee's Toyota Camry. She had once again been amazed by the persuasive ability that her best friend seemed to possess. While Regina usually enjoyed watching Renee weave her magic on unsuspecting subjects, she didn't find it quite as entertaining when she found herself as the victim.

"I don't know how I let you talk me into this, Renee." Regina watched as two men entered Uptown Tavern, a small bar affectionately referred to by locals as String Bean's after the owner's nickname.

"Talk you into what?" Renee's full attention was focused on the task of applying eyeliner.

"You know what I'm talking about."

"Relax, girl." Renee placed the eyeliner back in her purse, then grabbed her lipstick. "You need a night out."

"A bunch of kids hang out here, Renee."

"That's on weekends. It's Monday."

"My children think I'm at bingo."

"Since when do your children have to be informed of your whereabouts?"

"That's not the point, Renee."

"Look, let's go in and have a drink. If you're ready to leave after that, we will." Renee tucked her purse under her arm and opened her door. "OK?"

Regina followed Renee through the front door of String Beans. There was a relatively small crowd scattered throughout the bar. The room was dark, and the jukebox played R.Kelly's "12 Play."

Renee had the full attention of the male portion of the crowd as she strutted directly toward the bar. She was a very attractive woman. Not the kind of attractive that one would see on the cover of *Vogue*, but the kind of attractive that men who frequented places like String Beans went nuts over. She had a beautiful, dark-chocolate complexion with incredibly smooth skin. She was about five feet, six inches tall and weighed 150 pounds. While some would consider that to be slightly overweight, Renee wore it well. She had large shapely thighs, and beautifully curved hips. The source of men's madness, however, was Renee's behind.

Renee had a perfectly round, improbably oversized butt that remained remarkably firm. It was impossible to hide, even on the few occasions when Renee had attempted to do so. And on a night like tonight, when Renee's choice of clothing was a skin-tight black catsuit, her behind took on a personality of its own. And predictably, that personality was now dominating the atmosphere in String Beans.

"What are you ladies drinking?" String Bean asked as Renee and Regina approached the bar.

"Let me have a rum and Coke, Mr. String Bean," Renee answered before turning to Regina.

"A wine cooler, please." Regina would much rather have ordered a Coke, but she knew that such a request would invoke a heated protest from Renee.

"How have you been doing, Mr. String Bean?" Renee reached in her purse as he fixed her drink.

"OK, I guess," the gray-haired man answered. "I was about to ask you the same. Been a while since I've seen you."

"I'm fine." Renee answered. "Just working a lot."

"And you, Regina?" String Bean eyed Regina. "Didn't think I remembered you, huh?"

"I'm doing OK." Regina was shocked by the old man's memory. There was once a time when she had frequented String Beans quite a bit, but that time was long ago.

"All right," String Bean grunted as he placed both drinks on the bar. "You two enjoy yourself."

"I'm sure we will." Regina extended her hand toward String Bean, and with it a ten dollar bill.

"You girls go ahead. This round's on the house."

"Thank you, Mr. String Bean," both women murmured, almost in unison.

"I got a feeling you two won't be paying for any drinks tonight." String Bean left them in order to wait on another patron.

"Let's find a table." Renee turned suddenly, and with Regina following closely, walked away from the bar and toward the tables to their left. "I guess this one's all right. Loosen up a little, Gina. You might enjoy yourself."

"This just isn't my idea of fun, Renee."

"It used to be."

"That was a long time ago."

"A long time ago?" Renee scoffed before taking a sip from her drink. "You're thirty-four, not sixty-four, so how long ago could it have been?"

There was a lull in the conversation as the two of them listened to the music and evaluated the scene around them.

"You need a man." Renee boldly declared.

"I what?"

"It's been too long." Renee shook her head. "Not healthy." Bluntness was one of Renee's most dominant personality traits.

Regina dismissed Renee's words with a wave of her hand.

"Look." Renee said. "See that guy I'm smiling at?"

Regina turned to see a middle-aged man smiling back at Renee, wearing a simple pair of navy blue dress slacks and a white button-down shirt.

"That's Melvin Roy, the car dealer," Renee informed her.

"And?"

"And I'm tired of driving that old Camry." Renee gave her friend a mischievous smile before continuing. "His little brother likes you."

"What are you talking about?"

"He's the big one at the pool table. He ain't took his eyes off of your narrow behind since we stepped foot in this place."

Regina glanced in the direction of the two pool tables on the opposite side of the building. There was, as Renee had said, a large man also dressed in slacks and a dress shirt, staring directly at her. Upon noticing Regina's awareness of his attention, the large man hurriedly looked away.

"That's Melvin's younger brother, Patrick." Renee continued her informative narration. "I'm going to ask them to join us."

Faster than Regina could protest, Renee, along with her rear end, had once again captured the attention of the entire male population in the room as the two of them walked across the small dance floor and stood in front of the jukebox. Regina laughed when, as if on cue, Melvin Roy slithered over beside Renee. After a brief conversation, Melvin motioned to his brother, who laid his pool stick down and lumbered over in Melvin and Renee's direction. After another short conversation, Renee returned to the table with both men following closely.

"This is my girlfriend, Regina." Renee spoke to the men as the three of them were seated. "Regina, this is my good friend Melvin, and his younger brother, Patrick."

There was a round of greetings at the small table.

"Can we get a pitcher of beer over here?" Melvin summoned a nearby waitress who quickly nodded her head in acknowledgment.

"Patrick used to play for the Atlanta Falcons." Renee never stopped talking when men were around.

"What position did you play?" Regina said, making an attempt at casual conversation.

"Linebacker." Patrick replied. "Sounds like you know a little about football."

"Just what I pick up from my son."

"Oh, yeah." Renee was talking again. "Patrick coaches at Ball High. He might know Pooney."

"Pooney?" There was a puzzled expression on Patrick Roy's face.

"Allen." Regina smiled, amused by the look on the coach's face. "Allen Richards."

"Allen Richards is your son?" Patrick was disbelieving.

"Yes, he is. Do you know him?"

"Oh, yeah." Coach Roy nodded as the waitress appeared with their pitcher of beer. "I know him."

(2)

Pooney was awakened by the sound of music and the smell of bacon frying. He grabbed the clock from the nightstand beside his bed. 5:45. Sheila had gone crazy. He rolled from under his sheets and slipped into his house slippers before staggering toward the front of the apartment.

"Mama?" Pooney was shocked to see that the early-morning chef was his mother.

"Who did you expect?" Pooney detected an unfamiliar drag to his mother's voice. "I was going to wake you and your sister when breakfast was ready. I thought it would be nice for the three of us to eat breakfast together."

"How long you been up?" Pooney was now sure of the cause of the slur in his mother's speech.

"I haven't been to sleep yet." Regina pulled open the oven door, extracted a pan of rolls, and began applying butter to them. "So used to working nights, I guess."

Pooney watched his mother as she continued buttering the rolls. He felt an inexplicable tinge of anger toward her as he deduced that she had been out extremely late last night.

"I owe you an apology, baby." Regina spoke suddenly.

"Huh?"

"You were right. You are too old for spankings." Regina placed her utensils on the table before walking toward her son and giving him a warm embrace. "I was way out of line."

"I guess I'll forgive you this time," Pooney joked as his mind frantically searched for the date and time of the last apology he had gotten from his mother.

"I was scared, baby." Regina's embrace now threatened to suffocate him. "You had me worried to death." She finally let go.

"I'm sorry, too, Mama." Pooney took a step back, and upon seeing the tears in his mother's eyes, he truly was sorry.

"I met someone last night who thinks very highly of you." Regina wiped her eyes almost bashfully as she returned to the kitchen.

"Who?"

"Coach Roy."

"Coach Roy?" Pooney repeated. "Where did you see Coach Roy?"

"I ran into him." Regina avoided her son's question.

"What did he say?" Pooney's anxiousness was obvious.

"He said," Regina opened the oven door once more and placed the freshly buttered rolls back inside, "that you are an incredibly gifted athlete and a very good student."

"Really?"

"He also said that he is expecting big things from you next fall."

"What y'all doing?" Sheila appeared, still rubbing her eyes.

"You hungry?" Regina asked her daughter.

"Uh huh." Sheila nodded.

"Well, sit down and tell your brother about the summer music school you're attending this summer. I'll be through in a minute."

Pooney listened as Sheila very excitedly told him about her classroom performance and the conversation with Mr. Comeaux that followed. While he would probably never admit it, he couldn't help but feel proud of his baby sister.

"Well, say something." Regina urged Pooney as she placed two large plastic bowls, one filled with scrambled eggs and the other containing bacon, in the center of the table before returning to the kitchen.

"About what?"

"What do you mean about what?" Regina returned once again with plates and silverware before returning to the kitchen and reaching in the oven.

"About what?" Pooney was intent on being stubborn.

"About the news your sister just told you." Regina placed a third plastic bowl on the table. This one was full of buttered rolls. She also placed a pitcher of Kool-Aid and three drinking glasses on the table before sitting down. "Isn't it wonderful?"

"Yeah." Pooney grabbed a plate and proceeded to pile equally heaping servings of eggs and bacon onto it. "Just great."

CHAPTER 5

Pooney stepped from the shower and struggled toward his locker. Today had been an especially brutal practice. Coach Roy saw to it that Pooney led every exercise the team had done. And whenever one didn't go as the coach desired, Pooney had to repeat it. Alone. Although happy to oblige since Coach Roy had taken care of the problem with his teachers as he said he would, Pooney's body now protested vehemently. He could only imagine the pain that the morning would bring. He dressed as quickly as was possible in his present physical state, grabbed his backpack from his locker, and headed toward the front door.

As he stepped into the now slightly less menacing sunlight, his thoughts turned to Ms. Dawkins. She had apologized, and of course given him the "it's for your own good" speech. Pooney had sworn to himself that he would hate Ms. Dawkins forever, but then she smiled, and any resentment he attempted to harbor was instantly melted away.

Fortunately, his mother had reduced his sentence to one week's punishment. Easy enough. He had figured her leniency had everything to do with her conversation with Coach Roy. Oddly enough, when Pooney attempted to thank Coach Roy for the comments he had made to his mother, Coach Roy avoided the subject.

Now that he thought about it, although Coach Roy had been extremely hard on him in front of the team today, there was a noticeable timidness in the coach when the two of them had talked alone. Pooney had even become aware that Coach Roy had purposely avoided eye contact with him.

"Allen!" Pooney breathed heavily, his thoughts suddenly interrupted by the voice of trouble.

Pooney stopped and turned slowly to face his nightmare. Trouble, namely Chantaye Johnson, wore a pair of white "Daisy Duke" shorts. Made to fit tight, Chantaye's barely permitted movement. She wore an equally tight-fitting, light blue blouse that almost succeeded in covering her navel. Chantaye's skin, which she presently displayed to the world, was a beautiful shade of dark brown. She had wavy, jet-black hair that reached the center of her back, and she possessed a set of brilliantly white teeth that contrasted perfectly with her skin-tone. A slightly chipped front tooth, a remnant of a skateboarding accident during her tomboy stage, only served to enhance her already dazzling smile. As beautiful as Chantaye was, Pooney considered her to be twice as dangerous.

Two years older than Pooney, Taye, as she preferred to be called, was the girlfriend of Arthur Johnson, better known as Lil' Arthur. Lil' Arthur was a high-ranking member of the Four-trey Gangsta Bloods and known to be violently jealous. He had once stabbed another boy over an altercation stemming from Taye's repertoire of sexy dance moves. Lil' Arthur had once caught Pooney and Taye talking in the school cafeteria and went ballistic. Pooney's fear over the possible consequences of his argument with Lil' Arthur was the reason he had talked to Tony about joining the Deuce-nine Crips.

"What was you doing in there?" Taye asked. I've been waiting an hour since practice was over."

"Takin' a shower." Pooney looked around nervously to see who was watching.

"What happened?" Taye touched his eye, which was
mercifully just one color now: black.

"My helmet came off during a blocking drill."

"Uh huh." Taye smirked as she shook the key chain in her
left hand. "Wanna ride home?"

"Who let you drive their car?" Pooney asked.

"My mama's boyfriend let me use his car." Taye stepped
closer. Close enough that if Lil' Arthur happened on the scene
there would be big trouble. "You wanna ride or what?"

"Where's Arthur?" Pooney asked.

"Arthur?" Taye laughed. "So that's what you're afraid of. I
was startin' to think it was me."

"I ain't scared of nothing," Pooney told her.

"Let's go, then." Taye eyed him mischievously while
running her tongue along the chip in her tooth.

"You still haven't answered my question." Pooney was
visibly uncomfortable. Taye stood so close to him that their lips
almost touched.

"What question?"

"Where's Arthur?"

"Arthur's in jail again." Taye was growing impatient.
"Forget him. I don't fool with him no more anyway."

Pooney briefly considered the consequences of being
seen in a car with Taye. He certainly didn't buy her story about
not fooling with Arthur anymore. But looking at her, how could
he resist?

"I guess I could use a ride home," Pooney finally said.

"Good. I've been wanting to talk to you."

Pooney followed her toward the park adjacent to the field
house. He was impressed when Taye stopped in front of a late
model white Nissan Maxima.

"How'd you talk your mother's boyfriend into letting you
use this car?" Pooney asked as they got inside.

"The same way I got you to get in it." Taye smiled
seductively as she sped away from the curb.

(2)

Regina pretended to be totally immersed in paperwork when she saw Renee hustling off the elevator and heading toward the nurse's station.

"Hey, girl." Renee sat her purse on her desk before hurrying for the time clock on the far wall. "Damn, I'm a little late, huh?" she whispered upon her return.

"So what else is new?" Regina kept her eyes on the open file before her.

"I'll tell you what's new."

"Renee," Regina said as she closed the file and turned to her best friend. "Don't even get started because I don't want to hear it!"

"OK, but just one question," Renee pleaded.

"What?"

"What time did you get home last night?"

"What kind of question is that?"

"A very good question since I rung your phone until four o'clock this morning." Renee paused to read her friend's face. "Needless to say there was no answer."

"We didn't leave the club until one thirty," Regina explained.

"One o'clock," Renee corrected her.

"Maybe my ringer was off. A lot of people turn their ringers off at night."

"Or, maybe you were at Patrick's house."

"Don't be silly."

"Where else would you be at that time of night?"

"Getting something to eat. I mean...we could have." Regina covered her face then laughed softly, realizing Renee had backed her into a corner.

"Where'd y'all go?" Renee pulled her seat closer.

"OK." Regina let out a huge sigh while scanning the room for eavesdroppers. "After we left you and Melvin, we went to The Kettle."

"And?"

"We rode around for a little while, then we parked on the beach."

"Where on the beach?" Renee was thoroughly enjoying herself.

"You would make one fine investigative reporter, you know that, Renee?"

"Yeah, yeah girl. Come on with the rest of the story." Renee pulled her chair closer.

"We parked on the Seawall, got out, and walked for a while."

"On the Seawall?"

"Uh huh." Regina shook her head slowly. "On the sand."

"What?" Renee's eyes widened. "Did y'all hold hands?"

"Hold hands? Why would you ask me that?"

"Patrick looks like the hand-holding type." Renee backed up just far enough to grab a folder from her desk, then returned to her perch. "Well, did y'all?"

"Yeah, silly," Regina finally admitted. "We held hands."

"Then what?"

"Then he took me home."

"Did he kiss you before or after y'all left the beach?"

"Both."

"You harlot!" Renee used her hand to cover her gaping mouth.

"Girl, be quiet." Regina spoke in a hushed voice, noting the glances they were getting.

"When y'all going out again?" Renee asked.

"I don't know, Renee."

"What do you mean you don't know?"

"I don't know if I'm ready for all of this."

"Ready? Girlfriend, you're way past ready."

"But, Renee, he's Allen's football coach."

"What's that got to do with it?"

"I don't know how Allen will feel about it."

"You're the mother, Regina. He'll just have to accept it."

"You know it's not that simple, Renee."

"And why not?"

"He's been through so much." Regina walked over to the mini-refrigerator and returned with a Diet Coke. "He's just getting over what happened to his father."

"Regina, Big Al has been in prison for six years." Renee now understood the problem. "And you might have Alzheimer's by the time he gets out."

"He still writes, Renee."

"So what?"

"Ms. Franklin, I'm ready for my Epsom bath." They were suddenly interrupted by an extremely wrinkled, elderly black man who hung over the counter showing the mouthful of beet-red gums he possessed. "You promised, and it's eight." He pointed to the clock on Renee's desk.

"Here, Mr. Parker." Renee handed him a full carton of Epsom salt. "Wait for me in your room. I won't be long."

"OK." You could hear the enthusiasm in Mr. Parker's voice. "Hurry, I'll be waiting."

"We'll talk later, girl." Renee threw the file she was holding back on her desk.

"What's wrong, Renee?"

"I hate bathing that old freak."

"Why?"

"He gets turned on."

"That never upset you before." Regina laughed.

"It's not funny, Regina," Renee whined. "You ever see an eighty-seven-year-old man with an erection? It's disgusting!"

Regina burst into laughter while watching Renee storm toward Mr. Parker's room.

(3)

An hour had passed since Pooney accepted Taye's offer to drive him home. However, he was no closer to home than he was before Taye called his name in front of the field house. While he knew that he was pushing his luck with his mother, Pooney found it impossible to tell Taye that he needed to get home because his mother would be angry if she called and he wasn't there.

They had spent the last hour laughing, talking, and listening to the radio as Taye made one stop after another. Pooney had always been physically attracted to Taye, but now that he was finally getting a chance to talk to her alone, he found himself surprised by her intelligence and personality.

"What are you doing now?" Pooney asked as they pulled into the Burger King parking lot.

"I gotta get me a Whopper." Taye reached for the purse under her seat. "I'm hungry."

"Hurry up." Pooney turned up the music.

"What do you mean, hurry up?" Taye was now standing outside the car. "Come with me, baby."

Maybe it was the way her lips puckered when she called him baby, but at that moment Taye could have gotten him to bungee jump from the Causeway Bridge that connects Galveston to the mainland. Pooney turned the radio off, jumped from the car, and followed Taye to the restaurant's entrance.

There was only a small line, but with one cashier working, the progress was slow.

"I'll be right back, Taye. I need to use the phone," Pooney said suddenly.

"To call who?" Taye's voice was stern.

"I need to check on my lil' sister."

"You better not be calling no other woman." Taye's voice was soft, but her facial expression was very serious.

"I'm not." Pooney smiled as he hurried for the phone just outside the store's entrance.

Once outside, Pooney dropped his money in the slot and quickly dialed his home phone number.

"Hello." Sheila answered on the second ring.

"Sheila."

"Boy, where are you?"

"Did Mama call?"

"Yeah, she called."

"What did you tell her?"

"Tell me where you are first."

"I ain't got time to be playing with you, girl."

"You think I'm playing?" Sheila challenged before hanging up the phone.

"Sheila! Sheila!" Pooney yelled in vain.

After fishing more change from his pocket and feeding it to the phone, Pooney dialed the number once more.

"What, boy?" Sheila answered on the first ring this time.

"What did you tell Mama?"

"I told her you were in the shower, bye!"

"Hold on." Pooney was getting angry. "What did she say?"

"OOOOOh, you're getting on my nerves!" Sheila was just as angry with him. "She said she'll call back."

"What's your problem?"

"You're stupid!" Sheila's voice was cold. "And I'm tired of lying for you."

"Thank you anyway." Pooney giggled and awaited Sheila's reply. To his surprise, he heard only a click and a dial tone.

Pooney reentered the Burger King lobby just as Taye was ordering.

"Anything else?" The cashier was a girl Pooney recognized from school.

"Hold on, let me see what my man wants," Taye replied with enough volume and attitude that the handful of customers all watched Pooney as he approached. "What do you want, baby?" Taye placed one hand around his waist while dangling a twenty-dollar bill over the counter with the other.

"Let me get a Whopper," Pooney answered.

"My baby wants a Whopper with cheese combo." Taye turned to the patiently waiting cashier.

"What kind of drink would you like, Allen?" The cashier, a cute blonde, surprised Pooney.

"A Coke."

"So that's two Whopper with cheese combos, both with Cokes?" The cashier repeated the order.

"That's what we said, ain't it?" Taye snapped.

"That'll be $6.44." The cashier ignored Taye's belligerence. "Out of twenty." The twenty-dollar bill was exchanged between the two girls. "Your change is $13.56. Your order will be right up. Thank you. "

"Why are you actin' crazy with that girl?" Pooney asked Taye once the two of them stepped away from the counter.

"That heifer disrespected me!"

"Disrespected you? How?"

"Don't play dumb." Taye clutched his chin in her right hand. "You heard how she said your name."

"You trippin'."

"What kind of drink would you like, Allen?" Taye mimicked the white girl's voice in an extremely exaggerated fashion.

"One thirteen," A man called out. Taye approached the young man at the counter holding the large Burger King bag. "Two Whopper with cheese combos with Cokes?"

"Yeah." Taye snatched the bag from his hand and inspected their order.

"Anything else?" The young man asked politely.

"Could you put your eyes back in your head and get me some ketchup please?"

A small ripple of laughter traveled through the handful of patrons as the red-faced employee grabbed some ketchup packages from under the counter and threw them into the bag.

"Thanks, playa," Pooney mercifully intervened, grabbing both sodas and leading Taye to the door.

"You're crazy, Taye." Pooney laughed as the two of them waltzed across the parking lot toward the Maxima. "You love making things hard for people, don't you?"

"Shoot, homeboy lookin' at me like he's starvin' and I'm a pork chop sandwich," Taye mumbled through a mouthful of French fries.

"Look how you're dressed, Taye." Pooney hoped she didn't take his comment offensively. "What man wouldn't look at you?"

"I wore this for you, not him!"

Pooney climbed into the passenger side of the Maxima, not quite sure what to think of Taye's last statement.

(4)

"Who is it?" Sheila queried in response to the knock at the door.

"Is Pooney home, Sheila?"

Sheila opened the door, but left the chain lock attached. "He's not here, Tony."

"You know where he is?"

"He called and said he was at Burger King."

"Say, lil' mama," Larry said as he stepped from behind Tony. "Can I use the bathroom and get a cup of ice?"

"I'm not supposed to let anyone in the house when I'm here alone," Sheila answered.

"C'mon, baby girl," Larry persisted. "It'll only be a second."

"We can go to Tim's," Tony intervened.

"I can't make it to Tim's. What's your name? Sheila?" Larry started a pitiful looking dance. "Please, Sheila."

"OK." Sheila giggled then closed the door momentarily to take the chain off. "You got two minutes."

"Move, fool." Larry pushed Tony out of the way and danced his way through the door. "Which way, Sheila?"

Sheila giggled loudly as she pointed him in the right direction.

"So what you been up to, Sheila?" Tony asked.

"Nothin'."

"You look different without all those big barrettes in your hair."

"I comb my own hair now." Sheila smiled, remembering the assortment of gigantic barrettes her mother used to attach to her ponytails.

"You still eat dirt?"

"Of course not!" Sheila had been notorious during her early childhood years for making mud pies and actually eating them.

"Dirt must be good for you," Tony continued, "'cause you sure looking good these days."

"Thanks, Tony."

"Whew." Larry slammed the bathroom door behind him. "How do you spell relief, baby girl?"

"Watch your mouth, Larry," Tony scolded. "Let's go."

"Hold on." Larry ran outside and returned with a large blue cup. "My ice."

Sheila took the cup from his hand and walked to the kitchen. She opened the freezer and filled Larry's cup with ice, fully conscious that Larry was staring at her the entire time.

"What are you looking at?" Sheila asked Larry as she handed him the cup.

"Thank you, baby girl." Larry ignored her question. "Can I ask you one more favor?"

"You're out of favors." Sheila pushed him through the door. "Get out."

"C'mon Sheila, please." Larry clasped both hands beneath his chin in a praying gesture.

"Please what?"

"Light this Swisher for me." Larry pulled the marijuana cigar from his pocket.

"What the hell is wrong with you, Larry?" Tony voiced his objection.

"It's OK, Tony. I'll light it for him." Sheila took the Swisher from Larry's hand. "But you gotta wait right here. You can't come back inside."

"You all right, baby girl." Larry smiled. "If you was a little older, we'd hook up."

Sheila, Swisher in hand, turned toward the kitchen. She took one step before suddenly breaking the Swisher in two, smashing both halves, then turning and throwing the remains in Larry's face. She slammed the door and locked it before Larry knew what was happening.

"What the hell is wrong with you, Sheila?" Larry roared as he banged on the door.

"What's wrong with you?" Sheila was undaunted. "Bringing drugs in my Mama's house. Punk!"

"You owe me five dollars, ya lil' wench!" There was one last thud on the door.

"Hold your breath until you get it." Sheila watched through the peephole as her brother's friends walked away from the door, one furious, the other laughing.

(5)

After parking on Seawall Boulevard and eating, Pooney finally mustered the courage to tell Taye that he needed to get home. After assuring her that he wasn't expecting a phone call, nor company, she reluctantly agreed to drive him there. Pooney watched her from the corner of his eye as she drove down Heards Lane. Taye had now donned a pair of sunglasses to combat the setting sun, and was joyfully singing along with Mary J. Blige. Pooney had never had a steady girlfriend before, and Taye was not the girl that came to mind when he fantasized. But he had to admit, he enjoyed her company more than any girl he had ever spent time with. The prospect of spending more time with her excited him, but he had not forgotten about Arthur.

"Here." Taye reached in her purse and pulled out a small notepad and pen. "Write your number on this."

Pooney didn't even consider telling her that he was grounded and couldn't receive phone calls. He quickly scribbled the number on the pad and placed it back in her purse.

"I'll call you when I get home," she informed him as she pulled into the parking lot. "Which way?"

"Straight ahead." Pooney pointed. "Right past the mailboxes. Stop next to the Ford Escort."

Taye followed Pooney's instructions, stopping next to the car he had pointed to.

"Thanks for the ride, Taye." Pooney opened his door. "And the burger."

"What are you doing?" Taye took the sunglasses off.

"I'm getting out." Pooney was confused.

"You'd better give me a kiss."

"A kiss?"

"Yeah. A kiss."

Pooney closed the door and leaned in Taye's direction. He planted a clumsily placed kiss on her lips.

"What was that?" Taye frowned. "I want a real kiss. Come here."

Taye grabbed the back of his head with both hands and pulled him near. She placed her partially opened mouth against his and forced her tongue between his teeth. Not knowing what else to do, Pooney placed his arm around her and allowed his tongue to intermingle with hers. His pulse was rapid as his hands rubbed the baby smooth skin on Taye's back.

"I'll call you in twenty minutes." Taye pulled away slowly. "You'd better be home."

"I'll be here." Pooney grabbed his backpack from between his feet and exited the car.

"You haven't kissed many girls, have you, Allen?" Taye used the rearview mirror to aid her in positioning the sunglasses on her face just right.

.   "Why you asking?" Pooney stuck his head through the window. "You didn't like it?"

"We'll work on it." Taye smiled before backing out and driving away.

Pooney watched until she was out of the complex. Once again, Chantaye' Johnson had rendered him speechless.

"I done seen it all." Pooney turned at the sound of Larry's voice. He was surprised to find both Larry and Tony standing behind him.

"What y'all doing?" Pooney approached his friends.

"No. What you doing?" Crooked Tony frowned.

"Chillin'," Pooney answered.

"Yeah. You chillin' all right." Crooked Tony reached for the cup Larry was drinking and took a sip. "You know whose girl that is?"

"Yeah." Pooney answered. "Mine."

"I knew this boy was crazy." Larry's laugh was deep, loud, and obnoxious. "Is that what you gonna tell Lil' Arthur?"

"Fuck Lil' Arthur!"

"Fuck Lil' Arthur." Larry's laugh was even louder as he grabbed his cup from Tony. He then walked a full circle around Pooney. "I'll bet you the five dollars you owe me that you don't even have a pistol."

"I don't owe you five dollars."

"First things first." Crooked Tony approached. "You packin'?"

"Naw, I ain't packin'." Pooney found the question ridiculous.

"You're ridin' around The Island, cappin' with Lil' Arthur's girl, and you ain't even strapped?" Larry offered Pooney the cup.

"Lil' Arthur's in jail." Pooney declined the cup.

"How do you know?" Tony asked.

"She told me."

"I bet she also told you she ain't going to mess with him no more when he gets out," Larry said.

"I told you," Pooney was enjoying his own defiance, "she's my broad now."

"Just pay me my five dollars." Larry abruptly changed the subject.

"I told you I don't owe you no five dollars."

"Bullshit!"

"What is this fool talking about, Tony?"

"Let him tell you," Tony mumbled.

"I'm listening." Pooney turned his attention back to Larry.

"Yo' crazy ass sister crumbled up my damn Swisher Sweet!" Larry explained.

"What?"

"The crazy ass girl was supposed to light it for me but she smashed my shit and threw it at me."

Pooney looked to Tony for confirmation, but only received the Crooked Tony Shrug.

"What you doing trying to get my lil' sister to light a mothafuckin' Swisher?" Pooney dropped his backpack and took a step toward Larry with both fists clenched.

"Don't walk up on me, Loc." Larry sat his cup on the ground and struck a fighting pose.

"Y'all chill, man." Crooked Tony quickly jumped between his quarreling buddies. "We all cuz here. Save that shit for them slobs."

"I'ma see if you square off on Lil' Arthur like that." Larry relaxed and reached for his cup.

"Stay away from my sister." Pooney was noticeably calmer now.

"Skip that shit, Loc." Larry dismissed the matter. "We're here on business."

"What business?" Pooney took a seat on the stairs that led to the apartment above his own.

"We got a run to make Friday night." Larry was suddenly a military commander.

"We?"

"Yeah, we." Larry pointed at Pooney, then Tony, then himself.

"I'm grounded." Pooney was unconcerned with whatever Larry was talking about.

"Grounded? Talk to your boy, Crooked Tony." Larry walked across the parking lot and sat on the trunk of the LTD.

"What's up, Pooney?" Crooked Tony offered the Crip Shake.

"You know that's messed up, Tony." Pooney shook his head. "Askin' my sister to light a Swisher."

"I know." Tony maneuvered to where he could see Larry. "But Larry didn't mean no harm. Look at him. The boy is crazy."

Pooney looked across the parking lot at Larry, who was now sitting on the back of The Tank, twisting his hair into baby dreads.

"You right about that," Pooney laughed.

"About that run Larry mentioned." Tony scratched his head.

"I'm grounded, Tony."

"Why?"

"My Mama found out about yesterday."

"How?"

"My history teacher called her."

"That's fucked up."

"Tell me about it."

"Look, Pooney." Crooked Tony grabbed his shoulder. "You need to do this one."

"I told you, Tony, I'm grounded."

"I know, but," Tony paused to contemplate his next words, "Moe wants you to come."

"Moe?" Pooney's heart sank.

"He wants you to make a pick-up with us."

"What are you picking up?"

"Homeless puppies," Tony answered sarcastically. "Quit actin' stupid."

"Oh." Pooney nodded, pretending to understand. "Why y'all need me?"

"Moe wants you to see what's up." Tony sat next to Pooney on the stairs. "Don't your mama work nights?"

"You know my mama works nights."

"Well, we can pick you up after she goes to work."

"She might call."

"Sheila can tell her you sleep."

There was a brief silence as Pooney considered his options. He had no desire to cause his mother any more pain. However, he had to prove his loyalty to Deuce-nine.

Pooney stood abruptly. "Pick me up right here at eleven. Don't blow the horn, and don't knock on the door."

"Aw right, cuz." Crooked Tony smiled.

"Holler at y'all Friday." Pooney turned and walked toward his front door. Although he felt he could make the run and get back without his mother knowing, he couldn't help but wonder what her reaction would be if she did find out.

CHAPTER 6

Pooney lay in bed listening to the foreboding melody the heavy rain played against his window. His hopes were that the weather would cause the run to be rescheduled. To his dismay, Crooked Tony had phoned ten minutes before to let Pooney know that they would still be going.

It was now 10:55, and Pooney had just spent an entire hour trying to convince Taye that he was going to sleep. She protested fiercely, saying that it was Friday night, and that he could sleep tomorrow. She finally relented upon his promise to call her as soon as he opened his eyes.

Pooney leapt from his bed. Already fully dressed, he donned a blue pullover windbreaker with a hood, and slipped into an old pair of Nikes. He exited his bedroom and walked softly down the hallway. Sheila was asleep on the couch. He decided to gamble that she would remain there until he returned.

Pooney opened the door slowly, pushed the button on the knob, and shut it behind him. The wind was stronger than he expected, and it blew rain directly into his face. He pulled the hood over his head and held it there with his hand. A set of high beams flickered in his direction. As Pooney approached the burgundy Ford Taurus, the rear passenger door opened.

"What's up, cuz?" A man Pooney had never met before greeted him with the Crip Shake. Appearing to be in his early twenties, the wiry built, light-complexioned brother kept his hair neatly French braided, and wore a perpetual scowl. "King," he introduced himself.

"Pooney."

"This the young cat y'all say runnin' up in Lil' Arthur's broad?" King turned to Larry and Tony, who occupied the front seats.

"That's the one." Larry nodded.

"You ready to blast that fool, Loc?" King brought his hand next to his mouth, then took a bite of the beef jerky he held.

"Lil' Arthur?" Pooney laughed, wondering if he had ever actually seen anyone eat beef jerky.

"You laughing now, but if Lil' Arthur catches you slippin' after he finds out you runnin' up in his tramp, he's gonna bust a cap in yo' ass," King warned.

"It's like this, King." Pooney was starting to enjoy the game of shit-talking. "Taye is my girl now, and if Lil' Arthur got a problem with that, then I'll just have to handle my business. And that's on the C."

To a Crip, putting something on the "C" gave it the highest priority possible. Representing the "C" meant everything. Being a Crip meant eating, breathing, stealing, killing, living, and all too often, dying for the "C."

"I feel ya, Lil' Loc." King's approval was obvious. "Just watch yourself."

(2)

Pooney sipped on the sixteen-ounce Bull he had been holding for the last five minutes. It was his second since he had gotten into the car. After King had briefed him on the run, there had not been much conversation. The four of them had driven the last forty-five minutes in silence, save for the sound of the "Thunderstorm" playing on 97.9 FM.

Initially, Pooney had become very nervous as King explained the run. The four of them would be driving to Alvin, a small Texas town located twenty miles north of Galveston, to make a cocaine purchase from members of the Mexican Mafia. King was to be the purchaser, while the other three were more or less there for security purposes. Although King had assured him that he had been dealing with the Mexican Mafia for years, Pooney considered bailing from the car on several occasions. But now, after downing a beer and listening to half an hour of gangsta rap, his mood had changed. Still a bundle of nerves, Pooney was now consumed with more anxiety than fear.

"Here we go." Larry turned off the headlights as they crept down a narrow dirt road.

"Remember what I told you, Lil' Loc?" King inserted a clip into a semi-automatic pistol.

"Yeah." Pooney pulled the .38 that King had given him earlier from his pocket. He pretended to inspect his weapon as he saw the others doing.

The four of them stepped from the car with King leading the way. They walked across a mound of gravel, which effectively made a bridge over a ditch, before entering a wooden gate. Inside the large yard were a number of cars, half cars, and car parts. The grass was knee-high in some places, and there were beer cans, bags of trash, and other debris strewn throughout.

King led them around the side of the house and up a set of stairs that led to a small porch. He tapped four times on the screen door.

"Que paso?" A short, chubby-faced Mexican opened the door before yelling something to someone behind him.

"What's up, King?" Another Mexican, similar in build, but speaking English, entered the small room. He was wearing blue jean cut-offs and a pair of Adidas tennis shoes. Nothing else. "Come in, all of you."

"Nothin' much, Jorge." King pronounced his name "whore hey." "I hope y'all got some better stuff this time. That last shit was bunko."

Jorge said something in Spanish to the first Mexican, who then walked quickly toward the back of the house. He returned moments later carrying an album cover with both hands. Two scantily dressed white women followed him as he placed the album cover on the table, revealing the mound of white powder that lay on top of it. "See for yourself." Jorge grinned knowingly.

King handed Pooney the small brown satchel he carried and withdrew a twenty-dollar bill from his pocket. He rolled it into the shape of a cylinder and walked over to the table. One end of the twenty went into his nose as he leaned over the mound and inhaled deeply. He took a quick step backward, dropping the bill onto the table. He looked at Jorge, who was still smiling. King only nodded.

"Let me try some." Larry was always eager to get high.

"Help yourself." Jorge pointed to the mound of white powder. "All of you," he offered before turning to King. "Let's talk business."

King followed Jorge into the other room. He motioned for Pooney to join them.

Pooney followed Jorge and King down a long, dimly lit hallway. There was a single door at the opposite end of the hallway, which Jorge opened with a small key.

Pooney was hesitant as King motioned for him to join them in the room. Before entering, Pooney took one last look down the hallway. The Spanish-speaking man was guarding the exit with a pump-action shotgun.

"What do you want?" Jorge asked.

Pooney gasped at the sight before him. The floor was literally covered with large bricks of hardened powder. While he had no knowledge of drugs other than what he had seen on news broadcasts, Pooney knew that this had to be an incredible amount.

"Three wholes," King answered. "I got the five Gs I owe you too."

"Dump the money on the table," Jorge instructed as he rummaged through a closet.

"Dump it on the table." King, large beads of sweat now running down his forehead, said to Pooney.

Pooney thought about the Mexican with the shotgun as he walked toward the large wooden table. He unfastened the satchel and turned it upside down. Wads of money began to fall.

"Jesus," Pooney mumbled as he watched the dozens of rubber-banded wads of money hit the table.

Jorge laughed at Pooney while setting a triple beam scale on the table. Pooney recognized the scale as similar to the one in Mr. Lankford's biology lab.

"Thousand a stack?" Jorge looked at Pooney.

Pooney looked to King whose attention was now on whatever he saw as he peeked out the window.

"Yeah," Pooney finally answered, having no idea.

Jorge put the bills in five stacks of ten. "Fifty grand," he concluded.

Fifty grand. Pooney could have been knocked over with a feather.

Jorge took a small, hammer-like object and knocked two large chunks from the corner of one of the bricks. Pooney was amazed to see how hard the bricks actually were. He watched closely as Jorge played with the triple beam as a kid would a new toy. His mind raced with all sorts of thoughts. He smiled to himself, finding it amusing that while his classmates were either at home watching TV or at parties with other kids, he was packing a .38 caliber revolver and standing over fifty thousand dollars cash in a room full of cocaine, watching a Mexican named Jorge play with his triple beam, not to mention the other

Mexican at the end of the hall with the shotgun, or the two half-naked white women in the room with Larry and Tony.

"That's some good shit." King popped up at Jorge's side.

Jorge took a small quantity of powder that had fallen from one of the chunks and slid it in front of King. Once again, King went through the routine with the twenty-dollar bill before heading back to the window.

"Try some?" Jorge slid a small amount of powder in front of Pooney.

"No, thank you," Pooney spoke firmly. Jorge nodded approvingly, then resumed playing with his scale.

"Don't ever mess around with this shit, kid." Jorge was now filling a large plastic bag to capacity with white powder. "You'll have a future in this business."

Jorge placed the bag inside the satchel and handed it to Pooney.

"Let's go, King," Pooney called before exiting the room and walking toward the armed Mexican.

Pooney was halfway down the hall when he stopped and looked back. Jorge and King were just now entering the hallway. Pooney walked past the armed Mexican and into the room where Larry and the two white women, one who was now totally naked, were sitting around the table with the powder-covered album cover. Tony was guarding the front door as planned.

Pooney was usually excited by anything concerning naked women. However, the surprisingly frail white women failed to stir his interest.

"Let's go," Pooney barked, intoxicated with a power he had never before known. Larry's mouth moved, but nothing came out. Pooney recognized the pitiful look on his face. It was the same as the one King had worn just moments earlier.

"You got the stuff?" Larry finally managed.

"Didn't I say let's go?" Pooney walked past Tony and out the door. The others followed.

They exited the yard the way they came, all of them waiting impatiently as Larry fumbled with the lock on the door.

"Let me help you." Tony took the key from his hand and opened the door. "Maybe I'd better drive."

There was no objection from Larry who simply stood next to the back door and waited for Tony to open it.

Crooked Tony pulled away with Pooney in the passenger seat and both high-flyers in the back. As the Ford Taurus started in motion, Pooney observed the behavior of Larry and King. They were sweating profusely, looking out of their respective windows, and wearing ridiculous expressions on their faces. Pooney would never forget how pitiful they both looked. He made up his mind at that moment that cocaine would never be for him.

(3)

"Hello." Sheila was awakened by the phone but whoever it was had already hung up. She flipped on the light so that she could see the caller ID.

Chantaye Johnson, the same girl who had been calling for Pooney all day. Sheila was sure her brother was asleep, but she stumbled down the hallway toward his room anyway. His door was slightly ajar, so she pushed it open and stepped inside. The room was pitch dark and Sheila couldn't see a thing. She walked over to the side of the bed and reached for her brother. She felt nothing. She reached for the lamp on the nightstand and confirmed that which she had already deduced. Pooney was gone.

The clock on the nightstand read one thirty.

"You're stupid, Pooney," Sheila spoke to the empty room before turning off the light and returning to the living room.

(4)

Pooney had never been so happy to see the "Welcome To Galveston" sign that was directly before them. Moments later, the Ford Taurus cruised onto Broadway Boulevard.

"Where we going?" Pooney asked aloud.

"The clubhouse," King answered. "Give it here."

Pooney turned to the back of the car. Both King and Larry appeared to be themselves again. Pooney reluctantly handed King the satchel.

"Shake that ass, girl!" Larry hung out the window and yelled at Ms. Broadway, an overweight prostitute who worked Broadway Boulevard, known for her tight-fitting clothing and provocative dancing.

"Chill out, man," Crooked Tony spoke into the rearview mirror as he crossed the Forty-first Street intersection.

"Pull up at the Stop 'N' Go," King demanded.

"You crazy?" Tony replied.

"I'm thirsty, man," King continued.

"Me, too." Larry agreed. "And I gotta piss."

"Wait 'til we get to the clubhouse," Tony told them.

"Pull this muthafucka over!" Larry banged his head against the window.

"What's wrong with you, Larry?" Tony snapped.

"Pull over, man! Goddamn!" Larry screamed.

Crooked Tony switched to the left lane as they approached the intersection at 39th and Broadway. He made a sharp left turn and wheeled the car into the Stop 'N' Go parking lot.

"Y'all hurry up." Tony brought the car to a complete stop in full view of the front door.

King and Larry jumped from the car and ran into the store.

"What's wrong with them fools?" Pooney asked. "Got us in the middle of slob territory with all this dope."

"Them fools full of that bullshit," Tony answered.

"Did you do some?" Pooney tried to imagine Tony snorting cocaine through a twenty-dollar bill.

"Naw, did you?"

"Uh-uh." Pooney shook his head.

"One of y'all got a quarter?" A young woman was standing on Tony's side of the car crying.

"What happened to you?" Tony asked after viewing the bruises on the young woman's face.

"That muthafucka done put his hands on me for the last time." The young woman promised. "This time I'm filing charges on his ass. Fuck his parole!"

"We ain't got no quarter, home girl." Tony replied. "Wish I could help you." The nameless young woman ran in the direction of a middle-aged white woman who was pumping gas into a station wagon.

"Why'd you trip like that?" Pooney asked.

"Like what?"

"Why wouldn't you give her a quarter?"

"So she can call the police?"

Pooney watched the young woman climb into the station wagon with the white woman. The car then disappeared into the westbound traffic on Broadway Boulevard.

"Why do you think Moe wanted me to come?" Pooney asked while watching the passing cars.

"I don't know," Tony said, "but there must be a reason."

"Shit!" Pooney exclaimed while watching the police cruiser pull into the parking lot.

"Don't worry about it. Moe won't put more on you than you can handle." Tony was oblivious to the police car, which had pulled up beside them.

"Forget Moe." Pooney turned toward Tony and pretended to adjust the radio. "There's a cop on the side of us."

Tony strained to see out the corner of his eye, the whole time praying that Pooney was hallucinating. He wasn't. Tony turned his head completely around, interlocking gazes with the Chief Gillespie look alike.

"What the hell are these fools doing?" Tony turned toward the front of the store just in time to see King and Larry approaching, both with forty ounces in hand.

"Damn man, what the police doing here?" King looked as if someone had punched him in the stomach.

"Why the hell y'all had to get forties?" Tony displayed a rare tinge of anger.

"How were we supposed to know the laws was here?" Larry snapped back. "Just get the hell away from here!"

Tony put the car in reverse and eased out of the parking spot. He exited on the 39th Street side of the parking lot, turned right, crossed the intersection, and was once again traveling east on Broadway.

"He's behind us!" King was close to total panic.

"Stop looking at him, stupid!" Larry was just as nervous.

"Man, this is fucked up!" King whined.

"Quit crying!" Larry took a sip from his forty.

"What the fuck is wrong with you?" King went over the edge. "There's enough dope in this car to get us all twenty years!"

"Chill out, King." Tony was calm in the face of the storm.

"What's he doing?"

"Jesus Christ, he's on the radio." King answered.

"Maybe he has a call." Pooney tried to add some optimism to the scene.

"Naw man, he's callin' for backup." King was close to tears. "You gotta lose him, Tony."

"How the hell am I supposed to lose him?"

"Can't you drive this muthafucka?" Larry sided with King.

"Aw, man." Tony gasped at the site in his rearview mirror. "Ivy."

Galveston County's head narcotics officer pulled directly next to the Ford Taurus. He looked directly at Tony.

"Who's that in the car with him, Tony?" King asked.

"That new white boy." Tony answered.

"The runner?" King's eyes widened. "Aw man, we're up shit's creek. That muthafucka's fast, man."

"Not as fast as Pooney." Larry jumped in.

"What?" King looked at Larry.

"Lil' Loc got big-time boosters." Larry looked as desperate as he sounded. "He can outrun the white boy."

"What?" Pooney looked to Tony, already knowing he would get the Crooked Tony Shrug.

"You gotta do it, Loc." King looked at Pooney as if the fate of the world was in his hands. "You're the only one who can outrun him."

"Do what?"

"Look, Pooney," Tony said while keeping his eyes on the road, "I'm going to pull over real fast. You jump out and run to the clubhouse."

"The clubhouse?"

"Yeah." Larry's enthusiasm was growing. "Run through Cedar Terrace. That coward bastard might not even chase you through there."

Tony drove through the intersection of 29th and Broadway, contemplating how he could get Pooney to the opposite side of the street where he would have a better chance.

"Look." Tony had an idea. "The light at 27th Street is gonna be red when we get there. I'm gonna run it and make a left. I might not be able to get you all the way to the other side, but I'll try."

"OK." Pooney's lips quivered.

"Here." King threw the satchel onto Pooney's lap.

As Tony had anticipated, the 27th Street stoplight turned red as they approached. Ivy and the runner were still to their left, while the officer in the police cruiser continued to follow closely behind them. Tony slowed as he reached the intersection, then mashed hard on the gas pedal, sending the car barreling into traffic. He then maneuvered around a Ford Escort, driving over the walkway in the process. The Ford Taurus rocketed in front of the westbound traffic and came to an abrupt stop.

"Go, Pooney!" King yelled.

Pooney was out the door and running. He could hear nothing behind him. He sprinted to Sealy Avenue and turned left. He tucked the satchel under his arm like a football and accelerated to full speed. Pooney stole a glance behind him and ran even faster when he saw the sweatsuit-clad police officer running behind him.

"The gates are open in New Jack City," Pooney heard someone scream from the shadows.

New Jack City was the small apartment complex just ahead of Pooney. When the gates were open, it could be used as a short cut.

"Run, youngster!" Pooney heard another voice followed by the sound of a broken bottle as he crossed 28th and Sealy.

Pooney ran through the front gate of New Jack City, dashed across the small courtyard, and exited through the back gate. He crossed the alley behind New Jack City, then jumped a fence that landed him in someone's backyard. He ran around the side of a white two-story house, then hopped another fence, this one landing him on 28th Street and Avenue H. He ran across 29th Street and turned right, stealing another glance over his shoulder. The red-faced officer was just clearing the fence and trotting down 28th Street. Pooney had opened the gap but hadn't lost him. Turning left, Pooney was now in the deserted section of the Cedar Terrace Housing Projects. He zigzagged through the different sections enroute to 31st and Winnie, then switched into a gear he didn't know he had. He sprinted through the next section of units and directly to 33rd and Winnie. He looked behind him before trotting across the street, hurdling the small wooden fence, and running up the stairs to the clubhouse.

(5)

Pooney jerked violently on the screen door, tearing the locking mechanism from the doorframe in the process.

"What's wrong with you, Lil' Loc?" Big Lou grabbed him by the shirt, pulled him inside, and threw him to the floor.

"The runner." Pooney was unable to catch his breath.

"What?" Big Lou looked outside.

"Ivy. The runner. They're after me." Pooney panted like a small dog.

"Ivy?" Moe appeared from another room, running immediately to the window beside the door. "Where?"

"I jumped out the car on 27th. The runner chased me." Pooney took to his feet. "Here."

Moe left the window unattended to grab the brown satchel from Pooney. He dumped the contents onto the coffee table. He inspected each package briefly before looking to Pooney.

"You jumped out the car with this, Lil' Loc?" Moe's voice was a disbelieving whisper.

"Yeah." Pooney stood proud.

"With Ivy's runner chasing you?"

"Yeah."

"He must've lost him," Big Lou interjected. "I don't see him.

"What about the others, Loc?" Moe placed the plastic bag back in the satchel and withdrew a small cell phone from the pocket of his blue Dickies work pants.

"I think they got jammed up." There was a brand new swagger to Pooney's walk as he took a seat on the couch next to Moe. "My only concern was making it here with the package."

"You did good, cuz." Moe tapped a series of numbers into the cell phone.

"Good work, youngster." Big Lou squeezed Pooney's shoulder as he walked alongside the couch.

Pooney noticed for the first time that there were no lights on in the clubhouse. The only illumination came from the moonlight that shone through the large windows.

"Here y'all go." Big Lou returned with four sixteen-ounce Bulls. He gave one to Moe, another to Pooney, and returned to the front door with the other two.

"Say, Doc," Moe spoke into the cell phone. "Get yo' ass over here. Time to earn some cheese...Yeah...Yeah...Three whole thangs...Hurry up!"

Moe closed the flip phone and stuck it back in his pocket. He grabbed the beer from the table in front of him and opened it. He took a sip from the can and stood slowly.

"C'mon, Pooney." Moe motioned for Pooney to follow him toward the back of the house.

Pooney followed closely through the darkness while clutching his unopened beer. They exited the back of the clubhouse through another flimsy screen door and walked down a steep wooden staircase. Under the staircase was a small door leading to another dwelling. Moe used a key to open the door, stepped inside, and flipped on the light. The two of them stood in the living room area of the small apartment. Moe pulled a PlayStation 2 from the bottom shelf of an entertainment center, and after untangling a mass of wires, he placed it on the floor.

"I'm gonna jump in the shower, Loc." Moe turned on the floor model television set and offered Pooney a joystick. "Play the game 'til I finish."

"Aw right, cuz." Pooney sat Indian style in front of the television. He searched through Moe's collection of games until finding the Madden 2003 game disc.

"If Doc gets here before I finish, let him in." Moe headed down the hallway.

"OK.," Pooney nodded while watching his beloved Cowboys take the field for the opening kickoff.

Pooney searched the wall for a clock. It was approaching two o'clock. He was living dangerously. He considered calling Sheila, but quickly thought better of it.

Pooney allowed his mind to become consumed with the task of defeating the Rams. He and the Cowboys marched down the field at ease. Just moments into the game, the score was already 14-0 Cowboys.

Pooney's attention was diverted by the sound of an engine accompanied by the headlights that shined through the living room window. The sound of a car door slamming caused Pooney to place the control pad on the floor and walk toward the door.

"Doc?" Pooney cracked the door before the man could knock.

"Yeah."

"C'mon." Pooney opened the door wide enough for the man to step through.

Doc entered the room carrying a small nylon sack. He was a middle-aged, medium brown-skinned man with a potbelly, and suffering from male patterned baldness. Pooney could only assume that the extremely thick bifocal glasses Doc sported had something to do with his nickname.

"Where's Moe?" Doc asked.

"Takin' a shower," Pooney answered.

Doc moved toward the glass top table located in the small dining area. He untied the drawstring on the nylon sack and pulled out a *Houston Chronicle*. He covered the table with newspaper before emptying the rest of the bag and placing the contents onto the table. Pooney watched in amazement, wondering how Doc could possibly fit the vast assortment of items he carried into such a small sack. First, Doc pulled out six cases of baby food jars and placed them on the table. He then produced a small digital scale. Next he placed two small jars containing a flaky white powder on the table along with two empty milk jugs. Pooney almost laughed aloud when Doc finally pulled a small microwave oven from the sack.

"Hey, youngster." Doc took the empty milk jugs from the table. "Do me a favor and fill these up with water."

Pooney took the milk jugs and walked into the kitchen with them.

"What's up, Doc?" Moe entered the living room, heading directly for Doc's lab experiment.

"Nothin' much," Doc answered. "Just trying to make a dishonest living."

Both men laughed.

"I see you've met my lil' homie," Moe said.

"Yeah, I met the kid." Doc paused while observing Pooney. A grim look crossed his face before he finally returned to the task at hand.

"That kid," Moe reached in the brown satchel and placed the bag of powder on the table, "is responsible for saving this."

"Oh, is he?" Doc muttered before emptying one box of the baby food jars.

"Tell him what happened, Lil' Loc." Moe was proud of Pooney's heroics.

"I had to jump out the car on 27th and Broadway with the package." Pooney returned to the table and set the freshly filled jugs atop it. "Ivy and his runner was after us."

"You outran that peckerwood?" Doc's eyes, magnified through the bifocals, appeared to be as wide as the face of a grandfather clock.

"Yeah." Pooney retrieved the beer he had left in front of the television. "I lost him in C.T."

"You run track, kid?" Doc plugged in the microwave.

"Naw." Pooney opened his beer. "I play football."

"How old are you?"

"Fifteen."

Doc grimaced. "Who are your people?"

"Huh?"

"What's your mama's name?"

"Regina."

"Regina what?"

"Regina Richards." Pooney took a sip.

Doc stopped what he was doing and took a long hard look at Pooney. "You Big Al's boy?" The older man was excited.

"Yes, sir." Pooney suddenly felt like a child again.

"I'll be damned." Doc still eyed Pooney. "Boy, I remember the night you was born."

"You do?" Pooney felt sheepish.

"I was driving for Busy Bee Cab Company." Doc was overcome with nostalgia. "When your mama went into labor, Big Al called me, not the ambulance. I was always the fastest wheelman on the The Island."

"You wasn't fast enough to wheel yo' ass away from that fifteen years you got for robbing that jewelry store," Moe joked.

"Shut up, chump." Doc threw a playful jab to Moe's chin. "I got his Mama to the hospital on time. Where is Regina?" Doc turned to Pooney.

"At work," Pooney answered.

"So you snuck out after she went to work, huh?" Doc shook his head.

"How you know what he did?" Moe came to Pooney's defense.

"Cause I know Regina, and she don't play that shit." Doc took a knife, sliced the first bag, and emptied the contents into a large plastic bowl that lay atop the digital scale.

"Weigh right?" Moe asked.

"And some." Doc answered before asking. "How much you want me to hit it with?"

"Not too much." Moe reached in his pocket and grabbed a Swisher. "Get me about fifty cookies from each bird."

Pooney digested their conversation. He remembered Tony telling him once that a bird was a kilogram of cocaine, and that a cookie was an ounce.

"Give me four or five hours." Doc took a large bowl off the scale and replaced it with a baby food jar. He pressed the clear button on the scale before looking at Moe. "See ya."

"Aw old man, you a trip." Moe hung a blue bandana from his back pocket. "Let's roll, Loc. This old coon thinks somebody wanna sweat his technique."

"This old coon can still rumble, I bet you that." Doc looked up.

"Whatever." Moe laughed as he and Pooney left Doc to his work.

Pooney followed Moe down the alleyway. They crossed the street and walked down another alley until they reached a small, brown-brick apartment complex. There was a late-model, money-green Cadillac Seville parked there.

"This your car?" Pooney made a complete circle around the car, marveling at the Epic disc rims, and low-pro vogue tires the Cadillac rested on.

"Yeah." Moe opened the door, stuck the key in the ignition, and used a button on the driver's side door panel to open the passenger side door.

Pooney climbed in, opened-mouthed at the peanut butter leather interior. Moe pushed the lighter in and pulled a small ashtray from under his seat.

"Look in the glove compartment and find somethin' you wanna hear." Moe grabbed the car lighter and put the amber red end to the Swisher that hung from his mouth.

Moe started the engine and pulled slowly from the alley.

Pooney found a bootleg CD with the words "DJ SCREW" written on it with magic marker.

"Put it in, Loc." Moe took a hard drag from the Swisher, then placed it in the ashtray that lay on the seat beside him.

Pooney pushed the power button and placed the CD into the player.

They exited the alley on 35th Street and turned right. Pooney could see heavy traffic, both pedestrian and vehicular, about two blocks in front of them. He nodded rhythmically as the music began to play.

"Here you go, Loc." Moe placed the ashtray with the Swisher in it next to Pooney before pushing a button on the driver's side door panel that let all four windows down.

Pooney puffed lightly on the cigar, careful not to drop any ashes on the seat. He placed the cigar back in the ashtray and sat back in the seat as Moe drove toward the center of the action.

Moe turned the music up so loud Pooney felt his insides vibrate. They crept slowly in front of a small bar, which had dozens of people standing in front of it.

"Say, Loc," Moe turned the music down. "Run in there and grab us a pint of gin and two cups of ice."

"They'll sell it to me?" Pooney asked as he took a single bill from Moe's hand.

"You can get whatever you want in there with that." Moe motioned to the bill in Pooney's hand.

Pooney looked down to see that Moe had given him a one hundred-dollar bill.

Moe shifted the Cadillac into park right in the middle of the street, then turned the music up. Pooney clenched the bill tightly as he approached the door of the small bar. He looked back before entering, and found that the Cadillac had been engulfed by a small group of girls.

Pooney pushed the small wooden door open and stepped inside. He squinted to see through the dense fog caused by the many cigarettes that burned in the small room. The jukebox played loudly—a familiar tune—Johnny Taylor. Pooney had heard the same song many times before at his grandparents' house. There was a pool table in the middle of the room with a small group of spectators surrounding it. Pooney walked close enough to see a tall, well-dressed brother, straight from the pages of a Donald Goines novel, sink a three-cushion shot with an assist from the badly sloping table. There was a ripple of approval from the crowd as a short, thick-armed, heavily tattooed

Mexican reached into his pocket and threw a bundle of crumpled-up bills onto the table.

"'Scuse me, lil' bro'." Pooney felt a hand on his back. He moved aside to allow the passing of a heavily perspiring man who seemed to be in quite a hurry. Pooney saw that the door behind him led to the bathroom. Having to relieve himself, he entered.

"C'mon nine!" Pooney heard a shout, followed by the snap of a finger. Pooney turned toward the wall with the urinals attached to it. There he saw a half-dozen men crouched in a semi-circle.

"One time nine!" Pooney now saw that the man calling for nine was rolling a pair of dice.

"Ten he make." A shirtless fat man held a ten-dollar bill in front of Pooney.

"Naw, cuz." Pooney walked to the toilet in the far corner.

"Damn." Pooney heard the man calling for nine, yell.

"My dice," Pooney heard another man say as he finished his business and zipped his pants.

Pooney exited the bathroom just in time to see another victim throwing bills on the pool table after being defeated by the well-dressed brother. Finally Pooney made his way to the bar.

"What you want?" The young woman wiping the counter top asked harshly.

"Let me get a pint of gin and two cups of ice," Pooney barked with equal attitude.

The young woman smirked while surveying the teenage boy before her. She smiled broadly before filling his order. "Here you go." She was still smiling as she placed the two cups of ice on the counter and reached underneath for the gin.

Pooney handed her the one hundred-dollar bill. Her smile grew even brighter as she scurried to the cash register.

"Ninety-five dollars is your change." The woman gently placed the bills in Pooney's hand.

"Thank you." Pooney shoved the money deep inside his pocket.

"Come again." The woman resumed the task of wiping the counter.

Pooney felt that she was expecting him to say something, but had no idea what, so he turned and headed for the door.

Once outside, he walked quickly toward Moe's Cadillac, which was now parked legally with Moe and a female companion standing behind it.

"Damn, Loc. I thought I was going to have to come and get you."

"I was puttin' my mack down with old girl at the bar," Pooney exaggerated.

"You was rappin' to Pumpkin?"

"Yeah, that's her name, Pumpkin." Pooney handed Moe one of the plastic cups.

"Aw right, Pooney." Moe pried one hand from around his companion long enough to reach for the cup of ice. "Bust it open, Loc."

Pooney broke the seal and twisted the cap. He poured himself half a cup, then offered Moe the bottle.

"You gonna let that little boy drink that stuff?" The young woman spoke, causing Pooney to take serious notice of her for the first time.

"You gonna let that broad talk to me like that?" Pooney asked Moe, while never taking his eyes off of the flat-chested redbone.

"I know you didn't just call me no broad!" She pushed away from Moe suddenly, prepared to deliver a lethal tongue-lashing.

"Chill, baby. He didn't mean nothing." Moe grabbed her arm. "Anyway, you disrespected him first."

Pooney, now full of himself, glared at the redbone while taking a sip from his cup. Her frown turned to laughter as she watched him gag on the straight gin.

"There's some orange juice on the front seat, Loc." Moe laughed before pulling the redbone close to him and kissing her on the neck. "Don't be laughing at my lil' homeboy," Moe whispered into her ear.

Pooney sat his cup on the curb, then reached inside the Cadillac and grabbed the pint of orange juice before returning to the back of the car.

"Here's your change." Pooney offered Moe the ninety-five dollars.

"Keep it, Loc," Moe murmured as he reached for the orange juice.

"Keep it?"

"How you gonna romance Pumpkin if you ain't got no money?" Moe added a few drops of orange juice to his cup, then handed it back to Pooney.

After shoving the money back into his pocket, Pooney sat on the curb and poured orange juice into his cup. Now able to take large sips, he finished the cup off quickly.

"Page me. I'll come, I promise." Pooney heard Moe speaking to the girl.

Pooney stood on the edge of the curb when he saw the girl step away from Moe and join a group of girls in front of the bar.

"What was goin' on inside, Loc?" Moe turned to Pooney.

Pooney thought for a second before answering. "There's a man in there taking everybody's money on the pool table." Pooney answered.

"Drew." Moe locked the doors of the Cadillac.

"There's a crap game in the restroom."

"A crap game?" Moe seemed excited. "Let's check it out."

Pooney followed Moe back inside the bar, past the pool table, and into the restroom.

"What's up, Major?" Moe shook hands with a middle-aged black man sporting a graying beard. The man was dressed in army green pants, black boots, and a white tank top.

"Aw right, fool." Moe nodded to a bald-headed man.

The two of them were all that was left of the crap game Pooney had seen earlier.

Moe lifted the dice from the floor. "What they do?"

"Whatever you want." Bald head pulled a stack of bills from his pocket.

"You ever shoot craps, Pooney?" Moe asked his young companion.

Pooney shook his head.

"Here." Moe placed the dice in his hand.

"Man, c'mon." The bald-headed man protested, displaying a mouthful of brilliantly shining gold teeth. "What kind of shit is this?"

"His dice, chump!" Moe dropped a twenty-dollar bill on the floor. "You gonna fade him or what?"

"Yeah, I'll fade him." The bald-headed man matched the twenty-dollar bill that was already on the floor.

"Throw the dice, Pooney." Moe took a sip from his cup. "They have to hit the wall."

Pooney squeezed the dice in his hand before leaning over and tossing the dice so hard that they ricocheted off the wall and went bouncing all over the bathroom.

"No dice, man!" Baldhead angrily grabbed one die.

Moe retrieved the other die and returned to the circle. "Throw 'em a little softer, Pooney."

Pooney felt his palms perspire as he squeezed the dice once more. Once again he pitched the dice toward the wall, this time much softer. The two small dice bounced off the floor before kissing the wall gently. One die showed six immediately, while the other spun momentarily before landing on five.

"Eleven." Moe snatched one of the twenty-dollar bills from the floor.

Baldhead threw another twenty on the floor and everyone looked at Pooney.

"Lick him again, Loc," Moe encouraged.

Pooney threw the dice again. A four and a three.

"Seven." Moe picked another twenty from the floor.

"Go." Baldhead threw another bill on the floor.

Pooney threw the dice again. Both landed on two.

"Four." Baldhead yelled as he dropped two more twenties on the floor. "Forty he miss."

"Four's the point, Lil' Loc." Moe dropped two twenties on the floor. "You gotta make four again before you roll seven, got it?"

Pooney nodded.

"Let me get some of that." Major dropped two tens on the floor which Moe quickly matched.

Pooney threw the dice. Eight. He threw them again. Eleven. Five. Nine.

"Four!" Moe yelled when Pooney rolled a four on the fifth roll, then quickly snatched all the money from the floor before dropping a single twenty-dollar bill.

Baldhead took off his shirt and threw it across his shoulder, exposing an intricate maze of cuts, scars, and bullet wounds. This was punctuated by the zipper that ran from the top of his chest to just below his navel. Pooney wondered what could cause such damage. Baldhead reached for his full wad and held it in his hand.

"What that do?" Baldhead reached in his wad and threw a fifty-dollar bill on the floor.

Pooney took a deep breath as he watched Moe drop a second twenty along with a ten on the floor. The young boy unconsciously shook the dice in his hand, anxious to roll them again.

"Go 'head, youngster." Bald head barked.

Pooney kneeled on the floor, then threw the dice. Ten.

Baldhead threw another fifty on the floor.

"Let me get thirty of that." Major chimed in.

Moe matched both men's bets.

Pooney rolled another ten.

"Let's go, youngster." Baldhead threw another fifty on the floor. "You gonna have to break me."

Pooney rolled a seven.

Twenty minutes later, Baldhead's wad had been diminished to two twenty-dollar bills.

"Fade him, Major!" Baldhead was furious.

"Bullshit." Major placed an army green ball cap on his head. "That lil' bastard's on fire. He done already scalped your ass. I'm done."

"Coward muthafucka!" Baldhead called behind Major, who was now heading for the door.

"Go!" Baldhead threw his last money on the floor.

Pooney felt light-headed as he grabbed the dice and shook them in his hand.

"Break 'em, Loc." Moe stood over Pooney holding all of Baldhead's money.

Pooney rolled the dice again. Eleven. Baldhead was finished.

Moe snatched the money from the floor while Baldhead stared at Pooney. If looks could kill, Baldhead would be a double-murderer. The beaten man stormed from the bathroom without another word.

"I ain't never seen no shit like that, Loc." Moe enthusiastically counted the winnings.

"Like what?" Pooney stood up.

"Man, you was on fire." Moe separated a roll of twenty's from the stack and gave them to Pooney. "You didn't miss a point."

Pooney counted the ten twenties quickly, then placed them in his pocket before following Moe from the restroom.

Moe headed for the bar, but was cut off by two Hispanic teenagers dressed in khaki pants and blue T-shirts. Pooney stood a couple of feet behind Moe as the three of them conversed.

"It's about three-thirty now." Moe checked his watch. "Try me in about an hour."

The two Mexicans spoke briefly in Spanish.

"Four-thirty?" The taller Mexican held up three fingers to Moe.

"Yeah, cuz." Moe stepped around them and resumed his trek toward the bar. "Call me. It's on."

Pooney followed Moe as he maneuvered through the crowd, stopping occasionally to exchange the Crip Shake with blue-clad youngsters.

"What's up, Pumpkin?" Moe leaned against the counter.

"Hey, Moe." Pooney noticed the absence of the attitude she had shown earlier. "What are you doing here?"

"I'm just hangin' out with my lil' homie." Moe reached in his pocket and pulled out a twenty.

"We've met." Pumpkin smiled at Pooney.

"I heard." Moe leaned closer. "Let me get four sixteen ounce Bulls and three fat Swishers.

Pumpkin grabbed the four beers from the cooler then disappeared through a door Pooney hadn't noticed earlier. She returned moments later, took the twenty-dollar bill from Moe, and handed him a paper bag.

"Aw right." Moe looked in the paper bag. "Catch you later, Pumpkin."

"Come here." Pumpkin motioned in Pooney's direction.

Pooney slid between Moe and another man, then approached the bar.

"How old are you?" Pumpkin asked.

"Eighteen." Pooney fingered the trace of a mustache he sported.

Pumpkin smiled disbelievingly as she handed Pooney a small piece of paper. "One of these nights when you feel like getting away, call me. You can chill at my house."

"OK," Pooney stammered. "See you later."

"Bye," Pumpkin waved.

"I see you, playa." Moe tucked the paper bag under his arm and headed for the door.

Pooney could only smile as he followed Moe out the front door. Riding in a Cadillac with Moe, grown women offering to take him home, and with two hundred and ninety-five dollars in his pocket, things were beginning to look very promising. Or so he thought.

(6)

"What you know about that?" Moe pointed at the table where Doc had been diligently working for the last two hours.

Pooney stepped closer to observe the countless number of solid tan circles that covered the table. They reminded Pooney of the fatman cookies that he and his neighborhood friends used to pay a nickel for at Ms. Lucy's.

"It was good stuff." Doc used his hand to wipe the sweat from his forehead. "I ended up getting sixty a bird."

"Sixty?" Moe lifted a cookie from the table and examined it.

"Don't worry." Doc opened the beer Moe had given him and took a drink. "It's still better than anything else on The Island."

Moe, visibly satisfied, placed the cookie back on the table. "How you want yours?"

"Half and half," Doc answered.

Moe reached in his pocket and counted from Baldhead's money.

"Appreciate ya." Doc grabbed two of the cookies from the table and placed them in his bag. "See you playas later."

Moe followed Doc to the door and locked it behind him. He then ran quickly down the short hallway, entering a door to his left. He returned with a hand-held digital scale of his own.

"Check it out, Loc." Moe motioned for Pooney to join him. "Take these ten ounces and break 'em down to eight-balls for me.

Moe separated ten cookies and made two stacks next to the scale.

"Clear the scale with this button." Moe hit the button that said clear.

Pooney watched as the display window registered three zeroes.

"Make each ball 2.6 grams. This way you can squeeze ten from each ounce. Moe broke two small pieces from the first ounce and placed them on the scale. The window read 2.7.

"Close enough." Moe walked into the kitchen, returning with a handful of small, plastic Ziploc bags. "Put the balls in these. Got it?"

Pooney nodded while taking a seat in front of the scale.

Pooney began his task. The clock on the wall read five minutes until four. *I hope Sheila's still asleep,* he thought to himself as he pressed the clear button for the fifth time.

(7)

Moe and Pooney traveled slowly in the small blue Chevy Caprice. The radio clock now read 6:10. No longer intoxicated, Pooney was beginning to worry about his mother.

"This is the last one, Loc," Moe promised as they pulled in front of an apartment complex on 53rd Street and Avenue R.

Moe blew the horn twice. Moments later, a head protruded from the security gate, followed by an arm, which summoned them to come forward.

"Here, Loc." Moe handed Pooney another paper bag, the eighth one he was to deliver in the last hour. Pooney hopped from the car and ran to the gate. He recognized the Mexican man as the one he had seen Moe talking to at the cafe earlier. He and Pooney exchanged brown paper bags and Pooney dashed back to the car. Once inside, he pulled the money out and began to count it.

"Twenty-five hundred," Pooney told Moe.

Moe nodded and pulled away from the curb.

"Back Bay, right?" Moe asked.

"Right," Pooney answered.

"You hungry?"

"Starvin'"

"We'll stop by Jack 'N' The Box and get a couple of Jumbo Jacks."

"Cool." Pooney lay back in his seat.

Pooney closed his eyes and pictured himself driving a Cadillac like Moe's, surrounded by beautiful girls everywhere he went. He thought about the table full of dope they had left at the clubhouse, and decided that tomorrow he would ask Moe to put him down.

"Say, Loc." Pooney felt a nudge. "Say Loc, where's your apartment?"

It took Pooney a second to figure out that they were cruising through the Back Bay apartment complex.

"Straight past the mailboxes." Pooney sat up. "116."

"I got you two Jumbo Jacks with cheese and some curly fries." Moe placed the bag in Pooney's lap as they pulled up in front of Apartment 116.

"Thanks." Pooney grabbed a still hot curly fry from the bag and bit into it.

"And this is for you." Moe handed him two cookies twisted tightly in plastic. "A token of my appreciation for what you did earlier."

"Thanks, Moe."

"Thank you, Loc, and be careful."

"See ya, man." Pooney and Moe exchanged the Crip Shake before Pooney stepped from the car and Moe sped off.

Pooney stumbled toward his front door as the early-morning sun warned of another extremely hot day to come. He stuck his key in the door, turned the lock softly, and entered the apartment. Sheila was asleep on the couch, just as she had been when he left. Pooney tiptoed through the living room and walked to his bedroom. He slithered inside the half-open door and closed it softly behind him. Exhaustion began to weigh him down as he kicked off his shoes and grabbed one of the burgers from the bag. He placed the two cookies in the hiding place with the Swisher. He undressed between bites of his Jumbo Jack. He reached inside the bag and shoved a handful of curly fries in his mouth, and then sat on the edge of the bed and pulled the second burger from the bag. That's when he noticed the single sheet of folded notebook paper lying on his bed. He placed his burger on top of the bag and unfolded the paper. YOU STUPID POONEY!! was written in bold, black letters.

CHAPTER 7

Regina waved goodbye to Renee and turned for her apartment. She opened the door and found Sheila lying asleep on the living room couch.

"Hi, baby." Regina awakened her daughter with a kiss on the forehead. "Why don't you go and get in the bed, sweetheart?"

"I was waiting for you." Sheila rubbed her eyes furiously.

"Waiting for me?" Regina sat on the couch and kicked off her shoes.

"I had to make sure you made it home OK." Sheila stood up and folded the sheet she had used for a cover.

"Well, I made it home, grandma." Regina smiled. "You can go to bed now."

"I might as well get up now." The telephone in her mother's room rang as Sheila carried the linen to the closet. "I'll get it." Sheila placed the sheet in the closet and ran to the phone.

"Hello."

"Is Regina home?" A male voice inquired.

"May I ask who's calling, please?" Sheila disguised her nosiness with phone etiquette.

"Mr. Roy."

"Hold on." Sheila carried the phone to her mother. "It's a man on the phone."

"Hello," Regina spoke into the receiver.

"Hi, Regina."

"Patrick, how are you?" Regina met Sheila's disbelieving gaze.

"Fine. I know it's early but—"

"Patrick, could you hold on a second?"

"Sure." Coach Roy wondered if she could detect the anxiousness in his voice.

"What are you doing?" Regina asked Sheila.

"Nothing."

"Well, you can do nothing somewhere else, can't you?"

"OK." Sheila smiled and skipped down the hallway.

"I'm sorry, Patrick." Regina picked the receiver up again. "My daughter thinks she's Jessica Fletcher this morning."

"I understand." Coach Roy chuckled. "I know it's early Regina, but I was trying to catch you before you fell asleep."

"Well your timing is great. I just walked in the door."

"I called to tell you what happened to me yesterday." Coach Roy cleared his throat.

"You OK, Patrick?"

"Oh yeah. It was nothing bad." Coach Roy was surprised by Regina's concern. "As a matter of fact, it was good."

"Well, what happened?"

"I was listening to the radio last night and I called in and won two free tickets to see *Lord, What About Me* tomorrow night."

"Really?" Regina pretended to know what he was talking about.

"You've seen the advertisements, right?"

"Sure." Regina wondered where this was headed.

Coach Roy lay back in his Lazy Boy recliner. He was slightly disheartened by the lack of enthusiasm in Regina's voice. He closed his eyes while debating with himself whether or not to go any further.

"Patrick? You there?"

"Yeah, I'm here." Coach Roy sat up.

"Everything all right?"

"Just fine." Coach Roy felt like a fool. "Regina?"

"Yes, Patrick?"

"Would you like to go see the play with me?" Coach Roy couldn't believe he had finally spoken the words.

"Sure," Regina answered on impulse.

"Yes!" Coach Roy yelled into the phone before regaining his composure. "It starts at seven-thirty, but with the drive to Houston and all we'd better leave at about five-thirty."

"I'll be ready!" Regina couldn't believe she was hearing herself correctly.

"OK." Coach Roy's breathing was normal again. "Tomorrow at five-thirty."

"See you then." Regina wished she could tear her own tongue from her mouth.

"Bye, Regina."

"Bye, Patrick."

(2)

"Telephone, stupid!" Sheila's voice was followed by a heavy blow to Pooney's chest.

Pooney's eyes failed to open as he reached out in the direction of Sheila's voice.

"It's on your chest, dummy!" Pooney could see the disgust on Sheila's face through the small slits he was able to form with his eyes.

"Hello," Pooney mumbled after fumbling for the receiver.

"You got the phone upside down, retard!" Sheila snatched the phone from his hand, straightened it, then jammed it hard against the side of his head.

"Hello."

"What's up, Pooney?" Crooked Tony's voice was loud.

"What's up, Tony, man?" Pooney was suddenly awake. "What happened to y'all?"

"That fool King had about twenty dollars worth of powder on him so they took us all down."

"No shit?"

"They gave me and Larry some bullshit misdemeanors." Tony explained. "Moe got us out this morning. They charged King with the dope and the guns. You all right?"

"I made it, fool, but that runner was fast as hell. Hold on." Pooney held his hand over the receiver. "Excuse you," he spoke to his younger sister, who had been hanging on his every word.

"Ain't nobody listening to what you and that crooked teeth boy talkin' about!" Sheila snapped.

"Well, get your nappy-headed ass out my room."

"I know you didn't, punk." Sheila's head moved from side to side as she placed both hands on her hips. "Smellin' like you spent the night in a hog pen."

"Get out of here, girl." Pooney threw a pillow at his sister.

"Forget you." Sheila grabbed the pillow from the floor and threw it back at him before leaving the room.

"I'm back, Tony." Pooney placed the phone to his ear again. "Sheila's trippin'."

"Man, I was scared for you." Pooney could hear the sound of passing cars in the background. "The laws kept fuckin' with our heads, sayin' you got busted with it and that you told everything."

"Busted with it?" Pooney grabbed the remains of his half-eaten burger. "How'd they know what I had?"

"They didn't, man." Tony explained. "They was just trying to run that bullshit game on us."

"Oh."

"Moe said you caught fire in a crap game."

"Yeah, I broke some fool."

"I heard." Tony paused. "He also told us he dropped you a package."

"Yeah, looks like fatman cookies."

"Fatman cookies?" Tony laughed. "You definitely sittin' on somethin' fat. But it ain't no cookies."

"Sittin' on somethin' fat?"

"Hell, yeah. You about to come up like a fat rat."

"Yeah?"

"When you're ready, I'll show you how to make your money."

"I'm punished until Wednesday, so it'll have to be next weekend."

"Whenever you ready." Pooney heard a second voice in the background. "I'll holler at ya later. My order is ready."

"Where you at?"

"BK." Tony was at Burger King, but members of the Crips gang preferred the term BK because of the double meaning it held to them: Blood Killer.

"See ya later."

"Aw right, cuz." Pooney shoved the last of the burger in his mouth as he hung up the phone.

Pooney slipped into an oversized Deion Sanders jersey and a pair of white shorts, then headed for the kitchen.

"Good morning, Mama." Pooney passed his mother in the hallway.

"Good morning?" Regina frowned. "It's almost five o'clock."

"No shit? Oops." Pooney covered his mouth with his hands. "I mean, for real?"

"Boy, what is wrong with you?" Regina approached her son.

"Nothing, Mama. I'm just tired." Pooney tried to avoid making eye contact with his mother. "I stayed up late playing John Madden."

There was an uneasy silence as Regina gave Pooney the once over.

"I'm starvin'." Pooney turned away from his mother and hurried from the kitchen.

"Your sister put a plate in the microwave for you hours ago." Regina followed him closely.

Pooney opened the microwave and grabbed the Tupperware dish. He pulled the lid off, uncovering the three chilidogs, and a mountain of French fries his sister had left for him. Regina stood at the kitchen's entrance, still studying her son closely.

"What's up?" He smiled at her as he put the dish back in the microwave, closed the door, and pushed the start button.

"Who do you think you're talking to, Allen Richards?"

"What, Mama?"

"Asking me what's up." She grabbed the envelope containing the phone bill from the counter top and opened it. "Like I'm one of your homeboys or something."

"I didn't mean no harm, Mama." Pooney saw an opportunity to create a diversion. "The phone bill all right?"

"Why'd you ask me that? Do you have something to tell me?"

"Naw, Mama. I was just asking."

"Uh-huh. The same way you was just asking for two weeks straight before I got that bill with the four hundred dollars worth of calls you made to that phone sex line?"

"Mama that was two years ago," Pooney fussed. "I was only thirteen."

Regina put the phone bill down and studied her son closely while he reached into the microwave for his food.

"Your bathwater's gettin' cold, Mama." Sheila appeared from nowhere.

"OK." Regina finally turned from Pooney. "Thank you, baby."

Sheila shook her head at her brother before taking a seat in front of the TV.

Pooney bit into his chilidog as his sister switched the television to a *Saved By The Bell* rerun. Yes, she had saved him again.

(3)

Pooney turned the television to channel three and pressed the play button on the VCR. He had already put in his favorite tape, the one with the highlights of the Dallas Cowboys' 1999 football season.

Pooney clapped loudly as number twenty-one, Deion Sanders, lined up to receive a punt from the much-hated Washington Redskins. Deion fielded the kick at the twenty-yard line and headed straight up the field, directly into a crowd of Redskin defenders. Pooney jumped to his feet when Deion exploded from the pile and broke toward the left sideline.

"He's gone." Pooney yelled as Deion streaked down the sideline. "Go! Go! GO! Touchdown!" Pooney clapped and yelled loudly.

"What are you doing in here?" Sheila was standing in Pooney's bedroom door.

"That boy cold!" Pooney screamed.

"You done seen that video a thousand times, Pooney." Sheila fussed. "In here hollerin' and screamin' like you crazy."

"That's me in a few years." Pooney grabbed the football from the floor. "I'm going to play for the Cowboys, too!"

"Boy, please."

"You'll see." Pooney slammed the ball on the floor and raised both hands in the air as Deion crossed the goal line again. "Touchdown!"

"You're crazy." Sheila sat on the edge of Pooney's bed as the camera now showed a helmetless Deion Sanders. "He's cute."

"Cute?" Pooney laughed. "Football players ain't cute."

"I know one that ain't."

"Forget you." Pooney grabbed his soda from the nightstand.

"I'm bored." Sheila sounded pitiful.

"Call Janeen."

"She went out of town for the weekend."

"Watch TV."

"Ain't nothin' good on."

"Watch a movie."

"I already watched all those movies."

"Go to bed." Pooney turned his attention back to the television. The Cowboys offense was taking the field.

"It's too early," Sheila countered. "I know what."

"What?" Pooney asked disinterestedly.

"Let's play Monopoly."

"I'm watchin' something." Pooney quickly dismissed the idea.

"You can watch the game while we play Monopoly." Sheila insisted. "Please, Pooney."

While Pooney had no desire to play Monopoly, the pleading in his sister's voice proved persuasive. "Go get it."

"OK." Sheila jumped up from the bed and ran to retrieve the Monopoly game from the living room.

"Interception!" Pooney turned just in time to see Deion make a leaping grab of an ill-advised Washington Redskin pass.

"I'm the car." Sheila placed the box on the bed and removed the lid.

"I'm the wheelbarrow," Pooney declared as the phone rang. "Hello.'"

"Hi, baby." The softness of Chantaye's voice caused Pooney to forget about the car, the wheelbarrow, and even Deion Sanders.

"Hi, Taye." Pooney lay back in his bed.

"Finally awake, huh?"

"You called earlier?" Pooney asked.

"Twice." Taye informed him. "I was starting to think you were avoiding me."

"Never."

"I can't tell." Taye teased. "What you doin' tonight, baby?"

"I'm not allowed to leave the house for one more day." Pooney answered.

"Can you have company?"

"My mama didn't say anything about having company." Pooney met Sheila's disapproving gaze.

"Where is she?"

"At work."

"I can get a ride to your house." Taye paused. "But I don't wanna get you into any more trouble."

"Nobody's here but me and my little sister." Pooney flashed a glance in Sheila's direction.

Sheila frowned in return.

"She won't say nothin'."

"You sure."

"Yeah. C'mon."

"Alright." Taye committed. "Give me half an hour."

"OK"

"See you in a little while, baby." Taye hung up.

"Roll to see who goes first." Sheila offered her brother a die.

"Not right now." Pooney threw the die on the board and hopped from the bed. "I need to get ready for my company."

"But you said you was gonna play with me," Sheila protested.

"I'll play with you later." Pooney ran in the direction of the bathroom clutching a handful of clothing. Without thinking, he hit the light switch as he exited the bedroom.

"I hate you, Pooney," Sheila whispered into the darkness as she wiped away the single tear that slid down her cheek.

(4)

Pooney dressed hurriedly as he expected Taye to knock on his front door at any moment. He selected a pair of white Levi's pants, and a blue and white Tommy Hilfiger shirt. He slipped into his Jumpman tennis shoes and hurried toward the living room.

"She here yet?" Pooney plopped on the couch beside his sister.

"You see anybody?"

"What are you gonna do?" Pooney ignored his sister's sarcasm.

"What do you mean?"

"Why don't you go in the bedroom or something?" Pooney leaned over to tie his shoes.

"You must be crazy," Sheila roared at her brother before jumping from the couch and turning on the television.

"I'm having company."

"I don't care nothin' about your company!" Sheila returned to her seat. "Move! With your wet self."

"You can watch TV in the back." Pooney was rapidly losing patience.

"I'm watching TV right here." Sheila's propensity for stubbornness was legendary.

"You're about to make me mad, lil girl." Pooney used an open hand to push the side of his sister's head.

"Don't nobody care about you being mad." Her brother easily blocked the first punch Sheila threw. The second one surprised him, though, and caught him solidly on the cheek.

Pooney leapt from the couch, grabbed both of his sister's pants' legs, and pulled hard, bringing her crashing to the floor.

"Say you sorry," Pooney commanded.

"No."

"Say you sorry, or I'll put you in the figure four." Pooney threatened her with his favorite wrestling move.

"I don't care!" Sheila screamed loudly.

Pooney stepped between his sister's legs and twisted her left one violently. Sheila kicked and screamed until she was somehow able to shake free. Once on her feet, she lowered her head and charged into her brother full speed, driving him into the wall.

"Oh, you wanna get rough." Pooney turned his sister and pinned her against the wall.

Sheila fought with all her might, but was unable to push him away.

"Say you sorry!" Pooney ordered once more.

"Never!" Sheila continued to struggle in vain.

Pooney slapped his right arm around her neck, bringing her face to his side, then clamped on to her with a headlock.

"Let me go!" Sheila screamed.

"Say you sorry." Pooney rubbed his knuckles hard across the top of Sheila's head.

"Stop it!" Sheila screamed at the top of her lungs.

Sheila struggled wildly, sending both of them tumbling around the living room, bouncing off the walls, and knocking over everything in their path. Finally, in a last act of desperation, Sheila opened her mouth and sunk her teeth into her brother's side. Her eyes were closed and she squeezed harder than she ever thought possible.

"Ahhh!" Pooney was the one yelling now. "Let me go, girl!"

The two of them fell onto the couch with Sheila locked onto her brother like a rabid pit bull. Pooney's arms were no longer around Sheila's neck. Instead, he used both hands in an unsuccessful attempt at pushing her away.

"Aw right, Sheila," Pooney pleaded. "I'm sorry."

Sheila growled loudly, biting into her brother even harder. She then jumped up quickly and punched her brother once more in the face. "That's what you get," Sheila taunted. "Now leave me alone."

Pooney raised his shirt to examine the damage. There was a full circle of teeth marks, but miraculously the skin was not broken.

"I'ma kick yo' ass now." Pooney got up slowly from the couch and walked slowly toward Sheila.

"You'd better leave me alone." Sheila took one step backward for every step her brother took forward, causing the two of them to engage in an oddly choreographed dance routine.

Pooney jumped at his sister but wasn't quite quick enough. Sheila ran around the back of the couch, using it as a barrier between herself and her brother.

"I'm fixing to tear yo' ass up," Pooney promised as he angrily stalked his prey.

"Leave me alone," Sheila whined.   ..

Pooney ran around the back of the couch and the chase was on. The two of them circled the couch over and over again until Pooney finally hurdled it and tackled his sister.

"Get off me," Sheila fussed.

Pooney rolled Sheila onto her stomach and twisted her arm behind her back, causing her to let out a pain-filled yell.

"Say you're sorry," Pooney ordered again.

"I'm sorry!" Sheila yelled. "Please stop."

"Say it again." Pooney applied more pressure.

"I'm sorry, Pooney!"

"Let that girl go!" Taye was standing in the doorway. "Have you lost your mind?"

Speechless, Pooney quickly jumped to his feet.

"He tried to kill me," Sheila sobbed.

"You poor baby." Taye gave Sheila a warm embrace before aiming her wrath at Pooney. "What is wrong with you? I heard this child screamin' from the time I got out the cab."

"She bit me." Pooney raised his shirt to verify his claim.

"You had me in the headlock and I couldn't breathe." Sheila made her ordeal sound as horrible as possible.

"You ought to be ashamed of yourself," Taye scolded. "This is a little girl."

"She's always smartin' off," Pooney answered.

"He told me I had to stay closed up in the bedroom because he was havin' company," Sheila explained without being asked.

"Pooney," Taye sighed.

"She's just gonna be in the way."

"In the way of what?" Taye's hands went to her hips, and her head made the reptile-like motion that Pooney had seen from Sheila a thousand times.

"You know what I mean," Pooney mouthed despite the fact that even he didn't know what he meant.

What Pooney did know was that Chantaye Johnson was the finest girl he had ever laid eyes on. She presently wore a pair of black jeans with a tight-fitting blouse that once again failed to cover her navel.

"C'mon, baby," Taye spoke to Sheila. "Let's go wash your face."

Pooney watched as Taye and his sister walked to the bathroom. He was so fascinated by the way Taye's hips shifted as she walked that he could no longer concentrate on being angry with Sheila.

Pooney straightened up the living room while waiting for Taye to finish with Sheila. Luckily, he and Sheila had not broken anything during their fight.

"I'm the hat," Taye said as she returned to the living room.

"What?" Pooney frowned.

"You, me, and Sheila are going to play Monopoly," Taye said.

"Monopoly?"

"Yeah, Monopoly," Taye repeated. "You did promise to play with her, didn't you?"

"Yeah, but that was before you called." Pooney watched in disbelief as Sheila strutted before him carrying the Monopoly game.

"You're the wheelbarrow, right?" Sheila smiled while setting the game on the table and removing the lid.

"Naw." Pooney shook his head. "I'm the boot, and you know what I want to kick."

"You'd better be nice to my friend, Allen." Taye touched the tip of Pooney's nose with her index finger as she giggled her approval.

They were all quiet as Sheila counted out three stacks of Monopoly money. After placing one stack in front of each player, Sheila placed the three tokens on the square marked Go.

"You go first, girlfriend," Taye instructed. "I'll go next. Then he'll go last."

Pooney felt cheated but knew that a protest would be futile. He would soon discover that being forced to go last was only the beginning of his troubles. Taye and Sheila used a variety of tactics, both fair and unfair, to team up against him. They would excuse each other from paying due rent, make illegal property transactions, and loan each other money. The result was predictable. Pooney didn't stand a chance.

"You're on my property again." Sheila rubbed her palms together. "You owe me eight-hundred dollars."

"I'm broke." Pooney counted the last of his monopoly money and threw it on the board. "That's it for me."

"Where you going?" Taye asked.

"To get me a soda." Pooney's voice failed to hide his anger.

"I know you ain't catchin' no attitude." Taye tried in vain to hold back the smile that turned the sides of her mouth. "Bring me and my friend a soda too."

Pooney returned with the three sodas just in time to see Taye whispering into Sheila's ear.

"Baby, me and Sheila have decided to let you stop playing." Taye's smile was filled with mischief.

"OK." Pooney was sure there was a catch.

"But only on one condition." Taye continued.

"What condition?"

"First you gotta promise me you'll do it." Taye pressed.

"How can I agree to do somethin' and I don't even know what it is?"

"Let's see, Sheila." Taye reached for the two remaining property cards lying in front of Pooney. "Which one of these raggedy railroads do you want?"

"Pennsylvania!" Sheila, presently more amused than Pooney could ever remember her having been before, grabbed the property card from Taye's hand.

"Aw right, damn! I agree to the condition." Pooney had no intention of subjecting himself to more of their torture. "What do I have to do?"

"Tell him, Sheila." Taye stood behind her newfound friend and placed both hands on her shoulders.

"Remember that movie *The Last Dragon*?" Sheila asked.

"The one with Vanity." Pooney nodded.

"OK, then," Sheila went on, "when I say who's the master, you say Sho-Nuff!" Sheila imitated the movie's most colorful character.

"You must be crazy." Pooney opened the orange soda he held and took a sip.

"Allen." Taye's voice was firm. "You promised."

"Who's the master?" Sheila's smile covered her entire face.

Pooney's eyes dropped to the floor before Taye lifted his chin and forced him to face his sister.

"I don't think he heard you, girlfriend." Taye winked at Sheila. "Ask him again."

"Who's the master?" Sheila spoke loudly.

"Sho-Nuff," Pooney mumbled so low that even he wasn't sure he had actually spoken.

"I can't hear you, Leroy." Sheila flawlessly imitated another of Sho-Nuff's lines.

"Sho-Nuff!" Pooney yelled. "Sho-Nuff! Sho-Nuff! Sho-Nuff!"

Taye ran toward Sheila and the two of them exchanged high-fives in the middle of the living room. Pooney shook his head in disbelief at the pleasure derived from his suffering.

"I'll put the game up," Sheila volunteered.

"You mad at us, baby?" Taye stood directly in front of Pooney.

"Y'all cold." Pooney was still shaking his head.

"I'm sorry, baby." Taye kissed him softly. "But you shouldn't have done my friend like that."

"Like what?" That one kiss was enough to make up for everything Pooney had endured in the last hour.

"Puttin'" her in headlocks and twistin' her arm. You could have hurt her." Taye kissed him again. "Promise me you won't ever touch her again."

"I promise." Pooney would have agreed to just about anything.

"You wanna see my Black Barbie collection?" Taye was all set to kiss Pooney once more before Sheila tugged at her arm.

"Sure." Taye smiled a knowing smile in Pooney's direction. "I'd love to see your collection."

Pooney watched helplessly as his little sister led Taye toward the bedroom. Sheila allowed Taye to enter the bedroom first, pausing long enough to turn and stick her tongue out at her brother before following Taye inside. Pooney shook his head once more before taking another sip from his soda.

(5)

Finally asleep. Pooney poked his head through his mother's bedroom door once more for reassurance. Sheila was wrapped into a tight ball with both arms wrapped firmly around a small white pony. One of many stuffed animals in her possession, the pony was a gift from her grandmother. Watching Sheila sleep so peacefully, Pooney was stricken with the sudden urge to dash his younger sister with an ice-cold cup of water. The urge passed quickly as Pooney tiptoed silently toward the bed, and slipped his sister's glasses from her face.

"I wish I had a camera." Taye sounded oddly Southernish as she spoke from the doorway.

Pooney placed his sister's glasses on the nightstand and tiptoed back toward the door.

"That was so sweet." Taye wasn't about to let him off the hook.

"Be quiet." Pooney pushed her backward a couple of steps and eased the door shut behind him. He then led Taye by the hand to the living room.

"Don't be ashamed of your sensitive side, baby." Taye squeezed Pooney's hand as the two of them sat side by side on the couch.

"My sensitive side?" Pooney used his free hand to flip the remote control until he found ESPN.

"What do you mean my sensitive side?"

"Don't get all defensive." Taye unstrapped her sandals, slipped them from her feet, and leaned her back against Pooney's chest.

Pooney wrapped his left arm around Taye, inadvertently brushing against her breast. There was a momentary silence as Pooney anticipated a severe chastising. After regaining his confidence, Pooney placed his hand firmly on Taye's stomach. He was amazed by the way her body felt soft, yet so firm all at the same time. He gently tickled the area just under her belly button. He paused another brief moment before finding the courage to slip his hand under her blouse. While he did so, Taye stretched and moaned with what Pooney could only assume was pleasure.

"You know, that's why I liked you in the first place." Taye spoke softly.

"Why?" Pooney stopped suddenly, all the while wondering if Taye could feel the pounding of his heart.

"Because you're so caring and sensitive." Taye turned onto her stomach. She rested her head on Pooney's thigh.

"Huh?" Pooney placed his hand on the small of Taye's back.

"I still remember the first time I ever saw you." Taye began. "It was on a Friday, the first week of school, and it had been raining all week. It was flooded everywhere, and I was watching that little white girl in the wheelchair with all the buttons on it trying to go from the North campus to the South campus, but she couldn't find a dry path. At least twenty boys walked by that little girl like they didn't even see her. Then, here comes my baby."

Pooney blushed, already knowing the rest of the story.

"I watched you when you rolled up your pants' legs, and packed that little girl all the way to the South campus, then went all the way back to get her wheelchair. I knew then that one day you was gonna be my man."

Taye rolled over once more, raised her head, and kissed Pooney on the cheek. Not knowing what else to do, Pooney returned her kiss on the lips. The two of them continued to kiss as Pooney's hand once again traveled the entire smoothness of her torso before resting at the bottom of her bra. He slid the cups of her bra over her breasts before raising her blouse, rendering her breasts fully exposed. Pooney kissed Taye again as he slid his body from under hers, allowing Taye to lie flat on her back. He kissed her once more as he positioned himself atop of her. He unfastened her pants, then tugged gently at her waist.

"Pooney," Taye protested softly, the firmness of her grip surprising Pooney as she clamped her hand around his wrist. "Your sister."

"She's asleep." Pooney made a useless attempt at continuing his downward course. "She's not coming in here."

Taye relaxed while she and Pooney engaged in another kiss. Pooney briefly awaited a protest that never came, before pulling her pants away from the skin just enough to slide his hand beneath them. Pooney's breath came in gasps as his hand brushed against Taye's pubic hair. Having already gone farther with Taye than with any other girl, Pooney was overtaken with boldness. Taye's legs opened slightly as she allowed Pooney's hand to travel even lower.

"Uh uh," Taye moaned in protest.

Pooney sat up long enough to shed his shirt and pull at Taye's pants some more. This time, Taye lifted her hips in an attempt to aid him.

"Wait." Taye sat up suddenly and grabbed the waistband of her tights. "Go check on Sheila."

"Sheila's asleep."

"Make sure." Taye rolled over, grabbed her purse, and reached inside. "And take this with you."

Pooney stared at the condom Taye had just given him. He didn't know which shocked him more. The fact that she carried one in her purse, or the knowledge that by her giving it to him meant there would be no further protests.

"What's this for?" The absurdity of his own question struck him immediately.

"Either you can put it on, or we can play some more Monopoly."

Pooney hurried down the hallway. He stopped in front of his mother's bedroom door, opening it with the stealth of a cat burglar. He found Sheila lying in the exact same position as before. More importantly to Pooney, she was still sound asleep. He gently closed the bedroom door and looked toward the living room. To his dismay, Taye was fully dressed and headed in his direction.

"What's up?" Pooney threw up his hands.

"Let's go in your bedroom." Taye kissed him.

A knock on the door caused both Pooney and Taye to stop dead in their tracks. They stared directly at each other, both looking like the kid caught with his hand in the cookie jar. Neither of them dared to speak.

"They'll go away," Pooney finally managed.

There was another series of knocks, this time much harder.

"You'd better answer it before they wake Sheila up." Taye felt ridiculous that she was whispering, but somehow she felt compelled to do so. "I'll be in your room."

Pooney, growing steadily more irritable, rushed toward the door and placed his eye over the peephole. Whoever was on the other side was using their hand to block his view. Another hard knock caused Pooney to quickly unlock the door and jerk it open.

"What it wuz, cuz." Larry came barreling inside. He carried a half-filled bottle of Cisco wine in his right hand. "What you doin' runnin' around here with no shirt on like you all swole or something?"

"What's up, Pooney?" Crooked Tony entered behind Larry.

"What y'all doing?" Pooney wondered what else could possibly go wrong.

"Crippin', cuz, crippin'." Larry slurred as he took a seat in the living room.

"We came to bring you some business." Tony explained.

"Some business?"

"Remember I told you I'd help you move your package?"

"Oh." Pooney thought about the fatman cookies under his bed. "How much y'all want?"

"Half-ounce." Tony answered.

"How do I divide it?" Pooney asked.

"Larry has a scale," Tony answered.

"Whose purse?" Larry held the strap of Taye's purse in his right hand.

"My sister's." Pooney answered quickly.

"Bullshit, Loc." Larry shot back. "Lil' Arthur's bitch been over here."

"Watch yo' mouth, fool." Pooney snatched Taye's purse from Larry.

"Aw man, Lil' Loc got a rubber in his hand," Larry yelled into his bottle.

"Be quiet before you wake Sheila up!" Pooney fussed.

"OK. Shhhh, OK." Larry laughed. "Where is she? Is she naked? Can I look?" Larry laughed and offered Pooney the bottle of wine.

"Fuck you, Larry." Pooney snatched the bottle from his hand and took a sip.

"Chill out, Larry." Tony jumped in. "Say Pooney, go get the cheese, break us off, and we're outta here."

"Hold on." Pooney handed Larry the bottle and left the room to retrieve the fatman cookies.

"Who is that, baby?" Taye asked as Pooney burst through the bedroom door.

"Larry and Tony. They just..." Pooney suffered from instant paralysis at the sight of Taye's black bra and panties set.

"Get rid of them, baby."

"OK." Pooney reached under the bed and grabbed the paper bag. "I just gotta give Tony something real quick."

Pooney ran from the bedroom, failing to close the door behind him.

Larry and Tony were both seated on the couch with the scale on the table.

"One quarter is for my Mexican homeboy, the other one is for me and Larry." Tony turned on the scale. He took the ounce of crack from the plastic bag, then placed the entire piece of dope on the scale.

"26.8." Larry read the digital scale aloud. "Moe gave you love, fool."

"How much does a quarter weigh?" Pooney asked.

"Get out the way, Tony." Larry slid the scale in front of him and started breaking the ounce of crack into smaller pieces. "It's that hard dope, too!"

The other boys watched as Larry began to place small chunks onto the scale.

"That's good enough for the Mexican." Larry pulled two empty sandwich bags from his pocket.

Pooney walked around the coffee table to get a better look. The scale read 5.9.

"Now, I know you're gonna break your boys off something proper." Larry placed the portion he had designated for the Mexican customer on top of one of the sandwich bags. He then reset the scale in order to weigh his and Tony's portion. Pooney watched uneasily as Larry continued to place small pieces of crack on the scale, even though it already read 7.1.

"Now that's a fat quarter, Loc." Larry was extremely satisfied with the pile that lay before him.

"8.2 grams?" Pooney mouthed.

"We your boys, Loc." Larry explained.

"Aw right." Pooney just wanted them to leave as soon as possible.

"You might as well give your dope away." Taye entered the room fully dressed.

The three boys watched as Taye approached the table. She gathered all that had been broken from the first ounce into one pile and placed the scale before her.

"You count that?" Taye was all business as she began weighing the dope. Pooney grabbed the money, untangled the bills, and began counting

"What's up with this shit, lil' Loc?" Larry couldn't believe what was going on. "Check yo' broad."

"Check his broad?" Taye struck the python pose. "You check his broad."

"I don't want no trouble, lil' mama." Larry smiled while sticking both hands out in a gesture of submission.

"A quarter in powder is seven grams." Taye looked at Pooney. "In rock, it's six. Got it?"

Pooney nodded before speaking. "This is one seventy-five."

"Since you got a little extra," Taye continued, "you can give your customers a little extra." Taye stopped putting pieces on the scale when it read 6.3. "Where's your money?" Taye glared at Larry.

"What I do to you, baby girl?" Larry threw another wad of bills on the table. This time Pooney didn't have to be told to count it.

"We wanted to get one for a bill-fifty." Crooked Tony added. "If that's cool?"

"This is 140." Pooney held the money between two fingers.

"I know I'm good for ten dollars." Tony spoke to Pooney, but looked at Taye.

"That raggedy ass pager on your waist work?" Taye asked Larry.

"Yeah, it works."

"Give it here." Taye took the wad of money from Pooney, withdrew fifteen dollars and threw it in front of Larry.

"What's up?" Larry was totally baffled.

"You get a quarter for one twenty-five plus the pager." Taye was ruthless.

"What?" Larry was growing angry.

"Take it or leave it." Taye took the first quarter, put it in the corner of the sandwich bag, and tore the bag about two inches above the point where the dope stopped. She then tied the excess plastic in a knot and threw the package to Crooked Tony. She packaged the second quarter in the same fashion and stuffed it in her bra.

"Here." Larry gave Taye an especially nasty look as he threw the pager on the table.

"Dial the number." Taye handed the pager to Pooney with her index finger pointing to the number on the back.

An uneasy silence hovered over the Richards' living room as Pooney placed the receiver on its hook. Seconds later, the pager wailed loudly.

"Sold." Taye reached into her bra and threw the quarter ounce of dope to Larry.

"You got a cold woman there, lil Loc." Larry headed for the door. "She wanna leave a player broke."

"Later, Pooney." Tony smiled as he followed Larry out the door, finally leaving Pooney alone with Taye.

"Can I get a cab at 7200 Heards Lane, Apartment 116." Taye was on the telephone. "Uh-huh. Thank you."

"What are you doing?" Pooney was dumbfounded.

"Callin' a cab." Taye's anger was obvious.

"What's wrong with you?"

"No, Allen. What's wrong with you?"

"What do you mean?"

"What are you doing with that shit in your mother's house? Are you crazy?"

"Everything's cool, baby," Pooney assured her.

"No, it's not, Pooney." Taye took the money from the table and jammed it against the palm of his hand. "What you gonna tell your mama when one night while she's at work, the police knock her door down with a battering ram, and your sister happens to be standing in the way?"

After stuffing the money into his pocket, Pooney took Taye by the hand. "Just put your head on my shoulder." Pooney wrapped her in his arms while singing his favorite verse from Tupac Shakur's "Unconditional Love." "Don't worry about a thing, baby girl, I'm a soldier."

"You're crazy, boy." Taye managed a slight chuckle despite the sadness on her face. "But you don't know what you're getting into."

"I'll be all right as long as I got you on my team," Pooney whispered before kissing her.

Their kiss was interrupted by the sound of a horn blowing.

Taye ran to the door and waved for the cab to wait. "Get that stuff up before Sheila sees it." Taye pointed at the table before digging through her purse in search of a pen. "What's the number on your pager?"

Pooney held the pager so that Taye could see while she scribbled into her palm.

"Tell my friend I'll call her tomorrow." Taye tucked her purse under her arm and gave Pooney one last kiss before heading for the door.

"What am I going to do with this?" Pooney playfully held the condom in the air.

"You better have it the next time I see you," Taye said, and was gone.

CHAPTER 8

"Hello," Pooney finally grumbled into the telephone after at least a dozen rings.

"May I speak with Sheila, please?" The cheerful voice of an extremely polite young man sang into Pooney's ear.

"Who?" Pooney sat up in his bed, sure he had heard the boy correctly, but wanting to hear it once more for good measure.

"Does Sheila Richards live there?" the boy continued in his cheerful manner, stirring visions in Pooney of one of those young kids who always seemed to end up at his front door, soliciting pledges for one cause or another.

"Yeah, Sheila lives here." Pooney deepened his voice for intimidation purposes. "That's my little sister."

"May I speak with her please, sir?"

"About what?"

"About our date Friday night."

"Your what?" Once again Pooney was positive he had heard correctly, but he had to hear it once more.

"I'm taking Sheila to the 'School's Out' dance Friday night."

"You are, huh?" Pooney was taken aback by the news. "Who are you, lil homie?"

"Charlie Williams."

"Hold on a second."

Once both feet were firmly on the floor, Pooney pressed the power button on his stereo. The digital clock showed 10:15 a.m. He threw on a pair of purple Galveston Ball High sweatpants, and stormed through his bedroom door. He peeked first into his mother's bedroom, finding only his mother sound asleep. Next he walked into the living room where he found Sheila sitting upright on the couch. She was also sound asleep. There was a half-eaten bowl of Apple Jacks on the table in front of her, and an open *Source* magazine in her lap.

"Sheila." Pooney pushed the side of her head roughly. "Sheila."

"What?" Sheila opened her eyes.

"Who the hell is Charlie Williams?"

"Who?"

"Charlie Williams."

"A boy from my school." Sheila was wide awake now.

"And that's all?" Pooney stared his sister directly in the eye.

"What are you talkin' about?"

"You know what I'm talkin' about." Pooney lost control. "That lil punk on the phone talkin' about you goin' to some dance with him Friday night.

"On the phone?" Sheila repeated as she sprinted toward her brother's bedroom. "Hello!" She yelled into Charlie's ear.

Pooney, who had followed closely, stood in the doorway, watching and listening.

"Yes, Charlie. Of course I still want to go." Pooney was uncomfortable with the unfamiliar tone to Sheila's voice. "Oh, him?" Sheila continued now, glancing in her brother's direction, allowing Pooney a glimpse at the dancing eyes that accompanied her new voice. "He'll get over it."

Pooney took solace in the fact that his mother would never allow this date to take place.

"Lunch tomorrow?" Sheila now seemed oblivious to her brother's presence. "Sure, see you then." Sheila stood up. "Goodbye, Charlie."

"Goodbye, Charlie." Pooney angrily mocked his sister.

"What's up with you?" Sheila fired, pushing past her brother and skipping down the hallway.

"I'm talkin' to you!" Pooney grabbed her arm and spun her around.

"Get yo' hands off me, punk!"

"What's going on out there?" The racket her children made had awakened Regina.

"Mama, you need to come check yo' daughter." Pooney hurried to the front of his mother's bed.

"Check my daughter?" Regina wrapped herself in a bathrobe before getting out of bed.

"You need to tell your son to keep his hands to himself," Sheila yelled.

"She thinks she grown or somethin', Mama!"

"What?" Regina slipped into her house shoes and took a position between the warring siblings.

"You need to stay out of my business." Sheila was furious.

"See, Mama." Pooney looked to his mother, fully expecting her to back his stance.

"What are you talking about, Allen?" Regina was growing more confused.

"What she mean, her business? She ain't got no business."

"You ain't got no business, old stupid boy." Sheila rolled her eyes. "That's why you're worried about mine!"

"Will one of you tell me what's going on?" Regina tried to assert her authority. Her efforts were to no avail as her children yelled even louder.

"Stop it." Regina screamed over both of them. "One at a time. Allen, you first."

"Some lil punk called here talkin' about he's taking Sheila to a dance Friday night." Pooney crossed his arms.

"And?" Regina was impatient.

"Sheila don't go on dates," Pooney declared.

"Well, this will be her first one," Regina answered.

"You already know about this?" Pooney looked to Sheila, who smiled defiantly in return. "I don't think she's ready."

"Well, son, it really doesn't matter what you think because it's none of your business." Regina wondered if she would be able to speak so matter-of-factly when it was time to tell Pooney about her date with Patrick.

"But, Mama." Pooney was adamantly against all that was happening. "She's only thirteen-years-old."

"It's just a junior high school dance, Allen."

Regina walked to the nightstand and grabbed the bottle of Excedrin PM she had placed there just a couple hours before. She prepared herself for the headache she was sure to have in the next five minutes.

"We Richards' girls will do just fine on our dates."

"Mama, this is serious." Pooney dismissed his mother's statement. "You wanna play."

"I am very serious, son." Regina returned the pill bottle to the nightstand and reached for the now warm Diet Coke that lay there unopened. "The women in this house have their own lives, Allen, and from time to time those lives will include going on dates."

"When do you think you're going on a date?" Pooney was still skeptical of the seriousness of his mother's statements.

"I am attending a play with a friend this evening."

"Renee?"

"No. His name is Patrick." Regina could hardly muster the courage to continue. "Patrick Roy."

"Roy?" Pooney was incensed. "Coach Roy?"

There was a lull in the conversation as Pooney digested the information just given to him.

"Ain't this some shit," Pooney finally mumbled.

"You'd better watch your damn mouth, Allen."

"What you doin' goin' out with my coach, Mama?"

"He's my friend, Allen." Regina was rapidly losing momentum. "He won some tickets to see a play tonight, and asked if I'd join him."

"Aw, man." Pooney shoved his sister out of the way and stormed from his mother's bedroom. "This is messed up."

"You keep your hands off of her, Allen!" Regina was on him instantly. "You hear me?"

"Whatever." Pooney turned away from his mother.

"Boy, I almost hit you in your damn mouth!" Regina grabbed Pooney's chin, forcefully turning his head back toward her. "Do you understand me?"

"Yeah."

"Get your ass in that room."

"That's where I was tryin' to go in the first place."

Regina didn't reply. She hurried him through the door with a hand to the back before slamming the door shut. It was then that the first tears formed in the corners of her eyes.

(2)

Regina stepped into the living room where she was greeted by stares of approval from both Renee and Sheila.

"What?" Regina was not quite sure what to make of the stares.

"You look great, girl!" Renee was first to answer.

"Girl, please." Regina attempted to adjust the dress she was wearing so that the hemline would descend a couple of inches. "My thighs are much too thick for this hoochie mama dress."

"Stop trippin', Gina," Renee encouraged. "That dress was made with you in mind. Tell her, Sheila."

"You look beautiful, Mama." Sheila expressed her genuine admiration.

"I bet you haven't even looked in a mirror yet, have you?" Renee scolded, knowing her best friend all too well.

Regina acknowledged her guilt with a shake of her head.

"I'll get the one on your floor, Mama." Sheila ran down the hallway, only to return moments later dragging a mirror as tall as she was.

"Pull it around here." Renee helped Sheila slide the mirror around a chair and in front of her mother. "You lift that side, I'll hold this one."

"Ta da." Sheila felt the urge to accompany the occasion with music. "Open your eyes, Mama."

Regina found the image in the mirror before her to be surprisingly attractive. The mid-thigh length dress Renee had given her was cut in a way that perfectly accentuated curves Regina thought she had lost years ago. Regina turned to one side, then the other, frowning all the while so as not to give a hint to Renee and Sheila of her satisfaction.

"What's wrong, Mama?" Sheila was bewildered.

"I'm fine, ain't I?" Regina put both hands on her hips and the three of them shared a round of riotous laughter.

"Let me put a little make-up on you, Gina." Renee prodded despite the fact that she had been given a flat out no to the same proposition at least a half-dozen times during the last forty-five minutes.

"That's a little much, Renee. You already talked me into wearing this teenager's dress."

"C'mon, Regina. Just a little lipstick and eyeliner."

"I don't know, Renee." Regina was hesitant.

"Trust me, you'll like it when I'm done. Tell her, Sheila."

"It's just lipstick and eyeliner, Mama." Sheila gleefully sided with Renee.

"OK," Regina finally relented.

"Sit down while I grab my compact," Renee instructed.

Sheila led her mother to the dining room table while Renee rummaged through her purse.

"I can't believe I agreed to this," Regina laughed.

"Here we go." Renee rushed to the table, fearful that her friend was having second thoughts.

A hush came about the small dining area as Renee went to work on Regina's face. Nothing could be heard, save for the collective breathing of the three women. Renee applied the make-up with the precision of a heart surgeon. Sheila stood motionless behind her mother, hands clasped under her chin.

"There." Renee took a full step backward to admire her work.

"Mama!" Sheila mouthed unconsciously.

"Just lipstick and eyeliner, huh?" This time Regina was unable to sell them on her pretended indifference while gawking at herself in the mirror.

There was another short silence, which was interrupted by Pooney's sudden appearance.

"How does your mama look?" Renee took the empty plate from Pooney's hand and sat it on the counter.

Pooney silently scrutinized the woman standing before him. It had been quite some time since he had seen his mother dressed in anything other than her work uniform or the nightgown and robe she frequently sported around the house. The dress she wore was slightly shorter than he would like, but he had to admit it fit nicely. He could not recall ever seeing his mother wearing make-up. Pooney had always considered his mother to be attractive, even though she seldom paid any special attention to her appearance. However, seeing her now, in the cut-to-fit, tan dress and the small amount of make-up she wore, Pooney felt his mother now took on a movie-star type quality. And while he still struggled to keep his anger in check, he could not deny the truth.

"You're beautiful, Mama," Pooney spoke quietly.

"You mean it?" Regina's wide-eyed smile surprised Pooney with the obvious concern with which she regarded his opinion.

"Yeah, I mean it." Pooney gave up on anger. "You look like a movie star, Mama."

"Thank you, baby." The two embraced.

"I wish I had a camera," Renee remarked.

"I got two exposures left in mine." Sheila always seemed to possess whatever was needed.

"Go get it, girl," Renee exclaimed. "We might never get to see your mama dressed up again."

Pooney stepped into the kitchen. He poured himself a glass of orange juice while his sister retrieved the camera.

"C'mon, Pooney," Renee called. "I want to get a picture of you and Sheila with the movie star."

Pooney downed the orange juice and sat the glass next to the plate that already lay on the counter. He then stood next to his mother.

"That boy dwarfs you now, Gina." Renee ducked from behind the camera long enough to inform her friend.

"I know." Regina viewed the side of her son's head. "He's growing an inch a week."

"Say cheese!" Renee brought the camera to eye level and snapped the picture. "Now let's get the movie star by herself."

Pooney and Sheila stood behind Renee as she used the last exposure to immortalize their mother's movie star status.

"I'm getting these developed myself," Renee announced.

"When?" Sheila asked as she scurried toward the ringing phone.

"I'll drop them off when I leave here," Renee responded.

"Hello." Sheila's attention turned to the voice on the other line. "Hey girl...yeah...uh huh...we sure did...hold on."

Sheila sat the phone down and ran back toward the dining area. "It's for you, Pooney." She paused until she was sure she was the object of everyone's attention. "Chantaye said you'd better get yo' butt on the phone right now."

"Can I talk on the phone, Mama?" Pooney asked humbly.

"Go ahead, baby."

"Uh, who is Chantaye?" Pooney could hear Renee murmur behind him. "Ain't she something? Demanding people to the phone."

"Hello." Pooney unveiled his Barry White voice to the amusement of Renee and his mother. "I've been asleep, too."

"Ain't he about nothin'?" Renee cackled. "Look at him. I guess he's a playa."

"Girl, I don't know what he thinks he is, but he better not bring no grandbabies this way."

Pooney flashed them a disapproving glance. "It's a full house in here, Taye. Let me call you back from my bedroom...Alright...yeah...right back I promise...bye."

"I guess we're cramping his style, girl." Renee was still teasing as she placed the compact back in her purse.

"I'll cramp his style all right," Regina quipped.

"Hey, the man in the house got a life, too." Pooney smiled before strolling down the hallway and into his bedroom.

(3)
        "He'll get over it, you know." Patrick lowered the volume on his car stereo so that Regina could hear him.

"Huh?"

"Allen. He'll get over it."

"You didn't tell me you're a mind reader too," Regina remarked lightheartedly.

"Well, you're an easy read." Patrick laughed. "At least tonight, anyway."

Regina smiled, knowing that Patrick was correct. She hadn't spoken two words since they crossed the Causeway Bridge taking them from The Island to the mainland. She was totally preoccupied with Allen's reaction to her date with his football coach. While he did seem okay when she poked her head through his bedroom door to inform him of her departure, Regina was sure that her son's nonchalant response was for the benefit of the girl on the telephone.

"I'm sorry, Patrick," Regina answered. "I guess I haven't been much company the last twenty minutes."

"It's OK." Patrick's demeanor showcased his undying patience.

"This is the first date I've been on since Allen's father went to prison." Regina spoke more to herself than to Patrick. "So this is a totally new concept for him."

"I didn't know Allen's father was incarcerated."

"Yeah." Regina regretted her rambling. "He has a forty-year sentence."

"You wouldn't happen to be talking about Big Al, would you?"

"You know him?"

"You kidding? Everyone knows Big Al." Patrick paused for a second, a sudden faraway look suddenly masking his face, the look of one struggling to recall a long ago event. "Your son looks just like Big Al. I don't know why I never made the connection."

"Yeah, he does." Allen's striking resemblance to his father was a fact Regina couldn't deny.

"When I was about your son's age," Patrick stated, the memory now vivid in his mind, "I had a falling out with my science teacher. So one day, I cut his class and went around Wright Cuney Park, bought a joint and a bottle of wine, and sat on the benches next to the basketball court."

"What?" Regina turned suddenly, obviously intrigued by Patrick's unsolicited testimony.

"I've had my wild times," Patrick answered before getting back to the story. "Anyway, Big Al was there. He and a couple of guys his age were shooting craps and smoking weed. We lived on the same block so he recognized me. Big Al came over and asked what's up, so I told him about my disagreement with my science teacher, and a bunch of other stuff I thought he would be impressed to hear. Then I offered him a drink of my wine."

Patrick moved his Ford Bronco to the right lane in preparation to exit Interstate 45.

"He accepted, took a healthy drink, then put the cap on the bottle and sat the drink on the ground beside him. He looked me dead in the eye and asked, 'What the hell is wrong with you?' Before I could answer, he jerked me from the bench, slapped me upside the head, and kicked me in the behind. He started hollering and cursing, telling me I'd better take my ass back to school and he'd better not ever catch me around the park during school hours."

"I bet you were furious." Regina didn't know what else to say. "Did you hit him back?"

"Hit Big Al? Are you crazy?" Patrick laughed aloud. "I took my butt straight back to school and never came back around the park during school hours." Both of them laughed.

"Allen can be convincing." Regina wiped the tears of laughter from her eyes.

"Convincing?" Patrick too was still laughing. "Try terrifying."

"That, too." Regina agreed.

"You know though, Regina," Patrick was suddenly very serious. "I'll never forget what Big Al said next."

"What did he say?"

"I looked back at him one last time as I was leaving." Patrick remembered. "He was puffing on my joint and I swear I could see tears in his eyes."

"Tears?"

"Yeah." Patrick nodded slowly. "Big Al had tears in his eyes." Patrick uttered the words as if he didn't believe what he had seen now, any more than he had twenty years ago. "He blew a long stream of smoke through his nose and he said to me: 'Sometimes love hurts, young blood.'"

Regina was speechless. She had heard her husband speak the same words countless times before. It was at that very moment that Regina came to the realization that Big Al wasn't coming home for a very long time, if ever. He had already been gone six years, and it would be fourteen more before he would be eligible for parole.

"How's Big Al doing these days?" Patrick knew he had asked a ridiculous question.

"He 's . . ."

"I'm sorry, Regina. That was a stupid question."

"It's OK." She stretched the truth. "I've adjusted to the situation."

"Good." Patrick felt awkward.

"Is that Gerald Levert?" Regina was desperate to redirect the conversation.

"Yeah." Patrick was more than happy with the change of subject.

"I love that song. Turn it up."

CHAPTER 9

Monday's bus ride home provided Pooney with the much-needed opportunity to reflect on the last week's events. And what a fast-paced week it had been. Starting with being clicked into Deuce-nine last Sunday night, to the ride to Alvin, to his budding relationship with Taye, Pooney felt as if he had lived the last week in hyperspace.

Pooney exhibited a slightly perceptible frown as his thoughts turned to his mother's date with Coach Roy. Unable to sleep until his mother's return, Pooney lay awake for hours thinking about his early childhood years, before his father's legal troubles, when all was well in the Richards' household. Now that he was older, Pooney understood that by most people's standards his father was a bad man. But he also knew that those same people had never met the man he called Daddy. Pooney idolized his father, and no matter the opinion of others, he always would.

Admittedly, Pooney held Coach Roy in the highest regard. However, he refused to become a co-conspirator in any betrayal of his father. When Pooney finally heard his mother's arrival, sometime after two thirty a.m., he was more upset with her than he had ever been with anyone in his life. An hour later, as Pooney hovered somewhere between sleep and consciousness, he vowed that regardless of what Sheila and his mother decided, his loyalty to his father would forever be absolute.

Once the bus stopped, Pooney leaped from the side door and trotted across the parking lot of Tim's store.

"Say, Pooney." Crooked Tony jumped from behind the wheel of The Tank.

"What y'all doin'?" Pooney peeked inside the LTD and saw Larry asleep in the back seat. His left hand, knuckles bloodied, still clutched a twenty-two-ounce Schlitz Malt Liquor Bull.

"Waitin' for you," Crooked Tony answered.

"What's up with your boy?" Pooney laughed.

"Damn fool been over there fightin' with that ignorant ass girl," Tony explained. "We were at her Auntie's house and he had her pinned against the side of the garage. That clown is so drunk, he tried to punch her, but she ducked and he hit nothin' but brick wall."

"What happened then?" Pooney took another peek at his pitiful-looking friend.

"Leticia got away from him and ran into the house."

"One of y'all lil' brothers got a quarter?" Willie Coakley interrupted Pooney and Tony. Willie was a one-time baller, whose daily routine now consisted of standing in front of Tim's store and hustling quarters until he had enough for a cheap bottle of wine.

"Go get me a pint of strawberry ice cream." Pooney handed Willie two one-dollar bills. "And you keep the change."

Willie took the money from Pooney, acknowledging the teenage boy's instructions with a nod and a smile, before running up the stairs and through the convenience store door.

"Yeah, Loc," Tony continued his story, "her Auntie came outside and that damn fool pushed her down."

"Aw, man." Pooney thoroughly enjoyed Tony's recollection of Larry's clowning.

"Old girl called the police and shit, fool. It took me damn near five minutes to wrestle him into the car. I just knew we was going to jail." Tony shook his head before abruptly changing the subject. "So what you gettin' into today?"

"Nothin'."

"Let's get on our grind then," Tony suggested.

"What?"

"I forgot you was a rookie." Tony laughed. "Let's see if we can move that package you got."

"I'm with it." Pooney watched as Willie left the store with the ice cream.

"Well, let's go to your house and break your package down." Tony paused while Pooney accepted his ice cream from Willie. "Then we'll go around Cedar Terrace and see what's up."

"Cool with me." Pooney was already climbing into the car.

Tony eased out of the driveway, crossed Heards Lane, and pulled into Pooney's complex.

Grindin'. Pooney had picked up a new word. Unfortunately, he was clueless as to all the possible ramifications the term entailed.

(2)

Pooney was extremely apprehensive about leaving his dope in Larry's grandfather's car. Finally, after being assured and reassured that his package was safe, Pooney reluctantly agreed to leave all but two eight-balls and a dozen or so small rocks inside The Tank.

Crooked Tony parked The Tank alongside New Jack City, the small apartment complex Pooney had run through while evading Ivy's runner. Tony led the way, while Pooney and Larry followed him down 28th Street on foot. They stopped at an abandoned house on the alley corner, half a block from Broadway Boulevard.

"We stoppin' here?" Pooney frowned.

"Yeah. What's wrong?" Tony was puzzled.

"We're across the street from a church." Pooney stared at Jerusalem Baptist Church, the very church where he had attended Vacation Bible School a few summers before.

"I know you ain't fixing to trip like that, Lil' Loc." Larry was sobering up.

"Don't even talk about trippin'." Pooney took offense to Larry's statement.

"It's chill, Pooney." Crooked Tony was once again primed to use his skills of diplomacy. "Look, God is everywhere. So whether you're in front of a church or wherever, he still knows when you're doing wrong."

Pooney felt no need to reply. As usual, Tony made perfect sense. Pooney had always found it frustrating that most people thought so little of his best friend's mental capabilities. When in actuality, Crooked Tony had always possessed wisdom and insight far beyond his years.

"Check it out, Pooney." Tony took a small piece of foil paper from his pocket and stuck it in a patch of high grass next to the curb. "Don't ever hold your dope on you. Put it where you can see it, but don't stand too close."

Pooney walked over to the spot where Tony had stashed his package, but found it difficult to camouflage the much larger brown paper bag he possessed.

"Look, Loc," Larry was laughing hysterically while motioning for Pooney to join him next to an overstuffed trash can standing a few feet away from them. "Put it in here."

Pooney followed Larry's instructions, then joined his friends on the steps of the abandoned house.

"Tony." Thaddeus Lee, a thin, unshaven man approached. He walked at a high rate of speed and spoke loudly through two missing front teeth. "Let me see a twenty."

"Hold on." Tony jumped from the steps and ran toward the foil he had placed in the grass just moments before.

"What's up, Larry?" Lee offered Larry an oil-stained hand before turning to Pooney. "You're the youngster that new white narc was after Friday night, ain't you?"

Pooney nodded.

"I sure thought he was gonna catch you, boy." Lee handed Tony the twenty-dollar bill, then placed the rock under his tongue. "But when you hit that corner and put that burst on, it was all over then."

"Yeah, that muthafucka was on my ass." Pooney thought he sounded cool.

"Check it out. My lil' homeboy got some eight-balls," Tony explained. "So if you hear anybody want one, send 'em over here."

"What they goin' for?" Lee asked while Pooney marveled at how well the man was able to speak with the crack rock in his mouth.

"Seventy-five," Tony answered.

"That's love." Lee's eyes lit up.

"They fat too!" Crooked Tony turned salesman.

"I'll see what I can do." Lee turned to Pooney. "What's your name, youngster?"

"Pooney."

"Awright Pooney, Thaddeus Lee's on the job." Pooney watched as Lee motioned to a weary-looking, dark-skinned woman to join him as he disappeared down the alley.

"That's a hustlin' ass dope-fiend there," Larry said once Lee was gone. "He'll probably have all yo' shit sold before dark."

"Looks like he got a sale already." Tony pointed.

Lee was once again standing at the alley's entrance, this time accompanied by a teenage boy. Lee pointed in their direction and the teenager came running toward them.

"Which one of you playas got them balls for seventy-five dollars?"

"Me." Pooney hesitated before answering.

"Let me check one out." The youngster pulled out a handful of crinkled bills and counted them out.

Pooney, assuming he was doing the right thing because neither Tony nor Larry objected, ran to the trash can and grabbed a ball from the brown paper bag.

"Here you go, playa." Pooney handed his first customer the merchandise.

"This ain't that blow-up shit, huh?" The boy handed Pooney the money, then commenced to examine the package as would a highly suspicious jeweler.

"My homeboy don't sell no bullshit, cuz," Larry butted in.

"I hope not." The youngster closed his hand around the eight-ball. "Y'all gonna be right here?"

"Shops open, baby boy." Tony spoke again.

"If it's good, I'll be back," the young man promised before jogging away.

"I told you that was a hustlin' ass dope fiend," Larry remarked.

"Peep game, Pooney." Tony stood up. "Once you give a customer the dope and you got the money, cut the conversation short."

"OK."

"'Cause he's the one dirty now," Tony continued. "So you want him away from you as soon as possible."

As he would a number of times over the next few hours, Pooney had learned something valuable from Tony.

Twenty-eighth Street was unlike anything Pooney had ever experienced before. There was never a dull moment, and money changed hands continuously. Nervous at first, Pooney took to his new environment like a duck to water. He enjoyed the power he felt from knowing he possessed something that everyone wanted badly. There was no end to what people offered for his crack. Money, cars, jewelry, and the bodies of women he had never met before were readily at his disposal.

The words Larry had spoken earlier seemed prophetic now. It was shortly after seven o'clock, just before dark, when Pooney sold his last eight-ball. Three seconds later, he sold his last ten-dollar rock for seven dollars to a woman named Vikki. Vikki had already proven to be a loyal customer, and unlike most of the women Pooney encountered in the last few hours, he found Vikki to be very attractive.

"You sold out?" Crooked Tony came from around the corner counting money, something the three of them had been doing a lot of the last couple of hours.

"That was the last one," Pooney answered.

"I was going to get another one." Tony had already purchased three of Pooney's eleven eight-balls.

"Is it like this all the time?" Pooney was flabbergasted by the fact that he had just made a little over a thousand dollars in about three and a half hours.

"Today is check day," Tony explained. "Otherwise it wouldn't be rolllin' like this on a Monday. But you ain't seen nothin' yet. Wait 'til Friday."

"Say, youngster." Lee came from the alley waving a dirty baseball cap above his head. "Let me get something for thirty dollars." Lee's mouth twisted and turned, causing a hilarious contortion of his face.

"I'm out, Lee," Pooney answered.

"What? You ain't got no more?" Lee looked as if someone had just told him the sun would never rise again.

"I got these last two twenties," Tony interjected. "You can take 'em off my hands for thirty dollars."

"OK." Lee acted like a crying baby who had just been given a pacifier. "Y'all gotta score, man. It's poppin' out here. I got customers coming."

"If we go and get a nice-sized package, do you think it'll go tonight?" Tony asked.

"Didn't you hear me, Tony?" Lee used a washcloth to wipe the sweat from his forehead. "I got clientele around here. I don't care if you bring a kilo around this muthafucka, Thaddeus Lee can move it."

All three boys rolled with laughter.

"Y'all hurry up and take care of your business," Lee urged. "It's check day, Tony. You know it's money to make out here."

"Aw right, Lee." Tony tugged at the cramps in his side. "We 'bout to handle our business right now."

"Go ahead, then." Lee was still fussing as he departed. "Y'all hired Thaddeus Lee to do a job, now go get the work."

"Now, that's a fool." Pooney laughed.

"He's a money-making fool, though," Larry added.

"Still feel like grindin'?" Tony asked Pooney.

Pooney thought about the American History exam he had at eight tomorrow morning. He should go home and rest. He already had more money in his pocket than he knew what to do with. He also knew that his mother would be extremely angry if she called and he wasn't home.

"What you got in mind?" Pooney hoped the grimace that accompanied thoughts of his mother went unnoticed.

"Let's go to the clubhouse and see what Moe'll do for us."

"I'm with it," Pooney answered.

"Let's get in The Tank and see how much money we got," Tony suggested. "Then we can either put our money together or, you can score from Moe, and we can score from you."

The three boys walked in the direction of The Tank. This time Pooney led the way.

"You think you a baller now huh, Lil' Loc?" Larry playfully pushed Pooney's shoulder.

"You didn't know?" Pooney mused while feeling the sizeable lump in his pocket.

The three of them piled into The Tank, enroute to the clubhouse. Pooney lounged in the back seat, deeply contemplating his future in hustling, fancying himself driving a Cadillac like Moe's with beautiful girls at his beck and call. *A baller*, Pooney thought, *that's exactly what I am.*

(3)

"One thousand, two hundred fifty dollars." Pooney had to speak the amount aloud in order to believe it himself.

"Let me give you this two-fifty." Crooked Tony handed him more money. "Then you can get three ounces."

"OK." Pooney arranged the money into two bundles and stuffed one in each pocket.

"We'll pull up and drop you off, Loc." Larry slipped the idle engine into drive and crept slowly toward the clubhouse. "I'll make a couple of blocks, then park close enough to see you when you come out."

Pooney took the odd five dollars and handed it to Larry as The Tank rolled to a stop in front of the clubhouse. "Get us something to drink, man."

"Aw right, Loc."

Pooney closed the door behind him and The Tank pulled away slowly. He walked hurriedly through the open gate and ran up the stairs.

"What's up?" Big Lou stood in the doorway.

"Moe here?"

"What you need?"

"I need to score." Pooney's voice was unsteady.

"Hold on." Big Lou closed the door, leaving Pooney alone to ponder the first lieutenant's reluctance to grant him entrance to the clubhouse.

"OK, come on," Big Lou barked over the squeaky hinges.

Pooney stood just inside the doorway. He wondered if there was a permanent smell of marijuana in the clubhouse, or if once again, his timing had been just right.

"What's up, cuz?" Moe entered the living room wearing nothing but his boxers, and carrying a mixed drink.

Pooney turned to Big Lou, cognizant for the first time that the first lieutenant, too, was clad only in boxers.

There was a third man standing in the doorway leading to the bedroom. He was just under six feet tall and well over three hundred pounds. Like the others, he wore only boxers.

"I'm ready." Pooney uttered the words that Tony had advised him to use.

"Already?" Moe was surprised.

Pooney was still wondering why none of the three men wore any clothes when he said, "Let me get three of 'em."

"I see ya, Loc." Moe took a sip from his glass, frowning immediately. "Damn Lou, where's the juice, cuz?"

"You said a stiff one." Big Lou was now standing in front of the door where the obese man had been standing moments before. A fourth man, whom Pooney could only assume had been inside the room, was standing behind Big Lou. Pooney was not surprised to see that he too was wearing only boxers.

"Want some pussy, Loc?" Moe asked suddenly.

"What?" Pooney grinned.

"You want some pussy?" Moe motioned for Pooney to follow him toward the bedroom. "Look."

Pooney stood in the doorway. The obese man was lying on top of a woman and humping vigorously. The motion caused his heavily dimpled behind to appear as if there were gigantic tidal waves rolling under his skin.

"C'mon, fat boy," a female voice urged from beneath the massive mound of flesh.

The pitch of the woman's voice led Pooney to believe that she was white.

"C'mon, fat boy. Don't quit so soon." The woman continued to urge as the tidal waves decreased in size and speed.

Finally, fat boy came to a halt with a loud grunt.

"That bitch is a freak, Loc," Moe whispered in Pooney's ear as fat boy climbed from atop the woman and stepped into the bathroom, allowing the woman to finally become visible to Pooney.

Pooney stared at the white woman. Her eyes were closed and her legs were wide open. Pooney, who had never been so close to a naked woman before, watched as the woman's hips moved in a circular motion, rising from the bed with each rotation.

"Her husband's a doctor." Moe told Pooney. "She don't do no dope or nothin', Loc. She just likes to fuck."

The woman's eyes opened and Pooney thought his heart would escape from his chest. She was staring right at him. No, through him. There was a hunger in the woman's eyes, the likes of which Pooney had never before seen, but somehow knew could never be satisfied.

"Gon' hit it, Loc," Moe offered.

The woman's eyes closed again as she placed her right hand between her legs. The rhythmic motion of her undulating hips increasing in speed, appealed to Pooney to accept Moe's offer.

"Naw, cuz." Pooney turned his head, suddenly ashamed by the entire scene. "Let me get the package."

"C'mon." Moe smiled a knowing smile.

Pooney followed Moe through the backdoor and down the stairs that led to the apartment below.

"You handled your business with that last package, Loc." Moe turned the light on as they stepped inside. "What you got?"

"Fifteen hundred," Pooney answered proudly as he pulled out both pocketfuls of money to corroborate his claim.

"Shit, you moved them so fast." Moe pulled on the plastic at the bottom of the refrigerator until the front of it came off. He then reached under the refrigerator and withdrew a small wooden box. "Tell you what."

Pooney watched as Moe pulled one fatman cookie after another from the box, six in all. He placed the box back in the hole and repositioned the plastic guard so as to make the hiding place inconspicuous once again.

"Give me the fifteen hundred for three." Moe held three cookies in his hand. "And I'll front you three more." Moe stacked all three ounces directly in front of the rapidly drowning teenage boy.

"OK." Pooney handed Moe the money.

"I see somethin' in you, Loc." Moe held the money with two hands. "Stick with me, and you'll come up big, cuz. Pooney was once again intoxicated with thoughts of being a baller.

As if Moe could read his mind, he said, "By the time school starts back in August, you won't have to ride no bus. You'll be drivin' your own shit."

Pooney exited the clubhouse with the same big dreams that had led to the demise of countless little boys before him. Money, cars, and women. All he wanted, free for the taking. Unfortunately, the lesson would reveal itself with the intensity of a bowling ball-sized hailstorm: nothing from the street is free, only borrowed. And when the street comes calling for its dues, the only payments accepted are blood and tears.

(4)

"What took you so long, Loc?" Larry handed Pooney the Thunderbird and Kool-Aid concoction.

Pooney told them all about the white woman and fat boy, and all about everyone standing around in their boxers.

"What you mean, you didn't hit it?" Larry bellowed upon hearing that Pooney had declined Moe's offer to have sex with the woman. "What's wrong with your boy, Crooked Tony?"

"Man, I wouldn't wanna get none after everybody in the house either," Tony replied.

"Both of y'all some busters." Larry snatched the bottle from Pooney and drank heartily. Wine fell from both corners of his mouth. "Lil' Loc, you probably a virgin."

"Be for real." Pooney waved him off.

"Yeah, you a virgin." Larry nodded his head. "You ain't never hit nothin'."

"How you gon' call my homeboy a virgin?" Tony smiled, obviously agreeing with Larry's assumption.

"I ain't no virgin," Pooney protested.

"Well, tell me one broad you done hit," Larry challenged.

The first name that formed on Pooney's lips was Chantaye. However, Pooney was reluctant to lie about having sex with her for fear that she may find out about it.

"Pam," Pooney finally replied.

"Pam who?" Larry was totally unbelieving.

"My cousin Kisha's friend, Pam."

"Pamela Sanders." Larry laughed loud enough to shatter the windshield. "I know you ain't never hit that, Loc. Stop lying."

Larry and Crooked Tony both shook with laughter.

"Fuck that." Pooney had the perfect subject changer. "What y'all know about this here."

Pooney turned the brown paper bag upside down, dumping all six ounces in the seat between Larry and Tony.

"Damn," Larry exclaimed.

"How'd you get all that, Pooney?" Crooked Tony's words came slowly.

"I bought three, and he fronted me three."

"That fool cut for you, huh?" Larry asked.

"Ballers recognize ballers." Pooney smiled as he put all but one ounce back in the bag. "Y'all already paid for half of that." Pooney was growing addicted to the power he felt. "Just give me the rest when y'all handle y'all's business."

"Thanks, Pooney." Tony held the fatman cookie in the palm of his hand.

"You're all right, Lil' Loc." Larry looked at Pooney through the rearview mirror. "But tonight you gonna have to hit somethin'."

All the boys laughed.

"Take us to my house, Larry." Pooney was giving orders now. "We can break our shit down there."

Larry redirected The Tank with a sudden U-turn, and just like that, the three of them were headed toward their destination.

CHAPTER 10

"What the fuck?" Pooney stared disbelievingly at his younger sister.

"What's wrong, Pooney?" Crooked Tony entered the apartment behind Pooney, alarmed by the tone of his friend's voice.

"What the hell is wrong with you?" Pooney yelled at Sheila.

"What the hell is wrong with you?" Sheila, obviously well prepared for an argument, stood to face her older brother.

"Who put that shit in yo' hair?" Pooney was furious about the extensions Sheila sported.

"Taye." Sheila said the name as if it were a protective shield against her older brother.

"Taye?" Pooney lost some of his steam. "I can't wait to see what Mama says."

"Mama already knows, 'cause I called her and Taye asked her," Sheila said matter-of-factly while peeking over her brother's shoulder and gaining confidence from his friends.

"I bet she didn't know you're in here dressed like a slut." Pooney was still angry. "I guess Taye gave you those clothes, too."

Sheila stood staring at her older brother. With both hands on her hips, and wearing black tights with a purple halter-top, Sheila was behaving in typical Chantayesque fashion. "Call her and ask her," she challenged.

Pooney snatched the phone from the table, then viciously assaulted the push buttons.

Tony and Larry squeezed behind Pooney and both took seats. They, along with Sheila, eyed Pooney with great anticipation.

"May I speak to Chantaye?" Pooney asked sternly, then took a deep breath as he listened to the fumbling sound of the telephone receiver changing hands.

"Hello." The sound of Chantaye's voice stirred memories in Pooney of two nights before, a time when he had been so close to finally making it with a girl.

"This is Pooney. Why did you..."

"Where have you been?" Taye cut him off.

"Hangin' out with Larry and Tony.

The two boys on the couch squirmed, sensing that their friend was already losing the battle.

"I waited at your house for hours," Taye angrily informed him. "What was so important that you couldn't even call home to check on your sister?"

"I was grindin'." Conscious of his friends' observance, Pooney tried to sound cool. "You know how it is, baby. A playa gotta get his scrilla."

"Save that hip shit for your friends, Pooney." Taye sounded tired. Not a physical tired, but a mental, fed-up type of tired. "Don't talk to me that way."

"Why is my sister looking like a prostitute?" Pooney quickly changed the subject, conceding the first round to Taye.

"What are you talking about?"

"I'm talking these booty girl pants my sister is wearing and the horse hair you put in her head. She looks like a hooker."

"She does not." The anger was gone from Taye's voice. "She's cute."

"She don't need to be dressing like that." Pooney was regaining momentum. "She's already fast."

"Why are you so hard on her?" Taye asked. "Your sister is sweet."

"She still don't need to be dressing like that."

"So, when are you going to find time for me?" Now Taye was the one shuffling topics.

"What you mean?"

"I mean." Taye's voice was lowered to a seductive whisper. "When are you going to take a break from playing with your friends long enough to come and play with me?"

"We gonna be in your room, Loc," Larry told Pooney.

The smile on Pooney's face told everyone all that they needed to know.

"Come over tomorrow." Pooney was almost begging.

"You sure you gonna have time for me?"

"Yeah, baby."

There was a short silence before Taye asked, "You going back out tonight, ain't you?"

"For a little while."

"Be careful, Pooney." Taye sounded more serious to Pooney than she ever had before.

"I will, baby." Pooney felt like he was going off to war.

"I'll be there tomorrow after school."

"OK."

"You'd better be there."

"I will."

"And you'd better have what I gave you."

"I will." Pooney smiled. "See you tomorrow."

(2)

Pooney sat in the passenger side of The Tank as Tony cruised Broadway Boulevard. After drinking most of the wine, Larry had once again fallen asleep in the backseat. Pooney used the downtime to sort through his feelings regarding the women in his life. His mother was dating Coach Roy, and as much as he hated it, there was simply nothing he could do about it. His loyalty to his father would never allow him to accept his mother having a relationship with another man, but he could see no sense in wasting any more time worrying about the matter.

The situation with Sheila caused a different reaction in Pooney. He would not tolerate his sister dressing the way she had today. Maybe Tony had been correct in his assessment of the situation. Maybe he was tripping. But Sheila was still his younger sister and she would mind, or else.

Then there was Taye. Besides his belief that she could become a negative influence on Sheila, Pooney thought Taye to be incredible. Pooney didn't understand why such a beautiful, "older" woman would be interested in him in the first place. He also wondered how he could possibly measure up, since his experience was zero.

"What's on your mind, Pooney?" Tony asked suddenly.

"Mo' money, mo' money."

"You ain't gotta front with me." Tony switched lanes. "What's bothering you?"

"I'm just thinking about Sheila." Pooney told him a third of the truth.

"Why does it bother you so much that she got her hair done?" Tony asked.

"It's not just the hair." Pooney opened up. "It's the attitude with it. And..."

"And what?"

"Some lil' punk called for her the other morning." Pooney spoke as if recounting the most horrific tale imaginable.

"Ohhhhh." A light went on somewhere inside Tony's head.

"The lil' punk talkin' about he's taking Sheila to a dance."

"So you get jealous when boys show your sister attention."

"That's not it."

"Yes, it is."

"No, it's not."

"What is it, then?" Tony gave Pooney the opportunity to explain.

Pooney frowned, then turned toward the passenger side window.

Tony decided not to push the issue any further, choosing instead to turn on The Tank's radio.

"The No Limit set, fool." Tony turned up the volume.

"Make 'em say uhhh nananana." Larry sat straight up in the back seat. He sang loudly along with Master P.

Pooney and Tony could only laugh at their drunken partner.

(3)

"Go ahead.   Handle your business, Loc." Larry was somehow still drinking.

"But she ain't got no teeth." Pooney stood in the alley outside the small house, eyeing the extremely slender blonde standing on the porch.

"That's the best kind, youngster." Tony and Larry snickered at Jerome.

Jerome was the blonde's "old man." He envisioned himself as a big time pimp, but in reality was nothing more than a fast-talking crackhead. Pooney had already decided that he didn't care very much for Jerome.

"Gone get your rocks off, lil' Loc." Larry offered Pooney the Styrofoam cup. "I told you, you was hittin' somethin' tonight."

"You in the game now, youngster." Jerome prepared his final sales pitch. "Treat yourself, don't cheat yourself."

"Yeah, treat yourself, lil' Loc." Larry was enjoying himself.

"Look at her." Jerome spoke, and Pooney took a look at the frail white woman on the porch. She brushed her hair back with her right hand while placing her left one on her hip in a feeble attempt at looking sexy. "She ready for you, youngster."

"What you gonna do, Loc?" Larry jumped in.

Pooney turned to Tony.

The Crooked Tony Shrug.

"Fuck it." Pooney broke the twenty he held in his hand and gave half of it to Jerome.

"Uh-oh." Larry slapped Tony on the back. "Lil' Loc found his balls."

Jerome motioned for Pooney to follow him inside.

"You know where we'll be, Pooney." Crooked Tony and Larry drifted down the alleyway that led to 28th Street.

(4)

Pooney had never smelled anything that could have prepared him for the aroma that met him at the door of the small house. He was reminded of the chitterlings his grandmother often fixed for him as a child. While rather tasty once prepared, the smell they gave off while cooking was intolerable. Throw in the smell of last week's wet gym socks, along with a barrel full of dirty diapers, and you may have something comparable to the putrid smell that presently attacked Pooney's stomach.

There was apparently no electricity in the small house, as there were candles burning in every room. The rail-thin woman looked much older to Pooney now that he viewed her from up close. The woman took Pooney's hand and led him through another room, this one with no candles burning. The only thing discernible to him through the darkness was six sets of large white eyes. The only sound was a chorus of low whispers accompanied by the continuous striking of an uncooperative lighter.

"It's OK." The blonde squeezed Pooney's hand in response to the mounting tension she felt in his body.

The two of them continued through the small room and into another room with identical dimensions, this one with candlelight. Once inside, Pooney's date closed the door behind them.

"Go ahead and get undressed," the blonde suggested. "I'll be right back."

The blonde hurried through the door, and the voices in the other room became louder. There was a large, dirty sofa along the only wall with a window. There had been a day, Pooney surmised, when the sofa had been off-white in color. Now, it was rain-threatening gray.

Pooney took a seat on the couch and removed his Jumpman tennis shoes. The voices in the other room grew even louder and Pooney began to regret his decision not to give Tony his money to hold. Because Thaddeus Lee had made good on his promise to move whatever dope Pooney and his friends returned with only half an ounce remaining from the two ounces Pooney had decided to bring with him. The half-ounce, along with approximately fifteen hundred dollars, was now in Pooney's pocket.

Pooney pressed the button that illuminated the face of the Nike watch he had purchased from a crackhead earlier in the night. The watch read four a.m. He then took a large buck knife, also courtesy of a neighborhood drug user, opened it, and placed it under the middle cushion.

"You ready, baby?" The blonde returned, her eyes now the size of flying saucers.

Pooney pulled off his pants, folded them, and placed them under the cushion that he planned to lay his head on. Next, he took his shirt off and placed it on the arm of the couch. Dressed only in his boxers, he lay flat on his back.

"What you want, hun?" The blonde quickly discarded her clothes.

Pooney watched her appreciatively as she walked slowly toward the sofa, allowing him to enjoy her naked body.

Pooney had no idea which fascinated him more, the small pear-shaped breasts that she allowed to dangle just inches from his face, or the feel of the warmth between her legs rubbing against his stomach.

"Everything," Pooney answered.

"What's everything, baby?" The blonde leaned forward and kissed the young drug dealer on the neck.

"I want a blowjob." Pooney tried to remember the exact words Larry had used. "Then I want you to ride it like a horse."

"Whatever you want, baby." The blonde laughed before lowering her face to Pooney's groin.

The perks that came with being a baller were becoming more appealing to Pooney all the time.

(5)

"What, Mama?" Taye answered angrily.

"Open the door, I gotta tell you something." The voice Chantaye Johnson had grown to despise the most in recent months beckoned from the other side of her bedroom door.

"I ain't got no money." Taye sat up in her bed and squinted to see the alarm clock sitting on the windowsill. "I have a final exam to take in three hours, so leave me alone!"

"I don't want no money, girl," Chantaye's mother explained. "Open the door. It's important."

Over the last few months, as Barbara Johnson's drug habit steadily increased, Taye began to find it harder to hide her hatred for her mother. When at home, Taye would usually spend her time in her bedroom, dreaming of the bright future she was determined to have. She would imagine herself as the anchorwoman of *Good Morning America*, a dream she had held dearly since early childhood.

Chantaye also dreamed of large houses, a loving husband, and beautiful children. Most of all, she longed for the day that she would never again have to see her mother's face.

Chantaye's classmates were sure that they knew Chantaye quite well. However, nothing could be further from the truth. None of them could possibly imagine the hell her life had become since her mother began using drugs. Knowing her only as the loose, fun-loving girl in the skimpy clothes, none of her classmates had any idea of the single-minded determination Chantaye possessed to be successful. None of them knew that she had never made anything less than an A in any class throughout her three years of high school. None of them knew that she had, just a couple of months earlier, scored over thirteen hundred on the SAT exam. None of them really knew Chantaye Johnson at all.

"Hold on, shoot," Taye fussed as she found some clothes to put on, then hurried toward the door. "Now, what's so important?"

"Arthur's here." Her mother's whisper sent chills down Taye's spine.

"Where?"

"In the living room." Her mother pointed.

"Why did you let him in here?" Taye's voice betrayed her struggle to conceal the terror she felt.

"It's OK, Ron's here."

The presence of the drunken, overweight longshoreman, one of her mother's many boyfriends, didn't exactly make Taye feel secure. She could only hope that Ron's size alone would deter Lil' Arthur from starting any trouble.

Taye took a deep breath and headed for the confrontation with the lunatic that she now cursed herself forever for becoming involved with. Her mother followed closely.

"What do you want, Arthur?" Taye's demeanor projected her frustration.

"I came to see my baby." Lil' Arthur sipped straight from the bottle of Seagram's Gin he held in his right hand.

Lil' Arthur was not a huge man. He stood five feet, five inches tall. He was solidly built at 160 pounds. His skin was charcoal-black and his hair was cut in a bald fade. He wore red pants and a matching tank top. Black and red were the only colors Lil' Arthur ever wore. A large gold chain dangled from his neck.

"Well, you're in the wrong place." Taye had no idea when Lil' Arthur had gotten out of jail. "'Cause you ain't got no baby over here."

"You got a smart mouth." Arthur looked gravely serious before flashing the gold-toothed grin that only served to make him look more menacing.

"I've got exams in the morning." Taye's voice broke, showing her nervousness.

"Let's go to bed," Arthur told her.

"I'm going to bed alone," Taye spoke firmly.

Arthur stepped closer to Taye. The smell from his breath, along with the redness in his eyes, answered any questions Taye may have had regarding Arthur's sobriety.

"What you say?" Arthur's voice was low and threatening, giving hint to the potential violence that Taye knew all too well.

"I don't want no shit out of you, Arthur." Taye's mother, who had been watching quietly, stepped between them.

"Why don't you mind your business, bitch!" Arthur now held the gin bottle as a weapon.

Before thinking better of it, Taye slapped him.

Lil' Arthur smiled broadly.

"Ron!" Taye's mother called loudly in anticipation of an imminent eruption of violence. As if on cue, Ron could be heard snoring loudly from the bedroom. Arthur took another sip from the gin bottle. Taye was certain that he could hear the frantic drumming in her chest.

"Let's go to bed." Arthur's eyes were now tiny slits of red fluorescent light.

"Yeah, y'all go to bed and we can eat a big breakfast in the morning," Taye's mother suggested.

Taye eyed her mother with disgust. "I'm going to bed alone."

Arthur was on her quickly, grabbing a patch full of the hair on the back of Taye's head, and forcing her to the floor. "Who the fuck you think you playin' with, bitch?" Arthur placed his knee on her chest while still clutching her hair.

"Let me go, you coward bastard." Taye struggled, but Arthur was too strong.

"Get off of her." Taye's mother added. "I'm going to call the police."

"And I'll burn this muthafucka down!" Arthur maintained his control of Taye while taking another sip of gin.

Taye's mother ran toward the bedroom in hopes of waking Ron.

"Wanna drink?" Arthur clamped a hand around Taye's face while attempting to pour gin in her mouth.

"Stop it!" Taye bit Arthur's hand.

"You don't want me in your bed no more?" Arthur slapped her hand. "Since you fuckin' wit' that crab-ass muthafucka?"

Taye's terror reached new heights as Arthur informed her of his knowledge of her relationship with Pooney. She struggled desperately, using her nails in an attempt to rake Arthur's eyes, but only managed to inflict a few harmless scratches. Arthur punished her with another slap to the face, followed by a hard punch to the stomach,

"Get off my goddamn daughter!" Taye's mother ran back into the living room, now clutching a small, wooden bat.

Taye rolled over onto her stomach, gasping for air, unable to even weep.

"What's wrong with you, man?" Ron forced his immense body through the doorway.

Arthur took a step backward upon sight of the grizzly bear-sized man.

Taye managed to climb to her feet at about the same time the tears began to fall from her eyes. She watched Ron move closer to Arthur. She prayed that the usually mild-mannered dock worker would hurt him badly.

"Chill out before somebody gets hurt!" Taye noted the unsteadiness of Arthur's voice.

"The only somebody gonna get hurt is you." Ron continued forward.

"I said mind yo' muthafuckin' business." Whatever fear Taye thought she had heard in Arthur's voice was now gone as he brandished the chrome-plated .357 Magnum that he loved so well.

Ron stopped in his tracks as the much smaller man aimed the death tool directly at his chest.

"The police is already on the way," Taye's mother told Arthur. "And they already got your name."

Taye was unsure whether her mother was bluffing or not. Whatever the case, the message stalled Arthur's aggression.

"Y'all win this one." Lil' Arthur exchanged gazes with the others in the room before settling on Taye. "But I'll be seeing you and your square-ass boyfriend around."

Lil' Arthur maneuvered from the living room, never once aiming the barrel of the pistol away from Ron's chest. A deathly silence hovered over the house until Lil' Arthur finally slammed the door behind him.

"You fool with trash, girl." Ron was first to speak.

"You all right, sweetheart?" Taye's mother attempted to console her.

"Yeah." Taye wiggled from her mother's grasp. "I'm all right."

Having no desire to converse about the night's events, Taye walked to her bedroom and closed the door behind her. She lay across her bed, grabbed the phone, and dialed Pooney's number in hopes of warning him of Arthur's release from jail. No answer.

Taye closed her eyes, attempting in vain to shut out the images in her mind of an unsuspecting Pooney somewhere on the street, with Arthur, gun in hand, sneaking up behind him. Chantaye frantically dialed Pooney's pager number. After entering her number, followed by the 911 code, she placed the telephone back on the nightstand and opened her top dresser drawer. She reached for her favorite doll from her own Black Barbie collection, and brushed its hair slowly. She would do so until it was time for her to get ready for school.

(6)

"Don't be a stranger." The woman who had just taken Pooney's virginity flashed a snaggletoothed grin.

"I won't," Pooney answered in all sincerity. "Here's a little something extra for you while Jerome ain't here to get in your business." Pooney gave her the other half of the 'twenty' he had broken earlier.

"Thank you." The blonde, Dawn was her name, smiled even broader. Pooney was sure he could see her tonsils through the gaps in her teeth.

Pooney hurried down the alleyway to join his friends. Unbeknownst to him, he stepped with a strut totally alien to anything anyone had ever seen from him before.

Pooney's attention was diverted by the vibrating pager in his pocket. A quick glance revealed Taye's number followed by 9-1-1. Pooney was definitely surprised. The time on his Nike watch was 4:25.

"Look at this character." Larry's voice was loud and merry. "Struttin' like the rooster that just left the hen house."

"What's up, cuz?" Crooked Tony's eyes were filled with questions.

"Ain't nothin' but a gangsta party," Pooney quipped.

"I don't believe this cat," Larry laughed. "How'd it go, killa?"

"She was all right," Pooney answered as seriously as possible. "I taught her a few things."

"Man, quit." Larry bent over, grasping his stomach. "Stop it, Loc, please."

"Hey." Thaddeus Lee came running down the street. "Give me a quarter."

"A quarter?" Larry repeated. "How much you got?"

"I got 150." Thaddeus Lee held the money out for all to see. "Ain't that how much they cost?"

Pooney took the money from Lee and counted it—150. He then reached in his pocket and produced the four remaining eight-balls. "Get the two you want."

Thaddeus Lee picked each package up and turned them in his palm, examining them from every angle.

"They're all the same size, man." Pooney grew impatient as his mind searched for a reason that Taye would page him at four thirty in the morning.

"This one." Lee clutched one of the eight-balls. "And this one." Thaddeus Lee was visibly satisfied with his selections.

"You handlin' yo' business, ain't you?" Larry patted Lee on the back.

"I told y'all," Lee answered. "I got clientele."

"You hit a lick, fool." Larry was curious as to the origin of the money that Lee had just spent.

"I save my twos and fews all day," Lee explained. "It's my time now. I'm 'bout to find me a couple of these girls and do it like my main man, Michael Irvin."

"I'm about ready to call it a night myself," Tony laughed.

"Y'all be here tomorrow." Lee was off and running.

"I need to call Taye," Pooney said after Lee was out of sight.

"This time of night?" Tony asked.

"Something's wrong," Pooney informed his best friend.

"What's up?"

"I don't know yet. One of y'all got a change?"

"Here." Larry pulled two quarters from his pocket and handed it to Pooney.

Pooney jogged across the street to the nearest pay phone. He pushed the money into the slot and dialed Taye's number.

"Hello," Taye, fully awake, answered on the first ring.

"What's up?"

Taye hesitated, unsure of just what to say. "Arthur," Taye choked on the name.

"Arthur?" Pooney repeated.

"He's out of jail, Pooney."

"So?"

"He came over here."

Pooney's mind conjured images of Arthur and Taye together the way he and Taye had been the other night.

"Pooney?" Taye was unsure what to make of the lack of response.

"I'm here."

"He pulled a gun on my mother's boyfriend."

"Why?"

"It's not important." Taye felt it unnecessary to relive the entire ordeal. "I'll tell you the whole story tomorrow."

"What you tryin' to hide?" Pooney was growing angry.

"Nothing, baby. It's just a long story and I want to get to the point."

"What point?"

"He knows about us, Pooney,"

"And?"

"Don't act like that, Pooney."

"So, what's the point?"

"He might try to get you, baby."

"So that's why you paged me?" Pooney fussed. "To tell me your boyfriend might want trouble?"

"He's not my boyfriend, Pooney," Taye sobbed.

"What are you cryin' for?"

"Because you're so stupid!"

Pooney thought about his sister Sheila, who would undoubtedly attest to the same thing.

"Not as stupid as you think," Pooney finally answered.

"No! Even more stupid!" Taye's sobbing increased.

"Taye?" Pooney began to realize that things were much more serious than he had initially perceived.

"I paged you because I was worried about you, asshole!" Taye unleashed her fury. "Arthur came over here, called my mama a bitch, hit me in the face, and threatened us with a gun! And now I got to put up with your fuckin' attitude!"

Pooney was speechless.

"I don't know why I even bothered!" Taye continued. "I'll let you get back to playing gangster!"

"Wait a minute, Taye." Pooney found his voice.

"What?"

"I'm sorry." Pooney rummaged his minds in search of words to describe his feelings. "I was jealous, baby. Look, I'll be there at seven to take you to school. We'll talk then."

"OK," Taye answered with a barely audible whisper. "Be careful, Pooney, he's out there."

"Don't worry." Pooney hung up the phone, the anger inside him boiling rapidly.

(7)

"Damn, that's messed up Pooney." Tony lit a Swisher and handed it to Pooney.

"I know." Pooney passed the Swisher without smoking.

"Me and Arthur grew up together. He was cool until he started slobbin'." Larry paused to blow marijuana smoke through his nose. "He's gonna come with it, Loc." The certainty with which Larry spoke sent chills up and down Pooney's spine. He looked to Tony, who added his affirmation.

"How deep do your feelings go for this broad, Loc?" Larry asked.

"That's my girl, what do you think?"

"I'm just askin', cuz." Larry hit the Swisher once more before passing it to Tony. "Because if your heart ain't in it, maybe you need to stay away from her."

"Naw, he'd better stay away from her," Pooney answered.

"You gonna make him?" Larry smiled.

"I'll make him understand."

"Look, Loc." Larry was no longer smiling. "Fools like Lil' Arthur only understand one thing."

"And what's that?"

"Pain. Lots of it."

"Well pain it is," Pooney declared.

"Pain it is." Larry chuckled.

"This shit ain't funny, man." Pooney vented his frustration at Larry. "That mark-ass slob hit my girl in the face!"

"Don't get mad at me, Loc." Larry stood up. "I'm on your side. Deuce-nine for life. I just wanna make sure you know what you're getting into."

"I feel you, Larry," Pooney stretched. "But that mark better know what he's getting into."

"The three of them turned toward a sudden eruption of loud voices coming from the alley. Two crack users were tussling over a crack pipe. The larger one was able to wrestle the pipe away from the smaller one. And just like that, the fight was over as suddenly as it had begun.

"Damn fools." Larry wasn't impressed.

"Y'all 'bout ready to call it a night?" Pooney sounded tired.

"Yeah man, I'm beat." Larry yawned.

"Drop me off at home, man. I gotta get ready for school," Pooney added before the three of them climbed into The Tank.

(8)

"You may begin." Pooney sat in the back row of Ms. Dawkins's classroom as his ex-favorite teacher gave the okay to begin the exam.

Under normal circumstances, the one hundred multiple-choice questions and three bonus essay questions would have presented Pooney with only a marginal challenge. But after spending all night on 28th Street and not getting one wink of sleep, his American History exam became a major obstacle.

Pooney attempted to work quickly since he would be allowed to leave once finished. Unfortunately, he found his mind totally unresponsive.

While struggling through questions regarding the Civil War, his mind's eye focused on the sight of Taye, complete with cut lip and scratches on her neck, meekly approaching the cab the two of them occupied together on their way to school. He had demanded that she tell the entire story about her confrontation with Arthur, and she had obliged. Taye went on to beg Pooney not to confront Arthur. She had been convincing. But he was a Deuce-nine Crip now, and he could not allow anyone, especially a Blood, to disrespect him in any way.

He imagined Arthur on his knees, begging for mercy in the school cafeteria. In his fantasy, Arthur approached Pooney in the school cafeteria brandishing a knife. Pooney quickly disarmed Arthur and issued a painful whipping. Arthur, on his knees, hands in prayer position, begged Pooney to hit him no more. While deliberating over Arthur's fate, a hand poked hard on Pooney's shoulder.

"Allen." The hand poked harder.

Pooney blinked twice at the frowning face of Ms. Dawkins. Once satisfied that Pooney was awake, Ms. Dawkins returned to her desk.

Pooney watched contemptuously as the woman he had once loved sat down and fixed a stern gaze in his direction. He looked down at his desk, finally turning his attention to his exam.

(9)

Ms. Dawkins watched with a guarded measure of sadness, as her students, one by one, filed from her classroom for the last time. All of them that was, except for Allen Richards.

She had already awakened him three times. Now after completing the multiple-choice portion of his exam, Allen had fallen asleep once more, presumably while contemplating his answer to the first essay question. This time she had allowed him to sleep.

Once the last student had exited the classroom, Ms. Dawkins stepped from behind her desk and walked toward her slumbering project.

"Allen," Ms. Dawkins spoke firmly.

Pooney's eyes opened quickly. His vision followed a second later.

"Didn't you get any sleep last night?" Ms. Dawkins stood directly in front of him.

"I was up all night with a toothache." Pooney recited his previously determined excuse.

"I see." Ms. Dawkins nodded. "Which one?"

"What do you mean, which one?" Pooney questioned her question while organizing his thoughts, a trick he had acquired in a debate class he had taken the year before.

"Which tooth is hurting you?" Ms. Dawkins, possessing a few tricks of her own, expressed overwhelming concern.

"Right here." Pooney placed a finger on his left jaw.

Ms. Dawkins gently touched the same spot. "Oh, it feels like it might be abscessed, too."

"I think it is." Pooney moaned.

"You have a fever, too."

"I do?"

"That may be from your allergies, though."

"My allergies?" Pooney stammered. "Yeah, my allergies."

"What else could explain that terrible redness in your eyes?"

"Yeah." Pooney's voice was void of confidence as he came to the realization that Ms. Dawkins was toying with him.

"So what are you going to do with yourself this summer, Allen?" Ms. Dawkins asked.

"I don't know." Pooney looked down at his unfinished essay questions. "I need to gain ten pounds for next football season, so I'll work on that."

"I've got an idea." Ms. Dawkins was suddenly brimming with enthusiasm.

"What?"

"There's a six-week writing workshop being given at the college," Ms. Dawkins explained. "It's for beginning writers of all ages. I'm going to attend. Why don't you join me?"

"I don't know, Ms. Dawkins." Pooney did know that he had no desire to attend any writer's workshop, but the prospect of joining Ms. Dawkins anywhere had a very strong appeal to him.

"Think about it." Ms. Dawkins still spoke with enthusiasm. "It starts in two weeks."

"I will." Pooney watched as Ms. Dawkins scribbled on the back of a small white index card.

"Here, this card contains the name and address of the instructor." Ms. Dawkins paused, knowing that with her next statement she could find herself in deep waters. "My number's on the back. Let me know what you decide."

"OK." Pooney hurriedly tucked the card in the pocket of his Levi's denim shirt.

"You have other exams today?" Ms. Dawkins looked to the wall clock. It read 9:15.

"Not until one o'clock."

"Well, I'll let you finish your essay questions." Ms. Dawkins smiled, displaying the dimples that Pooney still found irresistibly attractive. "If your toothache is cooperative, maybe you can find somewhere to take a nap." Ms. Dawkins turned to leave, then stopped. "Allen."

"Yes, Ms. Dawkins."

"If you need to call me for any reason," Cheryl Dawkins offered, "feel free to do so."

"I will, Ms. Dawkins."

She returned to her desk. There was so much she wanted to say, but she had done all she could. The lines of communication were established. And tonight, when Cheryl Dawkins knelt before her maker, her first prayer would be for the safekeeping of Allen Richards.

CHAPTER 11

Sheila sat quietly in her seat, sandwiched between her best friend Janeen and Janeen's mother. The six certificates, one for each class Sheila attended this past year, were stacked neatly in her lap. She had also been presented with ribbons for her participation in the Science Fair and Black History Program. Although extremely proud of her personal achievements, Sheila had been preoccupied the entire morning, save for the time spent accepting awards, with watching the auditorium door. Her mother had promised that if not too tired, she would attend the Central Middle School awards program.

The thirteen-year-old honor student had endured a morning in which each time the auditorium door opened, she was disappointed anew. She watched with silent envy as one classmate after another, accepted awards, then hurried to the open arms of smiling parents. Sheila also harbored a small degree of resentment for Janeen, who had earned no awards, but nevertheless enjoyed the companionship of her mother throughout the entire awards ceremony.

As the ceremony wound to a close, Sheila gave up all hopes of a late arrival by her mother. She promised herself that she had looked toward the door for the last time.

Sheila watched as Mr. Comeaux, who had already presented her with an award for outstanding achievement in music education, once again climbed the stairs to the stage.

"Ladies and gentlemen, we have one more award to present this morning." Mr. Comeaux's Creole accent echoed throughout the auditorium. "The teachers here at Central Middle School spent many hours of discussion in hopes of finding an appropriate way to recognize a very special student."

Sheila could see the auditorium door swing open from the corner of her eye, but staying true to her promise, she refused to turn in that direction.

"Finally, after weeks of debates and bickering, Ms. Ferguson," Mr. Comeaux pointed to the silver-haired English teacher standing against the far wall, "came up with the perfect idea."

The audience was dead quiet with anticipation.

"In light of the tremendous achievement of this very special talent, Ms. Ferguson advised the rest of us that a whole new award category would have to be added."

Sheila noted that Janeen and her mother were clutching hands.

"So I have been allowed the privilege of presenting an extraordinary young lady with an award, named in her honor."

Mr. Comeaux held a framed certificate over his head.

"The first winner of the Sheila Richards award for outstanding academic achievement is...Sheila Richards!"

There was a slight ripple of applause at Mr. Comeaux's humor, followed by a deafening round of applause as he motioned for Sheila to join him onstage.

Sheila had not been paying very much attention to Mr. Comeaux until hearing her name. She felt a twinge of self-consciousness as she marched toward the stage.

"Sheila is a very special young lady, who I am sure will contribute great things to our society." Mr. Comeaux continued his praise as Sheila climbed the stage stairs.

"Congratulations, Sheila." Mr. Comeaux's eyes told all that needed to be said regarding his feelings for Sheila. "It has been a true pleasure to watch the extraordinary strides you have made the last two years." Mr. Comeaux placed a hand on her shoulder. "I really hate to see you go, but I will take solace in the incredible future that is certainly yours."

"Thank you, Mr. Comeaux!" Sheila was unable to resist the incredible urge she felt to hug her music teacher.

The auditorium shook with applause as all present took to their feet.

"God bless you, Sheila." Mr. Comeaux withdrew from Sheila's embrace, wiped at his eyes, and then shuffled from the stage.

The applause continued as Sheila exited the stage and returned to her seat.

"That's right. That's my homegirl." Janeen was on her feet, clowning as usual, alternating between clapping loudly, and pointing at Sheila.

"Congratulations, Sheila." Janeen's mother smiled as Sheila sat down.

Mr. Williams, the school principal, took to the stage and offered a few words, bringing to an end the awards ceremony and, with it, Sheila's tenure at Central Middle School.

"I'll call you tonight, girl." Janeen hugged Sheila before heading for the door with her mother.

Sheila flipped through her awards disinterestedly while waiting for the traffic jam to subside. She watched as her classmates exited the auditorium, chattering and laughing with their parents.

They all spoke warmly to Sheila, both parents and students alike, while passing her on their way to the door.

Sheila gathered her awards and headed for the door as the crowd began to thin.

"C'mon, Mom. Let's go to Baskin Robbins." Sheila listened as a very excited little girl pleaded with her mother.

"OK, I guess so," the mother finally relented.

"Sheila." Sheila turned in the direction of the calling voice. Renee was standing against the wall conversing with an elderly gentleman, whom Sheila could only assume was the grandfather of the impatiently waiting boy standing beside them.

The boy got his wish as Renee came running toward Sheila with both arms extended.

"I'm so proud of you, mama." Renee, who had always referred to Sheila as "mama" in reference to her precocious nature, squeezed the young girl so hard that Sheila could barely breathe. "Let me see." Renee grabbed the stack of awards Sheila had won, and took a seat.

"You gonna call, ain't you?" The elderly man suddenly appeared behind Renee.

"Didn't I say I was gonna call?" Renee never looked up. "Now go on, I'm looking at my baby's awards."

Sheila lost a vain struggle with the giggles.

"Why'd you do him like that?" Sheila was still laughing.

"Who? Him?" Renee dismissed the subject with a wave of the hand. "I'm so proud of you, mama."

"What are you doing here?" Sheila took a seat opposite Renee.

"I was off last night." Renee read every word on each award. An act that brought Sheila more happiness than Renee could ever know. "Your mother mentioned it to me a couple of days ago."

"She did?" Sheila was glad to hear that the awards ceremony had at least crossed her mother's mind.

"I overslept, or I would have been here from the beginning." Renee studied Sheila's award in social studies. "Can't be."

"Can't be what?" Sheila was puzzled.

"Does the Mr. Coleman that taught your social studies class have really pink lips?"

"Yeah."

"Ain't that something. Pink-lip Coleman." Renee was gripped firmly by a distant memory. "He must be...what...sixty-years-old now."

"Sixty-four." Sheila was precise.

"He was my social studies teacher back in..." Renee hesitated while counting. "A long time ago."

"You're crazy, Renee." Sheila laughed loudly.

"Regina is going to be so proud of you." Renee held the framed award out in front of her. "I got here just in time for you to get this one."

"You were here?"

"Yeah. I heard all those wonderful things your music teacher said about you." Renee ran her finger across the surface of the award, tracing the letters of Sheila's name.

"Mr. Comeaux is a nice man." The thought occurred to Sheila that she may never see her favorite teacher again.

"Looks like you got company, mama." Renee smiled as a young boy approached Sheila from behind.

"Hello, ma'am." Charlie Williams spoke first to Renee. "Hi, Sheila."

"Hi, Charlie!"

"Congratulations." Charlie motioned to the stack of awards.

"Thank you."

"I can't wait until Friday." Charlie was noticeably nervous.

"Me, neither." So was Sheila.

A well-dressed, middle-aged woman stood behind Charlie. "Congratulations." Mrs. Williams had a generous smile.

"Thank you, Mrs. Williams," Sheila answered.

"You must be so proud." Mrs. Williams spoke to Renee.

"You better believe it," Renee replied with trademark boldness.

"You two have a nice afternoon." Mrs. Williams nodded. "We need to get going Charlie. I have an appointment to keep."

"OK." Charlie followed his mother. "See ya Friday, Sheila."

"Bye, Charlie."

"Look at you." Renee didn't speak until Charlie and his mother were beyond earshot. Even then, she spoke much lower than normal.

"What?"

"Bye, Charlie," Renee mimicked.

"Stop it, Renee." Sheila laughed.

"You hungry?"

"A little."

"How about some pizza?" Renee knew that Sheila loved pizza.

"Yeah!"

"Let's go." Renee picked up all the awards from the table and headed for the door. "Now I know you are going to let me put one of these in my living room?"

"We'll talk about it," Sheila teased as she followed Renee from the auditorium.

(2)

"Cuz, I was tired as a bitch!" Pooney stared at the alley's entrance, speaking indiscriminately to the growing crowd of hangers-on that hung on his every word.

"I bet you was." Tony spoke. "You was up all night."

"If y'all muthafuckas ain't spendin' no money, y'all need to move around." Larry's roar caused the tight ring around the three boys to become loose and unorganized.

Pooney and his friends watched as a little girl, no older than eight or nine, ran toward them.

"Which one of y'all name Pooney?" the little girl asked.

"I'm Pooney." Pooney was slightly bewildered.

"That man down there told me to tell you something." The angelic-faced little girl was obviously uncomfortable with the message she carried.

Pooney looked in the direction in which the little girl pointed. A small green Chevy Nova was parked alongside the Kentucky Fried Chicken on the opposite side of Broadway Boulevard. The driver of the vehicle waved a red flag outside his window.

"Arthur." Larry's voice was cautious but deadly.

Pooney inhaled deeply. "What does he want you to tell me?"

The little girl's head dropped, and she placed the tip of her pinky finger in her mouth.

"It's OK." Tony kneeled so that he and the little girl could see eye to eye.

"He said," the little girl looked up at Pooney, "bring your punk-ass across the street so y'all can handle y'all business like men." The message carried by the little girl's singsong voice caused the circle of onlookers to draw closer.

"Thanks, sweetheart." Tony patted the little girl softly on the head and she quickly ran away.

The ring grew tighter as Pooney contemplated his predicament.

"Didn't I tell y'all muthafuckas to move around?" Larry snapped at the crowd.

"What's up, Pooney?" Tony asked softly.

Pooney didn't answer.

"You gotta take care of your business, Loc." Larry's face was the picture of intensity. "You can't let it go down like this."

"Like what?" Pooney was beginning to perspire.

"You scared of that muthafucka or something?" Larry was yelling and waving his arms in a manner that reminded Pooney of the NFL's Bryan Cox. "You ain't gotta worry about no bullshit, y'all gonna fight one-on-one."

Arthur was standing in the street now, yelling obscenities in Pooney's direction. His three companions were still seated inside the car.

"Fuck it!" Pooney unhooked the gold rope necklace he wore and handed it to Tony.

"I'ma let them hos know what's up." Larry hurried toward the Nova.

Pooney handed Tony the money and drugs he had.

"What's up, cuz?" A car full of blue-clad youngsters pulled up. The young man in the front passenger seat got out and exchanged the Crip Shake with Pooney and Tony. Pooney recognized him as the man named Paul he had met a week ago.

"That slob ass ho', Lil' Arthur, wants to squabble with my homeboy over a broad." There was an unfamiliar edge to Tony's voice.

"So, what's up?" Paul asked.

"Larry's gettin' shit straight with Arthur right now," Tony explained. "Lettin' him know it's one-on-one."

"Park!" Paul instructed the driver before leaping from the car. "Don't worry about nothin', youngster! If them muthafuckas want to make war we got plenty of artillery."

"All right." Pooney was distraught by how drastic the situation was becoming. They all watched with great anticipation as Larry trotted toward them.

"It's on." Larry was animated. "One-on-one, no weapons. What's up, Paul?"

"You know I'm down for whatever, cuz."

"Here they come." Tony spoke as they watched the four young men cross Twenty-eighth Street on foot.

"I told 'em to leave the car over there." Larry said. "Y'all gonna take care of y'all's business in the gap." Larry motioned toward the alley.

Lil' Arthur and his grim-faced crew continued their march down 28th Street. The small crowd grew exponentially as the butterflies fluttered inside Pooney's belly.

"You can take him, Pooney." Tony's reassuring hand rested firmly on Pooney's shoulder.

Just a few yards away now, Arthur peeled his shirt from his body. He seemed much bigger to Pooney now that the black shirt with the red embroidered letters reading 'Lil' Arthur' was in his hand.

"Whip that ho', Arthur!" Pooney heard one of Arthur's friends yell.

Arthur bounced on his toes as he passed Pooney. Though a few inches shorter than Pooney, he was twice as wide. Arthur possessed extremely wide shoulders to go along with his heavily muscled arms and chest. He and Pooney interlocked gazes as Arthur continued down the alley and toward the gap. Pooney had seen the look in Arthur's eyes before. It was the same look he frequently saw while engaging pulling linemen, leading sweeps to his side of the field. Pooney was well aware of the ferocity that came with that look.

"Let's go, baby!" Paul slapped Pooney hard on the back.

Pooney and the mob who supported him followed Lil' Arthur and his friends to the gap.

The gap was a vacant lot midway through the alley running between 28th and 29th Streets. The only remaining sign of the house that once stood there was four concrete steps that must have led to the front porch. Various types of debris formed a heavy covering over the surface of the lot. Beer bottles far outnumbered all other types of debris. Two crackheads, who had been under the pecan tree that stood in the gap, left abruptly upon sight of the large crowd.

Lil' Arthur was in the middle of the gap now. "Let's go, bitch!" he yelled over and over as he continued to dance on his toes.

"Handle yo' business, youngster." An unfamiliar voice shouted encouragement as Pooney walked toward the middle of the gap.

"Bring yo' punk ass on over here." Lil' Arthur threw a flurry of punches at the air.

Just two feet separating him and Arthur now, Pooney remembered the advice his father had once given him: the man landing the first punch wins ninety percent of the time. Once within arms' reach of Lil' Arthur, Pooney threw a two-punch combination that landed squarely on Arthur's mouth. A collective "ooooh" came from the crowd.

Lil' Arthur, despite the blood flowing from his mouth, smiled at Pooney. Pooney threw two jabs that Lil' Arthur slipped easily.

Lil' Arthur threw a looping right hand that Pooney blocked with his left. The two of them clashed hard, going toe to toe, both men throwing, though not landing, a considerable number of punches. Lil' Arthur landed a short right hand and Pooney backed away quickly. He could feel the blood trickling from his left eye, even before brushing it with his hand.

Lil' Arthur charged with the force of a raging bull, slamming a left hand to Pooney's stomach, followed by a right-hand high on the side of Pooney's head, causing him to stumble backward.

Pooney considered taking a knee, hoping that someone would break up the fight before Arthur hurt him badly.

"Kill that ho', Arthur!" one of Arthur's friends yelled, striking a nerve in Pooney that was infuriating.

The two of them stood toe to toe again. Heads bumped and both men were hit repeatedly with fists as well as elbows. Possessing superior quickness, Pooney landed more punches, but Lil' Arthur seemed to be hitting him with a sledgehammer.

Lil' Arthur landed another hard right hand, this one to Pooney's forehead, sending the young boy sprawling on his back. "Get up, bitch!" Lil' Arthur jeered.

"That's it, man." Tony ran between the two combatants, Larry followed close behind.

"Fuck that!" Pooney climbed to his feet.

"You showed everybody you got heart, Loc." Larry placed both hands on Pooney's shoulders. "That's enough."

"Move." Pooney wiggled free.

"He's too strong for you, Pooney." Tony reasoned.

"Fuck that shit!"

"Let that ho' go!" Lil' Arthur's voice was hoarse.

"Y'all get out his way!" Paul yelled, instantly igniting a furor from the small crowd.

Tony stepped out of Pooney's way, shaking his head as he joined the others.

"Don't stand toe to toe with him, Loc." Larry whispered in Pooney's ear. "You're quicker than he is."

Heeding the wisdom of Larry's advice, Pooney stood just outside of Arthur's reach and hit him with two straight jabs, followed by a straight right hand. Arthur quickly became frustrated with Pooney's hit and run tactics, and began lunging wildly. When he did, Pooney unloaded on him with a barrage of punches.

Arthur backed up and paused momentarily, then charged full-speed at Pooney. Pooney hit him twice more, but to no avail. Arthur ran through the punches, grabbed Pooney, and lifted him from his feet, before slamming him hard to the ground.

Pooney was able to shield his face, but Arthur hit him repeatedly on both sides of his body. Pooney kicked and swung wildly, but found himself to be hopelessly pinned under the larger man.

"Five-oh." Pooney heard a distant voice.

"Five-oh," a closer voice yelled.

"C'mon, Loc." Pooney was being pulled up by the arm and led from the gap, toward the opposite side of the alley.

Pooney was vaguely coherent as he struggled to keep up with the running crowd. His body ached and his vision was blurred.

"Run, cuz! Run!" A hand pushed at his back as Pooney exited the alley and ran across 29th Street. "Right here." The same hand pushed Pooney toward a sky blue Buick Regal. Pooney collapsed into the passenger seat as the Buick eased away from the curb.

"Here you go, Pooney." Paul handed Pooney a towel. "Hold that against your eye, cuz, to stop the bleeding."

The side of Pooney's face throbbed as he placed the towel against his eye.

"We'll roll for a lil' bit until shit clears." Paul mumbled as he drove across Broadway. "Then we'll go to the clubhouse...hear me, Loc?"

"Yeah." Pooney lay back in his seat, the throbbing in his head and neck bringing him to the verge of tears.

"You got with that fool, Loc." Paul pounded the steering wheel with his fist. "He was just a little too big for you, cuz, that's all."

Paul continued to rant and rave as the Buick traveled steadily south on T29th Street.

"Don't worry about them slobs fuckin' wit' you no more!" The Regal picked up speed. "You got down for yours. It's a family thing now."

Pooney nodded, partly to prove to himself that he could. He attempted no words, opting instead to focus his attention on the streetlights the Buick passed as he contemplated a story to tell his mother.

(3)

"Damn, Loc." Moe frowned at the cut on Pooney's eyebrow. "You're going to need a couple of stitches."

"Let me see." Big Lou took a knee in front of Pooney. "I can stitch it up."

"What?" Pooney's right eye widened.

"I was a corpsman in the Navy, Loc." Big Lou was unconvincing. "It won't take five minutes."

"I don't know, man." Pooney shook his head before placing the towel back against his eye. Moe and Paul laughed hysterically as Big Lou headed toward the kitchen.

"I'm not laughing at you, Loc." Moe patted Pooney on the back. "What's up with you and Arthur anyway?"

"He's mad about me and Taye," Pooney answered.

"You and Taye?" Moe repeated. "What you mean?"

"He can't accept the fact that she's with me now."

Moe and Paul burst with laughter.

"You're a real character, Loc." Moe patted Pooney on the back again. "But that Taye, uh uh uh, you got yourself something there."

"For real," Paul agreed.

Pooney felt uncomfortable about the way the two of them discussed his woman. However, he possessed no energy to argue.

"On the real, though, Loc." Paul stopped laughing. "Youngster got heart."

"I already know," Moe grinned. "Pooney's the realest lil' G we got."

"I'm hungry, Moe," a female voice interrupted.

"Didn't I tell you I would take you somewhere when my homies leave?" There was real anger in Moe's voice.

"But I'm hungry now," the girl whined.

"Get yo' ass back in that room," Moe snapped.

"Man, you a trip." The girl pouted before noticing Pooney. "Hey Allen, what happened to you?"

Pooney looked hard at the girl. Finally, he recognized her. Her name was Tamara. He had taken a typing class with her last semester. She was a freshman, which meant she couldn't be older than fifteen.

"I had a fight," Pooney answered.

"Get yo' ass in there!" Moe was now furious. "Askin' people questions and shit!"

This time it was Pooney's turn to join Paul in laughter. "What you doing with that little girl?" Paul asked the question that was on Pooney's mind. "She can't be but—"

"Look Paul!" Moe's voice was violent. "Stay outta my damn business!"

"My bad, Loc." Paul put his hands up like he was being robbed. "I was just talkin' man."

"Aw right, Lil' Loc." Big Lou returned just in time to bring an anticlimactic end to the tension in the room. "One of y'all got a lighter?"

Paul handed Big Lou a Bic lighter. Pooney watched as the first lieutenant held the flame to a threaded sewing needle.

"How many times have you done this?" Pooney's voice broadcasted his apprehension. The room quickly filled with laughter.

"Get him a shot of Bacardi," Big Lou instructed. "Straight."

"Here you go, Loc." Moe grabbed the bottle of liquor from the coffee table and handed it to Pooney.

Under normal circumstances, Pooney would not have been able to drink the liquor straight from the bottle, but his fear turned him into a liquor guzzling fool.

"You ready?" Big Lou stood over Pooney, needle and thread in hand.

Pooney nodded, and the butcher shop was opened.

CHAPTER 12

Pooney spent much of the next three days in his bedroom. Although the physical pain from the beating he had endured from Arthur had subsided, he had no intentions of displaying the mess that was his face to the world. He left the house only once, to take his Biology exam. Of course, he had not been alone. Chantaye shared his every waking moment since his fight with Arthur. Taye was by his side even now, as he frowned at Sheila, who anxiously awaited the arrival of Charlie Williams.

Sheila stepped into the living room wearing the burgundy satin dress Taye had given her. The dress, which stopped just above the knee, hung off the shoulders by spaghetti straps. Not nearly as shapely as Taye, the dress fit loosely on Sheila's body. The shoes Taye had given her were of the same color and material as the dress. A bit large for her feet, Sheila remedied the problem by stuffing toilet paper into the toe of both shoes. Her hair was gathered atop her head in many curls which spiraled down the side of her face. From her hair hung a pink ribbon that brushed against her bare shoulder. Her face was lightly powdered, giving her a dream-like, angelic appearance. A trace of pink colored lip gloss added to an already dazzling smile.

"I still can't believe Mama is lettin' you do this." Pooney spoke between bites of a Texas Double cheeseburger.

"Shut up, Balboa." Sheila used her new nickname for her brother.

"After the dance you better come straight home." Pooney was the concerned father.

"She'll be all right, baby," Taye intervened. "Leave her alone."

"She too young for this," Pooney explained.

"It's just a dance," Taye laughed.

"You just come straight home." Pooney asserted his authority over Sheila. "Don't make me have to come find you."

"Boy, please." Sheila joined Taye in laughter.

A knock on the door brought an immediate silence to the Richards' household.

"I'll get it, girl." Taye too was filled with excitement.

Pooney watched as the two giggling schoolgirls briefly held hands, before the taller one broke for the door.

"You ready?" Taye, hand on doorknob, turned to Sheila.

A nod was the response, and Taye pulled the door open.

"Hi, is Sheila ready?" the extremely nervous young man asked.

"Come in," Taye answered.

"Wow!" Charlie Williams lost all self-control at the sight of Sheila wearing Chantaye's dress.

"Wow, what?" Pooney stood up.

"Sit down." Taye pushed him back onto the couch.

"I mean...you look great Sheila." Charlie's eyes never left his date.

"Thank you, Charlie." Sheila answered softly.

"Your corsage." Charlie held a small box in Sheila's direction.

"Pin it on her," Taye encouraged the young Romeo.

Sheila clasped her hands behind her back and pressed her chest forward in a subtle gesture of willingness.

"Oh, no!" Pooney stood in protest. "You ain't pinnin' nothin' over here, playa!"

Sheila frowned. Taye laughed. And Charlie's face went dim with confusion.

"I'll pin it on you." Taye took the corsage from Charlie's hand. "You're silly, you know that?" she asked Pooney while positioning the flower just right.

"Hold on a minute before y'all go." Taye snatched her purse from the table and fumbled with the contents inside until her hand came upon the small camera she had been sure to bring with her.

Pooney watched helplessly as Taye snapped picture after picture of the young couple.

"I hate to interrupt your Kodak moment, partner." Pooney stared directly into Charlie Williams's eyes. "But my lil' sister comes home directly after the dance."

"Let's go, Charlie." Sheila was finally angered by her brother's antics.

"Y'all have fun." Taye followed Sheila and her date to the door and locked it behind them. "What is your problem?"

"How would you feel if it were your sister?" Pooney asked.

"You act like she's been diagnosed with some type of horrible disease." Taye pushed Pooney onto the couch once more before taking a seat beside him.

There was a brief silence as Pooney toyed with the remote control.

"Allen?" Taye laid her head on his shoulder. "If you could eliminate anything from the world you wanted, what would it be?"

"Charlie Williams." Pooney settled on an old episode of *New York Undercover*.

"Be serious, Allen." Taye seemed to prefer addressing him by his given name.

"I don't know."

"Think about it, baby." Taye was determined to get an answer. "There has to be something you would want to rid the world of."

Pooney took a deep breath before answering. "AIDS, I guess."

"AIDS."

"Yeah." Pooney nodded. "AIDS."

"Why AIDS?"

"You don't think AIDS is a worthy cause?" Pooney was offended.

"Of course I do." Taye sensed his rising emotion. "I just wonder why you chose AIDS."

"One of my best friends growing up got AIDS from a blood transfusion." Pooney spoke with horrible sadness. "He died six months ago."

"That's terrible." Taye wrapped both arms around Pooney's waist.

"I remember how we both used to get Dallas Cowboy uniforms for Christmas when we were kids." Pooney paused as the memory grew stronger. "David was a hemophiliac, so he wasn't supposed to play tackle football. Every day, David went home bleeding, and an hour later he would be right back. He was tough."

Taye squeezed tighter.

"What about you?" Pooney asked.

"Huh?"

"What would you rid the world of?"

"Crack." Taye responded with little more than a whisper.

"Why crack?" Pooney smiled at his chance to press Taye for answers.

"Because," Taye stalled. "Because nothing has devastated as many families as crack cocaine."

"You sound like one of those 'just say no' commercials." Pooney laughed loudly.

"Don' t make fun of me." Taye lifted her head from his shoulder.

"I'm not. I just—"

Taye halted his speech with a firmly placed kiss. She clasped both hands behind his head and pulled him forward as she lay back slowly. Pooney's pulse raced as he lay on top of her.

"Where is it?" Taye whispered in his ear.

"Where's what?" Pooney's breath was shallow.

"What did I tell you to have when I see you again?" The kissing stopped.

"It's in my room." Pooney was referring to the condom Taye inquired about daily.

"Go get it."

"I showed it to you yesterday."

"Go get it."

"You just saw it yesterday."

"I'm not telling you to get it so I can look at it," Taye fussed. "Well, don't get it then. " She pushed him away from her.

"You're a trip!" Pooney stormed off, returning moments later with the condom. "See."

"I told you I don't want to see it." Taye's anger had subsided and was replaced with amusement.

"Would you make up your mind?"

"I have." Taye smiled. "Go in the bathroom and put it on."

"Huh?"

"You'd better hurry before I do change my mind."

Pooney did exactly as instructed. Taye had no change of mind.

(2)

Pooney believed his fight with Arthur would lead to ridicule from the regulars of 28th Street. However, nothing could be farther from the truth. After an entire week away, Pooney finally mustered the courage to return. When he did, he was surprised to find that he was greeted with respect and admiration, the likes of which he had never experienced before. It was plain to see that this would be the day that Allen Richards fell in love with 28th Street.

"Where you been?" Vikki, the one woman on the block whom Pooney considered attractive, stood very close to him as they conversed. "You know I don't like to deal with anyone but you."

"I've been chillin', baby." Pooney slowly chewed a wad of gum. "But I'm back now."

"For good, I hope." Vikki reached into her pocket. "I got twelve dollars, baby. Do something for me."

"What you gonna do for me?" Pooney flirted.

"Name it." Vikki reached her hand just inside of Pooney's mouth, far enough to withdraw the wad of gum. Then, for a brief moment she held the gum on the tip of her tongue, before slowly rolling her tongue to the back of her mouth and swallowing.

Pooney was keenly aware that Tony and Larry were watching closely as he stepped to the curb and bent at the waist. "Here you go." Pooney gave Vikki his largest twenty-dollar rock. "Check me out later. I might want to go somewhere and chill."

"Don't make promises you can't keep." Vikki's face registered a half-smile before hurrying toward the alley.

"Go get the Thunderbird, cuz." Pooney handed Larry the ten-dollar bill Vikki had just given him.

"That's what I'm talkin' about." Larry snatched the bill and ran toward the 7AM store on the corner of 28th Street and Broadway.

"Man, why you gonna go and get that fool started on that shit this early?" Tony shook his head.

Pooney didn't answer. He took a seat next to Tony on the porch of the abandoned house and watched the traffic, both motorists and pedestrians, as it passed before him. He marveled at how everyone moved with such speed and purpose. He was reminded of the ant farm he kept as a child.

"You been chillin' with that broad?" Tony broke the silence.

"Who? Taye?" Pooney masked his emotions.

"Who else?"

"I got a lot of women."

"OK, Pooney." Tony surrendered. "Have you seen Taye?"

"Yeah, I seen her." Pooney smiled.

"There's my homeboy." Thaddeus Lee came running from the alley. "Where you been? Vikki told me you was around here."

"I've been hangin' around the house," Pooney answered for the umpteenth time that day. "You know how it is."

"I saw you mixin' it up with that cat the other day." Thaddeus Lee began to shadow box. "Reminded me of myself when I was your age."

The three of them paused to watch a passing patrol car.

"They was outta fifths." Larry pulled a tremendously over-sized bottle from the brown paper bag. "I got us a gallon."

Tony shook his head in disbelief.

"Let me spend this thirty dollars and get out of your boy's way." Thaddeus Lee too shook his head at the bottle.

While Pooney and Lee stepped to the curb to finalize their transaction, Larry busied himself with mixing the small packages of cherry-flavored Kool-Aid into the cheap wine.

"Y'all stay close, 'cause Thaddeus Lee is on the job once again," Lee instructed before bailing for the alley.

Pooney was comforted by the fact that Thaddeus Lee was "on the job." The nine ounces Moe had brought to his home three days ago had not been touched until now. Moe would be expecting his money soon, and Pooney had no intentions of disappointing his O.G.

"Here you go, lil' Loc." Larry held a freshly poured cup of his favorite blend just under Pooney's nose.

Pooney took two large sips, then sat the cup on the porch.

"How many eight-balls you bring with you?" Tony asked.

"Twenty." Pooney had barely finished speaking when a young man riding a bicycle, sporting a towering afro, and clutching three, crisp one-hundred dollar bills, purchased four eight-balls from him.

During the next four hours business took place at a frenzied pace. Twice Pooney returned to his home, each time retrieving two ounces of crack cocaine. Twice he sold every last crumb. On the third trip, he retrieved only one ounce, as he did not plan to be out much longer.

"Man, it was rollin' today." Pooney observed the fiery red sunset as he and Larry finished off the last of the wine.

"I told you about Fridays," Tony reminded him. "How much you sell today?"

"This one'll make seven."

"Damn, Nino." Larry, who had been surprisingly quiet throughout the day, spoke loudly.

"And it's gonna be rollin' like this all night," Tony promised.

The sun was so low now that Pooney was sure he could reach out and grab it. While continuing to admire the sun's descension, Pooney's thoughts were of Taye, and the night they had spent together.

"How much you got at the house?" Tony asked.

"Two," Pooney answered.

"Well, let's get something to eat, then we'll move the last two."

Pooney was famished. He found the first part of Tony's plan somewhat appealing. However, he had plans of his own after that, and they did not include returning to 28th Street.

(3)

"Uh-uh." Taye turned her nose in disgust as she peered through the back window of The Tank, and directly at the dust-covered backseat.

"What's wrong?" Pooney asked.

"That seat is filthy," Taye pointed out.

"Who the hell she think she is?" Larry, now intoxicated and no longer quiet, yelled from behind the steering wheel. "I thought Princess Diana died."

"Shut your retarded ass up!" Taye caused Crooked Tony, who occupied his usual seat in The Tank, to double over with laughter.

"Retarded?" Larry was steaming. "Who you callin' retarded with Mr. Ed's tail swinging from the back of your head?"

"This is my hair for your information. You need to do something with those cuckabugs on top of that acre of head you got." Taye continued to crack Tony up. "Maybe if you untangled a few of those naps, your brain could get some oxygen."

"Say, Pooney." Larry's voice was pleading for help.

"C'mon, baby," Pooney whispered into Chantaye's ear. "You can sit on my lap.

Taye hesitated before answering. Not so much to consider Pooney's proposition, as she had already made her decision, but in order to let all present know just who was in charge. "I guess so."

Pooney opened the car door and climbed into the backseat. Taye sat in his lap. Larry mumbled something under his breath, and The Tank was in motion.

Larry traveled westward on Avenue S, en route to the Two Pesos restaurant on 61st Street. He and Crooked Tony rode in silence with the car stereo playing just loud enough so that they could not hear the whisperings of the love bugs occupying the back seat. Minutes later, The Tank rolled to a stop in the parking lot of the restaurant, and the four of them walked toward the entrance.

"Table for four?" A strawberry-cheeked young woman greeted them at the door.

"Yes, please," Crooked Tony answered.

"Smoking or non-smoking?" The cheeriness in the young woman's voice couldn't possibly be an act.

"Smokin'," Larry drawled.

"Non-smokin'." Taye was louder.

The confusion registered on the young lady's face as her gaze alternated from Taye to Larry.

"You heard me right, lady," Larry added.

"And you heard me right, too!" Taye was unrelenting.

The hostess looked to Tony for help.

The Crooked Tony Shrug.

"Look, Pooney, you really need to check yo' broad," Larry said.

"You sure do." Taye looked at Larry in a way that caused the meaning of her statement to become perfectly clear to him.

"What you tryin' to say, tramp?" Larry was violently angry.

"I'm tellin' you that my man is your pimp, ho'." Taye was not afraid.

A nearby couple laughed loudly at Taye's remark, sending Larry's anger to an entirely different level.

"What you say to me, slut?" Larry took a step toward Taye.

"What are you doin', man?" Crooked Tony quickly intervened.

Larry looked at Tony, then Taye, then Pooney, before turning to the trembling hostess, and offering a coy smile.

"Smoking." Pooney spoke to the hostess.

"I want non-smoking," Taye complained.

"Smoking," Pooney repeated sternly.

"Right this way." The cheeriness with which the hostess had spoken earlier was gone as she led them toward the table.

The four of them took their seats and immediately reached for their menus. The only remnants of the earlier altercation was the barely noticeable pout that framed Taye's face.

"Is this going to be all on the same ticket?" An olive-complexioned Hispanic waitress approached the table, pencil and pad in hand.

The four of them exchanged glances before Pooney answered. "Yes."

One by one, they all ordered and handed the waitress their menus. All sorts of dishes were ordered. Some they could pronounce, others they didn't dare try, preferring instead to call the number of the entree. In the process, the foursome filled three entire pages of the waitress's order pad.

Once they had all ordered, and settled back into their seats, Tony and Larry proceeded to converse about cars, women, rap music, and all sorts of gangsta families. Meanwhile, the love bugs resumed their whisperings.

Whatever tension that may have been hovering over the foursome dissipated immediately as the waitress unloaded two large platters full of plates onto their table. Seconds later, there was no conversation. Only the smacking of lips and pleasure-filled groans to accompany the melody the four sets of silverware made as they continuously struck the assortment of plates.

Twenty minutes later, Larry, leaning back in his seat and rubbing his now enormous belly with both hands, brought the feast to an official end with a belch so loud that every head in the smoking section turned in his direction.

"Don't you have any manners?" Oddly enough, there was no anger in Taye's voice.

"Sorry, princess." Larry grabbed the pack of Newports from his shirt pocket and lit one. As if on cue, the waitress returned with the bill.

"Seventy-four, twenty-five," Pooney read the total aloud.

"Let me see." Taye grabbed the bill and inspected it thoroughly. "Half of this stuff is yours, Larry," Taye concluded.

"Bullshit! Let me see!"

"Don't worry about it. Dinner's on me." Pooney was sure he had heard the same line in an old gangster movie. "Let's go."

Pooney dropped a ten-dollar bill on the table before heading toward the cash register with a handful of money. With Taye at his side, and his henchmen following closely, Pooney felt like he was the king of his world, and that nothing in it, or beyond, could ever stop him.

CHAPTER 13

Regina reached out for the wall of Tim's store in hopes of finding some relief from the wind and rain that threatened to pummel her to the ground as she sprinted across the convenience store parking lot. Once her back was squarely against the wall, Regina looked both ways as far as she could in hopes of locating Patrick's truck. No such luck. Granted, she had arrived five minutes early, but she still had little hope of Patrick showing up. From the looks of things, there was no one else on The Island foolish enough to be on the street during such a nasty storm. The only thing preventing her from returning to her home was the dread of being pelted once more by the metallic feeling raindrops.

The sound of an approaching horn struck the last chord of hope in Regina's heart as she watched two gigantic headlights coming toward her. She ran for the passenger side of the approaching vehicle, even though she was unable to discern the vehicle, or its driver. The door swung open and Regina stepped inside.

"I got here as fast as I could." Patrick's voice was barely audible as the rain somehow fell harder, and an explosion of thunder shook the automobile. "Jesus, you're soaking wet."

"No shit." The wind made even closing the door a formidable task for Regina.

"Let me help you." Leaning to his right only slightly, Patrick reached over Regina and grabbed the handle on the door.

"I got it." Regina pushed his arm away and used both hands to slam the door closed.

"Sorry." Patrick backed out of the parking lot, then drove cautiously down Heards Lane. There was a CD already inserted into the CD player. Patrick pushed the power button, and a classic Isley Brothers tune provided Regina with the much-needed relief from the sound of the pounding rain.

"I'm the one who should be sorry." Regina kicked two water-filled shoes from her feet. "I just can't believe we're doing this, on a night like this."

"It's OK." True to form, Patrick proved to be exceedingly patient and understanding.

"No, it's not." Regina felt an inexplicable urge to argue. "I'm a thirty-four-year old mother of two and I'm sneaking around like some damn schoolgirl."

"The sneaking part is your choice." Patrick turned right on 61st Street and cautiously proceeded toward the seawall.

Regina made no further comment. Patrick's serenity was driving her nuts. The Ford Bronco turned right on Seawall Boulevard, as both driver and passenger contented themselves with the melodic crooning of Ronald Isley.

"Put this on." Patrick shed his purple windbreaker and placed it in Regina's lap.

"Huh?" Eyes closed and totally immersed in the music, Regina was unaware that the Bronco had pulled into the Driftwood Apartment complex and was parked in front of Patrick's apartment. Regina donned the oversized garment as instructed. The sweet smell of cologne stirred long-forgotten feelings of intimacy from deep within her. Regina's door opened and mammoth hands gripped both of her shoulders, gently but firmly pulling her from the car.

The rain was falling so hard now that Regina was virtually blinded before a bolt of lightening turned the dark and stormy night into a midday Fourth of July celebration. Daylight came just in time to allow Regina to see her tall, dark knight form a cradle with his arms before lifting her from her feet, and trotting slowly for the door of his apartment. She pulled the collar of the windbreaker over the back of her head in an attempt to shield herself from the rain.

Regina clutched Patrick's neck tightly with both arms while he reached in his right pocket for the key to the door. Seconds later they were inside. Regina was immediately greeted by the smell of a well-prepared meal. Patrick sat her down on her feet, then headed immediately for the thermostat control. After turning up the heat, he opened the linen closet located in the same hallway. He grabbed two towels.

"You can have the big bathroom." Patrick laughed, his words obviously a private joke he thought to be quite amusing. He pointed to a door that was visible through the master bedroom. "There's nothing in your size, but the closet's open."

Regina took one of the towels from Patrick's hand and proceeded toward the bathroom.

"I hope you're hungry," Patrick called behind her.

(2)

"This is fucked up," Pooney declared once the rain had slacked just enough so that he was sure his voice would be heard.

"Tell me about it." Crooked Tony took a drag from the Swisher and handed it to Pooney. Once the rain started falling, the two of them sought shelter under the porch ceiling of the church across the street from their 28th Street hangout.

"Ain't no money out here tonight." Pooney puffed softly on the Swisher Sweet. "We need a ride."

"A ride? Shit, we the only fools in Galveston crazy enough to be outside tonight."

Both boys laughed at their plight.

"We shouldn't be smokin' weed on church property."
Pooney passed the Swisher back to his friend.

"Do I have to explain to you again?"

"Explain what?"

"God is everywhere. So wrong is wrong, no matter where
you're at." Tony took a drag. "Anyway, marijuana grows naturally
from the earth. That means it comes from God."

Crooked Tony's logic made sense to Pooney. It always
did.

"Why'd you quit school, Tony?" Pooney had always
wondered why his best friend had stopped attending school
when they were both seventh graders.

"School ain't for me." Crooked Tony passed the Swisher.
"School is for kids."

The conversation was suddenly interrupted by an almost
frighteningly loud noise. An old Ford Thunderbird, muffler
dragging the street, zoomed in front of the church and across
Broadway with no regard for the stop sign at the corner.

"Damn fool." Tony shook his head.

"Remember junior high school, when we played football
together?" Some of Pooney's fondest memories were of the days
when he and Tony were the starting safeties on their junior high
school football team.

"Yeah, I remember." It was evident that Tony enjoyed
the memories as much as Pooney did. "We had a defense, didn't
we?"

"Hell, yeah!" Pooney agreed. "We should've won district."

"That fool John fumbled at the end of the game against
La Marque," Tony recalled. "They ran it all the way back. We lost
by one point."

"You returned a kickoff for a touchdown in that game."
Pooney finished the Swisher and threw the butt into the street.
"You sure was fast, Tony."

"Not as fast as you." Both boys had always respected the other's physical ability. "But you know what I liked best about returnin' kicks?"

"What's that?" Pooney asked.

"The high," Tony answered.

"The high?" Pooney repeated.

"Yeah. It's like, right before the kickoff, I'm aware of everything. The band playin', people callin' my name, little kids chasin' each other in the stands." Crooked Tony grinned at the picture in his mind. "Then the kicker starts forward, steps, picks up speed...plants...boom! Now, I don't hear nothin'. It's like there's no sound in the whole world. No motion either, except for the ball. And it's like the football is weightless or something...like it's headed straight to the moon. Then, it starts to come down. It gets bigger, and bigger, and bigger. My feet move under it on their own. The ball keeps growin' until it looks like a big, brown pumpkin or somethin'. Once I got it in my arms, all the sound comes back at once. The band, the cheerleaders, the children giggling, and the eleven crazy muthafuckas trying to break my neck."

Pooney laughed in approval. "Man, you're crazy."

"You know, Pooney," Tony said in a somber tone. "It was easy for me to walk away from school and football because I wasn't that good at either one of 'em." Tony paused to gather his thoughts. "But you're big-time Pooney. Books or football, you can make it man."

"Think so?" Pooney had always been uncomfortable with the way in which others had always spoken of his abilities.

"I hate that I ever got you into this Deuce-nine shit." Tony's voice contained more emotion than Pooney had heard since the time they were kids and Pooney had fallen during a raid on old lady Hightower's plum tree, breaking his arm. That day, Tony loaded Pooney on the handlebars of his bicycle and pumped his fallen comrade over forty blocks to the emergency room. "This ain't for you, man."

"What do you mean?"

"You got a future, Pooney," Tony added. "This street shit is for people like me and Larry."

"I'm down for Deuce-nine."

"Man, fuck Deuce-nine." Crooked Tony was animated. "Dope, guns, this shit with Lil' Arthur, man..." Crooked Tony didn't finish his sentence. The way he shook his head said it all for him.

Neither did Pooney reply. He withdrew a second Swisher from his pocket, lit it, puffed twice, and passed it to his best friend.

(3)

"Smells good." Regina stood behind Patrick, leaning over the counter still drying her hair while watching the sweatsuit clad football coach prepare the plates.

"Well, have a seat," Patrick invited without turning to look at his dinner guest. "Another minute or so and we'll be ready to go."

Regina continued to watch as Patrick heaped enough food onto two plates to feed the entire offensive line of the Dallas Cowboys. There were pork bones, collard greens, cabbage, black-eyed peas, yams, cornbread, and a whole sweet potato pie. It was obvious that Patrick had at least two loves other than football: cooking and eating.

"Will someone else be joining us?" Regina placed the towel on the counter.

"I see that I'm entertaining a comedian." Patrick turned toward Regina for the first time, and was stopped cold in his tracks.

"What's wrong?"

"Nothing." Patrick tried to peel his eyes away from Regina, but found his efforts to be futile. "I didn't know your hair was so long."

While true that this was Patrick's first time seeing Regina's hair combed to full-length, the source of his amazement was the sight of Regina wearing the old football jersey she had found in his closet. Almost knee length, the jersey was no more revealing than a Sunday dress. However, Patrick was positive that he was looking at the sexiest woman who had ever walked the face of the earth.

Regina smiled as she took her seat. Although slightly uncomfortable, she appreciated the attention. The two of them sat on opposite ends of the table, launching simultaneous assaults on the plates before them. Regina astounded herself with the quantity of food she was able to consume. She found Patrick's cooking to be so delicious that she ate almost as much as he did.

"I'm stuffed." Regina finally sat back in her chair, rubbing the palm of her hand between the two fives on the front of the jersey she wore.

"I'm sure you are," Patrick joked.

"You should talk," Regina pouted.

"Just joking." Patrick laughed. "I'm just happy you like my cooking."

"I was going to give you a compliment."

"Was?" Patrick began the task of clearing the table.

"Yeah, but that was before you hurt my feelings."

"How'd I hurt your feelings?" Patrick asked against his better judgment, fully aware that Regina was slowly ensnaring him into one of those dangerous cat and mouse games women love to play.

"You talked as if I was a glutton." Regina used the most girlish voice she could muster.

"I was just making conversation." Patrick raked what little food was on the plates into the garbage disposal, then placed the plates in the dishwasher. "I didn't mean anything by it."

"Sure you didn't." Regina finished the Big Red soda Patrick had poured for her.

"I didn't," Patrick persisted. "Want some more soda?"

"What else you got?"

"I've got some orange juice, and there may be a can of Sprite in the refrigerator." Patrick poured the detergent into the dishwasher, closed the door, and turned the power on.

"I don't want soda."

"What do you want, Regina?"

"Something stronger."

"A glass of wine?"

"Stronger."

"I've got a bottle of E&J Brandy," Patrick offered.

Patrick opened the cabinet above the sink and grabbed the unopened bottle of brandy. He watched with a bemused half-grin as Regina walked slowly across the living room floor toward the entertainment system. He grabbed an ice tray from the refrigerator freezer, then returned to his perch atop the kitchen counter. Regina was now sifting through his collection of CDs. He continued to watch her as he fixed drinks for the two of them.

The sound of Master P's "I Got the Hook Up" began to play, and Regina danced slowly. Patrick was totally fascinated by the way she moved. He walked slowly toward her with both drinks in hand. Regina continued to dance, her back to Patrick, totally oblivious to his presence.

"Regina." Patrick was just loud enough to be heard over the music. There was no response.

"Regina." This time the call was accompanied by a gentle touch to her back.

Regina turned slowly. She continued to dance as she accepted the drink Patrick had prepared for her. She took a sip, then reached high with her left arm, placing it around Patrick's neck as she continued to hold her drink with her right. She pressed her body against his while Master P continued to provide the perfect background music for her performance.

Patrick shifted his weight from one foot to the other in an effort to keep up with the wild woman who inhabited Regina's body. The feel of her warm breath against his neck, along with the softness of her body as it pressed against his, caused Patrick to feel inebriated before he had even taken one sip from his glass.

Regina pushed Patrick away as suddenly as she had pulled him near. She stared in his eyes while taking another drink. She loved the surprise she saw. Another sip and she was dancing again, this time alone all over the room, intoxicated with the liberation she felt at knowing that no one in the world, but the two of them, had any idea of her whereabouts.

Tonight, Regina would have no insomniac patients to pester her. No having to listen to Renee's endless scoldings about her lack of a love life. No worrying about Allen—the big one or the small one. Tonight was hers, to live in the moment. Tonight she was just a woman, listening to music, and enjoying a private evening with a friend.

(4)

"Turn the fuckin' lights out, Peanut!" Lil' Arthur said.

"I can barely see with the muthafuckas on, Arthur." Broderick Senegal, aka Peanut, Lil' Arthur's best friend and most trusted triggerman, killed the headlights of the Oldsmobile as instructed. "How the hell do you expect me to get those suckers?"

"They can't move 'til the rain stops." Lil' Arthur struggled to see the rival gang members through the sheets of rain. "When they do, we'll be here."

Peanut took the AK-47 assault rifle, which had been resting on his lap, and placed it across the backseat of his car. He then pushed the vehicle's cigarette lighter in and sat back in his seat.

"What the hell them suckers doin' at a church?" Peanut asked, mostly to himself.

"I don't know," Arthur declared. "But what better place could there be to get your cap peeled?"

Peanut grabbed the lighter and lit the Black 'n' Mild cigar that had been in his top shirt pocket. Never partaking of alcohol or drugs, Peanut's "Blackie Milds," as he pronounced it, were his only vice. He smoked them endlessly.

"We should've got 'em before the rain started." Peanut was still talking to himself when a bolt of lightening provided a momentary reprieve from the total darkness that had hovered over The Island for the past hour, allowing him a perfect look at his intended victims.

"Think they saw us?" Lil' Arthur couldn't hide his anxiety. "They were looking this way."

"It don't matter." Peanut took a long draw from his cigarette. "They're just standin' there. Let's handle our business."

"OK," Lil' Arthur agreed. "But check it out, go ahead and back out, so we can creep up behind 'em."

"Yeah." Peanut's face became a wickedly grinning Mardi Gras mask.

"We'll jump out on 'em," Lil' Arthur continued. "They'll never know what hit 'em."

Peanut pushed the lighter in once more as he eased the Oldsmobile from the alley. No more words were spoken. There was no need for any.

(5)

Pooney and Tony stood in silence as they continued to pass the Swisher back and forth between them. The rain slowed steadily until the sound was no more than that of a score of leaky faucets running simultaneously. A small dog could be heard from afar, obviously pleased with the respite from nature.

"Let's get away from here while the rain has stopped," Pooney suggested.

"Maybe we can catch a cab at the Stop 'N' Go." Tony's somber demeanor had gone unchanged.

The two boys stepped from the shelter of the church into the slight drizzle that remained. They ran down the alley behind the church, racing stride for stride, exactly as they had done a million times before as small kids playing on the beach. Two sets of footprints in the sand, running at breakneck speed into the darkness before them; caution to the wind, with only the hand of God protecting them from the obstacles in their path.

(6)

"Fuck Peanut, there they go right there!" Arthur couldn't believe his eyes when Pooney and Tony came running from the alleyway.

"Shit." The Oldsmobile veered into the middle of the street as Peanut reached for the AK-47. Once his weapon was in hand, the determined triggerman leapt from the car without bothering to slow the vehicle.

"Get 'em Peanut." Arthur slammed the car into park, inciting a heated protest from the Oldsmobile's transmission. Arthur reached for the chrome .357 laying on the dashboard.

Peanut lifted the barrel of the gun in the boys' direction but dropped his weapon when he lost his balance. Undaunted by the stinging he felt in both hands and knees while sliding across the pavement, Peanut was quickly rearmed and on his feet. He watched as Pooney and Tony turned left on 27th and Broadway, then quickly gave chase.

Once at the corner, Peanut once again lifted his weapon to a ready position, but lowered it once seeing that Pooney and Tony were already sprinting across the Stop 'N' Go parking lot on 26th Street.

Peanut's scowl deepened as he watched the boys' get inside a parked cab.

"Here." A nudge to Peanut's rib caused him to turn quickly. "Chill." Arthur held a Nike tennis shoe in Peanut's direction. "Let's roll, we'll get them hos."

Peanut looked down at his feet before reaching for the shoe. He had been totally unaware he had lost it. He didn't bother to put it on as he and Arthur returned the Oldsmobile.

CHAPTER 14

"I'll get it." Pooney, hearing the knock on the door, pushed Taye's arm from around his neck and leapt from the couch, knocking over the orange plastic bowl she held in the process, and leaving her with a lap full of popcorn.

Moe had called from his cellular phone minutes before, warning Pooney of his imminent arrival.

"What's up, Loc?" Moe seemed to speak even before the door was open.

"What's up, cuz?" Pooney returned his greeting, and to Moe's amusement, offered the Crip Shake.

Moe stepped inside the Richards' home wearing a spotless white jumpsuit and carrying a plate covered with aluminum foil.

"Here's the plate my mama sent you." Moe handed Pooney the plate then looked around the room. "Hi, Chantaye."

"Hi, Moe." After placing the last kernel of popcorn back in the plastic bowl, Taye allowed her eyes to rest on Moe a little too long for Pooney's liking.

"And how are you?" Pooney could hear Moe speak as he carried the plate containing the nine ounces of crack cocaine to his bedroom.

"I'm all right," Sheila answered with attitude, already disliking the extremely arrogant man standing in her living room.

"You must be..."

"Way too young for you." Taye cut Moe off in mid-sentence.

"I was going to say Pooney's sister." Moe was not upset. Instead, he seemed to enjoy the challenge. "Sheila...right?"

"Right." Sheila was still laughing at Taye.

"Sheila, could you do a friend of your brother's a real big favor?" Moe asked.

"What?" The attitude was back.

"I'm really thirsty." The arrogance was gone, and Moe suddenly sounded pitiful. "Could you please bring me a glass of water?"

"I guess so." Sheila finally climbed from the love seat and headed for the kitchen.

"You're such a darling." Moe never took his eyes off Sheila as she fetched the water.

"You'd better watch yourself, fuckin' pervert!" Taye spoke so only Moe could hear. Knowing Moe very well, Taye was extremely wary of the way he watched her young friend.

"But she is a darling." Moe spoke in an equally low tone. "Sort of reminds me of you at that age."

"Asshole," Taye hissed.

"Bitch." Moe chuckled to himself.

"Here you go, cuz." Pooney re-entered the room suddenly, carrying a brown paper bag.

Totally oblivious to the wall of tension that stood between Taye and Moe, Pooney handed his mentor the paper bag stuffed with more money than his mother would earn in the next three months.

"Me and my girl are taking a short vacation," Moe stated. "That's why I wanted to make sure I left you with something."

"Appreciate it." The look on Taye's face told Pooney that something was not quite right, although he couldn't even began to figure out what that something could possibly be.

At about the same time, Sheila walked from the kitchen carrying the requested glass of water.

"Thank you, beautiful." Moe was sure to make eye contact with the young girl as she handed him the glass.

Sheila smiled broadly as she returned to her place on the love seat.

"What y'all watchin'?" Moe referred to the movie the three of them had been watching prior to his arrival. His eyes however traveled in whatever direction Sheila did.

"*Dead Presidents.*" Pooney spoke sharply as he, too, watched his still blushing baby sister.

"*Dead Presidents.*" Moe nodded before taking a drink from the glass of water. "You oughtta have quite a few of them stashed away somewhere."

Pooney laughed half-heartedly while avoiding Taye's disapproving gaze. The room was disturbingly quiet as Moe finished his water.

"See ya when I get back, Loc." Moe handed Pooney the empty glass

"Aw right." Pooney followed Moe to the door, while for the first time, thinking of his sleeping mother.

Moe paused in the doorway and looked over his shoulder before saying. "Bye, Sheila."

"Bye," was Sheila's carefully measured response.

Pooney closed the door slowly behind Moe. Then he turned in Taye's direction. One look in her eyes, and Pooney knew without a doubt that later there would be a major argument.

Pooney knew that by declining to watch the remainder of the movie, he risked sending Taye's fury to never-before-seen heights. But Taye would have to understand. There was work to be done, and not much time left before his mother awakened.

After locking the bedroom door behind him, Pooney peeled the foil from the plate, uncovering twelve perfectly shaped fatman cookies.

Pooney grabbed the scale and the plastic bags he kept in his closet. Then he began the tedious task of breaking the 'fatman' cookies down to eight-balls. He had barely begun his work when the phone rang.

"Hello." Pooney answered immediately.

"Allen?" A familiar voice beckoned.

"Yes, ma'am."

"Listen at you," the woman continued. "You sound like a grown man."

"Hi, Mrs. Fisher." The memory became clear. The voice was Delores Fisher's, Pooney' s one-time Sunday school teacher, and his mother's present work supervisor. "How's Mr. Fisher doin'?"

"He's doing okay, I guess. Just a little frustrated now that he can't get around the way he did before the surgery." Mrs. Fisher's rambling had always reminded Pooney of his own grandmother. "You know how stubborn he is."

"Yes, ma'am." Pooney was extremely fond of Mrs. Fisher. As a kid he and Tony had to have spent at least two summers worth of Sunday afternoons at the Fishers. They had always gotten a kick out of driving Mr. Fisher's riding mower.

"Is Regina in?" Mrs. Fisher abruptly changed subjects.

"She's still asleep," Pooney answered. "Want me to wake her?"

"Well," Mrs. Fisher hesitated. "Is she feeling any better?"

"Better?"

"She assured me that she wouldn't need more than one night off. I just called to make sure." There was a brief pause. "You know how those summer colds can linger on."

"Oh, yeah." Pooney had already surmised the exact nature of his mother's malady. "I think I should wake her."

"Maybe that would be best."

"Hold on." Pooney dropped the receiver on the floor before shoving the plate, the scale, and the baggies under his bed.

Once all was secured, he stormed off toward his mother's bedroom.

"Mama!" Pooney was screaming as he pushed his mother's bedroom door so hard that it slammed against the wall.

"What's wrong?" Regina Richards sat straight up in her bed, her motherly instincts worked to a frenzy by the tone of her son's voice.

"You tell me!"

"Boy, have you lost your damn mind?" Regina's head began to throb.

"Mrs. Fisher's on the phone." Pooney watched closely for her reaction.

"Bring it here." Regina fumbled on the nightstand for the bottle of Excedrin she kept handy.

"Bring it?" Pooney frowned. "You too sick to get it yourself?"

"What?" Regina placed the two tablets in her mouth and swallowed.

"Mrs. Fisher wants to know if you'll be at work tonight." Pooney was oblivious to the fact that the volume of his voice had attracted both Taye and Sheila to his mother's doorway. "Since you were too sick to make it last night."

"Bring me the phone." Regina repeated firmly as she swung her legs around the side of the bed and placed her feet in her house shoes.

"Where were you?" Pooney's voice was lowered in volume, but not intensity.

"I'll get it, Ms. Regina." Taye attempted to diffuse the situation.

"You don't have to answer me." Pooney's anger reached the danger level. "I know where you were."

"Thank you, sweetheart." Regina accepted the phone from Chantaye.

Taye brushed against Pooney in an effort to lead him from the room. He didn't budge.

"Oh, I know Mrs. Fisher. He thinks he's one, too." The entire room hung on Regina's every word as she spoke into the telephone. "Yes, ma'am. I feel much better. Don't worry, I'll be there...Yes, I'm fine. OK, bye bye."

"Why didn't you tell her where you were last night?" Pooney was yelling.

"Stop it, Allen." Taye placed both hands on his shoulders. Pooney shrugged her off.

Regina closed her house robe before standing to face the three vastly different faces peeking anxiously back at her.

"Good morning, Mama." Sheila's unsteady voice came from the most confused face of the bunch.

"Tell your daughter where you were last night!" The angry face continued to jeer, causing Regina's headache to worsen.

"Don't do this, Allen." The face of compassion pleaded with the furious young man.

"Tell her!" Pooney continued despite Taye's pleading. "Tell your daughter you was out making a booty call last night while you were supposed to be at work."

Faster than any of them could ever have anticipated, Regina slapped Pooney squarely in the mouth. The entire room was silent, save for the clearly audible sigh of regret that escaped from the depths of Regina's soul.

Shocked and ashamed, Pooney knocked both Taye and Sheila from his path as he ran for his bedroom. All three women were stricken with the same powerful urge to rush to Pooney's side. Yet all six feet remained bolted to the floor.

(2)

Taye tapped lightly on Pooney's bedroom door. It had been over two hours since Pooney had slammed the door shut behind him. Taye could only imagine what he might be doing in there.

"What?" Pooney answered with the ferocity of a famished grizzly bear.

"Can I come in?"

Taye had spent the last two hours conversing with Regina and Sheila. The three of them had talked non-stop, seemingly touching upon every subject in the world. Taye had thoroughly enjoyed the time spent with Pooney's family.

"What you want?" Pooney's voice was only slightly more inviting.

Taye turned at the doorknob and, finding it open, pushed her way inside.

"I'm lonely," Taye answered girlishly as she stepped into Pooney's bedroom.

"I can't tell. Sounded to me like you was havin' the time of your life."

"Without you?" Taye sat on the bed next to Pooney. "What are you looking for?"

"An apartment." Pooney never looked up from the classified section of the *Galveston Daily News*.

"An apartment?" Taye was almost able to cover her mouth before the first round of giggles escaped.

"What's so damn funny?"

"Nothing." The giggle was now a tight-lipped smile that Taye still struggled to control.

"You think I ain't got no money?" Pooney reached under his bed and grabbed a red and white tin container that had once contained Christmas candy. "That's what you think?"

Pooney slammed the container on top of his bed with his right hand on top of it, effectively eliminating Santa and his sleigh from the intricately detailed Christmas scene.

"I know you got money, baby."

"Naw, you think I ain't got no money." Pooney snatched the lid from the can and held it upside down. "I'ma show you."

Taye was unimpressed by the wad of bills that fell onto the bed.

"Each one is a hundred," Pooney explained as he began to count. "One, two, three, four..."

"Quit acting so childish." Taye grabbed both of his hands, abruptly ending his count.

"You thought I didn't have no money."

"I never said that, Allen."

"Don't you want to know how much I have?"

"How much do you have, sweetheart?" Taye no longer shouldered the burden of suppressed amusement.

"Thirty-five hundred dollars," Pooney answered proudly. "And it's all mine."

"Good for you." Taye breathed deeply.

"I'm going to get an apartment." Pooney spoke to himself as he packed the money back into the tin can. "Then I won't have to worry about all this bullshit around here. You can spend the night whenever you want. Everything'll be tight. Just watch."

"Allen," Taye intervened. "Listen to yourself."

Pooney returned his attention to the open newspaper.

"Don't ignore me." Taye placed both her hands between Pooney's eyes and the newspaper. "Sheila and your mother went to the store. When they get back, you need to apologize to Ms. Regina."

"Apologize for what?"

"You were too hard on her, honey." Taye moved closer. "You shouldn't have put her on the spot like that in front of me and Sheila."

"Maybe not." Pooney thought for a moment. "But I don't owe her no apology.

"Don't be like that, baby." Taye put her arm around his neck and kissed him softly. "Give your mother a break."

"She didn't have no right puttin' her hands on me." Pooney's pride was obviously scorched.

"She didn't mean to, honey." Taye kissed him again. "She really feels awful about it."

"Right." Pooney was disbelieving.

"She told me herself." Taye stretched the truth.

Pooney took a moment before responding. "She should feel bad. I ain't no child."

"I know, baby." Taye pulled Pooney near to her and squeezed tightly, lest he see the smile that suddenly reappeared on her face. "Let her make it this time."

"I'll think about it." Pooney returned her embrace.

"In the meantime," Taye wiggled free from Pooney's grasp and grabbed the newspaper, "let's find something worthwhile to spend that money on."

"Like what?"

"Like, buy a car."

"A car?"

"It would sure beat all those cabs," Taye reasoned. "Then I could spend more time with you."

"I don't have a driver's license."

"I do."

"I can't drive."

"I'll teach you."

"I don't know." Pooney shook his head. "A car is a big step."

All of Taye's self-control was lost as her entire body shook with laughter. "I think we can handle it, baby."

Taye pulled Pooney close to her again. Twice she brushed his lips softly with hers before pressing harder, thus initiating an extremely heated exchange.

"You really think we oughtta buy a car?" Pooney asked as their faces separated.

"Yeah, baby; then whenever we want to get away, we can just take a drive."

"OK." Pooney reached for her again. The kissing stopped as the two of them heard the front door open.

"Now you can go and apologize to Ms. Regina." Taye wiped at her lips.

"Man."

"C'mon." Taye grabbed his hand and pulled him from the bed. "I'll make it up to you later."

There were no further protests. Pooney followed Taye with the wide-eyed innocence of a lamb to slaughter.

CHAPTER 15

Pooney drove with extreme caution as he crossed the intersection of 45th and Broadway. Although incredibly excited about his newest acquisition, and even more so about driving it, Pooney knew that he was not yet proficient enough behind the wheel to drive the car the way he wanted.

He had purchased the 1990 Cadillac Seville the day before from Roy Contreras, a used car dealer with a small lot on 49th and Broadway. And while the title, registration, and license were in the name of one Chantaye Johnson, there would be no misunderstanding as to whom the car truly belonged.

The Cadillac was beige with brown interior, but Pooney had already decided to have the car painted money-green, just like Moe's, and with the same type of candy-coated paint. He would also have to find a fourth Dayton rim since the Cadillac presently rode on three rims and a hubcap. Maybe he would even find a fifth Dayton since the Cadillac was already equipped with a bumper kit.

"Your driving is gettin' better," Crooked Tony commented from the passenger side.

Pooney's only reply was a disinterested smile. His thoughts were of 28th Street, and of showing off the Cadillac.

Pooney pushed the power button on the Pioneer stereo system. The two six by nine speakers made a brief humming sound before 97.9 FM's Shellie Wade's voice became loudly audible. Pooney reached over to the seat beside him and grabbed his favorite Cash Money CD. Moments later, the Cadillac rolled to a stop on 31st and Broadway as both boys bobbed their heads to the tune of "Back Dat Thang Up." Pooney leaned farther to his left upon seeing the three teenage girls standing in the intersection. With his elbow protruding from the open window, head cocked to the side, chin resting between thumb and index finger, and right hand clutching the wood grain steering wheel, Pooney envisioned himself to be of the same breed of Cadillac driving, jive-talking hustlers he had grown to love as a small child, watching blaxploitation films with his father.

The three girls stepped closer to the Cadillac in hopes of getting a closer look at the driver. Pooney accommodated them by turning his head in their direction. All three girls flashed their best "I'm available" smiles as the light turned green and the Cadillac eased into the intersection.

"Damn, they on it." Crooked Tony peered through the back window at the teenage girls who still stood in the same spot, watching attentively, as the Cadillac drove farther and farther away.

"You think they're on it now." Pooney looked through his rearview mirror. "Wait 'til I get this bad boy painted."

Finally Pooney turned his pride and joy left at the intersection of 28th and Broadway. As usual, dozens of people lined both sides of the street.

After allowing a procession of lesser vehicles to pass him by, Pooney eased his Cadillac across Broadway and directly toward the waiting crowd. He leaned farther back in his seat as he pulled alongside a group of 28th Street regulars that included Vikki and Thaddeus Lee.

"What's up?" Pooney spoke through the window as the Cadillac rolled to a stop.

"Where you been, youngster?" Thaddeus Lee hurried toward the car. "I got customers."

"I've been chillin'."

"Chillin'?" Thaddeus Lee was dismayed. "Ain't no time for chillin'. We gots money to make."

"What you need?" Pooney grabbed a bag full of rocks from under his thigh.

"Hold on." Thaddeus Lee returned to the crowd.

"That fool always on his hustle," Crooked Tony remarked as he and Pooney watched Thaddeus Lee collect money from everyone in the group except Vikki.

"I got eighty-two dollars." Lee returned to the driver's side window. Vikki was standing two full paces behind him.

Pooney arranged an assortment of various sized rocks in his hand, then gave them to Thaddeus Lee.

"I love you, too!" Thaddeus Lee was visibly excited by the amount of crack given to him.

"What you think of my ride, Lee?" Pooney was slightly disappointed at having to ask.

"This your ride?" Thaddeus Lee gave the Cadillac a quick once over.

"Yep."

"That's a lotta car you got there, youngster."

"I know."

"Be careful," Thaddeus Lee warned before running toward the restless crowd.

"This yo' car, daddy?" Vikki spoke seductively now that it was her turn at the window.

"Yeah." Pooney was all smiles. "I bought it yesterday."

"Ooh, I like it, daddy." Vikki rubbed Pooney's arm.

"Wanna roll with me later?" Even though a little ragged at present, Pooney still considered Vikki to be a very beautiful woman.

"You're just teasin' like always." Vikki sounded terribly disappointed.

"No, I'm not," Pooney promised. "I'll pick you up later."

"OK." Vikki handed Pooney a few crumpled-up bills. "I got twenty-six dollars, baby."

"Here." Pooney reached inside the bag and gave Vikki two twenty-dollar rocks. "You can pay me the rest later."

"How much I owe?"

"We'll talk about it." Pooney released the brake, leaving Vikki to ponder his last statement. Pooney cranked the volume on the stereo system as high as possible while continuing his path down 28th Street. He sat all the way back in his seat while reaching for the Swisher in his shirt pocket.

Pooney passed the Swisher to Tony, motioning for his friend to light up. He then slowed the Cadillac to a crawl in order to allow a small boy to retrieve the multi-colored plastic ball that bounced in the middle of the street. Once the boy had returned safely to the sidewalk alongside New Jack City, the Cadillac resumed normal speed.

Pooney took a long slow drag from the Swisher. As his lungs began to fill with marijuana smoke, he experienced one of those euphoric highs that kept regular marijuana smokers coming back for more. Every muscle in his body relaxed as his senses became superhumanly keen. The bass thumped louder in his ear while the sweet smell of the burning Swisher engulfed the inside of the car.

Outside the Cadillac, all heads turned to admire Pooney and his new pride and joy. The young drug dealer was king of the world as he continued his one-car parade down 28th Street.

Pooney passed the Swisher to Tony while approaching the stop sign at the corner of 28th and Winnie. A dark-skinned young man wearing a North Carolina Tarheels short set walked alongside the Cadillac as Pooney made a wide left turn. Pooney hit the unknown youngster with the C sign as he steadily approached his ultimate destination.

The convenience store at the corner of 28th and Winnie was surrounded by the usual cast of neighborhood drug dealers and gangbangers. The crowd of boys, young men, and men that frequented this corner were predominantly Deuce-nine Crips. Pooney felt a great deal of pride as he prepared to show his Cadillac to "the family."

Pooney stopped the car and placed it in park right in the middle of the street. He grabbed the Swisher from Tony, took one long drag, and handed it back before exiting the Cadillac. He left the driver side door wide-open while walking limp-legged toward the crowd.

"Aw man, I know that ain't Lil' Loc." Paul stepped from the crowd. "What's up, cuz?"

"Ain't nothin'." Pooney exchanged the Crip Shake with Paul. "Just rollin'."

"That your load, Loc?"

"Yeah. That's my shit, cuz." Pooney smiled. "Like it?"

Paul stepped closer to the Cadillac. "Tight." He nodded.

"Just wait 'til I get it painted." Pooney could no longer contain his enthusiasm.

"What's up, Paul?" Crooked Tony tumbled from the passenger side of the car with the burning Swisher still in his mouth.

"What's up, Crooked Tony?" Paul and Crooked Tony exchanged the Crip Shake. "Lil' Loc comin' up, huh?"

"Ballin' out of control." Tony handed Paul the Swisher.

"What's up, Loc?" Big Lou appeared from out of nowhere, followed closely by a man Pooney had never met before.

"What's up, Lou?" Pooney had the Swisher now.

"That your Caddie?" Big Lou asked.

"Uh huh." Pooney's pager vibrated in his pocket.

"Nice." Big Lou nodded.

"What's up with that hubcap, youngster?" The unknown man with Lou inquired about the Daytonless rear passenger side wheel.

"Oh, I'ma take care of that, cuz," Pooney stammered as the rest of the family drew close. "I'm even going to get a fifth wheel."

"I saw that car on Roy Contreras's lot," someone yelled from the crowd. "I hope you got a warranty with that raggedy muthafucka!" The stranger brought the crowd to laughter.

"Quit hatin' on my lil' homie, J.D," Paul chastised between laughs.

"I'm just trying to tell the lil cat somethin' real." J.D. approached the Cadillac and peeked inside. "That a Sparkomatic?"

"Hell naw, it ain't no Sparkomatic!" Pooney was growing angry.

"Ignore that fool, Loc," Big Lou advised. "He's a hater from way back."

"I'm as playa as they come." J.D. turned away from the Cadillac, walked past Pooney, and returned to the crowd. "But lil' homie gotta come better than that."

A light-colored Dodge Neon suddenly turned the corner, barely missing the Cadillac's driver's side door.

"That's my lil' freak." Paul waved for the attractive young woman to wait. "I'll get back at you boys tomorrow." There was a series of murmurings from the crowd as Paul trotted toward the Neon.

"Your ride got potential, Lil' Loc." Paul closed the door to the Cadillac before heading for the Neon. "You don't wanna get the door torn off."

"What's up with that J.D. cat?" Pooney spoke so that only Tony and Big Lou could hear.

"Same thing wrong with the rest of these busters." Big Lou spoke as if the answer was obvious.

"What's that?" Pooney was bewildered.

"They hatin' on you, Loc." Big Lou put a hand on Pooney's shoulder. "You're comin' up too fast. They don't like that."

With no reply in mind, Pooney took the pager from his pocket and read the display window. "Larry."

"What's up?" Crooked Tony's voice showed concern.

"I don't know," Pooney answered. "But he left a 911 after the number."

"Here." Big Lou handed Pooney a quarter. "You'd better see what the fool done got himself into."

Pooney headed for the pay phones just a few feet away. He placed a quarter in the phone and quickly dialed the number on his pager.

"Hello." Larry answered on the first ring, the anxiousness in his voice sounding loud and clear.

"What's up?"

"Where y'all at?" Larry was yelling.

"Deuce-nine, what's wrong?"

"Come to the Seahorse Motel," Larry instructed. "And bring some water."

"What?"

"Look." Larry took a deep breath and attempted to compose himself. "I got these broads, four of 'em. Top-notch. They wanna smoke a couple of sticks."

"Larry, you must be crazy." Water was the street name for a mixture of embalming fluid and PCP. Waterbabies, as they were called, would roll pin-sized marijuana joints, then dip them in water before smoking. Pooney had never been around anyone who was watered-out. However, he had heard enough regarding the drug's hallucinogenic effects to be extremely wary of Larry's request.

"C'mon, Pooney, man. These broads all that." Larry pleaded with the intensity of a condemned man. "Get five sticks and come to Room 134. I'll pay you back."

Pooney considered Larry's pleadings as Tony waved frantically in the background, desperate to know the details of Larry's situation.

"C'mon, Pooney," Larry continued. "I already got the Cisco. One of these hos is comin' out of her clothes already."

"All right, cuz," Pooney finally agreed. "I need to show you somethin' anyway." "Don't be bullshittin', Pooney."

"I'll be there in twenty minutes, cuz, on the C."

"I'm waitin' on you." Larry was pacified for the moment.

"These broads better be as fine as you say," Pooney said before hanging up.

(2)

"Sheila." Cynthia Popovich suddenly appeared as Sheila stood in front of the fitness center at Galveston College's 51st Street campus. Tonight was Sheila's fourth night of piano class. Earlier she had wowed her classmates with her first performance.

"Hi, Cynthia." Sheila smiled.

"I loved that piece you did earlier. What was the name of it again?"

Cynthia Popovich was one of the thirteen other students comprising Mr. Howard's piano class. A year older than Sheila, Cindy, as she preferred to be called, was a tall, thinly built brunette, with deeply tanned skin. Cindy had waist-length hair, sparkling white teeth, and the most beautiful singing voice Sheila had ever heard.

"'Hello' by Lionel Richie." Sheila smiled bashfully. "Did you really like it?"

"I loved it!" Cindy yelled in sincerity. "You think you could teach me the words?"

"I'll write them down and bring them tomorrow," Sheila promised, while noting the headlights that launched themselves into the fitness center parking lot.

"Fantastic!" The headlights were accompanied by two rapid beeps of the horn. "That's my mom. See ya tomorrow." Cynthia Popovich ran toward the waiting Nissan Maxima.

"See you tomorrow," Sheila whispered to no one.

"You need a ride?" Cindy yelled as she plopped into the passenger seat of the car.

"No, thank you." Sheila had barely spoken the words when the door slammed shut, and the Maxima zoomed away as quickly as it had come.

Sheila stepped a couple of feet closer to the entrance of the fitness center so as to be in full view of the desk attendant. On most nights her mother's friend, O'Neill, who had driven cab number fifty at Busy Bee Cab Company for longer than anyone cared to remember, picked Sheila up once her piano class was over. But Fridays was O'Neill's night off, and Sheila was forced to go through the normal avenues of obtaining cab services on Galveston Island.

Sheila's mind drifted back in time to the performance she had given earlier in Mr. Howard's piano class. Her classmates were dazzled, and Sheila relished every moment she had spent center stage. She was becoming aware of the fact that performing for crowds was quickly becoming her favorite thing in the world to do.

The thirteen-year old girl could vaguely hear the sound of approaching music as she pictured herself bowing to the thunderous ovation given to her just seconds after her performance at the Apollo Theater. The music was getting louder, but not yet loud enough to drown out the words of Steve Harvey as he continued to praise Sheila's performance. The music in the distance quickly became a deafening force, causing Sheila's whole body to vibrate along with the ground beneath her. Another pair of headlights entered the fitness center parking lot, and moments later, a money-green Cadillac stopped alongside the curb, directly in front of Sheila. The music was lowered and the darkly tinted driver's side window came down slowly.

"Sheila," a male voice called to her. "Come here for a second."

"Who is that?" Sheila took a step sideways, positioning herself directly in front of the fitness center door.

"Moe." Sheila remembered the man who had visited her brother at their apartment two days before. The aspiring pianist reluctantly walked toward the car, extremely curious as to what Moe would want with her.

"What you doin' standing out here at this time of night?" Moe was the concerned adult.

"Waiting for a cab," Sheila answered. "What are you doin' here?"

"Just ridin'." Moe hit the switch that unlocked the doors. "Save the three bucks. Get in."

"I already called the cab." Sheila could think of no other excuse.

"They'll get over it." Moe took a sip from a red plastic cup that had been sitting between his legs. "What's wrong? You don't trust my style?'

"It ain't that."

"Well, what is it?"

"I don't know."

"I won't tell Pooney."

"Why would I care if you told Pooney?" Sheila was slightly offended.

"I just figured he might jump your case if he found out you were in a car with a boy."

"Puh-leez. Pooney don't tell me what to do."

"I can't tell." Moe reached over and opened the door.

Sheila looked behind her. The extremely interested desk attendant was now standing in the double doors at the entrance of the fitness center.

"C'mon, lil' girl. I'm going to run out of gas waiting for you to make up your mind."

Sheila hesitated a second longer, then climbed inside the Cadillac. Moe reached over her and closed the door before hitting the switch to raise the windows. Seconds later, the Cadillac pulled away from the fitness center parking lot and turned west on Avenue U.

"You any good?" Moe broke the silence.

"At what?"

"Playing the piano, silly. What else?"

"I guess so." Sheila was uneasy about assessing her own ability out loud.

"You guess?" Moe smiled. "What you mean, you guess?"

"People tell me I'm good." Sheila failed to notice that Moe was now heading toward the Seawall.

"People like who?"

"People like my teachers."

"That's all?"

"No."

"Well, who else?"

"My classmates tell me I'm good, too."

"That's all?"

"Who else is there?"

"What do you tell yourself?"

"I'm good." Sheila was all smiles now.

"How long you been playin' football?"

"Football?" Sheila laughed. "I don't play football."

"You must do karate or something?"

"No, I don't do karate." Sheila chuckled heartily.

"So how in the world did your legs get so big?" Moe viewed the portion of Sheila's legs that was visible under the white sundress she wore.

"I don't know." Sheila pulled the bottom of the dress below her knees. "Where are you going?"

Moe was now traveling east on the Seawall, in the opposite direction from the Richards' home.

"I'm just riding for a couple of minutes before I take you home. Chill out."

Sheila sat back in her seat. The last thing she wanted Moe to see was the nervousness that was growing steadily within her.

"You got a boyfriend?" Moe asked.

"No." Sheila didn't know if the Cadillac had picked up speed or if the suddenness of Moe's question made her feel that way.

"Why not?"

"I just don't."

Moe smiled to himself, making Sheila even more uncomfortable. Sheila's mind raced with all sort of thoughts as the two of them rode in silence for a full five minutes.

"I'm just going to pick up my food," Moe said, as if reading her mind. He turned left on 35th Street.

The Cadillac shot through the yellow light on the next block and pulled in front of the building on the corner. The sign read Queen's Barbecue.

"I'll be right back." Moe jumped from the car and disappeared inside the restaurant before Sheila could reply.

Sheila watched as the door to Queen's Barbecue closed behind Moe. Her attention then turned to the Cadillac's stereo system. While searching the airwaves for something softer to listen to than the gangsta rap Moe had been playing, something flickered in the driver's seat, causing Sheila to turn in that direction. There was a wad of money, maybe bigger than Sheila could wrap both her hands around, lying in the seat with a gold money clip holding it together. Sheila looked toward the door of the restaurant before lifting the tight ball of money from the seat. She quickly flipped through the corners of the bills. All hundreds.

(3)

Against Tony's intense objections, as well as all rational judgment of his own, Pooney purchased five watersticks and headed for the Seawall. Now, as his Cadillac rolled slowly through the Seahorse Inn parking lot in search of Room 134, Pooney was certain he had made the wrong decision.

Larry was joined by a white woman so thin that with each step toward the Cadillac, it seemed as if her legs might snap in two. Larry was shirtless, sweating profusely, and clinging to a not-quite-empty bottle of Cisco.

"Gimme a fifty." Larry ran to the Cadillac.

"A fifty?" Pooney was irritated. "You didn't say nothin' about no crack! I know you didn't bring us all the way out here for some crackheads!"

"Told you Pooney." Tony shook his head.

"The hos is inside." Larry threw the now empty bottle onto the pavement, breaking it beside Pooney's car. "All I was doing was holding the lick down until you got here."

"Aw right, Larry." Pooney tried to calm his friend before he got any more animated.

The woman took a step backward as Larry flung both arms to his side and yelled even louder. "Every time I wanna do something, it's gotta be a mothafuckin' problem!"

"Chill out, Larry!" Tony got out of the car.

"Fuck that shit!" Larry was so furious that tears fell from his eyes. "Y'all act like everything I do is stupid or somethin'. Y'all suppose to be my homeboys!"

"I got some cheese, fool." Pooney jumped from the car holding a small sandwich bag half-filled with crack cocaine. "And the sticks too, five of 'em."

"If y'all don't wanna kick it with me, just tell me, cuz." Larry was highly intoxicated.

"It ain't like that, Larry." Crooked Tony was at his drunken friend's side. He placed his arm around Larry's neck and the two of them sat on the curb. Larry bawled uncontrollably as Pooney approached the frightened woman.

"You wanted a fifty?" Pooney asked.

The woman held the fifty-dollar bill in Pooney's direction. Pooney took the money from her hand and gave her a large piece of crack cocaine.

The woman smiled broadly. "I'll be back." And she was quickly gone.

Pooney turned back to his friends. What a pitiful sight they were. Larry's huge shoulders shook violently as the two-hundred-pound baby continued to cry. Meanwhile, the much smaller Tony continued his useless attempts at consoling his grief-stricken friend.

"Y'all 'spose to be my homeboys," Larry repeated over and over between sobs.

Unable to think of anything else that might quiet Larry, Pooney reached through the driver's side window, pushed the lighter in, waited for it to get hot, then lit one of the watersticks.

"We are your homies, Larry." Pooney sat on the opposite side of his friend, tapped him on the leg, and held the burning waterstick before him.

Larry raised his head slowly. He eyed the waterstick momentarily before reaching for it. Once in his hand, Larry slowly and deliberately brought the joint to his mouth. He closed his eyes tightly while pulling softly on the waterstick, causing the last of the tears to fall to the pavement.

"I'll die for y'all, cuz," Larry whispered before taking a second pull from the joint.

A door opened behind them, allowing the sound of rap music to become audible. Pooney turned quickly. A teenage girl stood in the doorway wearing red shorts and a white blouse. "Y'all smokin' alone?" the girl asked.

Larry stood up quickly, motioning with his head for the others to follow as he barreled toward the doorway. Larry handed the girl the waterstick before pushing her aside and entering the motel room.

"C'mon." The girl waved to Pooney and Tony as she placed the joint in her mouth,

As Pooney approached the room, he began to bob his head while singing along with the frantic flow of Mystikal. Another girl stood just inside the hotel room door. The petite and pretty light-skinned young woman wore an oversized #34 Miami Dolphin's football jersey. She smiled widely as Pooney passed her.

As Pooney entered the hotel room sleeping area, his mouth opened at the scene before him. A large speaker was turned on its side while a heavy-chested, cinnamon-colored young woman, clad only in black panties, danced atop of it.

"Pop that thang, girl!" Larry was seated on the bed next to the fourth young lady. A shade darker than the girl on the speaker, the seated young woman wore a pair of tight-fitting blue jeans and a solid black T-shirt. Freshly painted pink toenails showed through the front of the open-toed sandals she wore.

Larry lit a waterstick and gave it to the girl seated on the bed. He then reached toward the bottom of the bed and slid a small cooler along the floor, maneuvering it directly in front of him. He lifted the top and pulled out three forty ounces of Schlitz Malt Liquor Bull and two bottles of Cisco. He opened one of the bottles of Cisco, filled his cup, then replaced the top. He sat the remainder of the opened bottle, along with the four other bottles, on the top of the small table next to the bed.

Larry then reached into his shirt pocket, grabbed the watersticks, and put his lighter to use once more. Next he placed the lighter inside the bag containing the remainder of the watersticks, and placed the bag on the table. While taking a pull from the waterstick, Larry motioned for all in the room to help themselves to the table.

Pooney was speechless as he shuffled toward the small table. He grabbed one of the forty-ounces, untwisted the cap, and took a sip. He then took a slight sidestep to his left, so as to get a better view of the girl on the speaker.

"Ow, girl." Larry sounded like Larry Blackman, the lead singer of Cameo, as he stood directly in front of the speaker and the dancing girl. \

Pooney laughed loudly as the dancing girl bent forward, allowing the jiggling mounds of flesh to slap against Larry's face.

"Larry was right this time." Crooked Tony stood behind Pooney long enough to grab a forty-ounce.

Pooney turned around to acknowledge his friend, but saw that he had already returned to the two girls by the floor. The first girl was now sitting on the floor fanning herself with both hands, while the second girl was pressed so hard against Tony that the two of them looked like Siamese twins.

"OOWWVW Girl!" Larry was having the time of his life, his mouth wide open now as the dancing girl continued to slam her generously proportioned breasts against his face.

Pooney stepped to his right as a tap on his left stole his attention. The girl seated on the bed reached for Pooney's hand, while gibbering something about her name being Paula and driving from Lafayette, Louisiana. Pooney sat down next to her.

Without speaking, the girl took the waterstick from her mouth and placed it between Pooney's lips. Pooney puffed lightly on the thinly rolled cigarette as Paula took his hand and placed it under her T-shirt, and firmly against her stomach. Pooney took another drag before placing the cigarette back in the girl's mouth.

Pooney surveyed the room once more. The girl sitting on the floor continued to fan herself. Beads of sweat were running down her face. Tony and the girl wearing the Ricky Williams's jersey were now stretched out on the floor, still Siamese twins, she on top of him.

The girl on top of the speaker was now completely naked. Larry was on his knees in front of her, both hands stretched outward, puffing vigorously on the waterstick protruding from his mouth.

"Wanna feel my baby?" Pooney could hear a faraway female voice beckon.

He turned back to the girl beside him. She stood slowly, so slowly that Pooney felt as if he was in the final climactic scene of an action movie.

The girl pulled the black T-shirt over her head and threw it on the floor. She then wriggled free from the blue jeans and kicked them aside. She stood in front of Pooney wearing only a dark green bra and panty set.

"Wanna feel my baby?" Paula repeated. Pooney nodded while taking another puff from the waterstick.

The girl took his hand and placed it over her stomach again. Pooney tried to slide the waterstick back in her mouth but she took it from him and placed it in the ashtray on the table. She then lay back on the bed and pulled Pooney on top of her. Pooney pressed down hard. He closed his eyes as he and the girl slowly grinded against each other.

"What did you do with my clothes?" Pooney could hear someone, maybe the girl on the speaker, talking.

"Faaaaaye!" The girl on the speaker was screaming now. "Faaaaaye, this muthafucka done took my clothes!"

"Get up." The undulating body beneath Pooney spoke softly.

Oblivious to everything except the warmth of the body beneath him, Pooney continued to press his body firmly against the girl's.

"What the fuck did you do with my clothes?" The girl on top of speaker screamed once more.

"Get up." The body beneath Pooney pushed him over onto the bed.

"What did you do to her?" Pooney watched as the girl in the Ricky Williams jersey interrogated Larry.

"I ain't don' nothin' to that crazy bitch!" Larry declared his innocence.

"You stole my clothes." The girl on the speaker began to cry while attempting to cover her exposed body parts with her arms.

"Here, Kisha." Paula handed a knee-length white T-shirt to the girl on the speaker. "Put this on."

"I don't want this." The girl on the speaker threw the T-shirt at Larry. "I want my clothes."

"Where are her clothes?" The girl wearing the Ricky Williams jersey pointed her finger at Larry.

"I don't know." Larry pointed to the other side of the bed. "Look back there."

The naked girl leapt suddenly from her perch atop the speaker and onto Larry, sending him sprawling backward. Larry struggled to push the madwoman off him, but Kisha was a woman possessed. She clawed viciously at Larry's face as the two of them slammed into the dresser.

Crooked Tony was first to Larry's rescue. However, his apparent discomfort with grabbing the naked young woman made his efforts useless. Pooney stood and headed toward the melee. Although only a few feet away from the fight, he felt as if he would never get there. Just as he came within arms reach of the naked girl, Larry drew back with an open hand and hit her in the mouth. The naked girl fell into Tony, who fell into Pooney. The three entangled bodies landed on the bed.

"Muthafucka." Paula swung wildly at Larry.

"All y'all bitches in here crazy." Larry ducked.

Kisha untangled herself from Tony and Pooney, then ran toward the small table next to the bed. She grabbed the full bottle of Cisco and took a step toward the brawl. She stopped abruptly, as if suddenly remembering something. The naked girl dropped the bottle on the floor, breaking it, then lifted the mattress from the bed.

"What you do with my clothes, muthafucka?" Everyone in the room moved aside as Kisha approached Larry clutching a dangerous looking butcher's knife.

"One of y'all get this crazy bitch!" Larry backed against the dresser, then side-stepped toward the patio in an attempt to elude the naked girl.

Kisha, wielding the knife as a sword, took two harmless swipes at Larry before a third swipe barely missed the side of his head.

"Man, y'all better get this crazy bitch!" The combination of anger and fear in Larry's voice was menacing.

The naked girl held the knife high over his head like Norman Bates in the *Psycho* thriller. Larry grabbed a chair from against the wall and held it in front of him as would a lion tamer.

"Where are my clothes?" the naked girl screamed hysterically.

"I ain't touched yo' clothes, you crazy bitch!" Larry cocked the chair at his side. The rest of the room was quiet as the standoff continued.

"Gimme my clothes!" Kisha took one ill-advised step toward Larry before being struck in the side of the head with the chair. The naked girl fell to a knee, grabbing at the side of her head with one hand, while still clutching the knife with the other.

Kisha jumped to her feet and made another charge at Larry. Larry hit her once more, much harder this time, sending her entire body crashing into the wall. A steady stream of blood flowed from the wound high on the side of the naked girl's head.

"Somebody call the police." Paula stood in the doorway screaming to anyone who would listen.

"Chill out, girl." Crooked Tony ran toward Paula with hopes of calming her down.

"Get away from me," Paula screamed even louder. "Help! Somebody call the police!"

"Fuck!" Crooked Tony exclaimed.

"What's wrong?" Pooney joined Tony at the door.

There was no need for any explanations as Pooney and Tony watched a middle-aged couple waving their arms frantically at a passing police cruiser.

Pooney turned toward the carnage behind him. The girl who had been fanning herself held a towel to the side of Kisha's head. Kisha wept loudly between threats against Larry's life.

"I told y'all to get that crazy bitch!" Larry's voice was unsteady as he nervously assessed the damage he had done.

"Y'all lucky my brother ain't here," the girl wearing the Ricky Williams jersey said.

"Fuck yo' brother." Larry finally relinquished the chair.

"Fuck you, muthafucka!" Kisha lunged at Larry once more before being subdued.

"Flush the sticks, Pooney," Crooked Tony instructed. "Here they come."

Pooney grabbed the bag containing the remaining watersticks and ran for the restroom.

"Here we go! Right here!" Paula called out to the police.

"Fuck this shit!" Larry barreled through the doorway, pushing Crooked Tony and Paula from his path in the process.

Once outside the door, Larry sprinted directly toward the police car, passed it, and kept running. The startled policeman barked into the radio while wheeling his car around to give chase.

"C'mon, Pooney," Crooked Tony yelled while watching the police car turn onto Seawall Boulevard in hot pursuit of Larry.

"You ain't goin' nowhere." The girl wearing the Ricky Williams jersey snatched Pooney's car keys from the spot on the bed where he had been laying.

"Hurry up, Pooney, shit!" Crooked Tony was outside the hotel room.

"Gimme the keys, girl." Pooney tried to sound threatening.

"What you gonna do? Hit me with a chair?" She reached inside her shirt and placed the keys in her bra.

"C'mon, Pooney!" The urgency in Tony's voice was multiplied by the sound of rapidly approaching sirens.

Near panic, Pooney reached out and grabbed the girl wearing the Ricky Williams jersey and wrestled her to the bed.

"Get yo' ass off me!" The girl struggled mightily as Pooney placed his hand down her bra. The other girls in the room quickly converged on Pooney. He could feel their fingernails raking every inch of his body as he continued to fight for the keys. Somehow he finally managed to grab the keys and separate himself from the raging girls.

Pooney ran quickly through the door and toward his Cadillac, paying no mind to the growing clan of observers scattered throughout the parking lot.

"Damn." Crooked Tony was looking at Pooney but talking to himself as his fifteen-year-old friend started the car.

As Pooney approached the exit leading to the boulevard, three police cars, lights flashing and sirens screaming, sped in front of the Cadillac.

"Follow 'em," Crooked Tony instructed.

Pooney turned west on the boulevard, carefully trailing the racing police cars. Six blocks later, he and Crooked Tony arrived at a corner saturated with police cruisers.

"They got the whole damn force out here," Tony remarked as Pooney drew closer to the action.

A cop standing in the street was directing all traffic away from the lane closest to the sidewalk.

"There's Larry!" Crooked Tony yelled.

Pooney struggled to see despite the dozen or so police cars obscuring his view. Larry stood on the sidewalk, head down and swinging wildly. Two police officers stood directly in front of Larry, spraying him with pepper mace. The others easily dodged Larry's punches while using their nightsticks to deliver blows of their own. Larry fought hard, but his body finally gave out. Once on the ground, the club-wielding cops engulfed him like piranha at feeding time. Larry rolled himself into a ball in an attempt to shield himself from the raining blows, and then he could be seen no more.

(4)

"I ain't even gonna ask you if you liked the potato," Moe joked after watching Sheila devour the potato he had purchased for her. The gargantuan potatoes served at Queen's Barbecue were a favorite among Islanders. Sheila's was stuffed and running over with barbecue beef, sour cream, and cheese. "You're the first person I ever seen finish one of those things."

Sheila could only smile as Moe's Cadillac slowed enough to make the turn into the Back Bay apartment complex. She had thoroughly enjoyed the time she had just spent riding with Moe.

After leaving Queen's, the they had traveled farther east on the Seawall than Sheila had ever been. A dizzying maze of unpaved roads led to a secluded area of the beach. Moe parked the Cadillac on the sand, lowered the windows, and turned the music low. Next, he reached into the brown paper bag lying next to him and handed Sheila the potato. He had purchased a chopped beef sandwich for himself.

Although more than just a little uncomfortable about being alone with this man she hardly knew, whatever apprehensions the young girl may have had were quickly put to rest. Sheila found that there was something very reassuring about Moe. And while she was usually very reserved around strangers, especially male strangers, she had no problems opening up to her new friend. In the brief time they had spent on the beachfront, the two of them had discussed every topic of relevance in Sheila's life. Sheila couldn't recall anyone ever talking to her the way Moe did. And she was sure that no one had ever listened to her the way he had. Sheila was extremely thankful to finally find someone who was genuinely interested in her thoughts and emotions.

"Remember your promise." Moe had gotten Sheila to promise to him that she would take one day this weekend to think about no one but herself.

"I will," Sheila answered as the Cadillac crept closer to her front door.

"I want you to have this." Moe held a fifty-dollar bill out to her. Sheila stared uneasily at the money.

"It's all right," Moe promised. "You and Janeen can go to the movies or something."

"OK." Sheila closed her hand around the money. "Thanks, Moe."

"And here." Moe handed Sheila a small piece of paper containing his pager number as he pulled the Cadillac in front of her apartment. "Call me anytime you need a ride."

"I will." Sheila immediately circled next Friday on her mental calendar while stepping from the car.

"See ya later." Moe drove off.

"Bye, Moe." Sheila watched the Cadillac until it reached the end of the parking lot and turned onto Heards Lane. She stood a while longer, disappointed that her brief excursion with Moe had come to an end so quickly. Finally turning toward her doorway, Sheila was met by the angry gaze of her older brother, and the equally dumbfounded expression of his best friend, Crooked Tony.

CHAPTER 16

It was just after noon when Pooney finally got out of bed. Tired and hung over, the young boy chomped slowly on a spoonful of Captain Crunch cereal. After all else that had transpired the night before, seeing Sheila climb from Moe's Cadillac had caused Pooney to lose it. During the ensuing argument, he had said things to her that had eaten mercilessly away at his conscience throughout the night. Pooney finally gave up on the bowl of cereal as he watched Sheila, who was seated on the living room couch, sorting through a load of dirty clothes. The guilt Pooney felt over last night's name-calling was overwhelming.

"What are you looking at?" Sheila snapped, obviously still upset.

"I was waitin' for you to finish." Pooney grabbed the small stack of coins from the coffee table, then, to Sheila's surprise, stacked the laundry baskets, one atop the other, before heading for the door.

The drearily overcast sky that greeted Pooney at the front door was the perfect complement to his present mood. Pooney stopped in his tracks just a few feet from his front door, yielding the right-of-way to a quartet of neighborhood kids on bicycles.

Once the young speed demons had passed, Pooney continued his path down the sidewalk.

Putting last night's turn of events into perspective was a daunting task for Pooney. Everything had started so well. The Cadillac, the booze, the girls. Then, one crazy broad who couldn't handle her buzz had ruined the whole night for everyone. Now Larry, after being thoroughly beaten by scores of policeman, was being held in the county jail on an assortment of charges. Because of the five-year probation he had received six months ago for unlawfully carrying a firearm, there would be no bail set.

After filling two washers full of the Richards' dirty laundry, Pooney walked around to the front of the building where the mailboxes were located. As usual, the mailbox was stuffed to capacity with "junk mail and bills," as his grandmother would say.

Pooney flipped through a small Circuit City catalog as he began the short walk home. He bypassed envelopes from the light and cable companies before stopping in his tracks upon sight of the fourth piece of mail. The envelope was addressed to Allen Richards, a rarity in itself, but it was the return address that caused every artery in Pooney's body to constrict at once. The letter was from his father.

Pooney dropped the clothes basket along with the rest of the mail on the ground. He stood in the middle of the sidewalk as he read.

My Dearest Son,

I can imagine your surprise at receiving a letter from your father. So much time has passed since we last communicated. I know that you are very disappointed in me, first for leaving, then for not staying in touch. But you need to know that I have always loved you, Sheila, and your mother with all my heart. My decision not to write you was based on the belief shared by your mother and I, that your transition to life without me would be easier if there was no contact between us. For your own sake, please do not choose to harbor any resentment toward me. I am who I am. Please accept that.

I am writing at this time to inform you, the man of the house, of my present predicament. The State Court of Appeals has affirmed my conviction. Son, there is a very real possibility that your father will never be a free man again. Do not grieve for me. I am only suffering the consequences of a lifetime of bad decisions. I can accept my fate. My concern is the three of you.

Son, I want so much more for you than I have accomplished for myself. I know at this point in your life, you are being bombarded with issues and pressures from every direction. Regrettably, I am of no use to you.

Allen, you must remain focused on your goals. Don't allow anyone or anything to get in the way of the dreams you have for yourself. You must be strong. I need to know that you are able to take care of yourself, and your baby sister. Son, you have been dealt a bad hand, and I am to blame for it all. But God has blessed you with the capabilities to overcome the obstacles before you. So don't let them defeat you.

I would love to hear from you, Allen. However, I understand if you do not choose to respond to my letter. I will always love you, son. Take care and please think about what I have said. Tell Sheila and your mother that I love them both.

Pooney used the collar of his shirt to wipe his eyes before shoving his father's letter in his pocket. He then gathered the mail he had dropped. He stepped onto the grass, once again yielding to the extremely amused bikers. He resumed the short walk home, every emotion possible dancing within his outwardly serene body.

(2)

"Y'all wanna play one more?" Renee laughed while shuffling the deck of cards.

"One more?" Crooked Tony looked across the table at his partner.

Pooney nodded while peering into the living room at Sheila. She had been on the telephone for at least two hours now. During that time, Pooney had been half-heartedly participating in a game of Spades. Renee and his mother had now beaten him and Tony three games to none.

Under normal circumstances, Pooney would likely have enjoyed a game of Spades. Especially against his mother, whom he rarely got the chance to share any activity with, but today was anything but normal.

Once his mother had awakened, she immediately questioned Pooney regarding the origin of the scratches covering his face. After an extremely tense conversation, Pooney was finally able to convince her that his wounds were the result of a wrestling match with a friend from the football team. Or so he thought.

Next, Tony arrived. And with him came the details of Larry's situation. Larry had been charged with aggravated assault for hitting the naked girl with the chair. He was facing anywhere from two to twenty years in prison.

Pooney had yet to speak to Tony or anyone else about the letter he had received. He simply didn't have the energy.

"Cut 'em." Renee sat the deck before Pooney.

Pooney took the deck of cards in one hand, pulled approximately half the cards from the bottom, then placed them on top. He studied Sheila's body language as he placed the cards in front of Renee.

Pooney was sure that Sheila had been lying when she told him that Janeen was on the phone. Everything from the way she tucked herself away in the corner of the couch, to the way she peeked constantly over her shoulder, to the barely audible whisper with which she spoke, suggested something suspicious to Pooney.

"I got four, girl," Renee sang.

"I'll get three." Regina was all smiles.

"Let's go eight." Renee had the pencil in her hand. "We're not playin' anybody."

"Oh, yes." Crooked Tony was enjoying the game. "I'll make four, Pooney."

"I might make one." Pooney shook his head at the handful of nothing he had been dealt. "Try five."

"I'll go ahead and put a minus sign by that five right now." Renee winked at Regina. "Go, Tony."

Pooney simply followed suit whenever play made it to him. That was all he could do with the pitiful hand he possessed.

"How many is that?" Renee was the master showman.

"Seven." Regina was the perfect complement.

"Well, I don't think these turkeys are going to make their bid." Renee dropped both jokers on the table.

"Man." Tony dropped his last two cards, conceding the fact that he and Pooney had come up short once more. Pooney almost smiled when his mother and Renee exchanged hi-fives across the table.

"My deal." Regina shuffled cards like a Las Vegas Blackjack dealer.

"Chantaye said call her as soon as you get through playin' cards," Sheila barked in Pooney's direction.

"Ms. Chantaye still callin' here." Renee smirked. "Must be love."

"Yep." Crooked Tony cracked with laughter.

"Y'all using protection?" Renee asked.

"Renee," Regina scolded. "Chantaye's a nice girl."

"Uh huh. We'll see how nice she is when there's a station wagon full of nappy-headed children at the front door looking for Grandma."

Crooked Tony was doubled over with laughter.

"Who is Ms. Chantaye's people?" Renee asked.

"She's Betty Johnson's daughter," Regina answered.

"From Oleander Homes?" Renee's eyes widened.

Regina nodded.

"So." Renee's mind pieced together the long-forgotten puzzle. "Chantaye is Tremaine's daughter."

Regina nodded.

"That poor child." Renee shook her head.

"What y'all talkin' about?" Pooney was suddenly curious.

"I'll make two." Regina regretted opening the door to the conversation.

"What, Mama?" Pooney was getting upset.

"There were some problems at Betty's house when Chantaye was younger." As much as Regina hated the direction of things, she had vowed to herself just days before to be honest and forthcoming with her children.

"What kind of problems?" Pooney wanted to know.

"Her father killed a man," Regina answered calmly.

"For what?" Pooney could sense there was more.

"Tremaine found out that one of Betty's boyfriends had touched Chantaye in an inappropriate manner," Regina explained.

"What?" Pooney's pulse quickened. "When?"

"Years ago, handsome." Renee stepped in. "Chantaye couldn't have been but seven or eight-years-old."

"That's cold." Crooked Tony felt the need to say something.

"Tremaine had been to prison twice already," Regina continued. "The jury sentenced him to life in prison."

"For defending his daughter?" Pooney raised his voice.

"There was no evidence to corroborate his story," Regina answered.

"Tremaine shot him at a nightclub," Renee added.

"No evidence?" Pooney thought for a second. "How did he find out about it?"

"Chantaye told him." Regina's voice was but a whisper now.

There was a short silence as the four of them dealt with their own thoughts and emotions.

"Where's Tremaine now?" Pooney had learned just this morning that his own father was being held at the walls unit in Huntsville.

There was another uneasy silence before Regina answered. "He's dead, sweetheart."

"How?"

"He was killed in a prison riot." Renee spoke up.

"Aw, man." Pooney moaned as further words failed him.

"That Betty really turned out to be one sorry bitch!" Despite Renee's wild personality, Pooney was sure he had never before heard her utter one word of profanity. "Puttin' that child through all that nonsense."

"Who would have thought?" Regina was talking to Renee now.

Sensing that the conversation would now be reduced to a mere gossip session, Pooney slid his chair from the table and headed for the living room. He had to call Taye. Just to hear her voice, to know that she was okay, to tell her that he was thinking of her.

"Bye, Janeen. Talk to you later." Sheila hung the phone up suddenly as Pooney approached.

The two siblings stared unflinchingly at each other. No words were spoken.

(3)

"Ain't you gonna finish your onion rings, baby?" Taye asked Pooney as the two of them sat in the Cadillac Seville, munching on cheeseburgers and onion rings purchased from the small store on the corner of 38th and Broadway.

"Naw, you want 'em?" Pooney slid the small tray in her direction.

"Yeah, let me have them." Taye was already applying ketchup to the onion rings. "I need to build up my energy for the walking we are going to be doing."

Today was the nineteenth of June, or better known to the black community as Juneteenth. Juneteenth commemorated the date in history when Union Major General Gordon Granger landed in Galveston with news that the Civil War had ended and that the freedom promised to slaves by Lincoln's signing of the Emancipation Proclamation was now a reality. Throughout the state, African Americans were celebrating with parades, backyard barbecues, and parties of all kinds.

After purchasing their meal, Taye parked the Cadillac Seville in front of her aunt's house on 35th Street and Avenue H. The two of them would wait there until the parade made it to them. Then they would follow on foot, as would hundreds of kids of all ages, as the parade continued its path down Avenue H to 25th Street, then turn South and proceed to Seawall Boulevard, before finally making its way to Menard Park located on 28th and Seawall Boulevard. Once at the park, a wide variety of activities were planned.

"Wanna talk about it?"

"Talk about what?" Pooney responded dryly.

"Ooh, excuse me." Taye raised her top lip and rolled her eyes at him.

"I'm sorry, baby." Pooney couldn't help but laugh.

Taye leaned sideways and delivered a gentle peck on his cheek before saying, "It's OK."

"All this stuff's just got me kinda messed up," Pooney finally admitted. "I mean, first Larry gets whipped by the cops and goes to jail, then I catch Sheila in Moe's Cadillac." Pooney paused while inhaling deeply. "Then, my Daddy."

"I know, baby." Taye kissed him again. "But let's enjoy ourselves today, and then we can take care of that stuff tomorrow."

"Take care of it how?" Pooney was unmoved by Taye's optimism.

"For starters, you can put some money on Larry's books." Taye stuffed the last two onion rings in her mouth. "At least that way, you know he has everything he needs."

"Yeah." Pooney nodded, feeling a little better already.

"Then," Taye grabbed his hand, "you can write your father back."

"I already tried," Pooney told her. "I don't know what to say."

"Just tell him how you feel, baby." Taye squeezed his hand firmly. "You'll feel a whole lot better when you do."

Pooney stared at the toes of his Jumpman tennis shoes.

"And, as for Ms. Sheila..." Taye knew that this was the most delicate of the three issues. "Me and girlfriend are going to have a long talk tomorrow. Don't you worry."

Pooney and Taye both heard the unmistakable sound of an approaching drummer as revelers lined both sides of 35th Street and Avenue H.

"Here they come, baby." Taye jumped from the car. "Let's go."

Pooney followed Taye to the corner where the largest group of spectators was congregated. There they joined the rest of the crowd, both young and old alike, as they all looked anxiously in the direction of the oncoming parade.

Leading the parade was a group of elementary-aged schoolgirls, all dressed alike in white shorts and yellow T-shirts. The words "I'm black and I'm proud" were written in bold brown letters across the front of each shirt.

"Gon', girl." Taye shrieked with delight as the young girls stopped directly in front of the crowded corner, then performed a high energy dance routine, culminating with the Salt Shaker dance that had been wildly popular a few summers before.

Following the dancing girls was a Cub Scout troop. The troop marched in two rows. Each row carried a banner. The first banner read: Den 101. The second: I have a dream.

Next, a line of fancy cars passed them, starting with a red convertible Mustang occupied by four beautiful young women wearing two-piece bikinis.

Then came a purple Humvee with young men waving to the crowd from every window. A dozen or so vehicles passed before a group of men wearing dark-colored suits and bow ties came walking down the street.

"Here comes those brothers from the Nation!" An extremely excited young man screamed into Pooney's ear.

Pooney watched as the score of solemn-faced Muslims marched in front of him. A few among them were carrying posters, some bearing images of Elijah Mohammed or Louis Farrakhan, while others bore an assortment of wise messages.

A few more vehicles passed before the Central Middle School band and pep squad came walking down 35th and H. All were decked out in blue and white. The girls in the pep squad danced impressively as the band backed them with a rendition of "I Got Five On It."

Next came the Tornettes, Ball High School's version of the pep squad. The long, bare legs of the baton-twirling young girls had Pooney mesmerized until a punch in the arm from Chantaye brought him back to his senses.

"Why you trippin'?" Pooney smiled in her direction.

"You ain't seen trippin'."

"You know you the sexiest thing out here, baby," Pooney leaned over and whispered into her ear.

"Why you whispering, then?" Taye yelled loud enough so that those around them looked. "Scream it like you mean it!"

"You the sexiest thing out here," Pooney said loudly to the amusement of all within earshot. Satisfied, Taye stepped closer and kissed Pooney on the lips.

The Tornado band stopped directly in front of Pooney and Taye. Pooney pumped his fist in the air as the band played one of the many familiar tunes that Pooney had somehow always failed to learn the name of.

"Go Tors! Go Tors!" Two boys started a chant that quickly spread throughout the crowd.

Next the blue-and-gold-clad band of Booker T. Washington High School of Houston strutted down Avenue H, led by a quintet of high-stepping young girls carrying batons. This time, Pooney was sure not to give the girls too much of his attention.

The Eagle band was silent until the horn section began to softly play "On Broadway," theme music from the movie *All That Jazz*. The horn players played louder and louder until the boys carrying the snare and tom-tom drums joined them. A few seconds later, the two boys carrying the large bass drums added thunder to the party. The crowd clapped loudly with the rhythm of the song. All were totally captivated as the Eagle band continued to play while stepping in place. The drummers stopped drumming and tapped their sticks against each other as the horn section steadily slowed the tempo of the song to a crawl. The horn section stopped playing, leaving total silence. A whistle blew, a voice shouted instructions, and the Eagle band was playing again. Now the band played a heavily bass saturated version of Teddy Pendergrass's "Love TKO."

Seconds later, just as the crowd began to sway to the mellow groove, the music stopped suddenly. Another whistle, more instructions, and Eagle band was playing again. This tune, an extremely funky one, was one Pooney had never before heard. People everywhere danced, loving every minute of the performance.

The crowd cheered loudly as every member of the Booker T. Washington Marching Band began to dance while playing their instruments. The cheers grew in intensity when the boys in the horn section, all except the trombone players, dropped to the pavement and began doing one-armed push-ups. The horn section took to their feet again and swung their instruments from side-to-side while playing. Another whistle, more instructions, and the band was moving again. After the last of the drummers passed, a handful of girls, unencumbered by instruments, yet wearing the same matching blue pant and shirt set with the gold stripe down the side, followed with a banner that stretched nearly the entire width of the street. The banner read: We Wrecked Shop!

(4)

"Let's sit down." Taye sounded incredibly tired as she sat on the picnic bench. Pooney and Taye had been amongst the hundreds of celebrants at Menard Park for over six hours now. They had played together on a winning softball team, a losing volleyball team, and had participated in the potato sack races. They had also walked endlessly about the eight-block perimeter of the park. They were having a blast, but the heat and humidity of early summer were taking its toll on Taye.

"You OK?" Pooney used a napkin to wipe the sweat from Chantaye's face.

"It's hot out here." Taye repositioned herself atop the picnic table in an effort to better utilize the shade of the umbrella.

"I'll get us something to drink." Pooney hurried in the direction of the makeshift concession stand on the side of the large stage.

Pooney's only thoughts were of retrieving drinks for himself and Taye, until his eyes came to rest upon the sea of red and black engulfing a table to his right. A painfully familiar face was amongst the bunch of Blood gang members. Lil' Arthur, Pooney's only enemy in the world, stared violently back at him.

Pooney kept walking forward, praying to himself that the Bloods would be content with enjoying a peaceful Juneteenth celebration. Pooney could still feel Lil' Arthur's eyes boring into the back of his head as he stepped to the counter.

"Two Cokes." Pooney snuck a peek over his shoulder. Arthur was still watching.

"Two dollars and fifty cents." The teenage girl's fatigue showed in the not-very-warm smile she gave.

Pooney handed the girl three one-dollar bills, grabbed the drinks, then hurried from the counter. He looked back toward the picnic table to see if Arthur was still watching. To Pooney's dismay, the group of Bloods were still there, but Arthur was nowhere to be seen.

Pooney frantically scanned every inch of the park in hopes of locating Lil' Arthur.

"Pooney!" Pooney turned in a complete circle before fixing his gaze on Crooked Tony.

"What's up, Tony?" Pooney's relief was obvious.

Crooked Tony, along with J.D. and a mob of Deuce-nine loyalists, approached Pooney.

"You OK?" Tony asked.

"Yeah." Pooney took a sip from one of the sodas.

"You act like you're geekin'," J.D. stated. "You ain't smokin' that shit, is you?"

"Fuck you, J.D.!" Pooney was in no mood for J.D.'s act.

"What's wrong, Pooney?" Crooked Tony was growing concerned.

Pooney motioned across the park toward the table full of Bloods.

"Aw man, that's why you trippin'?" Tony smiled. "Don't worry about them. We got a truce for the day."

"You sure?" Pooney was unconvinced.

"Shit, they ain't yo' problem." J.D. was at it again. "Ain't that yo' broad over there?"

Pooney looked toward the table where he lad left Taye sitting. Lil' Arthur was standing close behind her. Once sure that Pooney was watching, Lil' Arthur placed both hands over Taye's eyes and uttered something in her ear.

Taye spun around angrily, no doubt bellowing obscenities at her ex-boyfriend. Arthur laughed heartily while glancing in Pooney's direction.

Watching Pooney's approach, Lil' Arthur left quickly, walking in the opposite direction.

"What's up, playa?" Pooney slammed both drinks on the table and began to follow Lil' Arthur.

"Pooney, don't." Taye grabbed his arm. "He's just meddling, baby. Don't worry about it."

Pooney looked toward Arthur, who was still laughing after completing a semi-circle about the park and rejoining his friends.

"Hey, Taye." Tony showed up with a bunch of Deuce-nine soldiers.

"Hi, Tony." Taye spoke affably.

"Everything chill?" Tony grabbed Pooney's shoulder.

"Yeah." Pooney hesitated before answering. "It's chill."

"Baby, let's go see what's going on over there." Taye pointed at the stage where a crew of workers seemed to be assembling a sound system as a large crowd gathered around.

"C'mon." Pooney grabbed the two Cokes from the table and handed one to Taye.

"What's up, Taye?" J.D. spoke to Chantaye as she passed him.

"Hi, J.D."

"I see you and my lil' homie—"

"Bye, J.D." Taye cut him off, causing the group of boys surrounding them to laugh.

Pooney and Tony led the way as Tony and the others followed them toward the stage. Pooney grabbed Taye's hand as they ventured into the rapidly growing crowd. A young man tapped twice on the mike before speaking. "All right fellas, here it goes. The main attraction of today's Juneteenth celebration: the bikini contest!" The emcee clapped, igniting cheers from the crowd.

Pooney watched as a long table and six chairs were placed in front of the stage.

"Before we get started," the young man with the microphone said, "are there any more young ladies out there who think they have what it takes to stand next to the beauties on this stage?" The emcee challenged, while motioning to the group of bikini-clad girls who had joined him onstage.

Young girls rushed the stage from every direction as excited young men whistled and cheered loudly for the contestants of their choice.

"Uh uh baby, hold my shorts." Taye had already unbuttoned the blue jean shorts she wore and lowered them just enough to reveal the peach-colored bikini bottom hiding underneath. "I got to show these hos."

"You what?" Pooney grabbed her arm before she could lower her shorts any farther.

"I'm just teasing, baby." Taye fastened her shorts and kissed Pooney on the cheek. "I just wanted to see if you would stop me."

"Oh yeah, I was going to stop you." Pooney was more embarrassed than angry.

"Here comes the winner!" Lil' Arthur's voice carried enough volume to turn every head in the large crowd. He kissed a tall, leggy, dark-skinned young woman before allowing her to walk for the stage.

Pooney looked at Taye in an effort to gauge her response. She was expressionless.

"Well, damn!" The emcee made a comical face at the dozens of young women who had flooded the stage at his request. The young man brought more laughter to the crowd when he pulled a handkerchief from his pocket and wiped at his brow. "It's gettin' hot up here."

"It's a good thing Lil' Loc stopped you, Taye." J.D. was standing next to Crooked Tony. "Looks like it's some stiff competition up there."

"Well, why don't I loan you my bikini, J.D.?" Taye had always been highly proficient at using her tongue as a weapon. "I'm sure you'd give them a run for their money."

"That's cold, fool!" Crooked Tony laughed loudly.

J.D. was smiling, but he still gave Taye a look of scorn. "If you wasn't my lil' homie's girl..." J.D. threatened.

"Then you wouldn't have your punk ass over here." Taye finished the sentence for him.

Crooked Tony was bent at the waist with laughter as J.D. shuffled through the crowd and mingled in with the other Deuce-nine members.

"What?" Taye smiled in response to Pooney's glare. "He started it, baby." Taye was instantly transformed into a helpless young girl.

"OK fellas, listen up." The young man on the microphone was calling again. "I need six volunteers! That's right, six volunteers to sit at the judges' table and get a firsthand view of the collection of talent we have here on this stage!" He motioned once more to the group of girls. "And after each contestant's assets have been thoroughly examined," the emcee paused for the laughter to subside, "the six of you will be asked to declare a winner. Now I know this is a hard job, but can I please get six volunteers?" Every male hand in the crowd shot up instantly, including Pooney's.

"Don't play with me, Allen!" Taye snatched his arm from the air.

"But I'm a good judge of talent, baby." Pooney's hand went up again.

"Don't make me get ugly!" Taye struck the python pose.

"I'm just playin', baby." Pooney placed his arms around her.

"Playing my foot." Taye allowed herself to be held.

Pooney kissed her softly, then pulled her near. He opened his eyes to see Lil' Arthur staring back at him. Lil' Arthur used the thumb and index finger of his right hand to form the letter C. With his other three fingers, he formed the letter K. In gangbanging circles the literal translation of such a gesture was Crip Killer! It became crystal clear to Pooney at that very moment that he and Lil' Arthur would clash again, one day very soon.

CHAPTER 17

Sheila had only been waiting a couple of minutes when Moe's Cadillac pulled into the parking lot. For the third Friday night in a row, Moe had come to drive her home.

Sheila was beginning to grow very fond of Moe. Unlike everyone else in her life, Moe always seemed to make time especially for her. During the past two weeks, she had spent every night talking on the telephone with Moe. They would talk until Sheila fell asleep, usually with the telephone in her hand. Twice, Moe stopped by the Richards' home to see Sheila. And last Friday night, he had taken her to the clubhouse. Of course, the two of them had to be very careful. Moe had explained to her that their friendship would have to remain a secret because some people would not understand. He told her that those same people would try to twist things around so that it would appear that there was something improper about the friendship they shared. Sheila listened attentively. In Moe, she had become all trusting.

Another major obstacle to Sheila's friendship with Moe was her older brother. Pooney had gone berserk the night he had seen Sheila getting out of Moe's Cadillac. Since that night Pooney had watched her every move with great scrutiny. A few times, Sheila had had to hang up the phone in Moe's ear, fearful that Pooney might snatch the receiver from her.

As Sheila approached the Cadillac, she ran her hand down the front of her blouse and reached for the gold rope chain with the M charm that had been hidden from the world. Only Moe was to know that she was wearing his latest gift to her.

"Hi, baby," Moe greeted as Sheila sat down.

"Hi, Moe." Sheila closed the door and the Cadillac was moving.

"I gotta take you straight home tonight," Moe started. "Something came up."

"OK." Sheila's disappointment showed clearly.

"You mad at me?" Moe was traveling at a high rate of speed.

"No." Sheila was partially honest.

"I'll make it up to you." Moe reached for Sheila's hand. "I promise."

"OK." Sheila smiled.

"I bought you something to eat." Moe released Sheila's hand and reached for the bag resting on the backseat. "Chinese. I remember you saying you like it."

"Thank you." Sheila sat the bag in her lap.

The Cadillac was now speeding down Heards Lane. Sheila could tell by Moe's driving that there really was some urgent matter that required his immediate attention.

"So you ready to answer my question?" Moe fired all of a sudden.

"What question?" Sheila knew very well what Moe was talking about.

"You know, the question I asked last night." Moe was perfectly willing to play her game. "Can I be your first?"

"I guess so," Sheila said meekly.

"You guess you're ready to answer my question?" Moe toyed with the young girl.

"No, not that." Sheila sighed.

"Well what, then?" The Cadillac stopped at the intersection.

"You can be my first." Sheila put her head down.

"Well, we'd better do it now." Moe turned in his seat.

Before Sheila could say a word, it happened. Moe lifted her chin with his hand, then pressed his lips against hers. Sheila tried pulling away when Moe forced his tongue between her lips, but Moe held her head in place. Sheila's breath stopped and she sat motionless as Moe ran his tongue over every inch of her mouth. A blaring horn signaled the end of Sheila's first kiss, and the Cadillac was moving once more.

The two of them were silent as Moe drove the rest of the way to Sheila's home. Sheila wanted desperately to speak, but her nervousness made conversation impossible.

"Here, baby." Moe handed Sheila the customary fifty-dollar gift as the Cadillac pulled into the Back Bay apartment complex. "I'm sorry I can't take you for a ride tonight."

Sheila nodded as she took the money.

Moe leaned over to kiss the young girl once more, and this time Sheila was first to use her tongue.

"You pick things up fast," Moe commented. Sheila smiled.

"See ya later." Moe touched the small of Sheila's back as she exited the car.

Sheila felt like she was walking on air as she made the short, dizzying walk to her front door. She struggled to fit her key in the lock as her entire body continued to tremble. Once inside, Sheila dropped the bag of food on the floor and ran straight to the telephone. She couldn't wait to tell Janeen.

(2)

"How you feeling?" Taye, who had been singing along with Foxy Brown as she told the world all about her "Ill Na Na," lowered the music just enough so Pooney could hear as the Cadillac Seville entered the parking lot area of the Walls Prison Unit.

"A little nervous," Pooney admitted.

"Me, too."

"What are you nervous for?" Pooney asked.

"I want to make a good impression." Taye slowed behind the car in front of them. "It's not every day that a girl meets her father-in-law."

Pooney's mind's eye zeroed in on the man he called Daddy. It had been six years since the two of them had seen each other face to face.

Upon receiving his father's letter, Pooney answered as Taye had suggested. It was also Taye who suggested this Saturday morning's visit. Naturally, Big Al was ecstatic.

Taye brought the Cadillac Seville to a complete stop as was instructed by a gray-suited corrections officer.

"How y'all doing today?" The officer peeked through Taye's window.

"Fine," Taye answered.

The officer looked at Pooney, then into the backseat. "Can I get you to open the trunk, ma'am.

"Sure." Taye was unusually cooperative.

Pooney was silently irritable as the corrections officer rummaged through the trunk of his car. Taye, as if sensing Pooney's discomfort, leaned toward Pooney's side of the car and kissed his cheek. The officer shut the trunk, then motioned for Taye to proceed before he approached the next vehicle.

Taye parked as close to the entrance as possible. Although just after eight a.m., the best parking spaces were already taken. Pooney and Taye walked hand-in-hand toward the double glass doors.

Taye led Pooney into a large waiting area. A small group of people waited in line to speak to the female officer at the desk. Pooney and Taye joined them.

The wall to Pooney's left was covered with framed photos of ex-wardens of the Walls Unit. Some of the photos were over one hundred years old, with all of the wardens seemingly wearing the same expressionless face as they stared right through Pooney and the other visitors.

"Next." After just a couple of minutes, Taye and Pooney stood before the young Hispanic woman at the desk.

"We're here to see Allen Richards." Taye was business-like.

"Identification." The state employee was cold and detached.

Pooney handed his identification card to Taye who handed them both to the officer. The woman checked the pictures on both cards against the faces in front of her, before vigorously assaulting the keyboard on her desk.

"Through the door." The officer pointed down the hall after staring at the monitor. "Give this to the officer at the podium."

Taye took the white slip of paper from the woman, along with their ID cards. Pooney followed closely as she led the way through the door to the podium.

"Hi." The woman behind the podium was much more approachable than the first state employee had been.

Taye handed the woman the small piece of paper as instructed. Pooney turned toward the room full of small tables. A dozen or so inmates were already joined by friends and family. The inmates were all dressed identically in white pants, white shirts, and black boots.

Pooney had never before seen such a wide range of emotions in one room. There were tears of both joy and despair, laughing children ran and played under tables, while impatient mothers soothed crying babies. There were conversations filled with hope-filled plans for the future, and body language that sang loudly of hopelessness. There were embraces that said I'll be here for you, and kisses that said, "Goodbye forever."

"C'mon, baby." Taye took Pooney by the hand. "We're at table fifteen. Pooney followed Taye down the second aisle to the table along the far wall.

"What kind of soda does your father like?" Taye asked.

"Coke," Pooney answered

Taye left Pooney and headed for the soft drink machines located to the right of the podium. While awaiting her return, Pooney couldn't help but overhear the conversation at the table next to him.

"Just like that huh, Karen?" The distraught inmate asked.

"No, it's not just like that." A young woman choked back tears.

"All your fuckin' promises were for shit!"

"I'm sorry, Leonard." The young woman released her sorrow. "Please don't hate me."

There was a lull in the conversation as only a duet of sniffles and sighs could be heard.

"All those lies." The young prisoner shook his head.

"I tried, Leonard." The young woman lost all control of her emotions. "But it's been so long."

"Don't you think I know how long it's been?" Leonard was loud enough to turn a few heads. "You think being here is easy?"

"I didn't put you here, Leonard!" The strawberry blonde matched Leonard's intensity. "You did."

Pooney was relieved to see Taye return with an armful of chips, cakes, and soda. Taye took one quick glance at the emotional couple before placing the food and drinks on the table.

"It's warm in here." She fanned herself with her hand.

"You're just not used to wearing so many clothes." Pooney joked.

"Forget you." Taye smiled.

Pooney grabbed a Minute Maid Orange and opened it.

"Sistergirl need to get on with all that damn crying." Taye spoke just a little too loud for Pooney's liking.

"Chill out, Taye," Pooney whispered.

A door behind the podium opened and all heads turned in that direction. A short, stocky Mexican man stepped to the podium, showed the corrections officer his identification card, and walked quickly toward the table where a beautiful woman and three small children were waiting.

Next, a slightly taller, and much younger, blond prisoner approached the podium. After conversing briefly with the officer, he hurried toward the waiting arms of his mother.

Then, Pooney sat up straight as the third prisoner stepped to the podium. Although he was much smaller than Pooney remembered, there was no mistaking the prisoner's identity.

"That's my daddy," Pooney mouthed to himself.

Allen Richards, Sr. showed the corrections officer his identification card, exchanged a few words, then turned in the direction of table fifteen. Pooney stared at the freshly shaven face. It was his own.

Allen Richards, Sr. fixed his gaze upon his sitting likeness, while quickly closing the distance between himself and his son. Pooney stood up, unconsciously pushing Taye and her chair from his path while moving to greet his father.

The two Allens crashed solidly, each clinging to the other as if the world was coming to its end. There were no words. Instead, the two men communicated the unspeakable pain in their hearts through the constantly tightening bear hug they shared. Pooney couldn't help the water that fell freely from his eyes.

"I missed you so much, man." The elder Richards was first to break the silence.

"Me, too," Pooney struggled.

"Let's sit down." The elder Richards held his son tighter before finally letting go.

"Hi, Mr. Richards." Taye, who had stood by silently, wiped at her eyes before offering her hand.

"Hi, Chantaye." A now much-more composed Big Al greeted the young woman to whom his son had devoted an entire page in his last letter. "You're as beautiful as Pooney said you were."

"Thank you." Taye wiped at her eyes again. The three of them were seated.

"I'm glad you two could make it." Big Al spoke with the self-assuredness that had always been his greatest source of charisma. "You didn't have any problems on the road, did you?"

"No." Taye shook her head.

"Good." Big Al nodded. "Now Pooney, tell me about this football thing."

"Last year, I was mostly used as a kick returner," Pooney explained. "But this year, I'm starting varsity corner."

"No way." Big Al feigned disbelief, but was unable to conceal the pride he felt.

"You ought to see my baby run with the ball." Taye couldn't help herself. "He's so fast, no one can catch him."

"What?" Big Al's face lit up. "Well, Mr. Hotshot, when you get to do your Deion Sanders thing this season, send your old man the clippings."

"OK."

"Here." Taye pushed the mountain of junk food toward Big Al.

"Took me six months to lose the extra weight and one Saturday morning to gain it all back," Big Al joked. "Thank you."

The three of them ate sweets and drank sodas while talking non-stop. For the most part, Taye remained quiet, allowing Pooney the opportunity to speak with his father. However, both men were sure not to make her feel left out. It was a joyous occasion with a truly festive mood. For Pooney, nothing could be more perfect. With Taye by his side, and in the company of his father, all voids within him were filled.

As for Big Al, he had never lived a greater day. So many nights he had fretted over the fate of his firstborn son, hoping and praying that somehow the family he left behind could manage without him. Now, while sitting across from the strong, intelligent young man before him, and the beautiful young woman at his side, Big Al knew that his prayers had been answered.

"You have fifteen minutes, Mr. Richards." The corrections officer walked by their table. All three of them checked their watches. The two hours couldn't possibly have passed so quickly.

"Man, time flies." Big Al leaned back in his chair.

"Yeah," Pooney agreed, the sorrow in his voice evident.

"I'm sorry, son." Big Al pulled his chair closer to the table.

"For what?"

"For leaving you, Sheila, and your mother alone to fix a mess that I made."

"You don't owe me no apology." Pooney was uncomfortable with the sudden seriousness of the conversation. "I know how it goes."

"Yes, I do," Big Al continued. "And I pray that you'll never have to give your son the same apology."

"I'm going to wait outside." Having known this time would come, Taye offered her hand to Pooney's father once more. "Nice to meet you, Mr. Richards."

"You, too, sweetheart."

"See you in a little bit." Taye kissed Pooney on the cheek before leaving.

"That's some woman you got there, son," Big Al commented.

"I know."

"Take care of her."

"I will."

"Your sister, and your mother."

"I will." Pooney felt as if he was losing his father all over again.

There was a brief silence before Big Al breathed deeply. "Son, please don't end up like your father. Understand?"

Pooney nodded.

"You can be anything and everything you ever wanted to be. You can turn this crazy mixed-up world upside down if you want. Dig?"

Another nod.

"Write me when you need advice." Big Al's eyes filled with tears. "You can tell me anything. I'll understand."

Pooney's lip began to quiver.

"I'm proud of you, son," Big Al continued. "You're already more man than I know how to be. Just keep on keepin' on."

With that Pooney lost control, and the tears fell in volume.

"I know, man." Big Al made his way around the table and placed both arms around his son. "I know."

Pooney buried his head into his father's chest. There was so much he wanted to say. So many questions he wanted to ask. But the rising tide of emotions he felt made it impossible for him to speak. He had never felt so powerless before. How could this man, his father, his hero, end up in such a predicament? Just another convict with nothing to show for his efforts except a double-digit prison sentence, possibly never to be a free man again.

"Time's up," The unsympathetic guard informed them.

"OK," Big Al answered. The two men finally separated. Pooney wiped his eyes as well as he could with the front of his shirt.

"Take care of yourself, son." Big Al offered a hand.

"You, too." Pooney used his firmest grip. The two men walked toward the podium.

"Drive safe," Big Al said.

"We will." Pooney looked through the glass door at the brilliant sunshine that awaited him.

Big Al reached for Pooney once more. He wanted to hold his son one last time before watching him leave for a world that he himself might never see again.

"See you later." Pooney pulled away.

"Goodbye, son."

Pooney turned and exited the door closest to the podium. The short walk through the lobby seemed so long he wanted to run. Once at the double doors leading to sunshine, Pooney turned for one last look at his father. Big Al was already gone.

(3)

"Damn Pooney, why you always playin' that bullshit?" Crooked Tony whined as his friend placed the Lil' Wayne CD in the CD player.

"You know these boys go hard, Tony." Pooney programmed his favorite track.

"I know them fools down with that ded shit!" A Deuce-nine Crip was never to say the word red.

"Quit trippin' man. It's just music."

"Tha block is hot." Crooked Tony scoffed as Lil' Wayne began to flow through the brand new fifteen inch woofers the Cadillac Seville now sported. "Why they got those damn flame throwers in the video if they ain't no slobs?"

Pooney laughed while turning the volume on his stereo system way up. He knew that Tony's attitude had nothing at all to do with Lil' Wayne, the hotboys, or whether or not any of them were Blood gang members.

Crooked Tony had been extremely temperamental ever since being told that Taye would be accompanying Pooney to visit Big Al. Crooked Tony had always revered Big Al, maybe even more so than Pooney or Sheila. As a child, Crooked Tony had spent so much of his time at the Richards' household, that he, too, called Big Al, Daddy. He felt betrayed that his best friend had not considered his feelings for Big Al.

"Ain't wearin' no suits 'cause we ain't trying to be president," Pooney sang loudly along with his favorite part of the song.

The eight days since the visit with his father had proven to be the most difficult period ever in Pooney's young life. Remarkably, his mind was able to recall every single detail of his visit with his father; from the expression on his father's face as he approached the podium, to the sophisticated manner in which his father enunciated every syllable of every word, to the last gut-wrenching hug Pooney shared with a slightly smaller, and much more vulnerable Big Al. Pooney's mind had vividly recorded it all. And the tape played non-stop, when Pooney wanted, and when he didn't.

Pooney had tried everything imaginable to eliminate the unsolicited images that continuously intruded upon his thoughts. From cruising The Island with Crooked Tony, to drinking Cisco wine and smoking Swishers, to hustling non-stop, to all-night sex with Taye, the tape continued to play.

Six days ago, Pooney had taken his Cadillac Seville to Flores's paint and body shop. Two days ago, he picked it up. The Cadillac Seville was now the candy-coated, money-green, hard-hitting, ghetto chariot Pooney had envisioned when he first saw it sitting on Roy Contreras's lot. Later that same day, Pooney purchased a brand new stereo system and a pair of fifteen-inch woofers to go along with the six-by-nines the Cadillac Seville already contained. But even now, as Pooney cruised the streets of Galveston showing off his prize, the victory was made hollow by the realization that his father was trapped in a cage, maybe never to return, and there was nothing that could be done to save him.

"I see you bobbin' your head." Pooney surprised Tony by turning the music down suddenly.

"You got me bent, fool." Crooked Tony adamantly denied grooving to Lil' Wayne as the track played out.

"You need to look past that gangbangin' shit, and give that boy his props," Pooney scolded.

"Look who's talkin'," Crooked Tony shot back. "Mr. Deuce-nine himself."

"What' s that supposed to mean?" Pooney turned off the Seawall at 53rd Street.

"I tried to tell you the same shit a long time ago."

"Maybe I wasn't ready to hear it then."

"And now you are?" Crooked Tony smirked.

"Maybe."

"You're confused." Crooked Tony waved him off.

"What about you?"

"What about me?" Crooked Tony turned to face Pooney.

"Let's get outta this Deuce-nine shit, Tony." Pooney spoke as if just popping the cork on a long-bottled secret.

"What?"

"You said it yourself, Tony. This shit ain't for us."

"I said this shit ain't for you, playa," Crooked Tony clarified. "I'm true blue through and through. You're different man."

"What the fuck is that supposed to mean?" Pooney had always hated being looked upon different.

"Pooney," Crooked Tony measured his words carefully, "I ain't got nothin' but Deuce-nine. It's different for you. That's all I'm sayin'."

Pooney turned left on Avenue S. A little league baseball game was being played in the ballpark located in front of Burnett Elementary School.

"Wanna catch a couple of innings?" Pooney asked.

"Why not?" Tony answered.

Pooney pulled into the parking area. He parked the Cadillac Seville right behind the bleachers along the third base line. Both boys climbed from the car and walked toward the ball game. Despite the fact that many good seats still remained, Pooney and Tony decided to stand along the fence in left field.

A quick look at the scoreboard and the boys realized that they had stumbled upon the climax of a pretty good ball game. The score was: Braves-3, Yankees-1. The Yankees had the bases loaded with two outs in the fifth and final inning when an extremely undersized boy stepped inside the batter's box.

"He can't even get the bat off his shoulder." Crooked Tony laughed at the weak stance of the batter.

"Five bucks he gets a hit," Pooney challenged.

"Bet that, crazy man. He ain't got a chance."

"Watch him." Pooney thought of his own days as the runt of his little league baseball team. Pooney played a decent second base for the ILA Bulls. Tony was a great shortstop. The ILA at the front of the team's name was in reference to the local union hall that sponsored them. However, the other teams in the league had given their own meaning to the three letters. Thus, Pooney's Bulls became forever known as the "I Lost Again Bulls" because of their pitiful play.

The first pitch from the large boy with the face full of red freckles was right above eye level, but the batter swung anyway. Strike one.

"That's all right, Shorty!" Pooney clapped and yelled. "Wait for your pitch."

"Yeah, right." Tony laughed.

The second pitch was in the same spot. Shorty's bat never left his shoulder. Ball one.

"Good eye, Shorty!" Pooney's cheers ignited Shorty's teammates, who had been much too quiet to be in the middle of a last-minute rally. Crooked Tony shook his head.

The sudden surge of encouragement seemed to energize the batter, who now held the bat off his shoulder in a much more aggressive stance. The third pitch was hard and inside. Shorty bailed out, barely avoiding being hit as he went sprawling. Ball two.

"He's nervous, Shorty." Pooney jumped up and down. "You got him now!"

The small crowd was getting into the act. Calls of "Get him, Shorty," echoed through the visitor's side of the ballpark, while the home side answered with "Strike 'em out, Clint." The volume rose exponentially.

The fourth pitch was right down the center of the plate. Shorty cocked his bat, stepped toward the pitcher, and swung mightily, just grazing the ball and fouling it backward.

"Good cut, Shorty!" Pooney was beside himself. "Good cut!"

"Two strikes," Crooked Tony reminded.

"C'mon, Clint." The Braves manager could be heard from the dugout. "This kid ain't got a hit all year."

"It's your time, Shorty!" Pooney encouraged.

Shorty settled back into the batter's box. Once again the bat was off his shoulder, and now it moved through the air in small circular motions as he awaited the next pitch. There was also movement in other parts of Shorty's body. His hips moved back and forth, and his lips moved as if he was talking softly.

The fifth pitch was identical to the last, very hard, and very straight. Shorty took a slightly bigger step forward, striding directly into the pitch. The bat came around in a blur, making solid contact with the ball. The tink sound that the aluminum made when hitting the ball was music to Pooney's ears.

"Run, Shorty! Run!" Pooney yelled as Shorty's line drive shot passed the third baseman's head.

The crowd cheered loudly as Shorty ran for his life, the too-big batter's helmet falling off his head as he rounded first base and ran for second.

Shorty rounded second base with a full head of steam at about the same time the ball arrived at third base. Shorty stopped in his tracks, turned and headed back for second base. The ball beat him there. The ensuing rundown drew riotous laughter from the crowd as none of the three participants seemed to realize that the game was already over.

"Juke 'em, Shorty!" Pooney laughed wholeheartedly. "Don't let 'em take you alive, soldier."

The comedic scene finally stopped when one of Shorty's teammates tackled him to the ground. Seconds later, Shorty was pinned under twenty screaming boys, all of them seemingly twice his size.

"I told you, Tony." Pooney never took his eyes off the wildly celebrating boys. "I knew he had it in him."

"Yeah. Yeah. That lil' fool got lucky and you know it."

Pooney leaned over the fence while continuing to watch the frolicking boys. He could see himself, with his teammates in a similar scene, five minutes after winning the 23-5A District Championship.

The boys finally untangled themselves and met the Braves at the pitcher's mound for the customary post-game handshake. Shorty broke from the group and bolted toward a middle-aged couple who waited for him at the opening in the fence next to his team's dugout.

He leapt into his father's arms with such force the large man stumbled backward.

"Now, that's all right," Crooked Tony whispered to himself while watching Shorty with his father. Shorty's mother joined them, kissing the grinning boy on the forehead.

"I need to work out." Pooney finally spoke.

"What?" Crooked Tony looked at Pooney.

"Two-a-days start in a month." Pooney thought about the drinking and drugging he had done all summer. "I'm out of shape."

"You know what you need to do," Crooked Tony replied.

"I'm blowin' it, Tony."

"Blowin' what?"

"Everything."

"You ain't blown nothin' yet, cuz"

"I gotta get my shit together." Pooney watched Shorty and his parents walk toward the parking lot. "I gotta be ready." Pooney shook the fence with both hands. "I gotta shine, Tony. Too many people believe in me."

Crooked Tony maintained his silence.

"My mama, Sheila, Coach Roy, Taye, my Daddy—they all believe in me."

"Don't forget me." Crooked Tony finally spoke. "I believe in you, too."

"You always did." Pooney turned and faced his long-time friend.

"And always will." Crooked Tony offered his hand.

Pooney grabbed Tony's hand and pulled him close. The two boys embraced briefly before remembering their "playa" status.

"C'mon, fool." Pooney hurried toward the driver side of the Cadillac.

"Where we goin'?" Crooked Tony asked while opening the passenger's side door.

"Wendy's," Pooney answered. "You owe me five bucks."

The Cadillac Seville backed out of the parking lot and Lil' Wayne started up again.

(4)

"Almost finished," Taye promised Regina as she tore the plastic containing the last of the hair extensions.

"You think he's still mad at me?" Regina had described to Taye in detail the spat she had with Coach Roy.

"He won't be when he sees your hair," Taye replied.

"He is so stupid," Regina fussed. "Let him be mad."

"I know what you mean." Taye had felt the same way about Pooney on more than a few occasions.

"You're incapable of understanding the complexities of dilemmas facing today's black man." Regina mimicked the most infuriating statement made by Coach Roy before saying. "Girl, I let him have it."

"I bet you did." Taye stitched the hair with the manual dexterity of a sushi chef.

"Where in the world is that son of mine?" Regina wondered aloud.

"He'll make it home soon." Taye laughed while continuing her work.

"I don't know what to make of that boy." Regina sighed. "He seems to be losing a little more of his mind every day."

Taye found it surprising that Regina could be so oblivious to the burdens of her firstborn child. What was wrong with her? Couldn't she see that her little boy was in pain? Couldn't she sense his frustration? Was Coach Roy correct? Was Regina incapable of understanding?

"My baby's going to be all right." Taye grabbed the scissors from the table and trimmed Regina's hair to perfection.

"I hope so." Regina paused. "You love that big head boy, don't you?"

"Why do you say that?" Taye was glad Regina couldn't see her face.

"I can tell how defensive you get when I talk about him." Both women laughed.

"Well, do you?" Regina pressed.

"Of course I love my baby." Taye made the final snip.

"I hope y'all using protection," Regina said boldly.

"What?" Taye laughed, caught totally off-guard.

"C'mon now, girlfriend," Regina continued. "I used to be your age." Both women were quiet.

"Let me see." Taye did a slow walk around Regina, examining her head from all angles.

"Lord knows the two of you don't need no child." Regina sounded three decades older than she actually was. "You going to college?"

"Yeah." Taye grabbed the comb from her shirt pocket and went to work on the left side of Regina's head.

"Where?"

"I always wanted to go to Spelman." Taye hesitated. "But, I'm not sure 'cause…"

"Because you want to stay close to that big head boy," Regina finished her sentence for her.

"Yeah." Taye nodded.

Regina turned to look Taye in the face. "Sweetheart, I know how you feel about Allen." Regina's words were the only sound in the house. "But you have to follow your dreams, baby. You'll never forgive yourself if you don't."

Regina turned around and Taye snipped the troubled spot away.

Taye smiled while handing Regina the mirror. It felt good to talk to someone who understood her feelings regarding Pooney.

"Girl!" Regina exclaimed.

"You like it?" Taye was unsure what to make of Regina's reaction.

"I love it." Regina turned her head to view her profile. "The girls in the dormitory are going to love you."

Taye looked fondly upon her future mother-in-law. Perhaps Coach Roy was wrong after all. One thing was for sure, Regina sure understood the dilemmas facing Chantaye Johnson.

CHAPTER 18

Pooney drove the Cadillac Seville all the way to his front door instead of using his customary hiding place around the corner. The car was still rolling when he killed the engine. He leapt from the vehicle and slammed the door behind him before running for his apartment. Promises to Chantaye of controlling his temper meant nothing to Pooney as he shoved the front door open.

"What's wrong with you, boy?" Sheila was startled by her brother's arrival.

Pooney ran straight for his sister and snatched the telephone from her hand. "Who the fuck is this?" Pooney roared into the telephone. The intensity of her brother's voice frightened Sheila to paralysis. "Sheila can't talk no more tonight." Pooney slammed the phone down after discovering that Janeen was on the other end.

"What's wrong with you?" Sheila slid toward the corner of the couch.

"What the fuck I tell you about riding in Moe's car?" Pooney hovered over his sister.

"What?" The fear showed in Sheila's eyes.

"You know what the fuck I'm talking about!"

"I needed a ride home."

"Don't give me that shit!" Pooney yelled. "What you do with the money Mama gave you for a cab?"

"I gave it to Moe for driving me home."

Pooney snatched Sheila's purse from the coffee table.

"Gimme my purse!" Sheila leapt from the safety of the couch.

"Get back!" Pooney pushed her down.

Pooney dumped the purse's contents onto the table. He found the usual: mirror, comb, brush, chewing gum, pencil, ink pens, calculator. But it was the additional items that caused him to snap. Seventy-six dollars in cash, a condom, and a small rope chain with an M charm.

"What the fuck!" Pooney glared at his sister.

"That's Janeen's stuff! I'm just holding it."

"Stop lying!" Pooney ripped the bills, first in halves, then in fourths.

"I'm not lying! Stop it!" Sheila grabbed at the necklace as her brother prepared to break it.

Pooney's anger soared to an all-time high. In a sudden fit of rage, he punched his younger sister in the chest. Sheila fell back on the couch, clutching her chest and trying desperately to regain her breath. Mercilessly, Pooney jumped on top of her, grabbing a handful of collar with both fists.

"What the fuck's on with you and Moe?"

"Nothing." Sheila was crying. "He just gave me a ride home."

"Stop lying to me, girl!" Pooney grabbed a patch of Sheila's hair and slung her to the opposite end of the couch.

"I'm not lying!" Sheila was mortally afraid of the madman hiding behind her brother's eyes.

"We'll see." Pooney jumped from atop Sheila and grabbed the telephone.

"What are you doing?" Sheila was dizzy.

"We're gonna call that punk muthafucka and ask him!" Pooney dialed the number.

"Don't!" Sheila broke down. "I'll tell you."

"What?" Pooney's pulse accelerated even more.

"Please, Pooney," Sheila begged. "I'll tell you."

Pooney sat on the couch next to his sister. Despite his anger, he had still hoped that nothing had happened between Sheila and Moe. Now he would have to sit and listen while Sheila recounted exactly what had.

(2)

Pooney eased the Cadillac Seville from the parking lot of the Stop 'N' Go store on 53rd Street and Avenue S, and headed north toward Broadway.

After Sheila's confession, Pooney's first thought was to go directly to the clubhouse and confront Moe. However, Tony had convinced him that challenging Moe at the clubhouse was not a good idea, so Pooney was now attempting to content himself with cruising the streets of Galveston until his anger subsided.

"Shit! The cops!" Crooked Tony yelled from the passenger side of the Cadillac Seville.

"Where?" Pooney put the cap on his forty-ounce.

"Right behind us." Nuts, a member of the allied 53rd Street Crips, and a recently released convict, spoke from the backseat.

"Just chill out." Crooked Tony eliminated one reason for them to be pulled over by lowering the volume on the stereo.

"Drive slow and don't look back." Pooney drove slowly down 53rd Street and Avenue M. The police cruiser followed closely behind him.

"Gimme the Sweet," Nuts called out.

"For what?" Crooked Tony asked.

"You want the law to find the muthafucka?"

Crooked Tony handed Nuts the Sweet as requested. Nuts broke the Swisher into at least a dozen pieces as the Cadillac Seville pulled up to the corner of Fifty-third and Avenue L. He then shoved marijuana and cigar paper into his mouth as fast as he could swallow.

"That's it?" Nuts frowned.

"Yeah." Crooked Tony stared forward.

"I gotta fifty in my pocket." Pooney spoke up.

"You what!?" Nuts lost his cool.

"I thought you wasn't hustlin' today?" Crooked Tony turned to Pooney.

"I was gonna hook up with Vikki later," Pooney explained.

"Stupid muthafucka!" Nuts yelled.

"Fuck you, bitch!" Pooney looked over his shoulder at Nuts.

"Fuck you, trick!" Nuts yelled back.

"Chill out, Pooney," Tony intervened. "Keep your eyes forward."

"Fuck!" Nuts saw the flashing lights a split second before the other boys. "Give me the shit!"

"What?" Pooney was all nerves as he pulled to the side of the street.

"Give me the dope, stupid muthafucka!" Nuts was yelling like a madman.

Pooney shifted the Cadillac into park, then grabbed the fifty from his pocket.

"Here." Pooney handed over the solid piece of crack. Nuts placed the dope in his mouth and swallowed.

"What about the beer?" Pooney inquired about the three open forty ounces in the car.

"It's too late," Tony concluded.

The three boys sat quietly as the police officer stepped from the patrol car. Pooney kept both hands on his steering wheel in plain view of the officer, in the manner he had been taught would least likely result in him becoming another statistic of excessive use of police force. Every muscle in his body tensed as the approaching officer unfastened his holster.

"Stay calm, Pooney," Crooked Tony whispered as the officer tapped on the driver's side window. Pooney lowered the window.

"License and registration." The officer was business-like. Pooney reached over Tony and into the glove compartment. A brief period of rummaging produced the vehicle registration card.

"Chantaye Johnson." The officer shined the flashlight on the card.

"My girlfriend," Pooney answered.

"And you are?"

"David Williams the third," Pooney lied.

Driver's license, Mr. Williams." The officer moved the light over every inch of the Seville's interior.

"I left it at home."

"Oh you did, huh?" The light rested on the forty ounce closest to Pooney. "You wouldn't happen to know your license number would you, Mr. Williams?"

"No sir."

"Any of you guys got a driver's license on you?" The light shone first on Tony, then on Nuts. Both men shook their heads.

"Do any of you guys have any type of identification?" All three were silent.

The red-faced officer let out a sigh as he pressed the button on the radio attached to his shoulder. Though not familiar with police radio language, Pooney knew the call was for backup.

"How much you drink tonight?" The officer asked Pooney.

"A little."

The officer unfastened his top shirt pocket and produced a pen and a small notepad. He scribbled quietly before asking, "And your name is?"

"Antonio Anderson," Crooked Tony uttered slowly.

"Jerome Fletcher," Nuts said when it was his turn.

"You all right, Jerome?" The officer voiced his concern while flashing the light on Nuts.

"Yes, sir," Nuts answered.

The officer spoke again into his radio. A second patrol car crossed the intersection of 53rd and Broadway then pulled up directly in front of Pooney's Cadillac. A young black officer climbed from the patrol car. The twenty-something bronze-colored man with the curly hair smiled nonchalantly at his coworker.

"What you got Frank?" The younger officer asked.

"Three kids. No ID's. Open containers." The first officer explained.

The younger officer shined his flashlight into the car, stopping on each boy's face one at a time. "Whose car?" He finally asked.

"The car's registered to a Chantaye Johnson." The first officer told him. "Driver says it's his girlfriend's."

"How old are you?" the second officer asked Pooney.

"Eighteen."

"Bullshit!"

"I'm waiting for a call back from warrants and gang file," the first officer continued.

"Crips," the younger officer said.

"Twenty-five go ahead," the first officer answered into the radio.

"You all right back there, cuz?" The black officer, speaking to Nuts, had a nasty edge to his voice. "You don't look so good."

"I'm OK," Nuts slurred. "Upset stomach."

"You're right, Roy." The first officer was finished on the radio. "Crips. Mr. Fletcher's confirmed. The other two aren't. Warrants were clear."

"What you gonna do?" The black officer asked. "It's your call."

"I don't know." The first man sounded tired. "Write some tickets I guess."

"You oughtta run all the bastards in." There was a shocking tinge of anger to the black officer's voice.

"I'm in a good mood," the older man countered. "Let's search the car. If they're clean, they ride."

"If you say so."

"OK, fellas." The first officer's light shone on the car again. "Any guns, knives, drugs, or anything else in the vehicle we should know about?"

"No, sir," Pooney answered.

"All right then. Everybody out the car."

Pooney waited for the officer to take a step backward before opening the door wide enough to step from the car.

"Come around this side." The black officer trained his light on Crooked Tony.

"C'mon out, young man." The first officer spoke to Nuts.

"I can't." His voice sounded strange to Pooney.

The first officer stepped closer to the car. "What's wrong?"

Nuts was leaning against the door. "I don't feel so good."

"You guys been getting high?" The first officer turned to Pooney.

"No, sir." Pooney was terrified.

The younger officer opened the door Nuts had been leaning against. Without the door to hold him up, his body collapsed totally. The black officer caught the slumping boy, then laid him gently on the concrete.

"What kind of shit is he on?" The black officer screamed in Pooney's direction.

Pooney stared blankly at the officer.

"Call an ambulance, Frank!" The black officer was near panic as Nuts' body began to shake with convulsions. Pooney was close to tears while watching Nuts flopping around on the ground.

"What kind of shit is he on?" The black officer was in Pooney's face now. The silence remained as Pooney began to cry.

"You gonna just stand there and watch him die?" The black officer snatched Pooney by the shirt. Pooney looked to Crooked Tony for help. None was given.

"He swallowed the dope," Pooney whimpered.

"What kind of dope?" The officer shook Pooney violently.

"Crack and marijuana."

"How much crack?" The shaking continued.

"Not that much."

"How much?"

"Half an eight-ball."

"You stupid kids." The first officer spoke to himself before kneeling beside Nuts. "Hold on, son. Help's on the way." Pooney could hear the siren.

"I'm going to put these two in my car, Frank," the black officer said. Frank didn't answer. Instead, the middle-aged father of three placed one hand on Nuts' chest, bowing his head in prayer.

"C'mon and join your homeboy," the black officer called to Tony as he shoved Pooney into the back of his police car.

Pooney and Crooked Tony watched silently as the ambulance pulled up beside Nuts. The two emergency workers leapt immediately from the vehicle and rushed to Nuts's aide. Pooney closed his eyes and said a prayer of his own. He knew that no one else could help Nuts now.

(3)

After suffering the indignities of being strip-searched, fingerprinted, and photographed, Pooney and Tony were shoved into the small holding tank along with the pitiful group of petty thieves, prostitutes, and drunks already present. Pooney's watch read 11:35 when he and Tony first entered the holding tank. It was now just after midnight. It had seemed like hours.

The holding tank in Galveston's city jail shared similar traits with the thousands of city jails across America. Two walls of concrete, the other two iron bars. The holding tank was much too small, much too dirty, and much too cold for human comfort. Adjacent to the holding tank was the sergeant's desk, positioned so as to allow a direct view of the tank to what officers were present.

The major difference between this holding tank and most others was that all suspects, male and female alike, unless obviously too rowdy for the rest, were held in this tank, thus setting the stage for more than just a few extremely interesting nights at the Galveston City Jail.

Pooney was being held on a variety of charges. Among them, unauthorized use of a motor vehicle and driving without a license and insurance. Tony was being held on public intoxication. The two of them had been threatened with much more serious charges in the event that Nuts didn't make it.

Pooney's one phone call had been to Chantaye. His hopes were that she could free him before his mother learned of his whereabouts.

Of the score of co-inhabitants in the holding tank, one face stood out from the crowd. The face was attached to the hulking body of the light-skinned brother sitting along the far wall directly opposite Pooney. For the past five minutes, Pooney had struggled to recall the other boy's name.

"You know that cat?" Pooney poked Crooked Tony in the side.

"Huh?" Tony was disturbed from a trance-like state.

"He looks familiar, but I can't remember his name," Pooney whispered.

"I don't know." Crooked Tony showed very little concern.

Pooney looked toward the other boy once more. This time, they locked gazes.

"What's up Pooney?" The afro-wearing youngster finally spoke.

"What's up, playa?" Pooney spoke back.

"You don't remember me, huh?" The young man asked.

"You look familiar."

"Herbert," the young man said. "Camp Sionito."

"Herbert Lattimore?" Pooney jumped from his seat on the iron bench, leapt over a drooling drunk, and offered the other boy his hand. "What's been up, man?"

"Nothing much." Herbert shook Pooney's hand.

"Damn you swole, fool!" Pooney couldn't believe this was the same timid little boy he had once chased half a mile with a dead lizard.

"I pump a lil' iron, fool." Herbert made an unconvincing attempt at modesty.

Pooney and Herbert knew each other from a summer camp they both attended as children. Camp Sionito, located in Bandera, Texas, was sponsored by the Church of Jesus Christ of Latter-day Saints. A very nice woman, known only to Pooney as Julia, sent Pooney and other neighborhood kids to Camp Sionito at her own expense. The kids Julia sent were among the few non-Mormons in attendance, and they were always the only Blacks. Nevertheless, many of Pooney's fondest childhood memories took place at Camp Sionito.

"What you been up to, man?" Pooney asked.

"Lil this, lil' that, you know how it goes."

"Yeah, I feel ya." Pooney remembered his surroundings.

"What you doin' in here, Pooney?" Herbert asked.

"No license and insurance," Pooney answered. "You?"

"Aw man, my baby mama filed that domestic shit on me. Ain't nothin' though."

Pooney smiled at how much Herbert reminded him of Larry. "You still live on the Island?" Pooney remembered riding with Julia to pick up Herbert and his sister, Mary, from the Palm Terrace Housing Projects.

"I still live 'round the trey," Herbert answered.

Pooney's body stiffened as the senseless world of gangbanging suddenly invaded his reunion with a childhood friend. Herbert was a Blood. The fact was obvious.

"Stay up, fool." Pooney retreated to the bench he and Tony shared, now designated Deuce-nine property.

"You, too," Herbert said.

The minutes idled away at a painfully slow pace as Pooney waited for Taye to free him from jail. He tried every possible position, but his search for comfort on the iron bench was fruitless.

Everything was deathly quiet now, save for the synchronized snoring of the two winos on the floor. Earlier the desk sergeant had remarked about the unusual quiet for a Friday night.

"Tony." Pooney poked his elbow into Tony's side once more.

"What?"

"What you thinkin' about?"

"Nuts," Tony answered.

"Me, too."

Pooney was also thinking of the fight he had earlier with Sheila. Things should have been done differently, but it was time to put his foot down.

A brief commotion interrupted Pooney's thoughts. The sound was a familiar one now, the iron gate opening as another wayward soul was escorted to purgatory. Pooney looked at his watch. It was now 1:45 a.m. He and Tony had been in the holding tank for over two hours, and they had no idea of what would happen to them next. A sudden deluge of female voices erupted through the maddening silence, alerting Pooney of the fact that something very different was happening.

Pooney watched as a smallish Asian woman wearing a gold-colored skirt and matching halter-top, appeared before the gate leading to the holding tank. He sat up straight when another

Asian woman, of comparable build and dress, stood next to the first woman. Suddenly a seemingly endless procession of Asian women wearing short skirts and halter-tops, lined the hallway leading to the holding tank.

"They raided them hos again." Herbert answered the question that was surely on Pooney's face.

Pooney turned to Tony.

"The bars downtown," Tony answered. "They turn tricks in 'em."

"Oh." Pooney nodded. The mental picture of the four or five nightclubs, all on the same block, where Pooney had probably seem some of these same women standing in the doorways, came to mind.

There was a buzzing sound and the gate to the holding tank sprang open.

"Go on, ladies. They don't bite." The amused officer addressed the women's hesitancy at entering the holding tank.

"Speak for yourself," Herbert yelled at the officer.

Herbert's comment sent a much-needed ripple of laughter through the holding tank.

The women filed into the holding tank, one by one, shuffling their feet slowly as if taking the final steps of the condemned.

"Wanna sit down, baby girl?" Herbert stood up, offering either of the women closest to him a seat on "his" bench. Three of the women squeezed onto the bench with Herbert.

There was a charged atmosphere in the holding tank now. The two slumbering winos were now wide-eyed and attentive. Even Crooked Tony's mood had picked up, if only a little.

Pooney moved closer to Tony in an attempt to coax the deeply-tanned, bow-legged Filipino girl standing in the middle of the floor to sit beside him. After a brief exchange of dialogue between bowlegs and an older, plumper Filipino woman, bowlegs and the other woman sat on the bench next to Pooney. To

Pooney's dismay, it was the older woman who sat closest to him. The six other women remained standing.

"So, what they got y'all for?" Herbert was the perfect host for the party. None of the women answered.

"I know you hear me, girl." Herbert was speaking loudly to the woman seated next to him. "What they get y'all for?"

"Shut up!" the heavily accented voice of a standing woman scolded.

"Wasn't nobody talkin' to yo' ugly ass." Herbert provoked another round of laughter.

The woman said something in her native language. It was the women's turn to laugh.

"Oh, y'all wanna talk that shit?" Herbert jumped up suddenly, startling the woman. He then headed for the gate facing the sergeant's desk. "Say, officer." Herbert waited until he was certain he had the officer's undivided attention. "What y'all got them for?"

"Prostitution," was the response.

"Ohhhhh." Herbert reacted as if a startling revelation had been made. "Y'all some hos."

"That boy's a fool." Crooked Tony smiled.

"One of y'all show a brother somethin'." Herbert remained at the gate.

"Shut up!" the heavily accented woman snapped.

"Nina and Sarah De Las Alas," The officer at the desk screamed. "C'mon out. Someone made your bond."

Pooney was pleased to see that one of the De las Alas sisters was the chubby woman seated next to him. When another woman attempted to fill the vacant seat, Pooney quickly slid over, forcing the woman to sit between himself and Tony. A look at bowlegs, and Pooney could swear that she smiled for just a split second.

"They got toll bridges in y'all country?" Herbert asked the De Las Alas sisters. Puzzlement graced the sisters' faces.

"Well, this is a toll bridge," Herbert explained as he blocked their path to freedom. "Except money can't help you. I wanna see some titties."

There were angry murmurings from every corner of the holding cell. The De Las Alas sisters looked toward the officer at the desk for assistance.

"Ain't no sense in looking at him," Herbert explained. "He wanna see some titties, too." Herbert looked to the officer for confirmation. "Ain't that right?"

A quiet nod and smile was the officer's answer.

The De Las Alas sisters chatted frantically with the other women.

"Let us out first." The smaller of the De Las Alas sisters spoke flawless English.

"What?"

"I'll show it once you let me out, baby." The woman raised her skirt a few inches.

Herbert's eyes followed the hemline.

"Promise," she added softly.

"Aw right." Herbert turned to the officer. "Open the gate."

There was the buzzing sound again, followed by the click of the electronic lock. The De Las Alas sister stepped through the gate, quickly closing it behind them.

"Aw right, gimme mine." Herbert placed his face against the bars.

The women ignored Herbert and walked hurriedly down the catwalk toward the waiting bail bondsman.

"OK! See how I got fucked over?" Herbert yelled at the remaining women. "The next one of y'all hos gonna show me y'all titties first." Herbert returned to his seat on the bench, visibly angered by the turn of events.

The women in the cell resumed their frantic indecipherable gibbering. While Pooney couldn't understand a word of what was spoken, he knew the women were plotting their strategy for dealing with Herbert.

"What's your name?" Pooney asked bowlegs.

"Autumn," the young woman whispered softly.

"You're beautiful, Autumn," Pooney told her.

"Thank you." Autumn smiled, showcasing a beautifully girlish smile.

One of the standing women spoke harshly to Autumn. Pooney had earned the young girl a scolding.

Two more women were called. They too had made bail. All eyes shifted toward Herbert.

"What the fuck y'all hos lookin' at?" Herbert yawned. "Y'all all 32Bs anyway." The tension level in the holding tank dropped dramatically.

Autumn was among a trio of women called next. Before leaving, the young Filipino girl slid a business card under Pooney's thigh, tapping him lightly on the leg to alert him of her craftiness. The business card advertised The Sweet Apples bar. Pooney surmised that this was the bar where Autumn had been arrested. The back of the card contained Autumn's name and number written in blue ink.

"You must have some black in you, girl." Herbert admired Autumn's ample rump as she exited the holding tank. "I saw that shit, too, Pooney. With yo' slick ass!"

Pooney's smile was wide.

Before long, all of the women were gone. As if on cue, the winos reassumed their positions on the floor. Meanwhile, Herbert stretched out on his bench, proceeding to snore much louder than both winos combined. Crooked Tony was wide awake, but depressingly quiet. Pooney wished that there was something he could do to lighten his friend's mood, but he knew Tony's depression would end only with news of the boy's survival. Hopefully, that would be the case.

Pooney's watch now read 4:25 a.m. He was so tired his head began to hurt. He cussed Taye in his mind as his anger became fixated on her failure to free him from jail. Another glance at his watch and it was 4:28. It seemed as if an hour had passed.

"Which one of you junior Boy Scouts is responsible for locking my baby up?" An angry female voice cut through the still of the night. Pooney stood at attention. There was no question as to whom the voice belonged.

"Don't you tell me to calm down you stupid bastard!" Regina was enraged. "I wanna know why my fifteen-year-old son is caged like some kind of wild animal!" There was the sound of sliding chairs and scrambling feet as officers appeared from nowhere. Pooney followed their movement in hopes of locating his mother.

"That sounds like your Mama, fool." Crooked Tony looked at Pooney.

"I know."

"Look." Tony pointed to a small window located at the far wall of the desk sergeant's arm. A group of officers huddled around the window. While Pooney and Tony couldn't actually see the object of the officer's interest, both knew that Regina was standing on the other side of the window. And she was mad!

"Ma'am," a white-haired officer spoke in his gentlest tone. "We can't help unless you tell us the problem."

"I'll tell you the fucking problem!" Regina's words cracked like automatic gunfire. "My son is somewhere in this God-forsaken place and if someone doesn't produce him now, I'm going to start wringing necks!"

"Shit!" Pooney looked to Tony.

The Crooked Tony Shrug.

"You think I'm just making threats?" Regina lunged at the middle-aged officer.

"Calm down, Regina." Coach Roy was somewhere on the other side of the gang of policemen.

"I want my baby!" Regina cried out while struggling against Coach Roy's grasp.

"His name is Allen Richards." Coach Roy's looming presence filled the window. "He's been arrested under an assumed name. The kid's fifteen-years-old."

"What name did he use?" The white-haired officer frantically shuffled through a pile of papers. Pooney and Tony watched as Coach Roy looked back for the answer.

"David Williams." Taye could be heard.

"Taye told my mama," Pooney whispered to Tony.

"That's probably the only way she could get you out," Crooked Tony answered.

Pooney listened as the white-haired officer told his mother of the events that had landed him and Crooked Tony in jail. He cringed when the officer explained about Nuts, and how he was in stable condition at John Sealy Hospital after having his stomach pumped because of a drug overdose.

"What's he charged with?" Coach Roy asked.

"Driving without a license and insurance," the officer answered. "Of course, there are many other charges we could file, but under the circumstances, I think that's sufficient."

"Thank you." Coach Roy nodded.

"The only reason we brought him and his buddy Anderson in was because of Fletcher's OD."

"We understand, sir," Coach Roy said. "Is there bail?"

"They're both free to go." The white-haired policeman motioned to another officer who hurried toward the holding tank.

"Thank God." The emotional release brought Regina to the brink of tears.

"Of course, he'll have to appear in court once a date is set." The officer handed Regina some papers and a pen. Regina nodded while reading, then she signed the juvenile release forms.

"You'll receive notification in the mail," the officer told her.

"OK," Regina answered.

The sound of heavy metal doors could be heard in the background, opening then closing, one after the other. The first was at a distance, then each grew steadily closer.

"One more thing, ma'am." The officer accepted the last of the papers from Regina. "Incidents like this are rarely isolated. You must respond firmly to nip this type of behavior in the bud."

"Yes, sir." Regina nodded. Finally, the metal door next to the booth where the white-haired officer stood was opened.

Pooney stepped into the waiting area with Crooked Tony following closely at his heels. The scowl on Coach Roy's face struck the fear of God in Pooney's every nerve. The pain on his mother's face broke his heart. And the sorrow in the faces of Sheila and Taye added immeasurable weight to his burden.

Regina couldn't help herself. As much as she wanted to take a firm stance with her son, she was only a mother. "Oh, baby!" She ran to embrace her firstborn child. "You OK?"

"Yeah." Pooney was slightly embarrassed.

"You sure?" Regina kissed him on the cheek.

"The boy is fine, Regina." Coach Roy was upset. "He's only been in a city jail holding tank for a couple of hours. He hasn't been to Alcatraz."

"Let's get out of here, baby." Regina ignored Coach Roy while leading Pooney to the front door. "You OK, Tony?"

"Yes, ma'am."

"You two must be starving." Regina had one arm around each boy as they all headed for the door. "We'll stop by the Kettle before we take Tony home. Coach Roy stood motionless, staring in disbelief as the others exited the Galveston Municipal Building. He could not believe the pampered treatment Allen was getting after getting into so much trouble. Later he would surely have a long talk with Regina.

CHAPTER 19

"What's up, Loc?" Moe pulled up on 28th Street, directly in front of Pooney and Tony driving a blue Impala Pooney had never seen before. "I was startin' to wonder about you."

"Chillin'," Pooney answered coldly.

"Where you been hidin'?" Moe hadn't seen Pooney in nearly two weeks.

"At the crib." Pooney stepped from the porch of the abandoned house. "Handlin' my business around the house."

"I feel ya." Moe took a puff from a Newport. "Turn that package yet?"

"I'm workin' on it," Pooney explained as he leaned forward into the car and saw the young girl lying across the backseat. "How old is she?"

"When you gonna be finished?" Moe dismissed Pooney's question with a breath of smoke.

"When I'm finished." Pooney turned and walked away from the car.

"Say Loc," Moe's voice was an unfamiliar mixture of surprise and frustration. "What's up with you?"

Pooney spun around angrily, storming back toward the car. "I'll tell you what's up! Keep yo' perverted ass away from my sister, that's what's up!"

"You better watch yourself, Loc." Moe stepped from the Impala.

"You better watch yourself, punk muthafucka!" Pooney's rage totally controlled him now. Crooked Tony ran to intervene as the shocked onlookers began to pay closer attention.

"You done lost your damn mind or something?" Moe's voice threatened.

"Help me find it, muthafucka!" Pooney peeled the blue and white Dallas Cowboy jersey from his body, and then waited for Moe in the street.

"Aw right, Loc." Moe unfastened the large necklace he wore, then unbuttoned his shirt. "That's how you wanna do it?"

"Y'all chill, man," Crooked Tony pleaded.

"Fuck that shit!" Pooney yelled as Moe stepped closer.

"Get yo' ass out the way, Crooked Tony!" someone yelled from the crowd.

Crooked Tony stepped out of the way in response to the obscenities hurled at him by the quickly maddening crowd.

Pooney, swinging wildly, charged full-speed ahead. The impact of the collision sent Moe stumbling backward until his back was against the Impala. Pooney continued to flail at Moe, who, for his part, managed to cover up effectively.

"Youngster done stole off on Moe," exclaimed one extremely excited spectator.

"That boy done went crazy!" another exclaimed.

Moe finally managed to wrap Pooney into a vice-like clench, reducing the fight to an actionless standstill.

"Let me go." Pooney struggled to free his arms. "Let's box, muthafucka!"

"You done really fucked up, Loc," Moe told him.

Moe leaned back suddenly, then delivered a vicious head butt to the young boy's mouth. Pooney could taste the blood immediately. Moe spun the young boy around, slammed him into the car, then landed a solid left-right combination. The young girl who had been sleeping inside the car, was now awake and frightened, and she leaped from the car and ran for the stairs of Jerusalem Baptist Church.

Pooney instinctively threw two harmless punches while falling forward onto his hands and knees.

"Do you know who you're fuckin' with, you lil' punk?" Moe kicked Pooney in the midsection. Pooney rolled over onto his back.

"You done fucked up, bitch!" Moe grabbed an empty forty-ounce bottle and threw it at Pooney, aiming for the young boy's head. Pooney was able to shield his face and head as the bottle shattered against his elbow.

Moe searched the ground for a more lethal weapon. He grabbed a brick that he found lying at the entrance of the alley, before returning to Pooney's battered body.

"You gon' fire off on me." Moe cocked the brick high over his head. "After all I did for you?"

"Say, Moe." Crooked Tony jumped in front of the embittered gang leader. "That's enough, man."

"Get out of my way, Tony," Moe ordered.

"Don't you hit that boy no more!" Thaddeus Lee, with Vikki at his side, came running from the alley.

"Mind yo' business, dope-fiend muthafucka!" a neighborhood Crip yelled from the crowd. Vikki stretched her body over Pooney's as Moe drew closer.

"You throw that brick, and it's curtains for you, boy." Thaddeus Lee was undaunted. "I'll call the law, tell 'em what you did, and testify on yo' black ass when you go to trial."

The last statement left Moe visibly fazed.

"I don't know what's wrong with you anyway," Thaddeus Lee said. "Why you wanna bash your lil' brother's head in?"

Moe watched a teary-eyed Vikki gently kissing Pooney's face before he dropped the brick in the street.

"And the rest of you lil' bastards," Thaddeus Lee waved his finger at the crowd of boys. "Always runnin' 'round here with your britches hangin' off your asses, talkin' about y'all 'bout it, and how y'all bar none. But where was you bad asses the other night when the task force beat your lil' homie half to death right there down the street?"

There was only silence from the crowd.

"Y'all 'spose to be soldiers, but I don't see you hurtin' nobody but each other." Thaddeus Lee reached inside his pants pocket and produced a pint of Wild Irish Rose wine. After a quick sip, the lecture continued. "When I was y'all's age we fought for things that mattered."

"Like what, who gets to hit the pipe first?" someone in the crowd used his wit to amuse his peers.

"Naw, like the right for you lil' illiterate bastards to get a decent education."

More laughter.

"And," Thaddeus Lee took a long drink from the wine bottle while holding one long finger in the air. "The most important thing was, we knew how to love and appreciate each other." Thaddeus Lee's head hung low momentarily before looking up at the now attentive crowd of boys. "In my day, our greatest danger was the hatred others had for us. Now, it's you fools who hate yourselves. I just don't get it."

"Some things just ain't for you to understand, old man." Moe spoke up.

"And you!" Thaddeus Lee's voice trembled. "You are just sickening! Recruitin' these children to work the deeds of the devil!"

"Fuck what you talkin' about." Moe turned to Tony. "Talk to your boy, Loc. Get his mind right."

Crooked Tony nodded.

"The rest of y'all get away from here," Moe commanded his flock. "Meet me around the store."

Pooney was on one knee, struggling to stand, while Vikki pleaded with him to relax.

"Let's go 'Trice," Moe called to the young girl still standing on the church steps. She hesitated.

"Get yo' ass in the car!" Moe was angry.

The girl stood firm.

"Fuck you, then!" Moe jumped into the car, rubber burned against the pavement, and the Impala went roaring down 28th Street.

"No! Fuck you!" Thaddeus Lee hurled the wine bottle in the direction of the Impala. The onlookers watched as the glass shattered harmlessly in the street.

(2)

Pooney was slumped over in the backseat of Big Heavy's cab. The Tylenol 3s the cabdriver had given him were doing wonders for the throbbing in Pooney's top lip. He had not yet developed the courage to examine himself in the mirror, contenting himself with poking at the swollen masses of flesh with his fingertips.

Big Heavy was a favorite amongst the young hustlers of Galveston Island. At just over six feet tall, and well over four hundred pounds, Big Heavy was an extremely imposing figure. He had also been endowed with the wit and colorfulness of a stand-up comedian. But the quality that most endeared Big Heavy to the young drug dealers of Galveston was his willingness to travel anywhere, any time of night, regardless of the circumstances. No questions asked.

"What?" Big Heavy was getting an earful as Crooked Tony nervously explained Moe and Pooney's altercation. "Youngster stole off on Moe?"

Pooney took a sip from the sixteen-ounce Bull he held with his right hand. He closed his eyes tightly, bracing himself against the burning sensation he felt along the inside of his upper lip.

"You OK back there, youngster?" Big Heavy asked, then continued talking to Tony without waiting for Pooney's reply. "Man, Moe is one dangerous cat."

"I know," Crooked Tony agreed.

"What's youngster gonna do?"

The Crooked Tony Shrug.

Big Heavy rolled the cab into the parking lot of the Circle K store on 51st and Seawall Boulevard. "I need a soda. Y'all want something?"

Pooney held his can high with one hand while pointing at it with the other.

"Get a six pack." Tony handed Big Heavy a ten-dollar bill.

"Got ya." The entire left side of the car rose as Big Heavy stepped out. The cabdriver lumbered forward, his attention directed at the trio of young, bikini-wearing white girls strolling down the sidewalk. "Say ladies, I can't chase y'all. Please slow down."

The young women giggled loudly at the huge man wobbling in their direction.

"Fat ass." Pooney almost laughed.

"They waitin' for him, though." Crooked Tony watched as Big Heavy entered the store along with the women, his arm around the waist of a tall, busty blonde.

Tony switched the radio to 97.9 FM. A commercial was playing, but he left it there anyway.

"I'm out, Tony," Pooney spoke loudly.

"What?" Tony lowered the volume.

"Out. Finished. Fuck Moe!"

"You ain't gotta hustle for that fool no more," Crooked Tony said.

"I'm talkin' about the whole thing, Tony." Pooney was crying now. "Crippin' too."

"Deuce-nine is for life, Pooney." Tony spoke somberly.

"Not my life," Pooney answered. "Fuck this bangin' shit!"

"Sayin' it is one thing, Pooney."

"Now watch me do it."

(3)

Regina held her breath while sliding her body from beneath Patrick's massive left arm. After finally disentangling herself from Patrick, Regina rolled slowly toward the edge of the bed and reached for the telephone. She then dialed her home phone number.

"Hello," Sheila answered cheerfully.

"Hi, sweetie."

"Hi, Mama."

"What are you doing still awake at this hour?" The clock on Patrick's nightstand said 11:55 p.m.

"Playing video games."

"Your brother there?" Regina got around to asking the question that was truly on her mind.

Sheila hesitated before saying, "Not yet, Mama."

"Oh." Regina felt the wind abandon her sail.

"Maybe he's with Taye, Mama." Sheila was conscious of her mother's disappointment.

"OK, baby. Tell your brother to call me as soon as he gets home," Regina instructed her daughter. "I love you, too, sweetheart...bye bye."

Regina gently placed the receiver on its cradle. Her mind raced with thoughts of her son in a variety of precarious positions.

Regina regretted not taking a harder stance with Allen the night she picked him up from the city jail. But the pitiful way in which her son looked to her from behind that damn iron door had made disciplining him impossible.

"Not home yet?" Patrick startled Regina before rolling over to face her. After waiting a few seconds for a reply that never came he asked, "When did he leave?"

"I don't know." Regina buried her hands in her face. "He was gone when I left."

"Regina." Coach Roy sat up. "You have to put your foot down."

"I know. I know." Regina stepped from the bed and lit a cigarette. "But things are tough for him right now."

"Tough!" Coach Roy repeated. "The tough ain't started yet. Wait until he sees how tough things are once he pisses off his future pedaling dope and playing gangster with the rest of the hoodlums!"

"What?"

"Don't act like you don't know, Regina." Coach Roy was on his feet and reaching for his house robe. "That boy is so full of that bullshit half the time he don't know whether he's coming or going!"

"Don't talk about my son that way." Regina's emotions were beyond her control. "We'll be just fine."

"No, you won't."

"And you'll save us, right?"

"I'd like to help."

"Me and my children have managed just fine all by ourselves." Regina reached for her clothes. "And no matter what anyone thinks, that's my son, and I'm raising him the best way I know how."

"No arguing that point."

Regina snatched the receiver from the hook once more and dialed frantically. "Can I get a cab at 8900 Seawall Boulevard, the Driftwood apartments...OK."

"What the hell are you doing, Regina?" Coach Roy reached for the light on the nightstand.

"Going home." Regina fastened her sandals.

"I'll give you a ride."

"I already told you me and my children don't need anything from anyone!" Regina snatched her purse from the floor and ran for the front door.

Once outside, Regina ran for the office, where she would catch the cab as it entered the apartment complex. Despite the bravado she had just shown, the thirty-four-year-old single mother was terrified by what was happening to her eldest child. Furthermore, she felt utterly powerless against the forces of the street, which seemed to have him firmly in their grasp.

CHAPTER 20

Pooney sat patiently on the porcelain throne, flipping through the latest issue of *Source* magazine, and waiting for nature to take care of itself. He paused, his page flipping long enough to admire the picture of the female rapper Eve, the woman who, as of present, was Pooney's choice for finest sister on the planet.

"I need to talk to you." Sheila burst into the bathroom and slammed the door behind her.

"Girl, what's wrong with you?" Pooney placed the magazine across his lap. "Can't you see I'm busy?"

"I don't care. We need to talk."

"If you don't get out of here, I'm callin' Mama."

"And she'll see those bruises on your face, too!"

"What you want?" Pooney knew Sheila had him in a compromising position.

"I told you we need to talk." Sheila leaned against the bathroom door.

"About what?" Pooney fussed.

"You and Moe."

"That ain't got nothin' to do with you." Pooney resumed his page turning.

"He told me y'all had a fight," Sheila said.

"What?" Pooney looked at her.

"He called to tell you he was sorry."

"I told you I don't want you talkin' to him!"

"He was calling for you."

"Fuck him!"

"What happened?"

"None of your business." Pooney turned pages again. "Just stay away from that punk!"

"I will," Sheila answered softly.

Pooney glanced briefly in his sister's direction before turning back to the magazine.

"If," Sheila continued, "you do the same thing."

"Now what are you talking about?" Pooney closed the magazine.

"You need to get out of that Deuce-nine stuff, Pooney."

"Go play, Sheila." Pooney lowered his head.

"Why?"

"'Cause I'm tryin' to shit!"

"You don't have to be scared," Sheila went on. "You can get Coach Roy to go to the clubhouse with you and tell Moe you quit."

"Sheila..." Pooney couldn't find the words.

"If that don't work we can call the police."

"It's not that easy, Sheila."

"Yes it is, Pooney." Sheila's eyes watered. "Just tell him you quit."

"What you cryin' for?" Pooney was frustrated.

"'Cause you stupid, Pooney." Sheila cried harder.

"Aw, man." Pooney shook his head.

"I don't want nothing to happen to you, Pooney."

"Nothing is going to happen to me, OK? Stop crying." The last thing Pooney wanted was for Sheila's crying to wake his mother.

"But Janeen said Moe kills people."

"Don't worry," Pooney told her. "I was gonna quit anyway."

"For real?" Sheila wiped her eyes with the back of her hands. "Promise?"

"I promise." Pooney answered. "Do you?"

Sheila nodded happily, then frowned and covered her face.

"What's wrong now?" Pooney was bewildered.

"You stink!"

"Get out of here!" Pooney flung the magazine at Sheila, but she was already gone.

(2)

Pooney and Crooked Tony pulled in front of the clubhouse at exactly three p.m. as instructed. The two of them stepped from the Cadillac Seville and headed for the stairs of the clubhouse. There was no need to knock. Big Lou stood at the front door.

"What's up, Crooked Tony?" Big Lou greeted as the two boys passed him in the doorway.

The front room of the clubhouse was dark and smoky as usual. Moe, Paul, and a man Pooney knew as Turk sat on the couch. Three young men stood behind the couch.

"What's up, Crooked Tony?" Moe took Tony's hand. The two men exchanged the Crip Shake, then an embrace.

"You stand here," Big Lou whispered firmly in Pooney's ear.

Pooney watched quietly as everyone in the room exchanged shakes and hugs with Crooked Tony. Afterward, Tony was handed a mixed drink and instructed to stand behind the couch with the other soldiers. Although drinks and marijuana circulated freely throughout the room, Pooney was offered nothing. The scene in the clubhouse was almost befitting of an informal get-together among old friends, if not for the lack of smiling faces in the room. Well aware of the fact that this meeting could end in tragedy, Pooney was already uncomfortable with the tension that filled the air.

"So, what's up?" Moe looked Pooney in the eye, officially bringing the meeting to a beginning.

"Like I told you on the phone," Pooney stopped to clear his throat, "I want out."

There were grumblings throughout the room, most notably from Paul.

"I told you, cuz," Moe shot in Paul's direction.

"It ain't nothin' against y'all," Pooney tried to explain. "Y'all showed me much love and everything, but I wanna do something else."

"You shoulda thought about that shit before you hooked up," Moe snapped. "Deuce-nine is for life." A short silence hung in the air.

"Damn, Pooney." Paul stood up. "What's up, playa?"

"Nothin. I just don't wanna bang no more."

"You ain't done no bangin'!" Turk exploded. "Moe put you on strong! You got a Caddy, money, hos, and you still ain't put in no muthafuckin' work!"

"That might be the problem," Big Lou added.

"For real," someone said from the back row.

"We all thought you was gonna lead the next generation." Paul was genuinely hurt. "Tell me what's wrong, Loc."

Pooney considered telling Paul of Moe's pursuit of his younger sister, but thought better of it. "It's just that two-a-days are coming soon, and then school starts after that. I need to concentrate on my education."

"Ain't nobody tryin' to stop you from going to school, Loc," Paul answered.

"I know, but between school and football practice, all my time would be taken."

"Regardless," Moe cut in "Deuce-nine is for life. Ain't no way out."

"Fuck that punk!" Turk said. "Let him go."

"What you mean, Loc?" Moe frowned.

"Let's jump the ho out and let him go," Turk answered.

Pooney grimaced. He knew that getting clicked out would be much more painful than getting clicked in.

"What about your homeboy, Pooney?" Paul asked. "Crooked Tony vouched for you from the beginning."

"Sorry, Tony," Pooney offered meekly.

"Fuck it! Let him go," Paul said.

"What?" Moe was furious.

"This is a volunteer army," Paul declared. "An unmotivated soldier is cancer in the ranks."

"And deserters is bad for morale," Moe fired back. "We can't let him just quit."

"Let's jump him out." Turk was intent on corporal punishment.

"Hold it! We need to talk about this shit!" Moe yelled. "Soldiers, downstairs! Pooney, wait out front!"

Big Lou held the front door open again. Crooked Tony offered Pooney a faint smile before he and the other soldiers headed for the back of the clubhouse.

"Don't go nowhere," Big Lou growled before slamming the wooden door shut behind Pooney.

Pooney walked halfway down the stairway and then took a seat. Alone, he now pondered the possibilities he faced. One more whipping didn't seem so bad if, in return, he would be granted his freedom. In any event, Pooney was determined that today would mark the end of his affiliation with the Deuce-nine Crips.

Each second was an eternity as Pooney impatiently waited for Big Lou to appear in the doorway. In the meantime, Allen Richards occupied himself by observing the foursome of barefooted kids who climbed the pecan tree across the street. Although the oldest kid could be no more than eight or nine-years-old, Pooney marveled at how the four of them reached heights that should never have been attainable to them. Pooney winced with every trembling branch as the kids traveled higher. He stood anxiously when he saw one child after another leap suddenly from the tree, screaming as if in terrible pain. Pooney laughed heartily upon realizing the source of the children's discomfort. The three small boys and one little girl had disturbed a colony of fire ants with whom they co-inhabited the pecan tree.

A young woman with rollers in her hair came running from the housing unit closest to the tree, obviously alarmed by the sound of the crying children.

"I told y'all asses to stay out of that damn tree!" The woman lost a house slipper as she grabbed the little girl by the arm and swatted her on the behind. "That's good for you."

Pooney watched as the rest of them received their swats, then scurried for the house.

The door to the clubhouse finally swung open, and Pooney turned to see Paul and Turk coming right toward him. The two men passed without speaking. Pooney watched anxiously as they climbed into the Ford Taurus parked behind his own car. Next, all the soldiers, save for Crooked Tony, passed Pooney. Scowls on their faces, they headed in the direction of the Cedar Terrace housing projects.

"C'mon," Big Lou said as he finally appeared in the doorway.

Pooney entered the clubhouse once more. No one remained but Moe, Big Lou, and Crooked Tony. Big Lou took his customary position by the door, while Crooked Tony and Moe were seated on the couch. Pooney stood in the middle of the floor.

"Well, Pooney, you got your wish," Moe announced. "We're gonna let your sorry ass go."

Pooney remained silent.

"But ain't nothin' in this world free," Moe continued. "Especially dissin' Deuce-nine."

"What's the deal?" Pooney stared at Moe.

"We've been having a little beef with those slobs from the trey. It's time to take it to that other level," Moe explained. "You're going to put in some work."

Pooney's eyes expressed the volume of questions running through his mind.

"A lot of them hang out on 43rd and H, right where Bulls used to be." Moe drank from his cup. "You know where I'm talking about?"

"Yeah." Pooney nodded. He was vaguely familiar with the area.

"Crooked Tony volunteered to help you handle your business," Moe informed him.

"What business?" Pooney was alarmed.

Moe looked at Tony.

"We gon' put some fire in their life," Tony said.

"Fire?"

"And we want a confirmed hit," Moe added.

"Wait a minute, man." Things were moving too fast for Pooney. "You talkin' about a drive-by?"

"What the fuck you think we're talkin' about?" Moe barked. "You're just lucky Crooked Tony volunteered to help your punk ass."

"Who are we supposed to shoot?" Pooney asked Moe.

"The muthafucka in the red shirt." Moe laughed.

Pooney shook his head, not quite able to come to grips with his predicament.

"Once we confirm the hit," Big Lou said, "you're out."

There was a long pause before Pooney finally murmured, "I'll think about it."

"You'll think about it?" Big Lou repeated in disbelief.

"I already figured you'd say some shit like that." Moe grabbed the remote control from the coffee table and turned the stereo on. "You got three days."

Crooked Tony stood and headed for the door, brushing Pooney as he walked by.

"Now get yo' bitch ass outta here." Moe propped his feet on the table. "The clubhouse is for soldiers and Gs, not punk muthafuckas."

Pooney turned and followed Tony out the door. Once at the bottom of the stairs, he stopped to view the scene across the street. The four barefooted children once again scaled the limbs of the pecan tree. Laughing merrily, they climbed higher, with no thoughts of gravity, angry fire ants, or any other dangers invading their young minds.

(3)

"Hold on, damn!" Pooney stumbled through his bedroom door and down the hallway. Puzzled as to Sheila and his mother's whereabouts, he hurried to answer the pounding at the front door. "She ain't here." Pooney frowned at Coach Roy.

"I know that." Coach Roy pushed Pooney backward as he stepped inside the apartment.

"You can wait," Pooney turned to walk away, "but I don't know when she's coming back."

Coach Roy walked right past Pooney and headed for the young boy's bedroom door. Once inside the bedroom, Coach Roy opened each dresser drawer one by one, and rummaged through Pooney's clothing. By the time Pooney entered the room, Coach Roy had made his way to the closet.

"What's up with you?" Pooney grew angry as Coach Roy sifted through clothes his star cornerback hadn't worn in months.

Coach Roy ignored the teenager's questions. After finishing in the closet, he went to the foot of Pooney's bed. Next, he stripped the linen from the bed, searching each piece thoroughly, discarding it all on the floor. Then, the giant of a football coach lifted the foot of Pooney's bed five feet off the floor.

"What the fuck you doing?" Pooney asked again.

"Where is it?" The bed came crashing to the floor.

"Where's what?"

"Don't play games with me." Coach Roy took the mattress and threw it on the floor.

"Man, quit tearing up my shit!"

"You gonna make me?" Coach Roy headed for the nightstand.

"I can." Pooney positioned himself between Coach Roy and the nightstand.

Coach Roy grabbed the shirtless boy by both shoulders and tossed him on the boxspring, leaving Pooney to ponder his feelings of weightlessness while continuing with his search of the nightstand.

"You done fucked up now!" Pooney leapt to his feet and charged Coach Roy. The mountain of a man stood firm. Pooney stopped abruptly, the scowl on Coach Roy's face frightened him to death.

"I'm tired of your shit, boy," Coach Roy growled.

"What you talkin' about?" Pooney took a step backward.

"Your mama works her ass off so you can have a chance in life." Coach Roy stepped closer. "And you show your appreciation by gangbanging and pushing dope!"

"You don't know nothin' about what I do." Pooney looked away from Coach Roy.

"You're not doing anything new," Coach Roy told him. "You're just another little dope-dealing punk who joins a gang because he ain't man enough to stand on his own two feet."

"Save the lecture, Coach." Pooney turned to exit the bedroom.

"What?" With astonishing quickness for a man his size, Coach Roy grabbed Pooney's arm and snatched him around. "You want more than a lecture?"

"Chill out, man." Pooney placed his hands forward in a gesture of submission. While no coward, he had no intentions of tangling with the much stronger man.

"Ain't no chillin' out." Coach Roy pulled roughly on Pooney's arm, leading him to the nightstand. Coach Roy then grabbed the telephone and placed the receiver to Pooney's ear. "Call your homeboys."

"Huh?"

"Call your locs and tell them I'm about to kick your ass!" Coach Roy's vice-like grip caused a dog-like yelp to escape from Pooney's mouth.

"C'mon, man," Pooney managed.

"I'm disrespecting you, huh?" Coach Roy slapped the side of Pooney's head with an oversized paw. "Ain't that what it's all about? Respect?"

"All right!" Pooney's anger was effectively negated by his fear.

"What would your homies think if they saw an old man handling you like this?" Coach Roy delivered another slap to Pooney's head.

"C'mon, man." Pooney tried to cover up.

"You ain't so tough one-on-one, are you?" Coach Roy grabbed the phone again. "Call your homeboys!"

"Why you trippin', Coach?" Pooney fought back tears.

Finally hearing the desired break in the young boy's voice, Coach Roy released his grip. "No son, why are you tripping?"

Pooney stared at the floor.

"Talk to me, son." Coach Roy was much gentler now. "What's wrong?"

"Nothin'."

"Something has to be wrong, Allen," Coach Roy surmised. "You're not a gangbanger."

"I made a mistake, Coach," Pooney explained. "But I'm taking care of it."

"What do you mean?"

"I told them fools I wasn't hangin' out with them anymore."

Coach Roy knew that leaving a gang was seldom so simple. "And they said OK?"

"Well, they was kind of upset." Pooney was the picture of innocence now. "They called me names and stuff, but so what?"

Coach Roy twisted the hairs on his chin while pondering the situation. "Look, Allen," Coach Roy was finally able to speak. "I don't want you around those boys anymore. Starting tomorrow, I want you at the field house every morning at eight a.m. Understand?"

Pooney nodded.

"The first morning you don't show, I'll be back." Coach Roy placed the mattress back on Pooney's bed. "And it won't be to talk."

"Gotcha, Coach." Pooney almost smiled.

Coach Roy and Pooney were quiet as the two of them worked together to fix the mess that was made.

"And not a word of this to your Mama," Coach Roy said once they were finished.

"OK."

"I'm gone." Coach Roy walked toward the front door.

Pooney counted his blessings that Coach Roy hadn't looked under the nightstand and found the three thousand dollars that belonged to Moe.

"One more thing, Allen," Coach Roy said while opening the front door.

"What's that, Coach?"

"I love you."

Pooney closed the door behind his coach and locked it.

CHAPTER 21

Pooney walked two full paces behind Coach Roy and Regina as the three of them approached the stairway leading to the Galveston College Auditorium. Initially, Pooney had been excited about accompanying his mother to Sheila's piano recital. That was before he discovered that Coach Roy would be joining them. Chantaye had also planned to attend, but a sudden problem with her mother caused her to renege at the last minute. Pooney considered reneging also, but he had promised Sheila he would be there.

Pooney's ordeal began as soon as Coach Roy's Ford Bronco appeared at his doorway. Pooney sat in the backseat, quietly listening as his mother and Coach Roy partook in the most ridiculous conversation he had ever heard. A chord of resentment stuck in his heart each time his mother laughed at one of Coach Roy's pitifully corny jokes. Pooney felt as if the two of them were totally oblivious to his presence. Worst of all, Coach Roy insisted upon listening to an Earth, Wind, and Fire CD.

"Oh no, they've already started." Regina walked a little faster.

The hallway leading to the auditorium's entrance was empty except for a smallish, red-haired security guard whose undivided attention was directed at the Gameboy with which he played.

There was a relatively small crowd inside the auditorium. So small, that only the first six rows of the middle section of seats were being used. Pooney maintained his two-pace comfort zone as he followed Coach Roy and his mother down the center aisle. The stage was occupied by a young Hispanic boy, sitting at a large piano, and laboring admirably at a piece that seemed just a little too demanding for him.

"Allen," a hushed voice beckoned.

Pooney looked behind him.

"Over here, silly," the same voice called again.

Pooney could discern a shapely female figure navigating its way through the seats to his left. Pooney recognized the girl immediately. Her name was Cynthia Popovich. Pooney and Cynthia had taken at least one class together ever since the sixth grade.

"What are you doing here?" Cynthia asked.

"My sister's performing tonight," Pooney answered.

"Really?" Cynthia thought for a moment, then smiled. "Sheila's your sister?"

"Yeah." Pooney ran his eyes over the tight-fitting, sleeveless white dress Cynthia wore. "Is she any good?"

"You've never heard her play?"

"Nope." Pooney shook his head.

"You're in for a treat, then." Cynthia smiled.

"Think so?"

"She's going to blow you away," Cynthia promised.

"You in her class?" Pooney would rather talk about Cynthia.

"Yes."

"So, you're performing, too?"

"That's right."

The two of them stopped talking as the crowd applauded generously for the young boy. Pooney clapped softly as a tall, lanky, red-haired young man wearing braces and bifocal glasses took his place in front of the piano.

"You any good?" Pooney stepped just a little closer to Cynthia.

"Judge for yourself." Cynthia stood up fast.

"I will."

"I gotta go. I'm next." Cynthia searched for her purse. "Here."

Pooney accepted the small piece of paper from Cynthia. Both her home and cell phone numbers were written on it.

"Call me and tell me what you think." Cynthia was already headed in the direction from whence she came.

Pooney stuck the card in his pocket and headed for the small crowd of spectators.

"Casanova!" Coach Roy attempted to whisper. "Over here."

Pooney chose the row directly behind the row that seated Coach Roy and his mother, a row that was only inhabited by himself. Pooney chose the seat closest to the aisle so as to put even more distance between himself and the lovebirds.

The crowd cheered loudly as the spectacled young man took a bow. Judging by the intensity of the cheers coming from the couple seated in front of him, Pooney was sure they were the boy's parents.

Next, Cynthia walked onto the stage. The crowd was quiet as Cynthia began to play a song totally unfamiliar to Pooney, classical, it sounded. Despite the exuberance with which Cynthia performed, it took but a few notes for Pooney to conclude that Cynthia Popovich was not a very good piano player. Of course, Pooney would tell her nothing of the sort later when he conversed with her on the telephone. A couple of minutes later, Cynthia was done, and she bowed to the same generous applause as the others.

Pooney watched disinterestedly as the procession of piano players continued. Although a couple of the players proved decent, for the most part, Pooney was unimpressed. As a matter of fact, if Sheila had already performed, Pooney was sure that he would be waiting in the car.

Occasionally, Pooney would steal a glance at the lovebirds. Coach Roy's arm had found its way around his mother's shoulder. Pooney frowned.

Pooney looked at his watch. He had been seated a little over an hour. Hopefully, it wouldn't be much longer.

Just then, a heavy-set, rapidly balding man walked onto the stage. He carried a microphone in one hand, and a small stand in the other. He placed the stand atop the piano before approaching center stage.

"I wanna thank you all for coming tonight," the piano instructor said. There was a trickle of applause from the crowd.

"Each of these kids worked very hard all summer, and it shows."

Cheers and applause.

"We're going to close with something special," the piano teacher promised. "This next young lady is one of the most prodigious talents I have ever had the pleasure of watching. I am sure you will agree."

The piano teacher sat the microphone on the stand and walked from the stage.

Sheila walked onto the stage amidst the scattered mumblings of the spectators.

"That must be the girl Jason's always talking about," the woman in front of Pooney whispered to her husband.

Sheila was dressed simply in a pair of black jeans and her brother's oversized Tommy Hilfiger shirt. She smiled broadly while waving to her mother. Her girlish enthusiasm was sending a ripple of laughter through everyone in the crowd, including Pooney.

Sheila was seated at the piano and began playing immediately. The tune was a vaguely familiar one that Pooney could not quite place until Sheila began to sing. "Harlem Blues" by Cynda Williams, and Pooney couldn't believe his ears. Not only was his little sister a gifted piano player, but she could sing. Boy, could she sing.

Pooney looked around to see if anyone else was as dumbfounded as he. All eyes were on Sheila.

Pooney had never been as proud of anyone as he was of his baby sister right now.

Once finished, Sheila stood and bowed. Everyone in the audience stood and cheered loudly. Pooney looked to his mother, who was crying now, but clapping loudly.

"I told you." There was a familiar whisper in Pooney's ear.

Pooney turned to Cynthia. He could only nod his agreement. Sheila waved once more, then ran for the curtain.

The ovation went on and on as some members of the crowd called for an encore. Pooney chanted along with the crowd as the piano instructor returned to the stage.

"This concludes our program, ladies and gentlemen. Goodnight." The piano teacher waved to the crowd.

Their answer was a thundering crescendo of boos, immediately followed by even more chants of "Encore!"

The red-faced instructor held his hands in the air in a fruitless attempt to quiet the crowd. A sudden eruption of cheers caused the piano teacher to spin on his heels.

Sheila, along with the other members of the piano class, walked across the stage. Her classmates stopped a few feet from the piano as Sheila repositioned herself in front of the piano. The cheers grew quiet as all waited for the young girl's next selection.

Pooney was amazed when Sheila began playing Mary J. Blige's "Mary." The crowd, still on its feet, swayed rhythmically as Sheila played. Regina dabbed at the corners of her eyes while singing along with her daughter.

Sheila ended her song to another ovation. The thirteen-year-old girl waved one last time and ran from the stage. Pooney took a seat as the crowd continued their cheers. Not that he was any less impressed than the others, but he was simply awestruck.

(2)

Sheila observed quietly as her brother crushed a large bag of Lay's Sour Cream and Onion potato chips into tiny pieces and poured them over the Meat Lover's pizza he had purchased for the two of them. Pooney then divided the pizza before taking the larger portion and placing it on the lid of the box.

Sheila took one slice from the portion of pizza Pooney left inside the box and placed it on one of the two saucers she had brought to the living room table.

"You're worse than a pig," Sheila commented as Pooney folded his pizza in half, then fourths, and took a bite.

"So."

"You're ugly, too."

"So."

"Let's play Mortal Kombat," Sheila asked, despite knowing her brother rarely played video games anymore.

"OK," Pooney answered with a full mouth.

"Really?" Sheila couldn't believe her ears.

"Turn it on." Pooney smiled.

Sheila ran to the television before her brother could change his mind.

"Where do you think Mama and Coach Roy went?" Pooney asked.

"I don't know." Sheila sat at the end of the couch, control pad in hand, as the game's theme music began to play.

"She could have at least spent one night with us."

"Quit trippin'." Sheila was happy enough just having her older brother at home. "At least she came to the recital."

"Let's see if she comes to any of my games."

"I'll come," Sheila offered.

Pooney smiled, but that wasn't the same. "You did good tonight."

"Huh?" Sheila couldn't remember the last time her brother complimented her on anything."

"I was surprised."

"Why?" Sheila twisted her mouth.

"I thought you could play a little," Pooney explained. "But I didn't know you could rock the house like that!"

"Really?" Sheila put her control pad down and turned to her brother.

"Hell, yeah," Pooney continued his praise. "You was all that."

"Boy, you're going to make me cry."

"Quit actin' silly, girl." Pooney was himself again. "Let's play."

OK." Sheila grabbed her brother, and before he could defend himself, planted a kiss on his cheek.

"Gon' girl." Pooney pushed her away.

"C'mon, sucker." Sheila grabbed her control pad, and the battle began.

(3)

"Call me when you make it home," Regina instructed as Coach Roy's Ford Bronco rolled to a stop in front of her apartment.

"OK." Patrick leaned over and kissed her.

"Don't forget." The clock read 4:55 a.m.

"I won't." Patrick kissed her again.

Regina stepped from the car and hurried toward her apartment door. She stopped to wave one last time before placing her key in the lock. She opened the door quickly, not wanting to wake her slumbering children, especially Pooney, who was undoubtedly furious with her.

Regina stepped inside and closed the door swiftly behind her. As she turned toward the living room, the sight before her touched her dearly. Pooney and Sheila were both asleep on the couch. Pooney, sitting upright against the couch's arm, and

CROSSROADS

Sheila, lying on her side, her head resting on a pillow placed against her brother's leg.

Regina tiptoed in their direction, kissed them both softly on the forehead, then headed toward the bedroom. She would forever have the snapshot just taken by her mind.

CHAPTER 22

Pooney wiped his face with the washcloth he carried in his pocket. This had to be the hottest day of the summer. "One hundred and humid," was what the weatherman had said.

Pooney sat the Dr. Pepper he was drinking on the porch of the abandoned house, and headed for the alley. Thaddeus Lee beckoned.

"I got sixty." Thaddeus Lee swatted at the imaginary creepy crawlers on his neck and back.

"Take the eight-ball." Pooney placed the package in Thaddeus Lee's hand. "You know how we do it."

"Thanks, Pooney." The heat had even knocked some of the luster from Thaddeus Lee's trademark enthusiasm.

Pooney turned and hurried for what little relief the porch of the abandoned house provided against the sweltering heat. Hopefully, he wouldn't be out much longer. His only plan was to make the rest of Moe's money, which he was still short of by four hundred dollars. After accomplishing his mission, his days as a hustler would be over. The three ounces of crack cocaine he still possessed would be a surprise gift to Tony.

"What did he want?"

"Eight-ball." Pooney grabbed his soda.

Crooked Tony nodded his satisfaction.

In addition to being a most unpleasant day for Pooney because of the heat, this day had also been the slowest in terms of business he had endured. After the first two hours of trickling sales, Crooked Tony was first to figure the problem. Moe had placed Pooney on the blacklist. Of course, his most loyal of customers were still showing support. That included Thaddeus Lee, Vikki, and a few other neighborhood crackheads. However, not one young hustler had purchased an eight-ball from Pooney today.

"Here comes Moe." Crooked Tony was first to see Moe's Cadillac.

Pooney said nothing.

Moe's Cadillac stopped directly in front of Pooney and Tony. Moe, seated in the passenger seat, motioned for Pooney to come to the car.

Pooney hesitated shortly before walking toward the car.

"You got the rest of my money?" Moe, a nasty edge to his voice, frowned from the passenger seat.

Pooney had already given Moe thirty-five hundred of the forty-five hundred dollars he owed him.

"She old enough to drive?" Pooney commented on the young girl sitting in the driver's seat of the Cadillac.

"You got my money?" Moe ignored the question.

"Six hundred," Pooney said.

"Give it here."

Pooney took the money from his pocket and gave it to Moe.

"Count this." Moe handed the money to the girl before turning back to Pooney. "About that other issue."

"I told you, I'm thinking about it," Pooney said.

"Time's up." Moe's voice was void of compassion. "You gonna handle your business or what?"

As badly as Pooney wanted out of the gang, agreeing to open fire on an entire neighborhood of people was an impossible decision to make. Tragically, Pooney had considered his options, and could see no other way. His entire body trembled as a deadly "yes" escaped from his lips.

"What?" Moe frowned at Pooney.

"I'll do it." Pooney stared back.

Moe glared at Pooney. "Tomorrow night at eleven o'clock, be yo' mark ass at the clubhouse." Moe snatched the money from the young girl. "Let's go."

Pooney returned to his seat on the porch. Mercilessly, Crooked Tony asked no questions. The two of them would be forced to discuss the matter soon enough.

Business continued to trickle along as the day somehow became hotter. Pooney peered down 28th Street, swearing he could see steam rising from the pavement. Through the haze, a familiar figure strode toward Pooney with an unmistakable gait.

"What the fuck?" Pooney said aloud.

"What's wrong?" Crooked Tony sat straight up.

"Larry." Pooney was on his feet and running toward the man who was a block away.

"That's right!" Larry was screaming at the top of his lungs. "The muthafuckin' villain is back!"

Pooney ran and wrapped his buddy in a bear hug. He didn't realize just how much he had missed Larry until this moment. Crooked Tony joined them and the three boys hugged and laughed in the middle of the street.

"How the hell did you get out?" Pooney asked.

"They dropped all the charges," Larry told them.

"No shit?" Crooked Tony was happier than any of them could ever remember.

"They had to," Larry explained. "The hos from the room never came to make a statement, and the laws whipped me so bad they was just glad I wasn't filing a suit."

"I bet you're hungry," Pooney said as the three of them began the short walk back to the abandoned house.

"Hungry? Fuck that shit. I'm ready to get fucked up!"

Pooney and Crooked Tony roared with laughter.

"That's right!" Larry called to a small group of young women staring from the front of New Jack City. "The coochie man is back."

"Take yo' drunk ass on down the street!" One of the young women called to the amusement of her friends.

"You didn't say that when I was laying this pipe to you." Larry gripped his crotch in a lewd gesture.

"In yo' dreams, broke muthafucka." The young woman's voice was not quite as cheerful as before.

A large man, wearing some sort of work uniform with steel-toed boots and a pair of goggles around his neck, appeared next to the woman. He stared at Larry.

"C'mon out here." Larry bounced on his toes, then threw punches in the air. "And get yo' muthafuckin' neck broke."

The working man took a step forward, but one of the women stopped him immediately. Perhaps telling him of the great peril involved with tangling with Larry and his friends.

"Chill out, fool." Crooked Tony attempted to pull Larry toward the vacant house. "You just got outta jail, man."

"Fuck that busta!" Larry yelled so that the working man could hear.

"You're throwed off, Larry," Pooney laughed.

"Y'all get me somethin' to drink before I screeeeeeam!" Larry yelled at the top of his lungs before bursting at the seams with laughter.

"Say, Fish," Pooney called out to a neighborhood drug user. "Go get me a fifth of Thunderbird."

"Cisco," Larry corrected.

"Cisco." Pooney handed the man a five-dollar bill. "Get you a beer or something."

"Gotcha," Fish agreed.

"I know y'all boys ballin' out of control." Larry headed for the porch. "Thanks Pooney, for the loot you put on my books." Neither boy spoke until they were all seated.

"How much paper y'all don' stacked since I've been gone?"

"Things been kinda slow lately," Pooney answered.

"Slow." Larry scoffed. "Ain't no slow around here."

"Shit's been fucked up," Crooked Tony answered.

"What's up?" Larry stood up while monitoring Fish's torrid approach. "Them slobs been trippin'?"

"Naw, it ain't that," Pooney answered.

"It's a long story," Crooked Tony said.

"Save it for later." Larry took the bottle of Cisco from Fish, opened it, and turned it up all in one motion. "I ain't in the mood for no long stories."

"Hey Pooney, hey Tony." Vikki approached while a woman who was a stranger to 28th Street waited at the entrance of the alley. "Hey, Larry. When did you get out?"

"What's up, Vikki?" Larry answered. "They let me go about an hour ago. Who is that?" He motioned toward the girl waiting for Vikki.

"Gimme a twenty, baby." Vikki handed Pooney a twenty-dollar bill before answering Larry. "That's my girlfriend, Stacy."

"Oh." Larry took another drink. "How much it cost for her to be my girlfriend too?"

"Ask her." Vikki laughed.

"Say, baby girl." Larry ran toward the alley.

"You been OK?" Vikki asked Pooney.

Pooney nodded, then handed her the dope.

"I've been worried about you." Vikki closed her hand around the dope without looking at it.

"I'm all right," Pooney answered.

"Good." Vikki started as if to hug the youngster, then backed away. "I'll be back."

"All right."

Larry came running. "One of y'all give me a rock."

"What?" Pooney looked at him.

"Give me a rock," Larry repeated. "She's gonna give me some."

Pooney handed Larry a ten-dollar rock.

"Later." Larry was running again.

Pooney and Tony both laughed. The six weeks Larry spent behind bars hadn't changed him a bit. But it sure was good to have him back.

(2)

Crooked Tony brought the gray Oldsmobile to a stop at the corner of 33rd Street and Avenue H. The boys had rented the car earlier from one of his regular customers. Larry had come up with the bright idea of letting Vikki and Stacy drive the car around the trey earlier to make a purchase. His reasoning was that once night fell, and the car was used to conduct business, the slobs wouldn't be as leery when they saw the Cutlass barreling down the street. Larry's theory made so much sense to Pooney that he sent the women to 43rd Street three times.

Pooney and Tony spent most of the day briefing Larry on the happenings since his jailing. They left out nothing. Larry was quite disappointed with Pooney's decision to leave Deuce-nine, but he understood. He also understood Pooney's anger over Moe's pursuit of Sheila. In any event, Larry was always game for puttin' in work, especially when that work meant warring with his sworn enemies from the trey. Pooney was quiet in the passenger seat as the Cutlass continued its path down Avenue H. Although Crooked Tony was traveling about twenty miles an hour, the car seemed to be moving much too fast.

Pooney took a swig from his forty-ounce before eyeing the death tool in his lap. Moe had insisted that Pooney use the AK-47. Larry chose a 12-gauge riot gun, while Tony, who was not likely to fire a shot since he was driving, stashed a .357 Magnum under his right thigh.

The plan was simple. Crooked Tony was to drive up alongside the largest crowd he saw. Pooney and Larry were to open fire. Afterward, they were to place the guns in an old Chevrolet Monte Carlo that would be parked in the alley behind the clubhouse. Once Moe and O.G.s received word of a confirmed hit, all ties would be severed between Pooney and the Deuce-nine Crips.

"One of y'all wanna hit this?" Larry placed a waterstick in his mouth and struck a match.

"You must be crazy." Crooked Tony sipped nervously on a sixteen-ounce Budweiser.

"What about you, Lil' Loc?" Larry offered.

"Naw, man." Pooney didn't even look back.

"A confirmed hit," Larry laughed while mimicking a portion of the speech Moe had given earlier. "I'm tryin' to smoke everybody 'round that muthafucka!" Larry's endless capacity for violence turned Pooney's stomach.

"Y'all ready?" Crooked Tony brought the Cutlass to a stop on 41st Street and Avenue H, just two blocks from their targets.

"Is an elephant heavy?" Larry chuckled between puffs of formaldehyde. "Is a monkey funky?"

"What about you, Pooney?" Crooked Tony stared intently at his friend.

Pooney wanted to say something but the nausea he felt made speech impossible. He simply nodded, then offered a weak smile.

"We don't have to do this," Crooked Tony spoke softly.

"Yes, we do!" Larry exclaimed. "I'm tired of them muthafuckas fuckin' with us!" Neither Pooney nor Tony had any idea what Larry was talking about.

The Cutlass approached the corner of 43rd and H, and the intended victims could now be seen. The scene was remarkably similar to the one Pooney saw every day around the convenience store on 29th Street. The only difference was that the dozen or so boys standing outside the old building that once was Bulls, wore red colored clothing, not blue. Some drank, others smoked, while they all awaited their next drug transaction.

Crooked Tony looked to Pooney one last time for confirmation.

"Let's do this." Pooney popped the thirty-six shot banana clip into the AK-47, carefully disengaging the safety mechanism as Big Lou had demonstrated to him.

The Cutlass pulled into the intersection of 43rd and Avenue H. Crooked Tony flicked the high beams once, then killed the lights altogether. Just as Vikki and Stacy had been instructed to do each time they had driven the Cutlass to the trey.

A young man stepped from the crowd waving a Kansas City Chief baseball cap in the direction of the Cutlass.

Crooked Tony drove directly for the unsuspecting Blood gang member, who was now stepping from the curb and into the street.

Pooney lifted the barrel of the AK-47 so as to be ready to stick it out the window.

"Deuce-nine, cuz!" Larry screamed as he fired the first shot.

The young man with the ball cap in his hand stopped cold in his tracks at the sound of Larry's voice. It was too late. Pooney could swear that he saw the boy's entire right arm leap from his body.

Pooney, heart beating rapidly and unable to breath, pointed his weapon into the scattering crowd. He squeezed the AK-47's trigger over and over and over again.

The Cutlass was stationary as Crooked Tony gave his co-workers enough time to spend their rounds. Pooney was having an impossible time fixing on a target through the mass of rapidly moving arms and legs. He was intent, however, on getting a confirmed hit.

Crooked Tony threw the Cutlass in reverse and moved rapidly in an attempt to follow the running boys. Once at the corner, Tony turned right, still trailing the crowd. Pooney counted three bodies on the ground, two were moving. Someone else was moving in the shadows alongside Rowe's grocery store. An injured man, limping badly, reached for the wall to steady himself while the trail of blood grew longer behind him.

"Get him Pooney!" Larry encouraged as the Cutlass pulled up behind the wounded warrior. "I'm outta bullets."

Pooney stuck the barrel out the window once more and pointed it at the man. Sensing his imminent demise, the injured man tried to move faster, but it was useless. He was badly injured.

"What you waitin' for?" Larry yelled. "Bust his ass!"

The wounded man fell to his knees, attempting to cover his head with his arms.

Pooney aimed the gun at him, closed his eyes, and pulled the trigger. Nothing. He pulled again. The gun was jammed.

"Shoot the bitch, Pooney!" Larry yelled.

"Here." Crooked Tony handed Pooney the .357.

Pooney jumped from the car and moved swiftly for the prone man. He did not want to miss.

"Now that's what I'm talkin' about!" Larry applauded. "Some big-time gangsta shit!"

Pooney, now five feet away from the man, pointed the .357 and cocked the hammer.

"Please don't shoot me, Allen," the injured man begged.

Pooney's heart froze upon hearing his name.

"It's me, man." The wounded man looked directly into Pooney's face. "Herbert."

A million thoughts ran through Pooney's mind at once, yet none proved murderous. He slowly lowered the weapon to his side and uncocked the gun.

"What the fuck you doing?" Larry yelled.

Crooked Tony blew the horn.

Pooney could taste the salt as tears ran along both cheeks into the corners of his mouth.

"Thank you," Herbert whispered softly, his eyes glazed, and his voice weak.

Pooney turned and walked slowly for the Cutlass. The sirens in the background were of little consequence to him.

"Get yo' crazy ass in the car!" Larry was angry.

Pooney took his seat without a word to anyone.

Crooked Tony sped off, turning right on Winnie, and heading east at a high rate of speed.

Pooney shut his eyes as tightly as he could, but the tears kept coming. He would never forget what he had just done.

(3)

Cheryl Dawkins rolled out of her bed. Although the extremely persistent knocker had awakened her more than ten minutes ago, she had remained in bed hoping that the early morning visitor would realize they were calling at the wrong door. They had not.

Ms. Dawkins reached for an oversized T-shirt to cover the bra and panties in which she slept. She hit the light on the nightstand. The clock read 3:35.

The knocker knocked harder.

"Coming," Ms. Dawkins called to the door while wondering what poor soul was lost in the steady downpour that battered The Island.

Ms. Dawkins placed her eye against the peephole. She stared harder, although she had already identified the knocker as Allen Richards. She hurriedly disengaged the deadbolt locks, then snatched the door open.

"What in the world are you doing here?" Ms. Dawkins grabbed Pooney's arm and pulled him inside. "You're soaked and wet."

Pooney didn't say a word.

"You OK, Allen?" Ms. Dawkins could see that there was something very wrong with Allen Richards.

Pooney grabbed Ms. Dawkins with both arms, holding on for dear life.

"It's OK now." Ms. Dawkins knew that asking questions at this point would be useless. "It's OK, sweetheart."

Allen Richards cried out loudly as whatever resolve he may have possessed just moments before dissipated completely. The young boy bawled uncontrollably now.

"You're OK now," Ms. Dawkins assured as she struggled to hold on to him despite the powerful spasms that shook his body. "Everything's OK"

Pooney tried in vain to shake the images from his mind of the explosion that had caused another youngster's arm to leap from his body, of the sheer terror in the faces of the running, screaming young boys caught on the wrong end of the gun barrels, of the writhing bodies, flapping on the ground, squealing like wounded animals, of the motionless body whose head was submerged in a pool of its own blood. Of Herbert, wounded and weak, left with strength enough only to beg for his life. Pooney tried in vain to forget that he had been responsible for it all.

"Let's see if I can find you some dry clothes before you freeze to death." Ms. Dawkins kissed her ex-student on the cheek before pulling away from him.

Pooney watched Ms. Dawkins as she walked down the hallway. She stopped momentarily to adjust the thermostat, then disappeared beyond his sight. Pooney used the bottom of his shirt to dry his eyes, suddenly embarrassed about crying in the arms of a beautiful woman.

A quick survey of the living room only served to reinforce what Pooney already knew about Ms. Dawkins. Her home was immaculately clean. The black leather sofa and loveseat set was classy but inexpensive. A beige-colored recliner was positioned directly in front of the television, the remote resting on the armrest. All four walls were filled with various sized pictures of people who Pooney could only assume were family. The brown oak table had a three-sectioned picture frame atop it. All three sections contained pictures of the same young boy during various stages of his life. In one picture, the young boy was a Cub Scout with a brilliant smile, a smile bearing a striking resemblance to Ms. Dawkins's. In the second picture, he was a fisherman, pole in one hand, small mouth bass in the other. In the third picture, the boy was number thirty-three, football tucked under one arm, the other arm positioned as if delivering a stiff arm. Pooney lifted the pictures from the table and studied them closely. There was no mistaking the resemblance.

"That's Derrick." Ms. Dawkins returned with a towel and some clothing.

"Your brother?" Pooney placed the pictures back on the table.

"That's right." Ms. Dawkins nodded. "These clothes were his. They may be a little big for you."

"Looks like he knew how to hold the rock." Pooney was trying to recapture his swagger. "Was he a running back?"

"Yes." Ms. Dawkins sighed heavily.

"Any good?" Pooney asked.

"All-State." She grabbed the picture from the table. "Two years in a row."

"What college did he go to?"

"He never made it to college."

"Bad grades?"

"No, Allen, bad choices."

"What?"

"Derrick was killed a month after taking this picture." Ms. Dawkins pointed at the picture of Derrick in his football uniform. "He and some friends got into a fight at a party. Derrick was stabbed in the heart."

"Man." Pooney was shook up all over again.

"I know." Ms. Dawkins placed the pictures back in their spot on the table then pointed. "The bathroom is through the bedroom. Turn right down the hallway."

Pooney struggled down the hallway toward the bedroom, his burdens growing heavier by the second. *At least I'm free,* he said to console himself while closing the bathroom door behind him.

CHAPTER 23

"Taye said she's ready, Mama." Sheila hung up the phone.

"What are you telling me for?" Regina quipped lightheartedly. "I'm not driving."

"Taye said she ready, Renee." Sheila was all smiles.

"I'm ready if y'all are." Renee stood and tucked her purse under her arm.

"I'm going to be stylin' this year." Sheila had never been so excited to go shopping for school clothes. "With Taye helping me pick out my clothes, I can't wait."

"You just make sure you call Mr. Roy and thank him," Regina said.

Coach Roy had given Regina full access to his credit cards to aid her in purchasing school clothes for her kids. He had instructed Regina to spend whatever was necessary.

"I already thanked him, Mama," Sheila pleaded.

"Thank him again," Regina snapped. Not so much at Sheila, but because she was finding herself to be quite uncomfortable at having accepted financial aid from a man after having been the sole provider for herself, and her kids, for such a long time.

"Yeah, mama." Renee, fully understanding of her best friend's awkwardness, put her arm around Sheila. "That was a very nice thing to do."

"I know Renee, but I..." Sheila's sentence was cut short by a tap on the shoulder, then the wink of Renee's eye.

"I'll call him as soon as we get back." Sheila smiled.

"Let me tell Pooney we're leaving." Regina started for her son's bedroom.

"I'll tell him." Sheila spun out of Renee's grasp and ran by her mother.

"That boy don't do nothing, but sleep," Regina complained.

"Maybe Ms. Taye is expecting," Renee joked.

"I told you about that stuff, Renee," Regina said.

"Pooney! Pooney! I'm talking to you, stupid!" Sheila yelled into Pooney's open bedroom door. "Mama told me to tell you we're leaving...Forget you, too, punk! Bye!" Sheila slammed the door closed.

"Girl." Renee laughed. "What in the world are you going to do with these characters?"

"I don't know," Regina answered. "But I'll be glad when they're both grown."

Thus, acting was added to Sheila's growing list of talents. Wanting desperately to assure that she and Taye remained the only two people in the family who knew that Pooney had not come home last night, Sheila had just given the performance of a lifetime.

"Let's go." Sheila skipped all the way to the front door. "Taye's waiting."

"Taye's waiting," Renee mimicked as she and Regina followed Sheila from the apartment.

(2)

Pressed for time, Taye moved quickly inside her bathroom. She turned on the shower, then stood in front of the sink while the water ran. A quick glance into the mirror revealed what Taye already knew. Her hair was a mess, and her face even worse. While spending the last few days constantly worrying about her mother and Pooney's problems, Taye had totally neglected herself. And while really not up to an afternoon of shopping, she did not want to disappoint Sheila again.

Chantaye pulled the nightgown she was wearing over her head and discarded it on the floor. She unhooked the clasp on her bra and threw it next to the gown. She then slid the black panties she wore down the length of her slender legs until she was able to step out of them.

The cool water from the shower was a welcome relief to Taye's heat-ravaged body. Her mother's latest crack spree had resulted in both air conditioning units being sold on the streets. Their home was a virtual inferno.

School would be starting in three weeks. Taye smiled. That would be less time she would have to spend near her mother. Nine and a half months from now, she would be a high school graduate, at which time she would put as much distance between herself and her mother as humanly possible.

Taye would have loved to spend all day in the shower, but was only working with minutes. She stepped from the tub, grabbed a towel from the rack, and slowly wiped at her body. She hadn't even begun to dress when she heard the knock at the door.

"Shit!" Taye quickly donned a fresh set of underwear.

The knocks at the door grew more intense as Taye ran to the door with shorts and blouse in hand. She stopped at the door and slipped into the clothing before reaching for the doorknob.

"Damn Sheila, you knock like a man." Taye snatched the door open. Slightly startled by what she saw, Taye pulled on the bottom of her blouse to cover her body.

Kyle, another one of Barbara Johnson's boyfriends, was dressed for severe weather in a two-piece yellow rain suit, and large black rain boots. His more than mini-fro was tangled and nappy, and his open mouth moved in constant motion, although nothing was inside it.

"You got early warning of the next hurricane or something?" Taye shook her head at the ridiculously overdressed man.

"Where's Barbara?" Kyle asked.

"She's not here," Taye answered. "I'll tell her you came by."

Kyle started forward. Taye tried to close the door on him, but was too late.

"Barbara!" Kyle pushed Taye aside and stepped inside the house.

Taye stood helplessly as the unwanted guest examined every nook and cranny of her home, fruitlessly calling her mother's name.

"Where's Barbara?" Kyle returned to the living room.

"I told you she ain't here." Taye was angry.

Kyle reached in his pocket and pulled out a small, glass, cylindrical object. Taye recognized the object. It was a crack pipe. In his other hand was a lighter.

"I know you're not about to smoke that shit in my house." Taye put her hands on her hips.

"It wouldn't be the first time," Kyle answered.

"My mama ain't here," Taye protested. "You could at least have a little respect for me."

"Ain't nobody botherin' you." Kyle placed the pipe in his mouth, then flicked the lighter. He placed the flame to the opposite end of the pipe and sucked slowly. The sizzling and sucking sound made by the burning crack rock made Taye's stomach sick.

She stormed by Kyle and returned to bathroom. She combed her hair back while mumbling obscenities to herself. She placed a hair band on the top of her head then applied just a tinge of mocha colored lipstick to her lips.

Kyle's reflection suddenly loomed behind hers in the mirror. He didn't say anything, just stared at Taye with the wide-eyed blankness of a crack smoker.

"What you want now?" Taye spoke into the mirror.

"Wanna drive my car?" Kyle moved closer to Taye, pressing himself against her.

"I got a ride already." Taye spun quickly around Kyle and dashed for the bedroom closet. She grabbed a pair of Nike Crosstrainers and kept moving until she was in the living room.

"Oh, it's like that now." Kyle made it to the living room, the crack pipe still in his hand.

"I need to lock up the house so I can wait outside for my ride, Kyle." Taye jingled her house keys to emphasize her point.

Kyle ignored her, his one hundred percent attention now on the crack pipe that was once again in his mouth.

Taye grabbed her purse, walked for the door and opened it before saying, "Let's go."

Kyle dropped the pipe on the floor and ran toward Taye. Now sweating like a madman, Kyle slammed the door shut.

"Aw man, I don't believe this shit." Taye had been through this with her mother too many times to count. "Muthafucka, don't start trippin'."

Kyle peered through the peephole before turning toward Taye. "Feel my heart." He stepped away from the door clutching his chest with both hands.

"You ought to know smoking crack makes your heart pump faster, dumb ass!" Taye was furious.

Kyle reached forward and touched the skin of Taye's chest.

"What the hell do you think you're doing?" Taye slapped at Kyle's hand.

"You oughtta know that smokin' crack makes a man horny." Kyle massaged his crotch.

"Uh uh, muthafucka." Taye stepped around him. "It's definitely time for your ass to go now."

Kyle grabbed her by the arm and swung her around. "I got some money."

Taye swung instinctively, striking Kyle in the face with her purse.

Kyle, undaunted, and still clinging to Taye's arm, smiled wickedly. "I knew you liked it rough."

Taye unfastened her purse, but before she could get her hand inside, Kyle snatched the purse away from her and threw it to the floor.

"C'mon, baby. I'ma give you what you want." Kyle clamped onto both of her arms.

Taye kicked her assailant between the legs. The blow didn't faze him. She struggled to free herself from Kyle's grasp, but he was too strong.

Kyle continued to backpedal slowly, pulling Taye with him as he did. Taye responded by raking her fingernails across Kyle's face.

The struggle escalated. Kyle tried in vain to pull the girl toward the bedroom, while Taye fought twice as hard to make it to the front door. Neither combatant could budge the other.

Kyle released her suddenly, and Taye went sprawling backward. Before she could react, Kyle clutched one of her ankles in both hands, dragging her across the floor.

"Somebody help me!" Taye screamed while kicking wildly.

Kyle managed to keep his grasp despite Taye's frantic struggle. "C'mon, baby, quit trippin'."

Taye held desperately to the wall that framed the door. Kyle jerked violently, finally giving up on the notion of pulling her to the back of the house and jumping on top of her.

Taye raised her knee as Kyle came crashing down on her. She pushed him off, then rolled over onto her hands and knees. She kicked Kyle hard in the face before leaping to her feet.

Kyle grabbed Taye's leg and pulled her back onto the floor. He used the waistband of her shorts to pull her near him. The crack-raged man then punched the young girl repeatedly in the face.

Taye kicked and screamed to no avail. Her hand gripped the small porcelain statue of the Virgin Mary that had fallen from the coffee table. In one swift motion, Taye smashed the statue against Kyle's head.

Still unfazed, Kyle made another mighty tug at the girl's shorts, ripping them from her body. He punched her twice more in the face, then snatched her legs open at the knees before climbing on top of her.

"Nooooo!" Taye continued to fight.

Kyle hit Taye with an open hand, then clamped the same palm over her mouth. He pinned her against the floor with a knee to the chest while pulling her underwear below her knees. Kyle stretched out atop of her once more. He pressed his face against hers.

Taye clamped her teeth onto Kyle's bottom lip and squeezed as hard as she could.

(3)

"Ms. Taye must be in there primping and thangs." Renee pressed the horn for the fourth time.

"I'll get her," Sheila volunteered.

"No." Renee wanted to see just how filthy Barbara Johnson was living. "I'll get her."

Renee stepped from the car and strode toward the house. She marched slowly through the open gate then up the stairs leading to the porch. The screen door was wide open and the window door ajar.

"Chantaye, baby, you in there?" Renee knocked twice on the door, then pushed it open. There was no answer. And no sound came from inside.

"Chantaye?" Renee stepped inside the house.

A sound like heavy breathing was coming from the back of the house. Renee hurried in that direction. She turned down the hallway and almost tripped on the crumpled body lying in the middle of the floor.

"Oh my God!" Renee was taken aback by the ghastly sight before her. "Reginaaaaaa!"

Chantaye was a battered mess. Blood was still running from her nose and mouth. Her right eye was completely closed and there were patches of drying blood in her hair. Her clothes had been ripped from her body, displaying an assortment of bruises and abrasions.

"He tried," Taye sobbed heavily. "He tried to."

"Reginaaaa!" Renee kneeled beside the battered girl. It's OK, baby."

"He tried to." Chantaye was finding it difficult to catch her breath.

"I know, baby." Renee held Taye in her arms. "I know."

"Jesus Christ." Regina appeared in the hallway.

"What's wrong?" Sheila struggled to see around Regina.

"Get back in the car, Sheila!" Regina yelled.

"What's wrong with Chantaye?" Sheila wanted to know.

"Do what your mother says, mama!" Renee was crying now.

"Jesus, what happened?" Regina backed against the wall then slid down the length of it until she was seated on the floor.

"Kyle, my mother's friend." Chantaye's body trembled. "I didn't let him. I fought him."

"No one's gonna hurt you now, baby." Renee rocked gently back and forth. "I promise."

"We gotta call the police." Regina stood suddenly. She, too, was crying.

"No." Taye shook her head.

"We have to, honey," Regina reasoned. "You can't let anyone get away with something like this."

Taye shook her head again. "My mama."

Regina and Renee eyed each other knowingly.

"You don't want your mother to get in trouble?" Renee held Chantaye closer.

Taye shook her head again.

"The hospital's going to call the police," Regina said.

"We're not going to the hospital." Renee spoke calmly.

"What are you talking about, Renee?" Regina was flabbergasted. "Look at her."

"She doesn't want to go to the hospital." Renee kissed the top of Chantaye's blood stained head. "Nothing's broken and he didn't penetrate her."

"Renee, we have to do something," Regina said.

"We are," Renee answered. "We're going to pack Chantaye's things and she's going home with me."

All was quiet except for Taye's heartfelt sobs.

"Taye?" Regina called softly.

Taye raised her head in Regina's direction.

"Did he penetrate you?" Regina asked bluntly.

"Uh uh." Taye shook her head then buried her face deep within Renee's bosom.

"Do you think anything's broken?" Regina asked.

"I don't think so," Taye answered.

"Which way is your room?" Regina asked.

Taye pointed in the direction of the bedroom.

"I'll start packing." Regina stepped over the two of them and headed for Chantaye's bedroom.

(4)

Pooney guzzled greedily at the bottle of Cisco, but nothing seemed capable of filling the huge void he felt in the pit of his stomach. Not the full country breakfast Ms. Dawkins fixed for him, complete with pancakes, scrambled eggs, grits, and summer sausage. Not the forty-ounce of Schlitz Malt Liquor Bull he drank just minutes after bidding Ms. Dawkins farewell. And not the shelf-warmed bottle of Cisco he drank now.

Last night, what little sleep Pooney was able to get served as brief intermissions for the continuously running tape that battered his tortured conscience. The constantly flashing images of urban warfare casualties set to the tone of Herbert's pitifully pleading voice, proved much too much to bear. Well before daybreak, Pooney had abandoned the blanket and pillow Ms. Dawkins had placed on the couch for him and positioned himself in the recliner. He was able to catch a Sports Center rebroadcast from the night before.

While eating breakfast with Ms. Dawkins, Pooney's pager began to vibrate. The message was 2-9.

Before leaving Ms. Dawkins's house, Pooney used the telephone to call Sheila and tell her that he would be home as soon as he took care of one last piece of business. Though first voicing her concern, Sheila agreed to cover for him a little longer.

"Keep the change." Pooney handed the cab driver a twenty-dollar bill.

"Thank you." The cab driver took the money.

Pooney stepped from the cab. The afternoon sun attacked him immediately as the beads of sweat gathered on his brow.

"C'mon." Big Lou stood in the door.

Pooney took the stairs two at a time, then slid by the lieutenant.

Larry and Tony were seated on the couch with Moe. No one else was present.

"I'm out." Pooney got right to the point. "Right?"

"You what?" Moe's scowl would have frightened the bravest of soldiers.

"I'm out," Pooney repeated with equal intensity.

"You out, all right." Moe stood and met Pooney in the middle of the floor. "Out of yo' muthafuckin' mind!"

"I handled my business! That's it!" Pooney drank from his bottle. "Tell 'em, Tony."

The Crooked Tony Shrug.

"You ain't handled shit!" Moe slapped the bottle from Pooney's hand. "You killed a civilian."

"Fuck you!" Pooney kicked the bottle.

"What the fuck did you say?" Moe stepped closer.

"Chill out, Moe," Big Lou intervened.

"On top of that," Moe continued, "you killed a dope-fiend."

"Look, man," Pooney spoke slowly. "All I know is I handled my business.

"Then," Moe went on as if Pooney hadn't said a word, "you let the slob muthafucka make it after he saw your face."

Pooney's mind replayed Herbert's plea once more.

"That cat can put all three of y'all away for good," Big Lou added calmly.

Pooney realized the seriousness of the situation, but as of present, only one thing mattered. "I'm out, Moe."

"Ain't nobody out of shit!" Moe yelled at him. "So, you might as well get that in yo' muthafuckin' mind!"

"I'm out." Pooney turned to leave. "Get that in yo' mind."

Moe punched Pooney in the back of the head, sending him flying toward the door.

Pooney braced himself against the doorframe, then spun himself around. Big Lou's large body stood between Pooney and Moe.

(5)

"Hello." Sheila answered the phone on the first ring.

"Sheila," Janeen screamed in her ear.

"Hey girl." Sheila didn't feel much like conversing with Janeen.

"Your brother there?" There was an unusual amount of anxiousness in Janeen's voice.

"No. Why?"

"Did he do it?" Janeen's voice was a whisper now.

"Do what?"

"I don't know why I asked you, anyway," Janeen snapped. "Pooney don't tell you nothing."

"Janeen, what are you talking about?"

"First, promise you won't tell Pooney I told you."

"I promise." After all that happened in the last hour, Sheila was finding it extremely difficult to maintain patience with her friend.

"Your brother killed somebody last night." Janeen was whispering again.

"What?" Sheila screamed.

"I was just at my friend Rachel's house." Janeen played reporter. "And her brother said Pooney, that crazy boy with the nappy hair, and that ugly boy with the crooked teeth, did a drive-by on Four-trey."

"You sure, Janeen?" Sheila's heart was pounding in her head.

"Yeah," Janeen said, then waited. "Somethin' else, too."

"What, Janeen?"

"They say they put a contract on your brother and his friends," Janeen said.

"A contract?"

"And that boy you like, Moe," Janeen kept on. "They say they're gonna kill him, too, because he set it up. They say they're getting their crew together right now."

"OK, Janeen, look," Sheila was shaking uncontrollably, "I'll talk to you later."

"Tell Pooney to be careful."

"OK."

"Bye." Janeen hung up.

Sheila held the button on the phone while plotting her next move. She released the button and dialed Pooney's pager number.

Sheila hung up the phone and sat back on the couch, her head spinning from the impact of Janeen's statements.

Seconds later, Sheila picked up the phone and dialed frantically. "I need a cab at 7200 Heards Lane, Back Bay Apartments, by the mailbox," Sheila told the yellow cab dispatcher. "Yes, ma'am...OK."

Sheila grabbed her purse and her mother's house keys from the table, and ran for the door.

(6)

"Let's do this!" The four young men broke from the huddle and ran for the '72 Impala. "That punk won't get away from me this time," Lil' Arthur, armed with a fully automatic Mac 10, declared from the passenger seat of the Impala.

"None of them crab ass muthafuckas." Peanut puffed on the Black 'n' Mild while starting the car.

"Goddamn right." E-Dog, the tall, lanky brother with the AR-15 stretched across his lap, sat behind Lil' Arthur.

The fourth passenger, Fat Dexter, remained silent while clutching the .41 caliber semi-automatic pistol.

Of the four in the car, only Fat Dexter had been present when the assault on the 'hood went down. He was the only one who had witnessed firsthand the trail of destruction left by the rival Deuce-nine Crips. The only one who had stood face to face with death less than twelve hours before. At this morning's meeting, Fat Dexter had insisted upon being part of the hit squad assigned the task of retaliatory attacks on Deuce-nine.

The Impala traveled slowly down the back road known to Islanders as Backtrack.

"They'll never expect us to hit the clubhouse." The thought amused Lil' Arthur.

"One thing's for sure," Peanut said as he held the Black 'n' Mild in his hand, "whoever's in that muthafucka'll never hear about it." The hit squad laughed as the Impala pressed on.

(7)

"Look, Pooney." Tony stood up. "Moe might not be tellin' it to you the way you want to hear it man, but we fucked up."

Pooney didn't answer.

"And right now, Pooney," Crooked Tony explained, "you ain't got no choice but to hang tight. It's gonna be war now."

"You ain't got a chance by yourself," Big Lou added.

"What the fuck you tryin' to dis' Deuce-nine for anyway?" Larry joined in.

Pooney went from face to face while considering the words of each man in the room. Admittedly, he had not given much thought to the aftermath of his actions. And possibly, the others did have his best interests at heart. But Pooney had no intention of being a member of the Deuce-nine Crips or any other gang ever again. "I'm out," Pooney repeated once more while staring directly into Moe's eyes. "And if anybody in here has a problem with that, let's take it outside."

"Fuck that shit!" Moe raised up his shirt, flashing a heavy caliber revolver, before snatching it from his waistband and handing it to Big Lou. "I'm fixin' to beat the shit out this lil' bitch!"

Pooney lunged through the clubhouse door, pulling off his shirt while running down the stairs. Once in the front yard, he turned to await the arrival of his opponent.

Big Lou came through the door first, followed by Moe, with Tony and Larry bringing up the rear.

"You didn't learn your lesson last time, huh?" Moe squared up with the teenage boy.

"Y'all need to stall that shit out, man," Larry said. "We all Locs."

"I ain't." Pooney held his fist in a fighting position.

(8)

"Pooney!" Sheila jumped from the cab while it was still moving.

Pooney's fists went to his sides as he turned toward the street. "What the hell you doing here?"

"Pooney," Sheila was out of breath when she exploded through the gate. "You gotta leave! All y'all gotta leave! They're coming!"

"Who's comin', Sheila?" Moe grabbed the frightened girl.

"Get yo' muthafuckin' hands off my sister!" Pooney shoved Moe hard.

"I know somebody better gimme my fare," the potbellied cabdriver demanded as he entered the fracas.

"I'm sorry." Sheila reached in her pocket. "I forgot to tell you I was picking somebody up."

"Put yo' hands on me again and it'll be the worst mistake you ever made, punk!" Moe threatened Pooney.

"Y'all chill, man." Big Lou was getting angry. "The girl got something to say."

"Here." Sheila handed the cab driver eight dollars.

"I need more if you want me to wait," the cabdriver said.

"Here, man." Moe gave the man ten dollars. "Now get yo' crazy ass in the cab and shut up!"

The cab driver stared at Moe as if to size him up, but quickly thought better of any further action. "The meter is running," he told Sheila before returning to his cab.

"OK, Sheila," Big Lou said. "Who's coming?"

"Four-trey!" Sheila was hysterical again. "C'mon, Pooney, let's go. They say they got contracts on all y'all."

"Did they say what for?" Big Lou was still calm as he questioned Sheila.

"They say my brother killed somebody last night." Sheila struggled through the last statement.

Silence prevailed as the five men considered the impact of what Sheila had just said.

"C'mon, Pooney, please." Sheila pleaded while tugging at her brother's arm. "Let's go."

"Look, Sheila." Pooney took her hand in both of his. "I want you to go straight home and wait for me there."

"Come with me, Pooney." Sheila couldn't help the tears.

"Do what I said," Pooney yelled loudly while pushing Sheila toward the gate.

"Say, Pooney, look out!" Crooked Tony leapt desperately in Pooney's direction, grabbing him by the arm and flinging him toward the clubhouse.

(9)

"Fo'-trey, muthafucka!" The Impala came roaring down the street with Lil' Arthur and E-Dog sitting atop the front and rear passenger side doors. Guns aimed over the top of the car, they opened fire on the small crowd standing in front of the clubhouse. Fat Dexter positively identified Pooney standing at the gate and aimed the .41 caliber pistol directly at him.

Pooney held tightly onto Sheila's arm as the gunfire erupted before them. He ran for the clubhouse, searching for something, anything, that could provide protection from the hailstorm of bullets.

Fire ran across the side of Pooney's head, just above his ear, just as someone tripped him from behind, sending him crashing headfirst into the base of the stairway.

Pooney heard only the screeching sound of rubber burning against the pavement, followed by an unearthly silence, then complete and total darkness.

The fallen boy struggled to raise his head. Through blurred vision, he could see that a puddle of blood was forming on the ground next to where his head had landed. He watched as the constant red drips caused the puddle to grow rapidly, realizing the blood was his own.

"Aw, naw!" Pooney heard a familiar voice, maybe Larry's, yelling loudly. "Hell naw!" Pooney tried to get up but a heavy weight pinned his legs to the ground.

"Tonyyyyy!" The distraught voice did indeed belong to Larry. "Y'all muthafuckas get an ambulance, man!"

Pooney turned to see the weight on his legs.

"I'm hit, too!" Pooney heard Moe's voice. "Fuck!"

Pooney's heart stood still upon discovering that the weight on his legs was Sheila. Though she spoke no words, the glossy, wide-eyed gaze the young girl wore posed a multitude of questions to her older brother.

"Oh God, no." Pooney eased his legs from under his sister and kneeled beside her. "You OK, Sheila?"

"It burns, Pooney." Sheila spoke softly. Pooney shuddered when he saw the large wound in the center of his sister's back.

"You're gonna be all right." He was unconvincing.

Pooney turned to someone for help, but the other men were just standing around. Tony had yet to rise off the ground.

"Pooney." Sheila's voice was weakening.

"Yes, Sheila." Pooney positioned himself so that he could no longer see his sister's wounds.

"Mama's gonna be mad at me, ain't she?"

"No, Sheila." Pooney could hear the all too familiar sound of sirens. "Help is on the way. Don't worry."

"You're bleeding, Pooney." Sheila looked at her brother.

"I'm OK." Pooney winced as the sirens grew rapidly closer, aggravating a headache that Pooney had not even realized he had.

Moments later, police cars, ambulances, and fire trucks were everywhere.

"Wait here." Pooney staggered toward the first paramedic he saw.

"Sir, could you sit down, please." A young white woman placed her hands on Pooney's shoulders and guided him gently toward the ground.

"My sister needs help." Pooney pointed behind him.

"Don't worry," the woman assured him. "Everyone's gonna get the best help possible."

"Please help my sister," Pooney begged as the endless number of city vehicles continued to pile up in front of the clubhouse. The number of spectators was also multiplying rapidly.

"We got a serious chest wound over here," Pooney could hear a frantic voice yell.

"Notify John Sealy," an authoritative voice barked. "Advise them we are en route with multiple gunshot victims."

"Just relax." The paramedic pushed Pooney onto his back.

Pooney stared at the cloudless blue sky as a helicopter hovered overhead. Everything began to spin rapidly, causing him to become nauseated. The sounds of the emergency personnel working behind him were terrifying. Pooney closed his eyes, offering a fervent prayer to God.

"Lift." Pooney felt himself being lifted off the ground and placed on something soft. He opened his eyes long enough to see the same female paramedic strapping him onto the stretcher.

"My sister?" Pooney asked the woman.

"She's halfway to John Sealy by now." The paramedic rolled the stretcher toward a waiting ambulance. "Now, let's get you there."

The stretcher with Pooney on it was placed in the back of the ambulance. The female paramedic and a much older, bearded man climbed into the back of the ambulance with Pooney.

"Please, Lord," Pooney spoke aloud as the ambulance raced on. "Take care of my sister."

CHAPTER 24

The days leading up to the funeral passed with a blur. The constant questioning by the doctors and policemen that frequented Pooney's hospital room left him both frightened and exhausted. And while Pooney's physical injuries were minor, his emotional pain was great.

The anguish seen in his mother's face during her brief visits to his hospital room was enough to break Pooney's heart. And the questions. Not the spoken ones. They were much easier. But the distant and pained stare in Regina's eyes presented the same questions to Pooney that Sheila had five days earlier. Questions that Pooney would never be able to answer.

Then there was Taye, who had spent every moment of Pooney's hospital stay curled up in a small chair next to his bed. Her bruised and swollen face was of much less consequence to her than the tragedy that had befallen the Richards' household.

Through it all, a rage had developed in Pooney the likes of which should never have been possible. Pooney vowed not to rest until Kyle, and every slob muthafucka in the '72 Impala, had expired.

"How y'all doing today?" A stern-faced man in a dark suit held the door for Pooney and Chantaye as they entered Field's funeral home.

The lobby of the funeral home was cold and quiet. A handful of people stood in line to sign the visitor's log. An organ could be heard in the distance.

"Sign the sheet while I get us a program," Pooney said.

Pooney approached the distinguished looking gentleman who was dressed similarly to the man at the front door.

"Thank you." Pooney accepted the program from the smiling man.

Pooney turned, then took a moment to observe Chantaye. She was striking in the simple, ankle-length, black dress she wore. Even with the Versace sunglasses and multiple layers of make-up that didn't quite hide the bruises which still remained on her face, Chantaye was definitely a beauty. Inside and out. Pooney would never understand why Taye would think that Kyle's attempted rape would cause him to think any less of her.

Pooney returned to his woman's side just as she reached for the gold-colored pen lying next to the visitor's log. On the next available line, Taye signed "Mr. and Mrs. Allen Richards."

"You ready, baby?" Taye turned to him once finished.

Pooney nodded but didn't move. A part of him wanted to turn and run, to put as much distance between himself and the funeral as possible. But he had to say goodbye.

"It's OK." Taye seized his hand and led him through the double doors.

Pooney was surprised by the number of people already seated. He had expected much less. Every head in the room turned at once when Pooney and Taye entered the room. Pooney purposely avoided all eye contact. He simply could not endure the condemnation he would surely see.

Pooney stared down the center aisle. At the end of the aisle lay the open casket. Pooney stopped suddenly. Taye squeezed his hand, reaffirming her presence and giving him the courage to continue forward.

A hand went up from Pooney and Taye's left as Larry motioned for them to join him.

"I saved y'all seats." Larry and Leticia stood to allow Taye and Pooney's passing. Pooney had never seen Larry so well groomed. He was wearing a pair of brown slacks, a white shirt, and a black tie. His hair was neatly French-braided, and he was clean-shaven. With his girlfriend and son at his side, Larry could have passed for a completely different individual, if not for the familiar stench of alcohol coming from his direction.

"Thank you." Pooney looked into Larry's bloodshot eyes. The pain was unbelievable.

"The police been fuckin' with you?" Larry asked.

"Yeah," Pooney answered. "You?"

"Yeah." Larry leaned close to Pooney. "Don't tell 'em shit! They ain't got nothin'!"

"OK." Pooney nodded.

"They don't give a damn who gets smoked in the 'hood anyway, lil' Loc," Larry continued. "Shit'll blow over, you'll see."

Pooney shifted in his seat. He looked to the right side of the room. Moe, immaculately dressed in a Versace suit, had his arm in a sling. He was accompanied by a full four rows of Deuce-nine Crips. The soldiers all wore blue Dallas Cowboys jerseys.

Pooney turned toward the casket, finally daring to take a peek inside. A storm brewed in the young boy's heart, but he could not cry. In fact, Pooney hadn't shed one tear in the last four days.

"Looks like he's sleepin', huh?" Larry held a stick of Wrigley's in Pooney's direction.

"Yeah." Pooney placed the gum in his mouth.

The organ player changed songs, a similarly depressing tune made exclusively for mourners.

Even in death, the smirk of a smile on Crooked Tony's face was capable of providing comfort during the most tumultuous of times. Tony was also dressed in a Dallas Cowboys jersey. Number eighty-eight. A large, gold rope chain with brilliantly shining diamonds cut into it was wrapped around Tony's neck.

When first informed of Tony's death, Pooney had simply refused to believe what he was hearing. Already heartbroken from learning the severity of his sister's injuries, and enraged by the details of Chantaye's ordeal, the death of his best friend proved almost too much for Pooney to bear. It was now, as Pooney peered into the open casket, that he had no choice but to face the harsh reality: Crooked Tony was lost forever.

The organ music stopped and a tall, well-dressed man, draped in white from head to toe, strode to the podium next to the casket. There was something very familiar about the man, but Pooney had yet to put a finger on it.

"You know who that is?" Larry whispered into Pooney's ear.

"He looks familiar," Pooney answered. "Who is it?"

"Your best customer." Larry smirked.

Pooney couldn't believe his eyes. He looked to the program he was holding for confirmation. He found it. The well-dressed man was none other than 28th Street's own Thaddeus Lee Anderson.

"Good afternoon." Thaddeus Lee's deep voice spoke softly. There were murmured greetings from the crowd.

"I wish we could be here under much more pleasant circumstances today, but the Lord had something different in mind."

Pooney was boiling inside. How could a neighborhood crackhead have been chosen to eulogize his best friend? Tony deserved better. Pooney looked around the room to see if anyone else was as upset as he, but to his dismay, everyone else was giving Thaddeus Lee their undivided attention.

"You know, I've done quite a few eulogies in my day, but I have to be honest with you," Thaddeus Lee warmed up. "Nothing I have ever experienced could have prepared me for this day. All the knowledge and experience I thought I had, is absolutely useless." The volume of Thaddeus Lee's voice rose with the intensity of his presentation. "Tragedies like this weren't discussed in those theology classes I bragged about doing so well in."

Pooney's anger subsided as Thaddeus Lee proved himself to be a skilled orator.

"In preparation for this eulogy, I combed through every inch of my Bible in search of just the right scriptures." Thaddeus Lee held a Bible high over his head before placing it on the podium and flipping through it. "Isaiah, Job, Proverbs, Psalms, Mark, John, first and second Corinthians, still I couldn't find what I was looking for." Thaddeus Lee closed the Bible. "I began to get concerned. I said 'God! I have to talk to these people tomorrow and I'm lost!'" The passion erupted. "'What do I say? What do I do? How do I comfort these people after such a terrible thing? How do I comfort myself?'"

The crowd eagerly awaited God's answer to Thaddeus Lee's questions.

"I opened my Bible again." Thaddeus Lee reopened the Bible.

Though Thaddeus Lee's presentation was quite stirring, Pooney found it hard to stay attentive. His thoughts were of Tony, and the life he would never get to live. Pooney thought also of how easily he could have been the one eulogized by Thaddeus Lee. And of how his thirteen-year-old sister, who may never walk again, was lying in a hospital bed after being hit in the back by a .41 caliber bullet meant for her brother. And of how some insane crackhead had beaten Taye to a bloody pulp and tried to rape her. And of how revenge was the only thing he truly had to look forward to now.

Pooney had no idea what had been said, but the thundering ovation grabbed his attention.

Pooney looked across the room to Tony's grandmother. The smallish, cinnamon-colored lady with the head full of snow-white hair dabbed constantly at her eyes. She had taken care of

Tony since infancy, and each of them were the only family the other had left. Pooney almost broke down under the weight of the guilt he felt while staring at the elderly woman. It was his actions that had set forth the chain of events that resulted in her loss.

"You see, Pooney," Thaddeus Lee jarred the young man's mind back to the sermon. "If we don't learn something from Tony's death, then he died for nothing."

There was a chorus of Amens from the crowd.

"Tony's legacy will ultimately be decided by whether or not WE!" Thaddeus Lee jabbed his thumb frantically into his own chest. "The people he loved, are able to use his untimely demise as the catalyst for our newfound desire to live our lives in a way Tony can be proud of."

The roar from the crowd was deafening.

"When I look at this fine young man's lifeless body lying in that casket, I ask myself," Thaddeus Lee walked slowly toward Crooked Tony's casket and stood over it. The crowd watched with hushed anticipation as he bent slowly at the waist, muttering words that only Tony could hear, and kissed the face of the young man's corpse.

Thaddeus Lee turned back to the crowd, tears falling now as he made his way back to the podium. "How much could it have cost Thaddeus Lee? How much could it have possibly have cost me to forget about my own self-destructive indulgences, to set aside my own selfish motives long enough to be the mentor, the brother, the friend, the father that my son, Tony, needed?" Thaddeus Lee seemingly made eye contact with every single parent in the room as the crowd felt the impact of his last statement. "That's right." Thaddeus Lee nodded slowly. "I, Thaddeus Lee Anderson, am father to the deceased."

Pooney was rocked by what was obviously the only secret Tony had ever kept from him. There wasn't a dry eye in the room.

"A lot of you know me, but for those of you who don't, I am a substance abuser. My son, Tony," Thaddeus Lee's voice broke, "was almost as ashamed of me as I was of myself. So, I never embarrassed him by acknowledging to his friends that I was his father."

Not a sound could be heard from the audience.

"I'm going to close now. But before I do, I have one more thing to say." Thaddeus Lee turned to the sea of blue to his left. "My son's death need not be in vain. Let us all heed the wake-up call."

The crowd responded loudly as Thaddeus Lee stepped away from the podium. Even Moe and the hardest of his soldiers were teary-eyed and clapping. Larry, the only person in the room still seated, held his head in both hands while sobbing loudly. The ovation continued as Thaddeus Lee greeted Tony's grandmother with a warm embrace.

The organ player began another impossibly touching tune as Thaddeus Lee led Tony's grandmother in the direction of the casket. Tony's grandmother kissed her last remaining link to this world for one last time before walking away.

A line had formed, and one by one, they all took their turn in front of Crooked Tony's casket for one last look, one last word, one last touch, one last kiss.

Pooney fell into the slow-moving line with Taye at his side. His heart pounded furiously, and his entire body trembled. Taye held his hand tightly. He thanked God for her presence.

The line seemed to be moving faster now. Maybe too fast. Pooney and Taye were next. Pooney took a deep breath in an attempt to brace himself for this dreaded last goodbye. With Taye at his side, Pooney now stood before his best friend's casket.

"Goodbye, Tony." Taye touched Tony's chest.

Pooney stared directly into his best friend's face. Realizing, but not believing that he was seeing Tony for the last time. Pooney's mind was bombarded by the lifetime of memories that would, from here on out, be his only connection to Crooked Tony.

"Say goodbye, baby," Taye urged, not quite sure what to make of the steely silence she was witnessing.

Pooney blinked away the blur and a single teardrop fell onto the side of Crooked Tony's casket. "I'm sorry, Tony!" Pooney placed his head on Tony's chest, his strength exhausted as he heaved heavily from his chest. "I'm sorry, man."

Taye gently touched Pooney's back but remained silent.

"I know I messed everything up," Pooney continued. "I'd take your place if I could man, I swear I would."

Thaddeus Lee approached Pooney from behind and placed both hands on his shoulders. "It's OK, Pooney. He knows."

Pooney stood straight and tall, never taking his eyes from the casket.

"Don't be giving the angels too hard of a time, man." What Pooney wouldn't give to see the Crooked Tony Shrug just once more.

Pooney gathered himself as Taye put her arms around his waist.

"I love you, Tony." Pooney was sure he could see his friend's smile grow broader. "And I'll never forget you, man. Never. Goodbye, Tony."

Pooney, with Taye on one side and Thaddeus Lee on the other, finally stepped away from the casket. He immediately searched the room for Tony's grandmother. Once the woman was in his sights, Pooney walked briskly in her direction. He had to speak with her. He had to tell her just how sorry he was for her loss.

"Big Mama." Once within speaking distance, Pooney called as Tony would. Further words failed him, however, as he collapsed into the old woman's arms.

"I remember you, baby." Big Mama spoke with gentle firmness. "You were always Tony's favorite playmate," Big Mama told him. "All of you boys need to get your lives together. I mean that."

"Yes, ma'am." Pooney found the soft-spoken lecture comforting.

"That's a pretty girl you got there." Big Mama looked to Taye. "You treatin' her right?"

"Yes, ma'am."

"Y'all come by the house after the cemetery and get something to eat," Big Mama instructed. "There'll be cold drinks, too."

"Yes, ma'am," Pooney and Taye answered together.

With no further words, Big Mama turned for the side door, heading for the limousine that would take her to the cemetery.

It was then that Pooney noticed that Larry was still seated.

Pooney stepped in Larry's direction, stopping only to ask Leticia, "What's up?"

"I don't know, but he 'bout to start trippin'." Leticia, baby in arm, brushed by Pooney and Taye. "I'm gone."

"What's wrong, Larry?" Pooney asked.

"Nothing." Larry was bent over with his arms resting on his knees.

"Ain't you gonna say goodbye to Tony?" Pooney was careful with his words.

"I can't." Larry struggled through the tears.

"What you mean?" Pooney was puzzled.

"Can't face him." Larry sat straight up.

"Why not?"

"I gotta handle my business first." Larry began to rock slowly to and fro. "Then I can face Tony."

"Hold up, man." Pooney knew well the business Larry spoke of. And admittedly, a part of Pooney felt the same way. But right now, he was totally incapable of violent thoughts. "What business?"

"What business?" Larry stopped rocking and frowned at Pooney. "You know what business I'm talking about."

Pooney faced forward, the intensity of Larry's gaze getting the best of him. "C'mon, Larry."

"We promised, Pooney. We always promised that if one of us fell, the other two would make it right."

"That's not what Tony would want." Pooney surprised himself.

Larry began rocking again, suddenly oblivious to Pooney's presence.

"We gon' make it right, Tony." Larry spoke aloud. "Then we'll say our goodbyes."

Pooney stood and walked away from his grief stricken partner. He felt for Larry, but had no idea how to help him. The exhausted young man retreated to the security of Chantaye's embrace.

(2)

Regina stood motionless before the plate glass window, the beautiful summer day before her going unnoticed. During the last four days, this spot, at the end of a remote hospital corridor, had become her only sanctuary when the pain of watching her youngest child battle critical gunshot wounds became too much to bear.

Unfortunately, Regina's frequent trips to the window provided her with more than a place to take a much-needed break from the gloom of Sheila's hospital room. The window at the end of the hall was also the place where Regina began questioning everything from her mettle as a parent, to her choice in men, to the existence of God. No matter how she turned the facts around in her head, she had failed her children. And because of it, her son was a street thug she hardly knew, and her daughter might never walk again.

"I've been looking all over for you." Patrick approached from behind and placed both arms around his saddened princess. "I should have known you'd be here."

Regina didn't respond, preferring instead to enjoy the comfort of Patrick's embrace, and hating herself for doing so.

"Hungry?" Patrick leaned into Regina's ear.

Regina shook her head.

"Sure?"

She nodded.

A few seconds passed before Patrick suggested, "Why don't we go to my place, have a drink or something, and relax for a while."

"What?" Regina shook free from Patrick's grasp. "Why don't we what?"

"Calm down, baby." Patrick took a step backward. "I just thought that since Sheila was resting, that you might want to get away from here for a little while."

"I know what you thought!" Regina was incensed, not believing that Patrick could be considering romance at a time like this.

"Relax, Regina," Patrick pleaded. "I'm on your side."

"I know." Regina was touched by the sincerity in Patrick's eyes.

Regina turned back toward the window. Patrick stood beside her, the gulf between them widening with each passing breath.

"Regina," Patrick spoke softly, never turning away from the window. "I know this is a rough time for you, but I want you to know that I love you and I'm here for you."

There was another long silence as Regina debated internally as to whether or not this was the time and place to tell Patrick what she had decided about their relationship.

"I love you too, Patrick," Regina finally stated. "And I appreciate everything you've done for me and my children, but I think it would be better if we didn't see each other for a while."

"What?" The surprise registered clearly in Patrick's face. "We're good together."

"Yes we are, Patrick. Maybe too good," Regina said. "'Cause God knows I haven't been much of a parent lately."

"C'mon Regina. Is that what this is all about?" Patrick turned her around in his direction. "You're blaming yourself for what happened to Sheila?"

"Who else can I blame, Patrick?" Regina argued.

"Allen, that's who!"

"I'm his mother, too, Patrick."

"He acted on his own, Regina. There was nothing you could do."

"Look, Patrick, all I know is that if I were paying closer attention to my son's life, none of this would have happened."

"You are not a superwoman, Regina." Patrick was terribly frustrated.

"No, Patrick, I'm a mama." Regina turned from the window and started walking down the hallway. "And right now my kids need one hundred percent of me. Please try to understand."

Regina took off down the hallway. Patrick made no effort to stop her. He watched sorrowfully as Regina walked further down the hallway, and out of his life. In another time, there was no doubt that Regina Richards would have become Regina Roy. Patrick was willing to wait patiently for that time to come. Even if the wait was forever.

(3)

Pooney sat in the darkness of the living room, hoping that the visitor at the front door would grow weary of knocking and search elsewhere for companionship. "Who is it?" Pooney finally asked once it became evident that whoever was outside his mother's apartment was not going away.

"Ms. Dawkins," was the answer.

Pooney stood slowly. The last thing in the world he wanted was company.

"Hi, Ms. Dawkins." Pooney opened the door.

"Hi, Allen." Ms. Dawkins gave a faint smile. "Can I come in?"

"C'mon." Pooney walked away from the open door and returned to his seat.

Ms. Dawkins stepped inside the apartment and closed the door behind her. The first thing she noticed once inside the living room was that Allen had been sitting in total darkness. Ms. Dawkins stepped to the patio and drew the curtains back halfway, just enough to allow the midday sun to give some illumination to the room.

"How are you feeling?" Ms. Dawkins took a seat on the couch.

"OK," Pooney answered.

"How's your sister doing?" Ms. Dawkins asked.

"Her condition has been upgraded to serious," Pooney answered.

"Keep praying."

"Yeah."

"I'm sorry about your friend's passing."

"Me too."

Ms. Dawkins shuffled in her seat, her mind searching for a way to penetrate the emotion-proof wall standing between herself and Allen Richards. "I'm worried about you, Allen."

"I'm OK." Pooney scratched the new growth of whiskers on his chin.

"You're banging, aren't you, Allen?" Ms. Dawkins asked.

"Naw." Pooney stared straight ahead.

"Look Allen, I'm no fool." Ms. Dawkins slid to the edge of the couch. "The paper reported a drive-by shooting around Palm Terrace about an hour before you showed up at my apartment. Then, half an hour after you leave the next morning, you're involved in a retaliatory shooting around Cedar Terrace."

Pooney declined to argue the obvious. "So what?"

"So, when's the payback?" Ms. Dawkins asked sarcastically.

"You the law?" Pooney was just as adept at sarcasm.

"Of course not."

"What's up with all the questions then?"

"Just concerned."

Pooney nodded appreciatively. Ms. Dawkins was friend, not foe.

"Remember the pictures of my brother you saw?" Ms. Dawkins flipped open the heart shaped locket dangling from her neck. She revealed a small picture of her deceased brother.

"I remember." Pooney observed the picture.

"My brother was an Insane Gangsta Crip. You've heard of the IGC, right?"

"Yeah."

"Well, he and his homeboys had some beef with some locs from another set." Ms. Dawkins wowed Pooney with her knowledge of gang terminology. "It went on so long, nobody even remembered how it started. One side would hit the other, then the retaliation. You know how it goes."

"Yeah." Pooney knew all too well.

"Well, that is how my brother lost his life."

Pooney nodded, fully understanding the theme of Ms. Dawkins's story. He waited a few moments before finally saying, "It's hard, Ms. Dawkins."

"I know it is." Ms. Dawkins touched his hand.

"My sister may never walk again." Pooney was determined not to cry again. "And Tony...Tony was my best friend since kindergarten. How can I let it go like that?"

"It's not about letting anything go, Allen," Ms. Dawkins answered. "Your family needs you now more than ever. What good are you to them behind bars?"

"But everybody's waiting to see what I'll do."

"The hell with everybody, Allen! It's time you matured past the point of worrying about what a bunch of hoodlums are thinking."

"I know." Pooney's determination was no match for his runaway emotions. "But every time I think about what happened to Tony and my sister, I just wanna..." Pooney didn't say the words, but they echoed through the room nonetheless.

"You think that's what Tony would want?" There was no scolding in Ms. Dawkins's voice. "Allen, please think before you throw your entire life away."

"I hate those muthafuckas!" Pooney slammed the remote against the front of the television. "Tony was my only friend! They took my only friend!"

Pooney fell out of the chair and onto the floor—all the anger, all the fear, all the rage, and all the guilt bombarding him at once. The overwhelmed teen curled himself into a modified fetal position, and cried like the frightened child he was.

"It's OK, sweetheart." Ms. Dawkins lay on the floor beside him. "Let it out, baby. Let it all out."

"But I got him killed, Ms. Dawkins." The tears kept flowing. "I was the one supposed to die."

Ms. Dawkins didn't interrupt. There would be time later for reason. Right now, she would content herself with providing what he needed most—a sympathetic ear to listen as the distraught young man struggled to come to grips with the same issues that have left thousands of urban youths emotionally crippled for life.

CHAPTER 25

Chantaye pulled into the 7AM store parking lot and parked next to the gas pumps.

"Blow the horn," Pooney said when he saw Vikki.

Chantaye did as instructed.

Vikki came running at the site of Pooney's Cadillac. She ran first to the driver's side of the car, but stopped when she saw Taye. Next she ran around the car and stuck her head in the passenger side window. "Hey, Pooney." Vikki squeezed his neck.

"Hi, Vikki." Pooney flashed a sheepish grin in Chantaye's direction. She was not smiling.

"Where in the world have you been, boy?" Vikki's smile covered her entire face. "Everybody's been worried."

"Just chillin'," Pooney answered. "Where's Thaddeus Lee?"

"Thaddeus Lee done went crazy." Vikki laughed. "He don't come around here no more. He say he through doin' the devil's work."

"Good." Pooney hoped Thaddeus Lee could hold up.

"You need to talk to Larry," Vikki said next.

"What's up?" Pooney was extra attentive now.

"He's really been trippin' lately," Vikki explained. "Talkin' to hisself, takin' people's money, and yesterday he bust the back window of my white friend's car because we wouldn't score from him."

"Where is he?" Larry was the reason Pooney had returned to 28th Street in the first place.

"'Round the corner."

"I'll be back, baby," Pooney told Chantaye.

"Don't get lost." Chantaye turned her nose up at Vikki. "Because I will come get your ass!"

Pooney felt as stiff as an eighty-year-old man as he stepped from the car. The first few days of two-a-day practices had proved brutal on his poorly conditioned body.

"Now, I see why you ain't been around here," Vikki said once they were safely away from the Cadillac.

"Why is that?"

"'Cause you been with that bitch!" Vikki said sharply.

"Girl," Pooney chuckled. "You crazy."

Pooney and Vikki shared a quick laugh before the sight of Larry, sitting in front of the abandoned house, instantly changed their moods.

"See," Vikki whispered, then hurried for the church across the street from Larry.

Larry sat alone in the same spot that had been headquarters for Pooney, Tony, and himself for most of the summer. His hair was tangled, and his beard had grown all over his face. He was drinking from a bottle of gin and sweating heavily.

"What's up, Larry?" Pooney approached with a smile.

"Pooney." Larry's face lit up. "I knew you was comin'."

Pooney sat beside Larry, placing his arm around his shoulder. "What you been up to, man?"

"You know how it is, cuz." Larry seemed excited. "Drinkin', smokin', fuckin'. The life of a young baller."

"I feel you." Pooney felt uneasy at hearing the odd tone to Larry's voice.

"Tony asked me about you last night." Larry took a drink. "I told him...just give him time, Tony. He'll come back when he's ready."

Pooney was speechless.

"Me and Tony rode the ferry last night, too. You know how that fool love the ferry." Larry passed the bottle to Pooney. "Man, we got high like a muthafucka. We blew 'bout fo' sticks, back to back."

The knot in Pooney's stomach tightened just as he prepared to take a sip from the gin bottle. He took a second sip, then passed the bottle back.

"Tony's been trippin' lately." Larry looked deadly serious. "He sayin' everything's changin' up on him. Says he feels lost."

"Everything's gonna be all right." Pooney didn't know what else to say.

"Tony says it's time for us to handle our business." Larry took another drink. "Says it's been too long already. Says retaliation should be swift."

"What does Larry say?" Pooney asked.

Larry went instantly silent. He stared into the bottle for what seemed like forever before finally standing. He threw the gin bottle as high in the air as he could. Everyone turned to look when the gin bottle landed in the middle of the street.

"What do I say?" Larry faced Pooney.

Pooney sat motionless, consciously trying to avoid any movements that might further excite the madman before him.

"I'm a muthafuckin' soldier, Loc!" Larry screamed at the top of his lungs. "What the fuck do you think I say?"

"Chill out, man."

"Fuck chillin' out!" Larry reached inside his pants and now brandished a small caliber pistol. He fired the gun in the air. "That's what I say, Loc!"

"Somebody's gonna call the police, man," Pooney reasoned.

"Fuck that shit!" Larry waved the gun as he spoke. "Are you ready to handle your business or what?"

"What business?"

"With them slobs from the trey!" Larry stared into Pooney's eyes.

"Let that shit go, Larry."

"Let it go?" Larry yelled. "Them hos smoke my homeboy, and you talkin' 'bout let it go?"

"I know it's hard, Larry." Pooney wanted desperately to reach his friend. "But we have to move on, Loc. That's what Tony would want."

"So you think Tony would want us to quit Crippin'? Go mark? Forget about what them slobs did to him?" Larry took a waterstick from his pocket, placed it between his lips, then lit it. "And you...you talkin' about movin' on after them muthafuckas put a .41 caliber slug in the middle of yo' sister's back?"

"Yeah." Larry's last statement had more impact on Pooney than he let on. "That's what I'm talkin' about."

"You do that, Lil' Loc." Larry sucked hard on the waterstick. "Go ahead and mark out. But don't worry 'cause I'ma stay true blue, through and through. And every time I catch one of them slob muthafuckas slippin', I'ma punch his ticket. And that's on the C."

Pooney didn't respond. No words seemed appropriate. Larry had made up his mind. And so had he. The two boys were traveling in opposite directions, at light speed.

"I know, Tony." Larry cocked his head in a peculiar fashion and nodded. "Lil' Loc good people. I love him."

"I love you, too, Larry." Pooney stepped from the porch of the abandoned house, then wrapped Larry in a bear hug. "Take it easy, cuz."

Pooney started down the street. A look back revealed Larry to be seated again, his head cocked in the same manner, his mouth moving slowly. "He'll be all right," Pooney consoled himself with one of his grandmother's favorite sayings. "The Lord looks after babies and fools."

"You got somethin'?" Vikki finally got around to asking the question that had been on her mind since first seeing the Cadillac Seville.

"I'm out the game, baby," Pooney said.

Vikki stopped cold in her tracks. Pooney didn't even seem to notice. He walked briskly toward the Cadillac Seville, where Chantaye was waiting to drive him to football practice. Just one of many doors the fifteen-year-old boy was finding open to him, doors that led away from the death trap of 28th Street.

(2)

Pooney stepped from the elevator, chocolate-covered cherries tucked under one arm, and proceeded in the direction of room 23C. Regrettably, he had not once visited Sheila during her twelve-day stay in the Intensive Care Unit. Though extremely concerned for his sister's welfare, Pooney feared that seeing her in the terrible condition described to him might prove more than he could handle.

But now, Sheila was out of the ICU, and by all accounts recovering miraculously. Moreover, Sheila had sent word through Chantaye that she would really like to see her brother. Pooney could hide no longer.

The door to room 23C was slightly cracked. Pooney stopped long enough to take a deep breath, then knocked softly.

"Yes?" Regina pulled the door open, then laughed. "Boy, what are you standing there for?"

"I don't know." Pooney stood still.

"C'mon, silly," Sheila's surprisingly cheerful voice sang from somewhere inside the room.

Pooney stopped just inside the door.

"Go on," Regina urged.

Pooney walked toward the center of the room.

"Howdy, stranger." Sheila beamed from her hospital bed.

Pooney couldn't believe his eyes. Sheila looked nothing like the reports of two weeks ago. She sat with her bed at an incline, smiling brightly. Her hair was freshly braided, and there was a half-eaten Junior Bacon Cheeseburger in her lap. The only visible sign of infirmary was the IV running into the back of her left hand. "Hi."

"It's about time you brought your butt up here." Sheila took a bite from her burger.

"I know." Pooney smiled. "I was kinda...you know."

Sheila waited patiently for her brother's explanation.

"I'm going to go and get us some sodas," Regina said to Sheila. "Want one, Allen?"

"Naw," Pooney answered.

"Be back in a few." Regina winked at Sheila.

"So stranger, exactly why did it take so long for you to come see me?" Sheila wasn't through with her brother yet.

"Because," Pooney tried to avoid his sister's gaze, "I was scared."

"Not as scared as I was." Sheila took another bite. "I guess I won't hold it against you, since you bumped your head and stuff."

"Thank you." Pooney laughed. "I'll make it up to you."

"You sure will." Sheila nodded.

"What they say about," Pooney swallowed before finishing, "about you walking?"

"I'll be on my feet in no time." Sheila took the last bite of her Junior Bacon Cheeseburger.

"Really?" Pooney was excited. "Is that what the doctor said?"

"Nope. That's what I say."

Pooney's countenance fell.

"Those doctors don't know nothing." Sheila threw her sheet to the side, exposing her bare legs. "Look."

Pooney watched closely as Sheila slowly wiggled the toes on both feet. Next, she rotated her left ankle in a semi-circle. Then, she bent her right knee ever so slightly.

"See." Sheila, though triumphant, spoke as if the small demonstration had caused her great physical strain. "That's three things those doctors told mama I may never do again."

Pooney's optimism was rising once more.

"Now they give me a fifty-fifty chance of walking again," Sheila continued. "But I know I'll be up and running soon."

"I hope so, Sheila."

"Sit down, boy, you're making me tired." Sheila pointed at the chair next to her bed.

Pooney sat down.

"I'm sorry about Tony." Sheila's voice was lower now. "I know how much you cared about him."

Pooney nodded.

"I wanna ask you something, Pooney."

"What's that?"

"You're through with all that Deuce-nine stuff, ain't you?" Sheila strained to look at her brother's face.

"Yeah." Pooney spoke softly. "Definitely."

"You promise?"

"I promise."

"No paybacks or none of that stuff?"

"No paybacks." Pooney shook his head. "Vengeance is God's."

"Good," Sheila said. "Now I can quit worrying about your stupid behind."

Pooney could only smile. Once again, Sheila had shown her natural selfless tendencies. It truly amazed Pooney that even during the turmoil of the past two weeks, Sheila's primary concern was not herself.

"When do you think you're coming home?" Pooney asked.

"In a few days, hopefully." Sheila pushed a button that lowered the head of her bed until she was in a prone position. "I'll definitely be at the football game next Friday night."

"Yeah?" Pooney would be thrilled if his sister could be present at next Friday's game against Ball High's archrival, the La Marque Cougars. It was to be his first varsity game.

"And y'all better win," Sheila told him. "Because Janeen is going with this boy that plays for La Marque, and all she talks about is how La Marque is going to beat Ball High."

"You know better than that." Pooney was animated. "We're going to smash those clowns, I'm tellin' you. Just wait!"

The light sound of Sheila's snoring took much of the steam from Pooney's enthusiasm. He stepped to the side of the bed and spread the sheet over her legs before taking the glasses from her face. Afterward, he couldn't resist doing something that would have been unthinkable just a month ago. Pooney kissed his sister softly on the cheek.

"That's so sweet." Sheila's eyes opened, a smile blanketing her face.

"Get some rest." Pooney laughed.

Sheila's eyes closed again and the snoring resumed almost immediately. Pooney took the chocolate-covered cherries he had bought for his sister and placed them on the table next to the bed. He then quietly exited the room, one more burden mercifully lifted from his heart.

(3)

As usual, Pooney was among the last handful of players to leave the field house after football practice. The beginning of school had marked the end of two-a-days. Now there was only a once daily, after school practice to endure. Pooney ran additional wind sprints after every practice. He wanted to make sure he possessed sufficient endurance after his drink and smoke-filled summer. Once finished with his sprints, the line for the shower had dwindled to nearly nothing.

"See ya tomorrow, Doc." Pooney said his goodbyes to the team trainer.

The sun was much lower in the sky now than when Pooney had come inside just moments before. He walked slowly across the Tornado practice field toward the Cadillac Seville. Taye was waiting inside. The two of them had already decided to stop at Blockbuster video and rent some movie about a witch project. Sheila had been babbling non-stop about wanting to see it ever since she came home from the hospital.

"What's up, cuz?" Moe's voice caused Pooney to drop his backpack while spinning to face his tormentor.

Moe was attired in a blue Dickies work uniform—the soldier's uniform. He stood stone-faced in front of Pooney.

"What do you want, man?" Pooney made no attempt to hide his displeasure.

"What's been up, Loc?" Moe asked.

"Pooney," he corrected. "My name is Pooney."

"It's like that, huh?" Moe smirked.

"Yeah." Pooney nodded. "Just like that."

"How's Sheila?" Moe changed speeds.

"Fine."

"Lot better than Crooked Tony, I imagine." Moe aimed low.

Pooney winced as if belted in the stomach with a baseball bat.

"And you know the worst of it?" Moe shook his head. "Crooked Tony died thinkin' he had a down-ass homeboy." There was a brief pause before Moe continued. "So what you gonna do, Pooney?" Moe spoke the name as if it tasted awful in his mouth. "Strike back like a soldier? Or fold up like a bitch?"

"I'm out, Moe." And that was all Pooney felt the need to say.

"You out?" Moe let go with a humorless laugh. "This ain't the glee club, muthafucka!"

"I don't give a fuck what it is!" Pooney was not afraid.

"You gon' respect Deuce-nine, you lil' mark!" Moe stepped closer.

"The hell with Deuce-nine!" Pooney stepped closer and the two of them touched noses.

Doc and a handful of Pooney's teammates appeared in the field house door. Meanwhile, Taye blew the Cadillac horn before leaping from the car and running toward the potential melee.

"You know what happens to defectors, don't you, Loc?" Moe spoke slowly.

"I don't give a fuck."

"Well, think about this." Moe smiled. "Friday night, when you're on that field, the whole crowd is going wild, and all those people are hollerin' and screamin'," Moe formed a pistol with his hand, "boom! No one will ever know where it came from."

Pooney remained quiet, lest Moe hear the fear in his voice.

"Everything chill?" Alfred Quintana, the Tors middle linebacker, posted his massive frame directly behind Moe.

Moe took one look at the gargantuan teenager and slithered two paces to his left.

"Yeah." Pooney smiled at Quintana. Pooney's teammates, who were well aware of his recent troubles, had proved much more supportive than Pooney could have ever imagined. Coach Hawthorne, the varsity head coach, had left it to the players to decide Pooney's status with the team. They voted unanimously in his favor. "Homeboy was just leaving."

"See ya Friday," Moe sneered.

"Let's go, baby." Taye reached for Pooney's arm, leading him to the car.

Pooney glanced over his shoulder. Quintana was walking with Moe, arm around his shoulder, explaining something in great detail to the smaller man. Pooney laughed himself dizzy all the way to the car.

(4)

The mood was electric. The butterflies churned continuously in Pooney's stomach as he and the rest of the Tors stood just outside their locker room, waiting eagerly for the opportunity to rip through the Tornado spirit banner. Pooney bounced on his toes amidst the sea of purple and gold, the Tornado band touching the very essence of his soul with the school fight song.

"Richards!" Coach Hawthorne motioned for Pooney to join him at the front of the pack. "Lead us out!"

His teammates clapped and yelled their agreement as Pooney made his way to the front of the manic pack of boys.

"Say Pooney! What's up, cuz?" Pooney's head jerked to his left, and he quickly scanned the bleachers located behind the north end zone. As promised, Moe stood amongst the excited fans.

Pooney turned his attention straight ahead. He and his grandfather had first dreamed of this night when Pooney was barely five-years-old. Moe was irrelevant.

"Let's go Tors!" Pooney blasted off as if fired from a cannon. He hurled his body through the center of the spirit banner, never breaking stride as the roar of the crowd urged him onward, faster, until he and his teammates had sprinted the entire length of the field.

The moment was magical. Nothing Pooney had ever dreamed of could have possibly been so perfect. Pooney bounced on his toes again in a futile attempt to control the fluttering butterflies. He watched anxiously as both sets of team captains took the field for the coin toss.

Pooney turned to the home section of the stadium, located directly behind the Tor sideline. He searched the stands thoroughly, hoping to find within the frenzied crowd of purple and gold pom-pom waving Tor-maniacs, the three faces he yearned most to see.

"Sounds like a winner!" Coach Hawthorne clapped a split second before the roar of the crowd. "Return team! Wedge right!"

Pooney took the field, every nerve in his body sending undecipherable messages to his brain as he sprinted full-speed toward the south end zone. The Ball High fight song played again, and Pooney's adrenaline level shot through the roof.

A look to his left, and the last puzzle pieces to the greatest night of Pooney's life shifted into place. Pooney smiled as a security guard helped Regina and Chantaye carry Sheila's wheelchair up the stairs leading to the bleachers. Sheila, no doubt looking for number twenty-one, searched the field until spotting her brother. "I told you," she said. Pooney read her lips.

Pooney waved to his family, then turned his attention to the maroon and white clad La Marque Cougars, especially number ten, who was now placing the football onto the kicking tee.

The time was now. Pooney rubbed the freshly done tattoo on his left bicep. It read: Tony 1 Love.

Number ten ran forward. Planted. Boom! All sound stopped as Pooney watched the ball shoot straight for the stars. Pooney backpedaled instinctively as the weightless pigskin soared. Then, the speck of brown against the light blue canvas began to grow bigger, and bigger, and bigger until it landed with a thud in Pooney's hands.

Pooney ran straight up the field and directly into a La Marque Cougar, whose helmet found the bull's-eye in the center of the kick returner's chest. Pooney stumbled backward, but didn't fall. He managed to shake free from the would-be tackler, then ran for the right side of the field.

No wedge. Cougars everywhere.

Pooney slipped a second defender, then stiff-armed another as he made his way to the sideline. Unable to turn the corner, Pooney spotted a sliver of daylight to his left, and exploded through the narrow opening, aided by a great block from a teammate.

Now in the open field, Pooney turned it on. The Cougars gave chase, but there was only one player on the field positioned between Pooney and the end zone. Number ten. No contest.

Pooney ran by the place kicker as if he was standing still. The crowd went berserk as Pooney ran the final twenty yards with the ball held high over his head. The young kick returner had just made ten thousand friends.

One face in the north end zone was not so friendly. Moe stood motionless, his expressionless face staring directly into Pooney's eyes.

Pooney slowed as he crossed the goal line, wary of the threats Moe had made to him. The young boy flinched when his former friend's hand came up suddenly, but he relaxed when he saw that Moe was only hittin' him up with the C.

Pooney walked slowly toward the back of the end zone, stopping just a few feet from where Moe was standing. He observed Moe closely. There had been a time in the not too distant past that any greeting by this man would have been returned with great enthusiasm. There was also a time when Moe's gesture would have incited great anger in Pooney, maybe even to the point of violence. But both those times were gone now. Looking at Moe now, Pooney could only see the ridiculousness of the man who had been his friend, mentor, and idol. Pooney shook his head at Moe, then dropped the ball and turned to join his teammates. Life was calling.

About the Author

Rochan Morgan was born and raised in Galveston, Texas. Rochan's love for reading began at the age of two while he sat each morning with his grandfather, drinking coffee, and listening as the morning paper was read to him. It was not long after that Rochan could read the paper on his own. But despite the academic potential Rochan demonstrated throughout his childhood, family instability during his teenage years contributed to an ill-fated decision to forego his final year of high school and enlist in the U.S. Navy.

In what was becoming a reoccurring pattern in Rochan's young life, he showed great promise as a seventeen-year-old sailor, earning meritorious advancement twice in the first six months of his enlistment, only to squander his naval career with more faulty decision-making.

The rollercoaster ride continued and Rochan became an enigma to all who knew him. While at times showing glimpses of the promise with which God had blessed him, continued poor judgment was threatening to destroy his life. Throughout it all, Rochan retained his deep love for reading, as well as a secret love for writing. Sometimes he wrote entire novel length manuscripts only to throw them away before allowing anyone to read them. When his penchant for poor decision-making finally caused him to hit rock bottom, it was writing that rescued his sanity. No longer ashamed of his passion, Rochan has decided to share his considerable talents with the world.

www.rochanmorgan.com

ALSO AVAILABLE FROM

DOUBLE BOOK!
DOUBLE BOOK!

DOUBLE BOOK!
DOUBLE BOOK!

LOOK FOR MORE HOT TITLES FROM

Q-BORO BOOKS

TALK TO THE HAND - OCTOBER 2006
$14.95
ISBN 0977624765

Nedra Harris, a twenty-three year old business executive, has experienced her share of heartache in her quest to find a soul mate. Just when she's about to give up on love, she runs into Simeon Mathews, a gentleman she met in college years earlier. She remembers his warm smile and charming nature, but soon finds out that Simeon possesses a dark side that will eventually make her life a living hell.

SOMEONE ELSE'S PUDDIN' - DECEMBER 2006
$14.95
ISBN 0977624706

While hairstylist Melody Pullman has no problem keeping clients in her chair, she can't keep her bills paid once her crack-addicted husband Big Steve steps through a revolving door leading in and out of prison. She soon finds what seems to be a sexual and financial solution when she becomes involved with her long-time client's husband, Larry.

THE AFTERMATH
$14.95
ISBN 0977624749

If you thought having a threesome could wreak havoc on a relationship, Monica from My Woman His Wife is back to show you why even the mere thought of a ménage a trios with your spouse and an outsider should never enter your imagination.

THE LAST TEMPTATION - APRIL 2007
$6.99
ISBN 0977733599

The Last Temptation is a multi-layered joy ride through explorations of relationships with Traci Johnson leading the way. She has found the new man of her dreams, the handsome and charming Jordan Styles, and they are anxious to move their relationship to the next level. But unbeknownst to Jordan, someone else is planning Traci's next move: her irresistible ex-boyfriend, Solomon Jackson, who thugged his way back into her heart.

LOOK FOR MORE HOT TITLES FROM

Q-BORO
BOOKS

DOGISM
$6.99
ISBN 0977733505

Lance Thomas is a sexy, young black male who has it all; a high paying blue collar career, a home in Queens, New York, two cars, a son, and a beautiful wife. However, after getting married at a very young age he realizes that he is afflicted with DOGISM, a distorted sexuality that causes men to stray and be unfaithful in their relationships with women.

POISON IVY – NOVEMBER 2006
$14.95
ISBN 0977733521

Ivy Davidson's life has been filled with sorrow. Her father was brutally murdered and she was forced to watch, she faced years of abuse at the hands of those she trusted, and was forced to live apart from the only source of love that she has ever known. Now Ivy stands alone at the crossroads of life staring into the eyes of the man that holds her final choice of life or death in his hands.

HOLY HUSTLER – FEBRUARY 2007
$14.95
ISBN 0977733556

Reverend Ethan Ezekiel Goodlove the Third and his three sons are known for spreading more than just the gospel. The sanctified drama of the Goodloves promises to make us all scream "Hallelujah!"

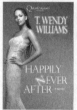

HAPPILY NEVER AFTER – JANUARY 2007
$14.95
ISBN 1933967005

To Family and friends, Dorothy and David Leonard's marriage appears to be one made in heaven. While David is one of Houston's most prominent physicians, Dorothy is a loving and carefree housewife. It seems as if life couldn't be more fabulous for this couple who appear to have it all: wealth, social status, and a loving union. However, looks can be deceiving. What really happens behind closed doors and when the flawless veneer begins to crack?

LOOK FOR MORE HOT TITLES FROM

OBSESSION 101
$6.99
ISBN 0977733548

After a horrendous trauma. Rashawn Ams is left pregnant and flees town to give birth to her son and repair her life after confiding in her psychiatrist. After her return to her life, her town, and her classroom, she finds herself the target of an intrusive secret admirer who has plans for her.

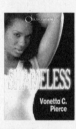

SHAMELESS- OCTOBER 2006
$6.99
ISBN 0977733513

Kyle is sexy, single, and smart; Jasmyn is a hot and sassy drama queen. These two complete opposites find love - or something real close to it - while away at college. Jasmyn is busy wreaking havoc on every man she meets. Kyle, on the other hand, is trying to walk the line between his faith and all the guilty pleasures being thrown his way. When the partying college days end and Jasmyn tests HIV positive, reality sets in.

MISSED OPPORTUNITIES - MARCH 2007
$14.95
ISBN 1933967013

Missed Opportunities illustrates how true-to-life characters must face the consequences of their poor choices. Was each decision worth the opportune cost? LaTonya Y. Williams delivers yet another account of love, lies, and deceit all wrapped up into one powerful novel.

ONE DEAD PREACHER - MARCH 2007
$14.95
ISBN 1933967021

Smooth operator and security CEO David Price sets out to protect the sexy, smart, and saucy Sugar Owens from her husband, who happens to be a powerful religious leader. Sugar isn't as sweet as she appears, however, and in a twisted turn of events, the preacher man turns up dead and Price becomes the prime suspect.

Attention Writers:

Writers looking to get their books published can view our submission guidelines by visiting our website at:
www.QBOROBOOKS.com

What we're looking for: Contemporary fiction in the tradition of Darrien Lee, Carl Weber, Anna J., Zane, Mary B. Morrison, Noire, Lolita Files, etc; groundbreaking mainstream contemporary fiction.

We prefer email submissions to: candace@qborobooks.com in MS Word, PDF, or rtf format only. However, if you wish to send the submission via snail mail, you can send it to:

Q-BORO BOOKS Acquisitions Department
165-41A Baisley Blvd., Suite 4. Mall #1
Jamaica, New York 11434

*** By submitting your work to Q-Boro Books, you agree to hold Q-Boro books harmless and not liable for publishing similar works as yours that we may already be considering or may consider in the future. ***

1. Submissions will not be returned.
2. **Do not contact us for status updates.** If we are interested in receiving your full manuscript, we will contact you via email or telephone.
3. Do not submit if the entire manuscript is not complete.

Due to the heavy volume of submissions, if these requirements are not followed, we will not be able to process your submission.